Inter Dimensional Spy

*Portals to Unknown
Intrigue and Tragedies*

By

Paul D. Escudero

WORKBOOK PRESS LLC
187 E Warm Springs Rd,
Suite B285 Las Vegas NV 89119 USA

Website: https://workbookpress.com/
Hotline: 1-888-818-4856
Email: admin@workbookpress.com

Ordering Information:
Quantity sales. Special discounts are available on quantity purchases by corporations, associations, and others. For details, contact the publisher at the address above.

Library of Congress Control Number:

ISBN-13:   978-1-965732-00-7   Paperback Version

PUB. DATE: 08/14/2024

Preface

Since this Novel is about Spies in advanced Alien Society, the names do not sound like human names we are accustomed to. Why would alien names sound like us?

To give an environment that speculates on Alien Civilization, I borrow words in Chinese, Russian, and other languages in constructing this book. In the back of the book is a Dramatis Persona that lists all the characters as well as a glossary that lists devices. In the text of the Novel when I use a new word constructed from these other languages, I have in parenthesis how to pronounce it and if necessary, what it means.

You might want to copy using your cell phone or a copy machine the Dramatis Persona and the glossary, so you have those explanations readily available to revert to if you get confused. If all else fails, cut those pages out to use and when you finish the book give it to one of your friends without the cribs and let them suffer before you come clean!

What will a spy use in the future? What do they do now in HUMINT?

In some cases, HUMINT uses traditional methods of espionage and low technology because the spy cannot be caught with any GIZMOS. In the non-fiction book "Operation SOLO," about Morris Childs, the most successful spy in U.S. history, he went to Russia for 29 years playing the role of CPUSA vice President. He and his wife met all the Soviet Leaders from 1959 until he bugged out in 1982 when Senator Frank Church blew his cover. He also met Mao and became friends.

Frank Church forced the FBI to brief him on Morris Childs along with a half dozen others. Morris Childs knew this was his death sentence because those people would be the source of a leak that would get him killed because the Soviets would chase him to the ends of the earth to find him and kill him from such an extraordinary betrayal.

Only 5 FBI agents knew about Morris Childs that ran him for 29 years. The CIA offered the FBI $10 Billion for a buy in on Morris Childs who in turn explained to his FBI handlers he would immediately end his spying career because the CIA had so many leaks you might as well call them a Swiss Cheese outfit. He has a point. Remember Aldridge Aimes and a few other traitors?

On behalf of President Ronald Reagan, the FBI convinced Morris Childs to continue spying on the Kremlin until one day the FBI had a request for 7 Congressmen to be briefed. How the hell did they know about it? Morris Childs quit on the spot in defiance of Reagan who thought he could coerce him into continuing. The FBI people that ran Morris Childs are in fact some of the best operators in the INTEL business during that era. The Soviets did not know Morris Childs was a spy until long after he was dead.

Morris Childs could not simply disappear, the Soviets would still find him and torture him to death using some of the techniques I described in my Novels *Sanctuary City, Brooklyn Galaxy Traveling Talking Dog, and Man of Birds Traveling to the Stars.*

As such Morris Childs handlers faked his death in such a good way, they convinced the CPUSA President Gus Hall, Morris Childs died from a heart attack. Note: Oppenheimers wife, a communist, was good friends with Gus Hall.

Morris Childs was betrayed by a Nosy Senator Church who was trying to stir up a Shit Show over assassinations carried out by our government and came across FBI funding for Morris Childs when he was investigating James Earl Ray and the Martin Luther King assassination that the average polar bear knows was carried out by rouge FBI agents, probably at the behest of Lyndon Johnson. My theory is LBJ might have been involved in killing JFK, RFK, and MLK. Was it the K in their names that upset LBJ?

In this Novel, the spy Adrak was betrayed by people he worked with. In a couple instances he came close to getting killed by such a betrayal.

Has betrayal happened in our military and intelligence agencies?

Certainly, John Walker, Aldridge Aimes, Charles Hanson, Ronald Pelton, Joseph George Helmich, James W. Hall III, and many others. The military has an issue. In the past they used the fact the man was wearing a uniform he was trustworthy. Sorry, that doesn't work.

Furthermore, why did the FBI bust a CIA man Aldridge Aimes and why did CIA bust a FBI man Charles Hansen? Perhaps those agencies Inspector Generals should have a boss from another agency their director can't touch, and we'd weed out the spies more effectively.

Is the WOKE business accelerating the Spy business? Sure, we can't go after certain ethnic groups unless there is overwhelming evidence because there will be huge outcry. Here's the reality, if you wait for overwhelming evidence, like in the John Walker case, a lot of damage will be done before you stop the spying.

Counterintelligence operations need to be color blind and if they go after an immigrant or a 3rd generation because of ties to the Ministry of State Security (China), so be it.

In this novel, an agency director is suddenly confronted with the possibility of having multiple moles within his organization. Can that happen?

Sure, it happened and that's why we ended up with the 1954 espionage act WRITTEN IN BLOOD.

Spies can have a dramatic impact on the outcome of a war. We know that because of several people such as Richard Sorge, Admiral Canaris, Mata Hari, and Fritz Duquesne. In this Novel in honor of such a successful spy, I have a character with the last name Duquesne.

A note on Mata Hari: she was made out to be a spy whose actions resulted in 50,000 French soldiers killed in a show trial for the sake of covering up French failures in World War 1.

In 1917, France had been badly shaken by mutinies in the French Army in the spring of 1917 following the failure of the Nivelle Offensive. France could have collapsed from war exhaustion.

Having the alleged German spy Mata Hari to blame for everything that went wrong during the war, was convenient for the French government.

Mata Hari was the perfect scapegoat. The case against Mata Hari received maximum publicity in the French press and led to her importance being greatly exaggerated.

The French Government needed a scapegoat, and Mata Hari was a notable target for that purpose. After Mata Hari's conviction she was executed by a French Army firing squad.

Mata Hari's sealed trial and other related documents, a total of 1,275 pages, were declassified by the French Army in 2017, one hundred years after her execution.

Mata Hari probably didn't contribute much to the outcome of the war, her value as a scapegoat was probably more valuable than what most spies did during the war. As a scapegoat, she had more to offer than sabotage or espionage.

The French Government created Mata Hari's legacy in the show trial, which gives a different perspective in what spies can do for a government. Was Lee Harvey Oswald used in the same way Mata Hari was?

In the case of Morris Childs his usefulness reached its zenith when he reported about Russian PROJECT RYAN that led to Reagan and Gorbachev seeing more eye to eye on events with a less bellicose attitude.

Throughout the Novel you will discover there are other traces to the history of the spy business. Be careful, if you follow those breadcrumbs, you will go down an infinitely long rabbit hole.

Finally, as you read this Novel, be advised, technological development ongoing will eventually allow us to do just about everything I wrote about. If you follow the breadcrumbs, I put in concerning signal processing, you will find you could spend the next five years reading all the references if you google that information or go to Wikipedia.

I personally met several world-famous signal processing experts during my travels attending meetings with them. I also met distinguished scientists at seminars. It's an ever- changing game and this Novel touches upon it briefly to explain how spies transmitting signals compromised their missions. Thanks to YouTube you can now go watch lectures done by very prominent scientists on signal processing in this vastly changing world.

Table of Contents

Chapter One

Insertion

The home on Davenkret Street in Praxiskrowtious was often dark as the single man named Geskar who lived there was gone most of the time.

Vekkar agents monitored Geskar extensively over a six-month period because he would have his life and identity stolen from him so that Vekkar Interdimensional Transport Directorate could use that stolen identity for this ongoing clandestine operation.

Intensive surveillance provided numerous breadcrumbs to investigate as Vekkar agents absorbed all the information they could glean about Geskar possible. They would pop in unannounced and often into Geskar's home in Praxiskrowtious while he was away, allowing Vekkar agents to research him thoroughly.

Geskar's watchers were always in position to trail him and record much of what he did as they built up their files with AI help to glean all pertinent information.

Bugs were planted in Geskar's home and at his office where he worked to record his voice systematically so that Adrak the Inter Dimensional Spy would get identity changed and voice modification to match Geskar appearance and his voice.

Geskar being somewhat a loner because his wife Mildrayd was taken from him at an early age in a terrible accident before they had children.

Geskar would be needed for a while as he might need to provide additional information to support Adrak the Interdimensional Portal Spy now on a crucial mission.

Vekkar Intelligence concerns and fears were now percolating at the tops of government. Their arch enemies, the Tramulars's were getting very close to mastering the ability to perform interdimensional portal missions. Pure chaos would reign down on the Vekkar's if Tramulars's successfully developed Interdimensional Portals allowing them to conduct nefarious operations Vekkar Security Forces could not prevent.

As soon as Adrak went operational on this mission and was getting acclimated to the safe house and the terrain, he started working on his milestones. Adrak was considerably more intelligent than Geskar and had been thoroughly trained in all aspects of his work and his coworkers.

When Adrak started showing up at the office portraying Geskar's identity he had stolen, he dressed and acted exactly the way Geskar would.

But as time went by Geskar's (a.k.a. Adrak) greater intelligence started making improvements in work performance, and his appearance slowly improved. To the office staff they merely thought Geskar had gotten over the loss of Mildrayd and was putting his life back on track for a normal life living without grief.

Geskar didn't have a lot of friends, but his co-workers were happy to see Geskar's overall stature was improving as it seemed he had left all his grief behind, which was also somewhat uplifting to his co-workers.

In a months' time Geskar's supervisor called him into a meeting and she explained: "I noticed your work has improved and I'm glad to see you are moving forward in a better trajectory." Geskar's supervisor said.

The supervisor didn't see or recognize the body snatch that had worked out flawlessly.

As soon as the rest of the preparations were completed, Adrak would then start attempting to penetrate Tramulite government secrets and discover the situation of their Inter-Dimensional Portal Development.

Adrak had leads to follow up with, but he had to go slow to not overturn the apple cart. Part of Adrak's transcendence into a local personality was to not draw undue interest by creating a scenario with a female to cement the essence of him appearing as Geskar during his clandestine activities.

That unique relationship he would develop manifested one day when Geskar (aka Adrak) went by the home of his wife's good friend Martilene Chares with some beautiful flowers.

Martilene wasn't expecting any visitors and the very last person she would think would ring her guest arriving button was none other than Geskar dressed for success with flowers to give to her. It was mildly shocking.

"Hello, I hope I'm not disrupting your evening," Geskar said.

"No not at all," Martilene said with a strange look on her face.

"Here's some flowers for you, I hope they brighten up your day," Geskar said then handed the flowers to Martilene who was in a semi-state of shock with Geskar's sudden appearance.

Martilene didn't know it, but plumbers (spies) had installed video and sound monitors in her home. Adrak planned on seducing and exploiting Martilene as part of his growing cover operation and the support team studied Martilene as well.

Martilene did not have male visitors very often and shied away from relationships after having her heart crushed by a fast-talking dude who promised her the universe then fled shortly after harvesting her planetary delights.

Martilene was prime for a relationship. Long after her lover abandoned her after he got his quick gratification on what appeared to be drive by sex, she had no recourse but to please herself which she did with robotic powered machines that did as well as a male and in many ways better since the robotic device did far more in stimulating her erogenous zones.

Martilene Chares felt sorry for Geskar who was very well mannered and never approached her explicitly in the past and according to her friend, Mildrayd was an ideal husband. That is the only reason why she invited him in after thanking Geskar (a.k.a. Adrak) the body snatcher into her home.

Geskar was the perfect gentleman and never revealed his fangs. Likewise, Martilene who wasn't dressed for success, wasn't looking like a gem, but she invited him in nevertheless where they visited for ten minutes and poured on the charm in a subtle manner.

After fifteen minutes, Geskar excused himself and left because he was the consummate social engineer knew better than a lot of people on Earth knew: The Romans didn't build Rome in a day.

As Geskar was outside of Matilene's front door saying goodbye to her he said, "Perhaps one day we can have dinner together?"

"Sure, why not," Martilene responded not in a convincing manner.

Geskar knew everything about Martilene including her utilizing her sex robotics later that evening. She was primed for exploitation.

Thanks to all the surveillance on Martilene, Adrak knew exactly everywhere she went including to the park to walk her pet *Labrodralger*, that resembled the typical small lovely fluffy dog.

Martilene had never seen Geskar's body and didn't know he worked out. She didn't know she was looking at a galaxy level top spy body as she bumped into Geskar on his current routine running at Martilene's favorite park. Afterwards she went home and utilized her personal robotics to satisfy her personal sexual needs.

Adrak, being the consummate social engineer, knew all this because of the secret cameras and microphones planted by the plumbers in Martilene's home.

It was during one of those chance meetings at the park when Geskar (a.k.a. Adrak) invited Martilene to dinner at a nice restaurant.

Martilene accepted the invitation to dinner only because she was almost bored to tears. This restaurant turned into a dance club after dinner hours with live performers up on a small stage about two feet above the dance floor.

Martilene didn't know she was being handled by a Galactic class spy who would drug her. While she went to the lady's room, Adrak put a special drug often called *Wild Dragon* spiked with *Damiana* and *Arginine* that affected Martilene's libido like a male who took twenty shots of a sex enhancer drug.

When Martilene started feeling the effects of her drugging she became a raging bitch in heat and said she wanted to go home and when they arrived there invited poor

Geskar in because she wanted some real gratification and not the robotic helper. Hence the evening ended with a *soiree on a theme by Paganini.*

Adrak then enjoyed the benefits of being a spy as he enjoyed Martilene's surreal cosmic flurry of celestial feasts.

It took Adrak several hours to fully satisfy Martilene's artificial drugged up needs.

The *Wild Dragon* dissipated in Martilene's system rapidly and if she had a notion she might have been drugged and went to authorities, all her lab work would come back negative.

But such a circumstance did not cross her mind. She didn't know it was mostly her needs. She misjudged the situation thinking it was all Geskar who had not been with a woman in quite a while and had all that pent up demand.

It was around midnight when the lovers tryst ended and Geskar politely said, "I need to leave now because I need to go to work in the morning."

"Alright, Geskar, I can't believe how much you turned me on. I didn't know sex could be so good."

"Perhaps it's because you motivated me." Geskar said.

"If that's the case, I'm very pleased." Martilene said.

Geskar gut up and put his clothes back on and the two had a phony goodbye. Martilene had no emotional bonding to Geskar. He was nothing more than a tool to her like her robotic toys. But she was grateful Geskar performed when she suddenly felt so incredibly horny not connecting the dots to what really transpired.

Martilene was attracted to Geskar for a new revelation. She had no idea he had such exquisite muscles and stamina. She knew none of her friends had ever ridden a guy like Geskar before. She wondered how Geskar developed such a great body. *Maybe he worked out a lot to help overcome the grief of losing his wife?*

Geskar knew there would be a welcoming committee back at the safe house as his security team had observed his performance. Their only regret the team had they were not having *Kokoshes* (like popcorn) available.

The "Doc" had Adrak take a bath, and then admonished him because he didn't use protection, "What was you planning in case you got her pregnant?"

"I sense there was no emotional bonding. When I left there was no lovey-dovey. I was merely her boy toy to take care of her needs from being drugged up. Watch her video closely, I expect her to take an anti-pregnancy medication tonight or tomorrow."

The next day the *Doc* reported to Adrak, "Your analysis was perfect. We saw her taking medication and placement into her medicine cabinet. After she went to work, the plumbers verified she took an anti-pregnancy pill."

"That's good to know," Adrak stated.

"You were not her first Rodeo; she apparently likes sex and used you like a cheap whore." The Doc said.

"I'm glad I could be of assistance," Adrak said with a smile.

Adrak looked at the Doc strangely and she wished she could polygraph him that very moment because she thought Adrak was thinking, *I wonder how the Doc would feel.*

Chapter Two

Train Ride

Geskar's supervisor approached him for some good news. After Geskar's wife Mildrayd died in the terrible accident, he burned up all his vacation time staying home dealing with events associated with her death, the memorial, closing out her estate, and removing all her personal belongings and donating them to groups that helped financially strapped people and people in need.

The real Geskar wasn't sure he would ever return to work. The only reason he returned to work when he did was out of boredom staying home alone. His productivity was poor until he was abducted and Adrak took his place with stolen identity.

Geskar had not taken any time off since Mildrayd passed and had accumulated some Holiday hours. Geskar didn't have enough vacation time to take a long vacation but his supervisor went to her boss and convinced him that Geskar's productivity had improved to the point he was now a better employee than he had ever been.

The supervisor wanted to reward Geskar for his turn around by giving him a few paid days off to show the sincere appreciation of his due diligence and seemingly more passion in the conduct of his job. Geskar's supervisor was given permission to reward Geskar with a few days off. Geskar could add to his leave total to give him enough time to go somewhere and do something fun.

Geskar's leave was announced in a private meeting with his supervisor and asked not to disclose the generosity of the company because the supervisor knew there would be line outside her office requesting a meeting for their *time off awards*.

Geskar was more than happy to promise he would keep the special reward confidential as this dove tailed nicely in his plans where he could do two important tasks that required some dedicated time. This would allow him some ISR time to help go find what he was searching for and provide another window of opportunity for the seduction of Martilene Chares to build up that relationship to give him a stronger cover and throw off any possible counterintelligence operations.

But where to take Martilene Chares and would she be available to go and have the desire to participate?

One thought was an ocean cruise, but that might be a risky plan and what if Martilene Chares didn't like going out on the ocean and got seasick?

Geskar asked his safe house occupants what they thought might be a good idea and they went about researching it and provided a half dozen suggestions. As Geskar thought about it, one suggestion had an element of adventure as well as an opportunity to survey the countryside in the most innocuous fashion.

That evening when Geskar took Martilene Chares out to dinner in his neverending efforts to seduce her and solidify her role in this significant operation. Martilene Chares would never know the real story, but her being seen in public with Geskar would help create the imagery of a couple to throw off possible investigators.

"Martilene , would you like to go on a trip with me?" Geskar asked.

"What do you have in mind, Geskar?" Martilene Chares asked.

"How would you like to go on a tourist train ride with me?" Geskar asked.

"How long would the trip last?" Martilene Chares asked.

"There are several options but if you are pressed for time the 5-day 4-night trip would good," Geskar replied.

"What train trip do you have in mind?" Martilene asked.

"There is a train that leaves Praxiskrowtious that will take us through majestic mountains and when we get to the destination, the City of Klamagore, we would fly back to Praxiskrowtious." Geskar said.

"What kind of accommodations will we have on the train?" Martilene asked.

"We could share a private room, but if you think you need to have a private room, I will arrange that," Geskar said.

"Staying alone in a private room would spoil all the fun," Martilene responded.

"Does that mean you are interested in going?" Geskar asked.

"I need to arrange time off from work." Martilene said.

"Alright, give me the dates you can be gone, and I'll make reservations," Geskar said.

The next day Martilene gave Geskar her timeline and the following day they were off on the train ride.

Martilene called Geskar when she was ready to leave. Geskar took a Skycar to her home and she immediately came out the front door carrying a small luggage piece. Geskar had a medium backpack with him loaded with essentials and a couple changes of tourist clothes.

The Skycar delivered the adventurous couple at the train station, and the driver paid in advance was delighted with the large tip and was very courteous and helpful with the luggage.

The trip was paid for and Geskar had their tickets on his personal communicator. The couple breezed through the train station and out on the platform where their train was waiting for them and many more passengers for this tourist trip across the mountains. This was an outdated mode of transportation but thrived on tourists who would not have any other means of seeing some of the majestic landscape that had no road access.

One the sides of each passenger car was large numbers on one corner easily to see and Geskar quickly spotted their car and led Martilene there with his backpack on and towing her small luggage on wheels since he was the perfect gentleman.

They climbed up into the passenger car and easily found their private room in the middle of the car. Geskar placed their luggage in the overhead bins at the rear of their room and they sat down on the sofa facing the side of the passenger car with a majestic picture window, designed for sightseeing.

Geskar said, "The windows were just cleaned and photographing the landscape through them will work out nicely if that's what you want to do."

"I may not have time to take pictures," Martilene joked and smiled.

The two were waiting for the train to start moving and sat there just enjoying each other's company. It was a very friendly atmosphere spiked with lust and desire. Martilene was already thinking three plays ahead of Geskar in her cosmic football game knowing she was going to want some big-A on the train, which she never did before.

This tourist train was powered by some antique locomotives that had been out of service to the public for a few years. It was the last generation of steam turbine electric locomotives. The locomotive would operate burning distillates out in the countryside, but in the city such as now where pollution standards were strict, the overhead catenary electric feed provided energy to the heaters in the boilers.

The closed loop steam system using a condenser to convert the used steam back into water significantly reduced the need for water stops even though the second and third cars on the train carried water and distillate. The train could make its destination Klamagore with no fuel or water stops. The second purpose of the large water tank car was to provide passengers with additional water for showers and toilet flushes even though passenger cars had water tanks.

The locomotive and its fuel tender all had electric trucks on them used for propulsion and dynamic breaking. During dynamic breaking the boilers were fed from the motor generators in the power trucks instead of the power source. If fuel to steam operation was being used at the time, the fuel was cut back to a minimum since dynamic breaks could provide all the energy required to keep up boiler pressure of 600 psi.

The five sets of trucks under the articulated locomotive and tender provided 16,000 horsepower which is all that was needed for the 1800-ton passenger train.

In the mountains speed was not the objective. Quality sight-seeing was.

Just as Martilene and Geskar were getting comfortable, the intercom in their room provided an announcement.

"Geskar, the waiter would like to enter your room and take drink requests now if you would like to have a drink while the train is leaving the station. May he enter at this time?"

"Sure, please enter." Geskar responded.

The waiter arrived momentarily and asked, "May I get you two any drinks?" Geskar asked, "Martilene what would you like?"

"Do you have Trambrosier Elixirs?" Martilene asked.

"Yes, we do Madam. Would you like me to shake your drink with a little ice or just chilled?"

"I would like it shaked with ice, thank you." Martilene said.

"And you sir?" The waiter asked.

"Can I get a È-long (pronounced uh long) elixir?" Geskar asked.

"Absolutely sir." The waiter said.

The waiter was gone for a few minutes and returned with their drinks. Timing was impecable because just as they were enjoying their first sips, the train started moving.

When they were alone the conversation started flowing.

"You know Geskar, I never would have taken this train if you had not invited me."

"I'm glad I could show you something you might like and remember, Martilene."

"Gānbēi (pronounced: Gun Bay, means: Cheers)" Martilene toasted Geskar.

The reason why Martilene liked Trambrosier Elixirs is because that substance loosened her up. She didn't want to be inhibited on the train in any way, but she thought she might wait until it was dark, and passengers were sleeping in their private nearby rooms to open the floodgates of passion.

For the first twenty minutes of the travel along the railroad right of way, there was nothing spectacular to see because it was all City Landscape and only the majestic buildings offered any sort of inspiration.

This rail line was once part of a major transportation system. In its heyday there were 4 sets of train tracks with 160 trains running in each direction per day. Because of the railroad right of way, buildings existed outside the perimeter of the original four sets of tracks. Three of the tracks had been recently ripped up but left a green area that was fenced off and produced a very long majestic park with sidewalks landscape and park like amenities. The last operating track was track #4 skewed to the far-right side of the right of way that provided the view to people in private cars such as Geskar and Martilene.

Since the sightseeing benefits of a city park were nothing compared to the mountains they would soon climb up, the train hustled at over 100 miles per hour cutting through this area. At this speed the train hit the outskirts of the city that was restricted from construction beyond a area marked off as a preserve for future generations. The land was still flat but within ten minutes the train started the ascent up into the mountains soon showing plenty of majestic views.

The train left the station one hour prior to mealtime for a purpose. After one hour of traveling, they were now in the mountains with majestic views perfect for the ambience in the dining car.

The intercom came alive again with an announcement: "Passengers in private rooms please proceed to the dining car now for first seating."

Coach passengers that only had reclining seats were forward of the dining car and the private room cars were aft of the dining car and only that access would be open for the first hour.

"Let's go to the dining car. I would like to be sipping on some nice elixirs or wine as we climb up into the mountains," Geskar said.

"Lead the way, I'm ready sweetheart." Martilene said.

Geskar being a spy and fully coherent quickly received the essence of Martilene's feelings with her statement. She was already exhibiting indications of capitulation which meant she would soon be a pawn in the game of superpower espionage and manipulation.

Both sides played this game. When it came to the spy business, nothing was sacred. The Tramular's were just as guilty as the Vekkar agents in using innocent bystanders in the game of clandestine affairs.

Everything is fair in love and war, and more so in the espionage business. Geskar thought as he was analyzing his situation.

Geskar and Martilene promptly walked towards the dining car. Many passengers in the private cars were procrastinating and took a while to decide to follow the two and in a while were stuck in a line.

Geskar informed the waiter they would prefer a table in the middle of the dining car which offered them the best view on both sides of the car and not be subjected to the noise of people entering from the adjacent private room car.

The waiter sat them down and took their drink orders. Mateline stuck with her Trambrosier Elixir while Geskar switched to Jiǎo Gǒu Yúyuè Qì (pronounced JiowGo You-Yea Chi) wine. This wine, known in many solar systems was a combined pleasurizer and some men thought it stimulated their libido. It was expensive and had quite an effect. Geskar wondered if the hearsay was true. He would find out later.

As the train continued climbing up the grade into the mountains it slowed, and the gentle ride consequently felt much more pleasing. The view from the center of the dining room away from noise in the back created the ambience that added greatly to their enjoyment of their meal. The ever-changing landscape could never be recreated in a restaurant. You had to be on the train to experience such an effect.

The waiters have this dining hall experience perfectly choreographed. Timing was everything and they had to move people in and out efficiently. The waiter was back soon after taking their meal orders.

Martilene, very conscious of her waistline and sure as hell didn't want to be carrying around a donut on her mid-section like some of her friends, ordered a seafood meal that was low in carbs and high in protein.

Since they were in an area of the world that had mountain climbing Tommie's, that was on the menu. Someone from Earth might say the meat tastes like lamb chops. Cooked in wine and a special brown gravy, the meat is very soft and favorable. Geskar ordered that which came with a potato tasting like sweet potatoes on Earth.

Geskar could investigate Martilene's eyes. They were full of expectations and surprise. She had no idea Geskar was the adventurous type. None of her girlfriends would ever guess Geskar took her on a train ride, and because women tend to be nosy, they would demand to know if she got ridden on the train.

She would toy with them and say, "I was ridden hard and put away wet."

The chefs on the train have the meals down to science. They learned long ago to precook, but not fully the meats leaving some rawness, then heat them up on the customer order with high heat and appropriate spices added only just before served. The flavor was thus incredible.

The two lovebirds would have engaged in precocious teasing had the waiter not returned in quick fashion with their orders.

The food tasted so great Martilene and Geskar could not concentrate on conversation and delved deeply into the satisfaction of their taste buds.

The meal was utterly fantastic and left Martilene and Geskar in a state of fulfillment. They didn't need the waiter to hustle them out of the dining car, on their own desires, they promptly left and went back to their private room and Geskar thought now would be a great time to relax, lay back on the sofa and hold Martilene in his arms.

Martilene at first wasn't too enthused but as her meal gripped her cognitive functionality, she reclined into Geskar's arms laying in such a way on the sofa looking forward observing the scenery as they passed by including waterfalls, green forests, and a few wild animals who saw the trains daily.

The combination of elixirs and wine and meal put the two almost into a state of comatose as they succumbed to the influence to take a nap. When you are extremely comfortable and happy and in the arms of a lover, time has a way of speeding up. They didn't realize but they were both out for a couple hours and only stirred because each of them needed a trip to their room's private toilet to drain their kidneys.

The two re-commenced their positions on the couch afterwards but they were now fully alert. Martilene was wondering when Geskar was going to make the first move. Martilene was fortified and more than ready for some big-A if that's what Geskar wanted to do. Martilene reached down with her left hand and felt Geskar's manliness. It was currently limp because sex was not on his mind. But Martilene knew if she kept squeezing it in a cyclical manner, she would take care of that problem.

Geskar was in for a big surprise as Martilene repositioned herself and zipped down his trousers and pulled out his manliness and started performing fellatio. There was now no doubt in Geskar's thoughts of what Martilene wanted.

Before Geskar could act, Martilene stood up, dropped her panties and climbed aboard Geskar and did to him what he thought he should be doing to her. Martilene's desires and expectations were unsurmountable. Martilene could feel all Geskar's responses to her application of great expertise.

Just like Martilene predicted, Geskar could not hold back very long and soon donated vast amounts of his silver serum to fulfill her desires. Thanks to the Trambrosier Elixir, Martilene was predisposed to perform in this wild fashion without being drugged.

After Martilene sucked the last of Geskar's essence with her muscle actions her robotic toys helped her develop, she laid down on Geskar's chest and started purring like a kitten keeping him inside her enjoying the lingering feeling. *The hell with the landscape, this feels better*, Martilene thought.

After a while as Martilene and Geskar's bodies recoiled into a post coitus stature, Martilene decided she wanted to get up and clean herself up and visited the toilet and took a sprite shower.

Geskar just laid back and observed the landscape waiting for Martilene to return to determine what their next actions would be.

Martilene returned, had a nice warm wet towel and wiped off all her essence that was all over Geskar's private area because she didn't want it to look like a glazed donut later.

After she cleaned Geskar nicely she kissed the head of his manliness then zipped up his trousers and took the wet towel and disposed of it in the slot the crew wanted all their wet towels to be deposited. While they were away for dinner, their beds would be made, and the towels removed and replaced with fresh towels.

About an hour before dinner time, the intercom announced, "The waiter would like to know if you would like him to enter and take drink requests."

"Sure, send him in," Geskar responded, and they repeated an earlier scenario and obtained new drinks.

The two were soon cuddling like they had earlier before the coitus, watching the landscape with Martilene's back against Geskar's chest.

At this point in time the train tracks went parallel to a river and in the background were snowcapped mountains. The majestic view was pleasurable and Martilene was now very happy she took this train trip. She never would have had sex on a train and seen the exhibit of such fantastic views had Geskar not invited her because it's the last thing she would ever thought of doing.

Three of the former tracks through this area had been ripped up and salvaged, but there were some passing lanes along the way. About this time the train slowed and soon came to a stop.

"I wonder why we are stopping," Martilene asked with a fearful look on her face.

Before Geskar could answer in a moment another train going in the opposite direction passed them.

"Looks like we stopped so the other train could go past us," Geskar said.

They could investigate the train and see the passengers and the fulfillment of life dreams shown in the other train passenger faces as they passed that was not going very fast for safety reasons on this meet.

Moments later the other train was long gone, and their train started moving. Martilene was now enjoying the experience and she never thought she would see another train passing out in the middle of nowhere.

Because of the way they were orientated they were observing in the direction the train was traveling. They were back near the rear of the train and could see it curve well in front of them.

"Looks like we are getting ready to cross over a large bridge," Martilene said.

Just before their car was on the bridge, they could see it was a long distance below them.

Geskar said, "The engineering that went into the bridge seemed to be rather genius."

Viewing all this, Geskar could not help but to have some positive feelings about the Tramular's. He knew it takes two to tango and unfortunately the Tramular's had a ruthless dictator, but so did the Vekkar's. Neither side really had the high moral ground in this ongoing dispute that Geskar increasingly thought was utter nonsense.

Both civilizations put these ruthless regimes in power. Had it not been for the thrill and excitement of being an interdimensional portal spy, Geskar would be leaving the VIA. He sometimes wondered: *should I just quit and move up into the mountains and live like a monk?*

Holding the sweet Martilene in his arms reinforced his notions of the utter nonsense that existed in this ongoing conflict. *Why can't we all learn to get along?* Geskar wondered while he was kissing the top of Martilene's head feeling the gravity of the situation.

Martilene was another fine example of Tramular's who have their fair share of lovely people. The last thing in the world he would want to witness is Martilene being severely injured or killed in wartime.

Thinking about musicians and composers and people that add so much pleasure to their lives also adds an element of regret in going about doing the things that Geskar accomplished in the past.

Geskar was highly brainwashed in his indoctrination into the spy business. But that brainwashing eventually wears out and spies get to see the enemy up close and eventually become free thinkers and eventually understand their support of a Tyrant makes them no better than the enemy.

But Geskar knew he was in over his head. He had traveled down the road too far now to consider turning around. The fact the Executive Director of Vekkar Interdimensional Transport Directorate, *Doctor Oxyuran Lepidotus Taipan*, was personally supervising this operation, meant he had no choice but to complete the mission. Otherwise, he too would disappear in a manner he knew he would not enjoy. *Would they take me to the hog farm if they thought I defected?* There was no greater fear in a Spy's mind of being tied up and dropped in the middle of a sabretooth hog farm where the hogs had purposely not been fed in a couple days.

Geskar knew that wasn't hearsay. He personally traveled with one of his superiors to such a place and watched his superior cut the prisoner in several places causing him to bleed so the hogs would smell the blood and go after the victim in a feeding frenzy orgy manner.

The person gagged and tied up was jerking and screaming as the hogs had their lunch. They didn't stick around but conversations with other agents said, *the hogs usually finish their meal in less than 15 minutes with not much left but bones and areas in the skull that were hard to get to, but later that night the rodents would take care of that.*

The truth of the matter was, both sides were vicious and disgusting in their approach. But Geskar knew the silver lining. It was spies who were a force multiplier. Some of their actions would save countless lives. So, he had to look at it with multiple perspectives. He didn't love his job, but he was stuck, and his most important role was simply to stay alive and reach the point when the end of his contract would allow him to leave the agency with a nice savings and spend the rest of his life trying to forget the horrors of what he experienced.

Martilene knew the affection Geskar exhibited was rare for Tramular males.

Geskar's whole persona was different. What Martilene didn't know is she was Geskar's *Temporal Oasis*, the calm before the storm, and the precious breadcrumbs of life Geskar knew to savor because there may not be a tomorrow in the business he was in.

If Geskar was betrayed by a double spy, he himself could end up in a hog farm hours after this train ride. Geskar knew he was living on borrowed time.

Martilene might have mistaken Geskar's demeaner for love. There might have been some love mixed in with the emotions as well as Geskar manners. Martilene recognized Geskar's behavior was much different than most Tramular males.

Even though Geskar might not have been in love with Martilene like she mistakenly felt, Geskar's appreciation for the temporal menagerie Martilene provided created this atmosphere and was the most any spy who was living on borrowed time could wish for.

Geskar was not demanding. He was only reactive and sweet in how he responded to Martilene. She had never felt such a positive valance from a man before.

If things were different Geskar might consider coming and taking Martilene faraway where they could live their lives privately together. But the reality is, after this mission completed, Geskar would never see Martilene again for the rest of his life.

Just before dinner the train entered a long circular tunnel, then it exited a tunnel and went at the present altitude for a while then it entered a second tunnel. As Geskar was watching when the train curved in the final direction before losing sight of the first tunnel entering another tunnel, Geskar realized they were moving about three hundred feet above the first tunnel they went through evidently designed to allow the trains to avoid serious grades that can be dangerous for trains.

Suddenly the train was in a long circular tunnel and when it exited the tunnel there was a completely different picturesque landscape as the railroad tracks were now entering a valley higher in altitude than the long climb up. The train also sped up and Geskar estimated based on timing the distance between passing ancient telephone poles that were no longer used, they were traveling more than 100 miles per hour. In all actuality, Geskar was not too far off the mark.

In thirty minutes, the train stopped in an alpine village where some passengers got off and others got on. The intercom stated people could get off the train for thirty minutes and stretch their legs.

Geskar was soon leading Martilene along storefronts near the train station where he purchased her a nice momento for their trip and a coffee cup she could take to work and show off to her girlfriends. Though she knew some of the women would feel kind of funny knowing Geskar was the widow of a woman that was killed in an accident.

Martilene being a realist, understood life goes on. The unavoidable past is the past. She could not hold Geskar accountable for something he could not prevent such as an accident nobody could predict and that he was not involved with.

About five minutes before the train left the station, Martilene and Geskar were back aboard the train in their private room relaxing. Then a short time later in approximately a half hour, the intercom announced, "Ladies and Gentlemen in the private rooms, you may now proceed to the dining car for evening meals."

AI on the train watched all private room entrances in case of nefarious activity and the necessity to intervene if necessary. The surveillance also allowed the staff to know when the private cabin was empty so staff could go in and make up the bed for the night.

The sofa turned into a queen size bed that had plenty of room for Geskar and Martilene. On one of the walls away from the head of the bed was a video display where they could watch movies in bed and fall asleep.

The other option was to go to the club-car and drink and mingle with other passengers. If Geskar was alone, that's where he would be heading.

The people in the club car were strangers they would never see again for the rest of their lives and Geskar realized staying out of there would enhance his personal security by avoiding chance discovery by a government agent.

After dinner and freshening up and sprite showers, the two love birds were in the bed watching videos together. It was getting dark so sightseeing was now finished for the day and Geskar closed the blinds so if they stopped at a train station nobody could look inside their private room from the station platform.

Halfway through the video the two lovers passed out and went to sleep. Artificial Intelligence monitoring the room for security reasons, analyzed the two sleeping and slowly dimmed and shut off the video to allow them to rest peacefully.

During the night, the train orders required them to slow down appreciably so that passengers would rest better, not feeling any movement of the train they might feel at higher velocities. Trains going in opposite directions were also going slower, so it added a measure of safety in case a signal malfunctioned.

Martilene was feeling more and more attached to Geskar and since he was a simple normal man with a good job, previously married to a beautiful woman, her esteem for him was gradually increasing. Sex for sex was on thing but when you start feeling emotions for your sex partner, that elevates the entire awareness and places you on a trajectory to estimated outcomes.

For Martilene, this was a losing cause she was unaware of. When the mission completed and Geskar vanished, she would start to question her own behavior, but nonetheless would be spooked because of Geskar's sudden disappearance, especially after the SMERSH 3rd Main Directorate took her in and started interrogating her.

Martilene was lucky the SMERSH female employees figured out Geskar was using her as a prop and had nothing to do with the espionage. Martilene's story and her lifelong experiences were easily vetted and even though she went through personal terror with all the interactions with the SMERSH people, she didn't crack.

After all that was over and Martilene reflected, her whole persona was uplifted one day when a special delivery agency left her a package that Geskar sent her that explained a few things but also conveyed to her, he had emotional attachment to her and one day in the future if things could be worked out, he would come and get her so they could live the rest of their lives together.

This alone uplifted Martilene's ego as well as her emotions because she knew for real one of the top enemy spies was indeed emotionally attached to her. It felt like one of the greatest honors in her life she had obtained, being chosen by such a distinguished person to be the source of his affection.

Whether Geskar (a.k.a. Adrak) embellished or stretched it or not, just reading the words stating, "Martilene, you are the most important woman in my life that I ever met," created an emotional tapestry in her life that nothing would ever compare.

Another one of her lucky days was the day Adrak's package arrived the day after the SMERSH people finally decided to leave her alone as the female SMERSH personnel had stated, *there was nothing more to be gained and all they were doing was punishing an innocent bystander.*

Those days were still off to the future, much would happen between now and then, but the present events created memories for Martilene that helped her survive the stressful period of dealing with SMERSH, some of the meanest people in the Galaxy.

Geskar (a.k.a. Adrak) could only sleep a maximum of 6 hours in a day. His body was wired for such a timeline. Early in the morning, Geskar awakened, went into the toilet, took care of business and took a sprite shower. He then went back to their bed and laid down next to Martilene and simply meditated while he awaited her arousal and the start of the next daily event on the train.

Martilene and Geskar would spend 3 more nights on the train, and after that when they reached City of Klamagore, they would take a flight back to City of Praxiskrowtious.

About forty-five minutes before the dining car opened for breakfast, Martilene woke and went to the toilet and took a shower. When she exited the bathroom, Geskar was watching the news on the video display. Just before Martilene asked why the hell Geskar would watch news and be distracted during his time off, the intercom announced:

"Ladies and Gentlemen, Breakfast will be served in the dining car in fifteen minutes for those passengers in the private rooms."

"Shall we go get breakfast?" Geskar asked.

"Yes, I feel like I want to get a stimulating drink," Martilene responded.

A lot of people were not quite awake and the enthusiasm for breakfast by the passengers developed slowly. In fifteen minutes, Geskar escorted Martilene to the dining car and there were only sparsely seated passengers. They would discover this was typical for the mornings. To make sure breakfast hours did not linger the Maître d', on the advice of the head waiter, invited coach passengers in for breakfast knowing those in private cars may not bother showing up.

The purpose of this train was strictly tourism. They had far more efficient methods of transportation, but the public enjoyed the fascination of these antique trains and the scenery they would likely never be able to see otherwise.

Geskar ordered what people on Earth would consider poached eggs on toast with a Hollandaise sauce.

"I'll have the Kratchen Eggs on toast," Geskar stated.

Morning drinks were elixirs full of caffein and chemicals that created stimulation and a buzz. A whip cream like substance was on top for decorations but people liked to dip the straw in it and taste the sweet creamy nature of it.

"Those Kratchen Eggs comes with a white tart *marmeladny sous* on top unless you prefer another type," the waiter explained.

"That will be fine," Geskar replied.

"I'll have what he's having," Martilene said.

"I'll be right back with your drinks," the waiter said.

After the waiter left, Geskar made an announcement to Matriline:

"According to the reservation description information, this afternoon the train will stop at a location called Potryasayushche Krasivo (pronounced Putra-seeya-su-cha Cra- seva) for four hours," Geskar stated.

"Why the long stop?" Martilene asked.

"The travel literature says they will service the train here and give us passengers time to explore this artist community."

"Sounds kind of fun," Martilene said.

Moments later their drinks were served and soon afterwards their meals. Geskar noticed the poached Kratchen Eggs appeared to be almost twice as big as where he came from which was delightful because he could dip into the egg yolk with bread and the delightful white tart marmeladny sous.

"These Kratchen Eggs have a delicious flavor that hits the spot well," Geskar said.

Martilene noticed Geskar had slightly poor table manners dipping the bread into the egg yolk with his fingers. *Geskar's probably lived like a Noble Savage after his wife died*, Martilene thought.

Geskar remembered reading in the travel brochure they would pass over a large bridge soon and see the majestic *Polina Raduga Waterfall*.

Geskar pulled his communicator out of his left front pocket where he always carried it and silently investigated a map application. He locked on his current location and clicked on the *Map Tracker Function*.

Artificial intelligence then started combining all the attributes of data available to them and immediately showed a scale model train resembling the exact one they were on traveling on the railroad tracks in a 5-mile scale.

Geskar then clicked on the landmarks icon and changed the scale to 10 miles.

BINGO! The landmark Geskar was wanting to locate now shown on the map and artificial intelligence gave statistics of based on current train speed they would pass over the bridge and see the *Polina Raduga Waterfall* in ten and a half minutes. "Martilene, in about 5 minutes, move to the chair next to me, we had an interesting landmark coming up," Geskar suggested.

"Alright honey," Martilene responded.

Geskar quickly noted the "honey" in Martilene's statement that gave him confidence the seduction phase of Martilene was well on its way, and he would have a prop that would go a long way towards reducing undue interest in him by officials who are always looking for signs a person might be up to nefarious deeds.

Martilene waited for a few minutes while she was finishing her Kratchen eggs on toast, then stood up and walked around the end of the table and sat down next to Geskar who was facing forward in the direction the train was traveling.

Several minutes later the first indication they were coming up on the *Polina Raduga Waterfall* was the giant rainbow they could suddenly see.

"Oh wow, look at the rainbow," Martilene said.

Geskar held back until he saw the first glimpse of the majestic waterfall, then held his hand out towards the train's window next to him and suddenly said, "Behold the *Polina Raduga Waterfall*."

Other passengers picked up on what Geskar said and soon the entire dining car was observing and some passengers on the other side of the dining car stood up and walked out into the isle so they could get a better view. People were taking pictures of the *Polina Raduga Waterfall* with their communicators, including Martilene.

The *Polina Raduga Waterfall* was probably a half mile from the tracks, and close enough to see the majestic natural imagery and the thundering vast amounts of water coming down.

Geskar pulled his communicator out of his pocket and looked at the same APP he had selected earlier and clicked on the landmarks icon which drilled down to the next layer of controls, and he selected descriptions. The information now populated his screen almost in a text message format which he stated aloud to Martilene.

"The waterfall is a half mile wide and the total distance from the Polina river to the bottom of the waterfall and Lake Valeriya is almost 1000 feet. Five acres of water fall each hour filling up Valeriya that has a dam and electric power generators that provide year- round electricity to all the towns and villages from the City of Klamagore all the way to the City of Praxiskrowtious."

"Does Klamagore and Praxiskrowtious get electric power from the dam generators?" Martilene asked.

Geskar had studied Praxiskrowtious for the purpose of sabotage in the future if required and knew the answer and assumed Klamagore was similarly structured. "Praxiskrowtious has a fusion reactor power plant that is built in underground tunnels in the foothills several miles from the city. There is a global power sharing network that allows cities in peak usage periods to borrow electricity from cities that are not, and due to the time of day when loading shifts due to change in demand, energy then flows in the opposite direction returning borrowed energy." Geskar said.

"Why do they do that?" Martilene asked.

"It saves them from building additional powerplants for standby energy. That results in better utilization of existing nuclear fusion power plants." Geskar responded.

"Whoever figured that out must be a genius," Martilene said.

"Actually, all of Praxiskrowtious nuclear power and distribution was designed by artificial intelligence," Geskar bluntly said.

"No people were involved?" Martilene asked.

"The government didn't want possible Tramular personnel errors, so it mandated Artificial Intelligence design the power stations and power grid."

"I would hope there would be a living being do an analysis of the plans to check up on AI to prevent design issues," Martilene said.

"Artificial Intelligence provided Holographic Discussion Point Presentations, that included an Artificial Intelligence narrator voice during the presentation. Because these were colossal scale engineering marvels, no living Tramulite would have enough time in their life to read and verify the millions of calculations required to build it."

"Are you telling me, Artificial Intelligence designed the fusion nuclear reactors and power grids without a living person actually having any part in developing the plans?" Martilene asked in a very curious manner.

"Not only did the Artificial Intelligence design it. They built it," Geskar stated nonchalantly.

"You got to be kidding me?" Martilene asked.

"The Artificial Intelligence used some people as workers in various modes, but if you think about it, what's the difference between a supervisor directing his men verses Artificial Intelligence holograph doing the same thing with direct oversight." Geskar said.

"That is rather astonishing," Martilene said.

"Artificial Intelligence had the ability to send work orders to whoever was required for any purpose needed. As such a lot of video cameras were installed in the work area, and mobile robots with cameras were walking all over the construction site filming where it was necessary that fixed camera positions didn't have sufficient coverage." Geskar noted.

"How did they maintain quality control?" Martilene asked.

"The entire Quality Assurance process was 100 percent robotic including initiating the fusion process in the nuclear reactors," Geskar noted.

"How do you know all these things?" Martilene asked.

"As you can imagine, when my wife Mildrayd died, I had a lot of spare time on my hands. My supervisor gave me several weeks off so I could stay home and commiserate my wife's death and take care of all her issues."

"And what does that have to do with knowing all this nuclear business?" Martilene asked.

"I needed to take my mind of Mildrayd and reduce the time I was living in sorrow, so I went to the library and randomly picked up a number of publications and one of them was an expose on our current power system and how it evolved from previous platforms and construction techniques," Geskar said.

"It sounds like you picked up a lot of information. What drove you to delve into it as deeply as you did?" Martilene asked.

"I was utterly shocked to learn how Artificial Intelligence took a commanding role in all of the design and construction of our current power grid and nuclear generators and my curiosity got to me and quickly finished the expose which gave me greater understanding in all of our power production and distribution," Geskar stated in a convincing manner.

"We take for granted our power system," Martilene said.

"Yes, I was puzzled why they dug the tunnels to put the fusion reactors in them," Geskar responded.

"What was the main reason for putting the nuclear reactors in tunnels?" Martilene asked.

"The first reason was to make them safe and available during wartime conditions."
"That seems logical."

"The second reason is all nuclear waste is taken to adjacent tunnels which eliminates shipment and also provides safety with underground storage."

"Can they build a powerful generator in a tunnel?" Martilene asked.

"They can scale the amount of energy produced simply by drilling additional tunnels and putting in new reactors." Geskar replied.

"Do they combine the outputs of the multiple generators?"

"Yes, and without Artificial Intelligence it might never have been possible."

"How do they do it?"

"The Generators produce alternating current of various frequencies based on their rpm's. The output goes through a rectifier making it DC Power. DC Power is how they tie the multiple generators together and then the DC power goes into an inverter that converts it back to AC power at regulated crystal-controlled frequencies. The higher frequency of around 150 kilocycles allows power transmission over long distances. The power is fed into sub stations that have inverters that convert the frequency down to what the legacy power requirements are. A lot of our legacy electrical equipment was designed to work at 200 Hertz, so that is what it's converted to 200 Hertz and then sent via underground cables to residences and business."

"That sounds so complicated," Martilene interjected.

"The Artificial Intelligence did a wholesale changeout in a very short period. The existing substations were simple and primitive, and they only had to secure power for a very short period to hook in the new power feeds. All the power company had to do was flip a switch and the new source of power was brought online. The original legacy power plants were soon demolished" Geskar explained.

"In all this power generation and power grid information you studied, what was your biggest surprise or what struck you the most?" Martilene asked.

"I would say what motivated me the most to read it completely was my curiosity into how much Artificial Intelligence involvement affected the outcome." Geskar responded.

"And how much of it do you think Artificial Intelligence did?" Martilene asked.

I came to the realization that Artificial Intelligence picked robots to do most of the physical work. It almost appears Artificial Intelligence was biased towards replacing all living people with a robot in practically anything they build," Geskar answered.

"That feels kind of strange just thinking about it," Martilene said.

"Here's another piece of information that was given in the holographic presentations and narrative: The statistics they showed indicate the new design over the legacy power plants, has 90 percent less down time," Geskar said.

"That's quite an astonishing number if it holds true to form over time,"

Martilene said.

"Sure does." Geskar added.

In due time they were done with their meals and wandered back to their private room to freshen up and figure out what they were going to do.

The train staff had converted their queen size bed back to a sofa and after each had a chance to visit the private toilet and freshen up, they were sitting on the sofa together enjoying the sights.

"How soon do we arrive at stop at Potryasayushche Krasivo?" Martilene asked.

"Let me check my APP." Geskar replied.

Geskar pulled his communicator out of his left front pocket and silently investigated the map application like he did before. He locked on his current location and clicked on the *Map Tracker Function.*

Artificial intelligence then started combining all the attributes of data available to them and immediately showed a scale model train resembling the exact one they were on traveling on the railroad tracks in a 5-mile scale.

Geskar then clicked on the landmarks icon and changed the scale to 50 miles. The landmark Geskar was wanting to locate now shown on the map and artificial intelligence gave statistics of based on current train speed.

Geskar then informed Martilene, "The train will arrive at Potryasayushche Krasivo in approximately ninety (90) minutes."

Martilene's internal computer started number crunching in her own biological manner and realized 90 minutes was a long time to kill and even though the spectacular landscapes were enjoyable to see, she started thinking she could get a quickie then take a sprite shower and clean up and put on new makeup easily in 90 minutes, so she initiated the transcendence into splendid euphoria on a theme from Paganini.

Geskar didn't have a physical embrace on his mind, but Martilene easily convinced him she was ready and willing to make him feel good without the need of pleasurizers or other stimulations.

While taking a commanding position, Martilene took care of all the logistics in preparation for launch into a new psychological domain and was soon on top of Geskar unfurling her carnal knowledge in a way that would make Mira Nair the director for the 1996 film *Kama Sutra: A Tale of Love* quite proud that a woman so skillfully enacted exactly what she crafted.

Geskar was starting to think *I could get used to being around a woman who initiates this type of activity so gracefully and skillfully in a spontaneous burst of passion.*

Geskar had an experience once before where his lover was in the state Martilene was in and softly said to her, "I think I love you."

Geskar didn't understand why he did it, perhaps he was curious to see if Martilene would react the same way the other woman did.

The psychophysical response of Martilene was rather incredible as it elevated the frequency of her being and the psychophysical response became rather intense as chemicals in her brain such as Dopamine (facilitates the experience of pleasure), Oxytocin (reinforces feelings of love and attachment and produces feelings of intimacy and bonding), and Serotonin (make a person feel happy and sleepy after having an orgasm) were opening like a flood gate. The logical part of Martilene's brain was shutting down while spatially remote areas of her brain were now activated.

It was like a cowboy riding a bucking bronco, but it was Martilene's body action creating all the kinetic forces. Geskar's statement created that bucking motion by Martilene's body responding to her psychological domains now in an emotional tornado.

Martilene had never experienced such a psychological response in her lifetime. And when she finally reached that point where her spatial gratification was tapering off, the Serotonin levels were quite high, and she simply laid down on Geskar's body as he held her for a long period. Martilene had become unconscious and entered a dream state fully enriched with splendid euphoria and gratification in higher frequency and in another dimension.

Geskar did the most noble and compassionate act possible and held Martilene tenderly avoiding arousing her as she recoiled from this special event. Martilene remained in this dream state for almost thirty minutes and Geskar regrettably only awakened Martilene because he seriously needed to visit the toilet and drain his fire hose.

The two then ascended to their next act which was Martilene in the shower while Geskar apologized and said, "I'm terribly sorry, but I have to go really bad."

"That's okay honey, do what you need to do."

When Martilene heard the noise level of Geskar draining his fire hose she chuckled and thought, *poor guy.*

Martilene was a realist. She had been around a few jerks who belonged to *Liars Anonymous*, and thus didn't know if Geskar's love pronouncement was fully legitimate, but she enjoyed it anyway and the effects it caused, nonetheless. She would take her time and find out if it were true.

Martilene finished her sprite shower and dried herself off and went out into the private room with a towel around herself and said, "Geskar, why don't you take a shower. I'm sure you don't want to spend the day walking around feeling like a glazed donut."

"Great idea, thanks." Geskar was soon feeling great with the shower and soon dried himself off and put his clothes back on and went out into the private room.

Martilene then went back into the private bathroom that had a good size mirror facilitating her doing the magic trick with the makeup making her look a lot younger and far more attractive.

After Martilene was dressed and ready she asked, "How much longer before we arrive at Potryasayushche Krasivo?"

"Let me check," Geskar responded.

Geskar pulled his communicator out of his left front pocket clicked on the *Map Tracker Function.*

Artificial intelligence then started combining all the attributes of data available to them and immediately showed a scale model train resembling the exact one they were on traveling on the railroad tracks in a 5-mile scale.

Geskar then clicked on the landmarks icon and changed the scale to 10 miles. The landmark Geskar was wanting to locate now shown on the map and artificial intelligence gave statistics of based on current train speed. He then informed Martilene, "The train will arrive at Potryasayushche Krasivo in approximately fifteen minutes."

"That's not too bad. What do you think we'll do when we get there?"

"This is an artist village; it will give us a chance to look at some fine artwork and go to a nice restaurant I'm sure serves great food."

"That sounds fun," Martilene responded and started thinking, *I never would have thought about going on this train trip if Geskar had not suggested it.*

The train was not going very fast because it was going through a series of curves in its mountain passage towards Potryasayushche Krasivo. Geskar looked down at the *Map Tracker Function* and clicked on statistics and confirmed the trains inertial velocity as thirty-five miles per hour.

Chapter Three

Adventures at Potryasayushche Krasivo

When the train eventually arrived at Potryasayushche Krasivo, the train did not take too long to stop since they were not traveling very fast.

Thanks to Martilene's earlier instigating their love making, they were already dressed and ready to leave the train. Other couples were not that far along as some women who took a long time to put on their makeup were still at it. Exiting the train was easy because of the small trickle of passengers leaving the tourist train.

Geskar was a man of the world and understood reality of a lot of things and said, "I know its slightly early, but let's go to a restaurant first, then we'll go look at the artwork later after the crowds do the opposite and settle down at restaurants."

"Alright dear, whichever you wish to do."

Geskar and Martilene walked down an old-fashioned boardwalk along what would constitute Main Street and saw several shops and restaurants. It was more of a random selection, and Geskar led Martilene into a restaurant named *Bustard Drofa*.

The lovely Maître d' met Martilene and Geskar and informed them, "The restaurant will not be seating diners for another fifteen minutes because it's early, but if you will please take a seat here in the waiting area, I'll seat you just as soon as the staff says they are ready."

"Thank you," Geskar responded.

"You are most welcome," the Maître d' responded.

Geskar and Martilene took chairs in the waiting area where they could also see some of the outside activity. Along the sidewalk were artists with little booths selling everything from hand crafted jewelry to oil paintings and sculptures. They would not have to walk far to see a lot.

In fifteen minutes, Martilene and Geskar were seated at one of the best tables in the restaurant with a great view of the mountains in the back view of the building.

There was a smell of baked products permeating the restaurant that was pleasant and added a little to their desires to eat something.

Geskar faced Martilene and in this position was able to get an excellent view of her face. Geskar realized Martilene was cute and when the mission was finished, he knew he would have some serious regrets during exit stage right.

But in the dangerous spy game Geskar (a.k.a. Adrak) was in where he could be turned by treachery and immediately subject to brutality, he knew that when he bugged out, he had to leave and never come back. This view of this beautiful woman reinforced his logic: obtain those few breadcrumbs of life and enjoy them while you can and don't look back for any reason.

Geskar also knew the obvious. If Martilene discovered he was a Vekkar spy, would she feel the same way? Probably not. Geskar estimated Martilene would feel she had been invaded and used as a prop by a spy and love would flash to seething hatred.

Geskar (a.k.a. Adrak) had far more credits available than the real Geskar could ever hope to obtain. And if he needed more credits, they would be forthcoming to support the mission to bribe an official or pay for some kind of nefarious activity.

With all the credits he needed Geskar ordered a bottle of Khrustal'ny Zverinets Wine (pronounced Crew-sh-tal-knee Zver-E-Nets).

Geskar was familiar with this red wine that had pleasurizers in it. It would taste a little like a cabernet sauvignon, with the added flavor of the pleasurizers as a bonus.

Looking over the menu, one entrée quickly caught Geskar's attention: Baked Phasianidae (pronounced Fay-she-awn-e-day).

Since Martilene was local and new the cuisine well, Geskar allowed her to decide on her own what she wanted and was patient and waited until she informed the waiter what entrée she wanted. Geskar could see the waiter acted anxious and appeared slightly annoyed that Martilene was taking so much time to decide.

In an obnoxious like manner the waiter asked, "May I make a recommendation Madam?"

Martilene then preemptively poked the waiter with her fast response:

"That will not be necessary, I will have the *Pastukhi Pie* (pronounced Puss-tue-he Pie)."

"And what can we get for you sir?" The waiter asked. "I'll have the Baked Phasianidae," Geskar answered.

"Baked Phasianidae takes almost double the time to prepare," The waiter advised. "I'm sure it's well worth the wait. Is that baked bread I smell?" Geskar asked.

"Yes, it is sir." The waiter responded.

"I would like a side order of a few slices of that fresh baked bread with butter on the side."

"Sure, that's not a problem." The waiter responded.

"May I ask if you have fresh butter?" Geskar asked.

"Sir, we are fortunate because there are nearby farmers in valleys who raise dairy animals and sell us fresh butter. I think you will like the taste." The Waiter explained.

"I'm looking forward to it." Geskar said.

In a short period the waiter delivered the bottle of Khrustal'ny Zverinets Wine and opened it and poured Martilene and Geskar wine glasses half full of the exotic substance. Geskar knew the waiter expected him to do a taste before he left the table to show approval, which came shortly.

"This Khrustal'ny Zverinets Wine is very good," Geskar announced.

"Thank you, sir, I'll check up on your entrée's," the waiter responded.

Moments later the waiter returned with slices of fresh baked bread and a white butter that had a creamy taste to it. The timing was perfect to accelerate the satisfaction of the Khrustal'ny Zverinets Wine.

"I've not had bread like this in a long time," Geskar said.

Geskar handed a small plate with bread and slices of butter to Martilene who immediately sampled it.

"This bread and butter really taste good," Martilene announced.

"It definitely hits the spot," Geskar replied.

Martilene and Geskar slowly worked on the bread and butter, not wanting to fill up their stomachs to make sure they had room for their entrée's.

The two lovebirds, chit chatted for what seemed like a relatively short time, then the waiter returned with a small cart that had their entrées on them.

Geskar was in for a big surprise. The Baked Phasianidae was half the bird with lots of meat on it. There were a few side items, but the Baked Phasianidae was the food Geskar was most interested in.

Soon Martilene and Geskar were slowly getting very satisfied with their food and the pleasurizers in the Khrustal'ny Zverinets Wine added greatly to the delightful meal.

There wasn't much conversation going on as the food consumed all their attention resulting in increased Dopamine production affecting the pleasure center of their brains.

While they were eating, the restaurant slowly received more diners, and the cacophony of sound slowly grew as more people were conversing waiting for their food orders.

Most of the diners were people that came from the tourist train. A line started forming at the entrance and no doubt several of the customers wished they had done what Geskar had done and put off looking at the artwork until after they had their noon meal.

After the bottle of Khrustal'ny Zverinets Wine was finished and half their entrées were down the pie hole, Martilene said, "I'm full, I can't eat anymore. How is your meal?"

"The baked Phasianidae is very soft and quite juicy. The chef really knows his methods," Geskar said.

When the waiter came by Geskar asked, "Sir, I'm curious do you know how the chef manages to bake the Phasianidae so soft and juicy? Geskar asked.

"Sir, part of our unique methods includes baking the Phasianidae in a special pressure cooker. The pressure cookers are divided in half and the top portion holds the Phasianidae and the lower half has a small reservoir that holds the liquid baking solution. A special rub is wiped all over the bird before we bake it to give it that special flavor. There is several holes in the divider that allow the steam cloud to rise and heat up the Phasianidae via computer controlled temperature. This allows precise cooking temperature and pressure that makes the meat extremely soft as you discovered," the waiter explained.

"Give me regards to the chef, I've never experienced fowl this tasty before,"

Geskar said.

"I will be delighted," the waiter said and smiled.

Soon, Geskar paid for the meal and the waiter was delighted to see the substantial tip.

Seldom did the train people tip him this much.

The two lovebirds left the restaurant and Martilene said, "I want to walk back to the train so I can freshen up."

"Not a problem."

Martilene was not the only train passenger who did such a procedure today, plus Geskar didn't mind having the opportunity to freshen up and get rid of some of his lunch.

After the brief excursion back to the tourist train the dynamic dual were out walking around looking at all the artworks. Martilene came across a beautiful oil painting she loved and made the disappointment comment:

"It's too bad we are on a train, I would love to buy this and take it home," Martilene spoke.

"Go ahead and get it, I'll pay for it as a momento for a reminder of this lovely train trip," Geskar said.

The artist showing all his paintings was more than delighted as Geskar paid him the credits that were written on the price on a sticker attached to the picture frame. *It's nice to have a customer who doesn't haggle with you about the price*, the artist thought.

The artist had some packing material and offered to encapsulate the oil painting to prevent damage during shipment. The painting was soon wrapped in something like bubble wrap and placed in a disassembled box the artist created to give added protection and held together after the bubble wrapped picture was inserted. He also surprised Geskar when he then wrapped a clear shrink wrap around it making all the packing material watertight in case a sudden rainstorm occurred.

The two walked down almost the entire Mainstreet looking at all the artworks and as they were about to head back, Geskar (a.k.a. Adrak) noticed five (5) men following them. As a spy who always does risk management made the command decision these five men were going to attempt robbing them at an opportunistic moment and they looked rough. Geskar decided he needed to call in the calvary.

As they walked along Geskar said in a low voice, I think those five men behind us are going to attempt robbing us, follow me into this alley where I can deal with them.

Martilene looked back and quickly surmised Geskar knew what he was talking about and suddenly was afraid. She dutifully followed Geskar who sped up their pace to get them down to the end of the alleyway where they would be out of sight if a confrontation was going to occur. He reached into his pocket and grabbed his communicator and clicked on an innocuous icon that was programmed if he tapped on it four times in quick succession, the Calvary would deploy to rescue him.

As he predicted, by the time they made it all the way to the end of the alley and a dead end the five criminal looking cretins were already halfway down the alley.

Vekkar rapid response people vectored into Geskar's location and saw him in a position in the alley with the five (5) cretins coming onto him and Martilene quickly.

"Keep walking and walk around the back of the store to the front and get near as many people as possible, these guys are criminals, I'll take care of them," Geskar stated in a very precise manner.

Martilene could see the men coming fast and didn't need a second thought to hustle doing as Geskar suggested hoping he would somehow survive.

Just as soon as Martilene went behind the store, several portals opened and well-armed men in planetary assault uniforms stepped out of them without the five criminals knowing, but Geskar knew the Calvary had just arrived and was emboldened.

"Which one of you guys want to get your ass kicked? Geskar asked in a very confident manner.

The five criminals stopped about 10 feet away from Geskar and the ringleader asked: "So, you are a wise guy punk?"

"Hey big mouth, don't you think you should turn around and look at the weapons that are being pointed at you?" Geskar responded.

One of the criminals turned around and said, "Okh, blyad' (means: oh fawk).

That got a couple more of them looking and one said, "Boss you need to turn around and see what's behind us."

With assault combat laser rifles pointing at them, the criminals suddenly were not so bold.

"Lay down on the ground or I'll tell them to shoot and kill you," Geskar said. The five criminals saw how nasty those shooters looked and decided to comply.

The Vekkar agents slowly approached and were soon upon the five criminals and put neurotic restraints on them. If they tried to move, they got a high voltage sting and quickly discovered they had better lay still.

"This guy here is the ringleader. Take the neurotic restraints off him. I think he wants to fight me. If he can beat me, we'll let all five of you go, otherwise we may have to kill you."

One of the Vekkar agents took the Neurotic restraint off the ringleader and stood him up.

"Okay cupcake let's see what you got," Geskar said.

The criminal thought he would get a fair fight and beat the hell out of Geskar, and they would then be free to leave and go pursue some other victims.

Geskar stood there in a calm state with no apparent hostile stance. The criminal gang leader came at Geskar attempting to get in a few blows and take him out. Criminals rarely get a chance to fight a galactic scale spy trained in the best combined martial arts ever assembled. The criminal had no idea how fast Geskar was and soon discovered his thoughts of beating Geskar were quite remote.

Geskar easily blocked the criminal's blows and landed a very strong punch to the solar plexus. The man stopped dead in his tracks and could not breath. Geskar then landed a nice powerful kick to the groin area of the man who then keeled over and fell onto the ground shaking like a leave.

Geskar then got down on one knee close to the man's face and said, "If you and your goons ever approach me again, I will hurt you worse."

The man was conscious but in the most pain he had ever felt in his lifetime. He had been in bar fights and street brawls, but never experienced this level of pain before.

Geskar then stood up and asked his rescuers, "Please give all five a disabled shot, then take off the restraints and leave."

The Calvary hit all five men with a blue beam that knocked them out really good and they would unlikely regain consciousness for hours.

About that time Geskar walked off, went around the end of the building in a prompt fashion to go find Martilene. After the five criminals were unconscious, the Vekkar agents took off the neurotic restraints, then gave the signal and walked back into a portal and disappeared. The criminals did not awaken until the tourist train had just left town. The ringleader was in excruciating pain and had to be helped back to their transportation. Whoever the man was they thought they were going to rob, was long gone with the woman.

Geskar had double clicked around the building and up to the public sidewalk and looked towards the center of the village and saw Martilene standing there, appearing in fear and wondering if she should contact the authorities.

Geskar approached her with all smiles completely alright with no indication of any type of trauma.

"I was just about to contact the local authorities," Martilene said.

"Not to worry, I handled them." Geskar said.

"How did you do that?" Martilene asked.

"I was trained in Martial Arts; they picked the wrong person to rob. No need to contact the authorities, they will be remembering this day for quite a while."

Martilene was suddenly wondering about Geskar. This was totally out of his character, and she had never heard of Geskar ever engaged in any type of violence before. Geskar grabbed Martilene and asked, "Is your artwork in good condition?"

"Yes, the artist packed it well, plus I didn't have and significant physical activity other than walk promptly around the back of the building and back out front of the stores."

"Glad to hear," Geskar responded.

"I want to go back to the train. I do not feel safe here," Martilene said.

"Sure, no problem. I could probably take a nap after that meal," Geskar replied.

Geskar looked at Martilene and thought she might feel more comfortable if she wasn't carrying the oil painting and said, "Let me carry that for you".

"Thank you, that's very nice of you." Martilene said as she now wondered how Geskar dealt with the five criminals.

Back on the train, they had some time to kill, but when Geskar suggested Martilene snuggle up close to him on the sofa with the curtains pulled down so that people at the station could not see inside their private room, she quickly felt good being held by a man who seemed to be a man of the world and knows how to handle himself quite well. If she knew how badly the swelling was in the criminal's groin area where Geskar kicked, she would have an added wonder.

The two napped until they felt a jerk of the train caused by the engineer who advanced the throttles too abruptly as he had the upcoming grade coming up, he didn't want any possibility of the train stalling and if he had enough momentum for the train to avoid a stall.

Geskar realized he didn't want to get cabin fever staying too long in their private room suggested, "Why don't we go to the club car, get a couple elixirs and socialize."

"Sure, that works for me." Martilene said.

The two got some exercise walking back to the rear of the train. They didn't have to walk through the dining car or coaches, so it didn't take too long.

People were just getting settled down in their private rooms or coach seats from enjoying four hours in the Artist village, so the club car was almost empty with just a couple of souls there who wanted to continue their conversations from the Artist village. They were riding in coach class, which they now knew was a blunder on their part. But at the next stop the following day, at the tourist mecca, *Jămbŏdià Càrŭzŏ,* some of the passengers would get off the train and their private rooms would be available for the tourist train crew to resell to coach passengers who now knew they needed the upgrade.

Many people who originated at Praxiskrowtious would not continue to Klamagore, they would take the train the following day or days later back to Praxiskrowtious.

Listening to the couple who met at a bar in the tourist village, they would share the private room just like a couple. The tourist rail line didn't care they were not a unified couple as this happened quite often when new love affairs formed out of chance meetings which could also stem from simply talking to each other in their coach seats.

While Geskar and Martilene were enjoying their elixirs in the club car, the conductor approached the couple he had dealings with previously and confirmed to them, their private room would be available in the morning after they stopped at *Jămbŏdià Càrŭzŏ.* The tourist train would stop at *Jămbŏdià Càrŭzŏ* for three hours which gave the passengers who would be continuing to Klamagore, time to stretch their legs, visit the gambling casinos, or take one of the terrain follower crafts out for an hour ride to sight see the area.

"When we get to *Jămbŏdià Càrŭzŏ,* would you like to go on a Terrain Follower with me and do some sightseeing of the local area?" Geskar asked.

"What's a Terrain Follower? Martilene asked.

"Terrain followers were a combination VTOL and Hovercraft. They can land on water on say a lake or fly along the mountain side close to the ground." Geskar answered.

"Is it a scarry ride?" Martilene asked.

"I'm sure they are gentle for the passengers if they want more passengers," Geskar replied.

"I'll try anything once," Martilene replied.

Slowly, the more passengers arrived the further the train left Potryasayushche Krasivo behind them.

Eventually the seats arranged on each side of Geskar and Martilene were occupied by tourists. Seats on the other side of the lounge car were also filling up. A cacophony of sound developed as the tourists were discussing their experiences back at Potryasayushche Krasivo.

A well-dressed lady sitting to the right of Martilene introduced herself. "Hello, I'm Karli Pauli."

"Greetings, I'm Martilene."

"Enjoying your trip?" Karli Pauli asked.

"Oh yes. Back at Potryasayushche Krasivo we had a very nice meal at a restaurant and my friend here Geskar bought me a nice oil painting."

"That's very nice of him."

"I do not have any artwork quite this nice back home. The colors in the painting are quite remarkable." (1) Moody Blues - The Promise (fantasy mid-70s LP) - YouTube

"The two of you are not unified?" Karli Pauli asked.

"No, we are juSst really good friends." Martilene said.

"You must be close friends if you are spending five days on a train together."

"Sure, I'm doing a great job of teaching Geskar I can be a naughty girl."

The two women chucked for a moment.

The passenger sitting next to Martilene, the very seemingly nice Karli Pauli had large beautiful blue eyes and lovely blonde hair that waved down like movie stars often wore for publicity pictures and reminded Geskar (a.k.a. Adrak) the woman seemed to have the appearance of Aida Valeriya, one of the top singers in the Vekkar worlds.

"Has Martilene taught you anything new?" Karli Pauli asked.

"Yes, do not underestimate what a woman is capable of," Geskar replied.

"And what was she capable of that impressed you the most?" Karli Pauli asked.

"She can keep her calm under pressure and take command of a situation and provide a unique approach to scenarios," Geskar said.

"I suspect I know Martilene is a scenario creator," Karli Pauli responded with a large cheshire cat smile and a slight giggle.

Martilene could not help but giggle a little herself as she knew Geskar had made her obtain satisfaction like she never experienced before.

"Are you two from Praxiskrowtious?" Karli Pauli asked.

"Yes, we are," Martilene replied.

Karli Pauli pulled a business card out of her small stylish purse and handed it to Martilene and said, "Here's my business card. If you are not busy give me a call in a couple weeks, maybe we can meet for lunch."

"Sure." Martilene replied.

Martilene looked at Karli Pauli's business card and saw she indeed was a singer under contract of *Glamour Entertainment*, one of the giants in the industry.

Then it hit Martilene, she recalled observing this woman sing during a holographic concert she observed at home one evening when she was relaxing and wanted to watch some music videos.

"Karli, I think I watched you on a music video about a year ago during one of those Lloyd Krutoy concerts."

"That sounds about right. I sang my new hit, *"How to Mend a Broken Wing."*

"Now I recall, that was such a beautiful song. I must admit it made me cry. I'm surprised you were able to sing it without breaking down." Martilene said.

"Paul, the composer and lyricist advised me to practice *How to Mend a Broken Wing* until it bored me so I would not break down in front of the audience," Karli replied.

"How many times did you have to practice it to reach that emotional stability?"

"To be honest, several thousand times over weeks. It's not that I do not feel emotional, but I at least can control my emotions while I sing it."

"I feel very special that I got to meet you, because your *Broken Wing* song really had an impact on me. At that time, I wish Geskar had been with me to console me." Martilene said.

"I hope to be there when you need me," Geskar interjected.

"You have such a sweet friend," Karli said.

"There is far more to him than you can imagine." Martilene responded.

"I'm sure there is," Karli said with an evil grin wondering how well he made Martilene feel during their love making.

The waiter making rounds without any sophisticated plan, almost ignoring Geskar and Martilene made his way to the couple and Karli now sitting next to them. He only went to them and not to other areas of the lounge car because he thought he recognized the celebrity.

Observing the three were conversing the waiter assumed they were together and asked, "What may I get you three to drink?"

Karli responded first and said, "I want to see what they are going to order because I might want to try it."

Martilene then spoke, "I'll have a Blue Bǎixiāng Guǒzhī (pronounced Blue Bye-schung Gwo-jhee) [Blue Passion Fruit].

Karli said, "I'll have what she's having."

Geskar said, "Make that three."

"Alright sir, would you like me to put this on a running tab?"

Karli interrupted before Geskar could respond and said, "Please put our drinks on my tab."

"May I ask you what your name is?" the waiter asked. "I'm Karli Pauli."

"Thank you for the information, Karli, I will start a tab for you." The waiter said then went to the bar and handed the order to the bartender via his communicator APP.

The waiter knew the glamorous woman was someone special and instead of asking other passengers for their orders as he normally would do, he waited for the bartender to pour the three drinks so he could check a global search APP on his communicator for the name Karli Pauli and immediately discovered this beautiful woman was none other than the famous singing Diva. And the woman looked exactly like the images he could scan through on the APP.

"That's a nice-looking woman you are serving," the bartender said as he handed the waiter the three drinks.

"That's none other than the famous singer Karli Pauli." The waiter said.

"No kidding." The bartender replied.

The bartender and the waiter would really be utterly shocked to learn the man sitting with the two women was one of the top spies in the galaxy involved in Inter Dimensional Spy Portals, and the enemy.

The waiter delivered the drinks to the three people having a good time, then went around the club car getting orders from other passengers who were gawking at the woman and one of the ladies who overheard the conversation passed on to her sister, "That's Karli Pauli the famous singer sitting there with the man and woman."

If you were in position to observe the club car you would see a human wave as the rumor circulated on the celebrity who was amongst them.

Martilene noticed Karli was by herself. She didn't know if she was traveling alone, but nevertheless enjoyed her presence and her conversation. The other thing that Martilene appreciated was the valence Adrak exhibited towards her and not the celebrity.

Little did Martilene realize, a galactic class Inter Dimensional Portal Spy was doing part of his mission seducing Martilene and would not be distracted by other women.

It seemed to Martilene that Geskar was allowing the two women to conduct the conversation and sat back smiling most of the time. Geskar had his arm casually around Martilene around her mid-section and she felt the warmth and the affection Geskar gave her that added substantially to her comfort especially observing Geskar placed all his focus on her and not the celebrity.

Karli was a very nice person and happy to see a loving couple where the male had his focus on the priority, ostensibly his future mate. In no way did Geskar come-on to Karli which further convinced Karli and Martilene that Geskar's sincerity and his common sense indicated genuine emotions.

It was almost like a breath of fresh air for Karli to be around genuine people

"What are the two of you going to do when we arrive at *Jămbŏdià Càrŭzŏ?*" Karli asked.

"I'm going to take Martilene on a ride on one of the terrain followers."

"That sounds fun. Is there enough room in one of them for a third party?" Karli asked.

"Yes, they hold up to five or six people," Geskar replied.

"When the train stops at *Jămbŏdià Càrŭzŏ,* may I accompany you two. I would like to try one of these terrain followers, but I do not want to go by myself."

Martilene could see the loneliness in Karli and understood an entertainer's life often lacked sufficient social contact from seclusion due to personal security and avoiding people with nefarious purpose in mind.

"Sure, you can come with us, we are just out having a good time." Martilene said.

The Blue Băixiāng Guŏzhī elixir had an immediate effect on the three and their satisfaction increased, and happiness seemed to flourish.

The experience for Geskar would be enough to humble other men, but he had his own universe and the lovely tapestry the two women provided, was just a shade of his total being having gone where he had in the past and achieved sometimes the impossible.

Chitchatting with the two women and enjoying scenic panorama the train went past in its journey to the next stop added greatly to Geskar's atmosphere. It was apparent to Geskar, the women were mostly engaged in conversations between them, and his participation was only casually requested a small percentage of the time. So, it was easy for Geskar to continue in this flight profile as it seemed to positively affect the women that he was more interested into hearing what they had to say vice what he must contribute during the conversation. This was all unfolding perfectly for Geskar as his flight path was automatic and his autothrottles took care of all the actions required in his mission profile.

The conversation lingered for quite a while and the time passed quickly, then the intercom announced: "Ladies and gentlemen in the private rooms, we'll be serving dinner in approximately fifteen minutes. At that time, you are welcome to enter the dining car and receive your evening meals."

"I'm getting kind of hungry; I missed lunch today looking over all the artwork, would you two like to join me in the dining car for our evening meal?" Karli asked.

"We would be delighted," Martilene quickly responded, which didn't seem to affect Geskar in any manner.

When the three stood up, the waiter knew they were leaving, and all their drinks had already been paid for when they were ordered and charged to Karli Pauli's tourist account. He did the polite goodbye to the three of them and immediately cleaned off their tables making them instantly available for the next passengers who wished to be in the lounge car.

It took about five minutes to walk to the dining car and they waited dutifully until the head waiter took down the access line allowing them entrance.

As before Geskar picked a table in the middle of the rail car offering fantastic views. As they were seated there were more spectacular views making dinner time extra special. The train was going through a Canyon known as Láng Xiágǔ (pronounced: Lang Sha-goo).

The waiter remembered the nice couple from the day before and felt slightly jovial noticing the couple was with the celebrity riding the train he had met yesterday.

Good afternoon, ladies and gentlemen, is there something I can get you to drink? The waiter asked.

Karli thought Geskar would likely order a bottle of wine for the table, so she remained quiet. Martilene also knew Geskar would likely order the wine.

"Would it be possible to order a bottle of Khrustal'ny Zverinets Wine?"

"Yes sir." The waiter responded then asked, "Ladies what would you like to drink?" "I'll have the wine too," Martilene said.

"I'll have the wine also, but I would also like a bottle of sparkling water?" Karli said.

The waiter was all smiles being in the presence of the celebrity, but he was also very happy the customer had given him a sizeable tip the previous day, said: "I'll be right back with your drinks."

"This canyon looks kind of scary," Martilene said.

"It would be terrible if one of those large boulders ever dropped down on one of the passenger cars," Karli said.

"I'm sure the railroad construction company shook loose all the boulders that would fall on us during construction," Geskar said.

The waiter arrived with a bottle of Khrustal'ny Zverinets Wine in a silver container full of ice water. One by one he flipped the wine glasses right side up and filled a good amount for each to taste and waited for a response.

Geskar did the official taste test and expressed: "It tastes fantastic, I'll have some more."

The waiter followed suit after the women all downed their sample and acknowledged the wine was satisfactory. He then took their order after all the wine glasses were full and the bottle back in the silver container full of ice water.

Geskar looked at the menu. There were four entrées to choose from and he picked Ròuzhì de Shīzi-bǐng (pronounced Roja da Shiyz-ea-bing) [succulent lion shank].

The other women copied Geskar's choice which made the waiter happy because since all three ordered the same entrée, he knew he would not get their orders mixed up or ask again who ordered what during the serving. Also, the entrée would be provided by the chef at the same time.

The train utilized as much artificial intelligence as possible to reduce crew size. The waiter had a conformal ear but fed information such as: "The entrées for table number five are ready to be served."

The Train Artificial Intelligence System scanning the room would also advise the waiter in his ear bud, "the diners at table number five appear to have finished."

The *Train AI System* would also alert the busboy would then approach table number five and ask, "May I remove your dishes?"

Three people can easily finish a bottle of Khrustal'ny Zverinets Wine. All the wine bottles were made with clear glass so that artificial intelligence could determine when the wine bottle was empty and notify the waiter who would ask, "May I get you another bottle of wine?"

Should the passenger answer in the affirmative, the auxiliary chef acted as a bartender and was just as busy as the club car bartender, would receive *Train AI System* alert then prepare the bottle of wine then alert the waiter via the waiter's ear bud from their *Train AI System* it was ready for pickup to deliver to dining table number five that ordered Khrustal'ny Zverinets Wine.

The Tramular planet Geskar (a.k.a. Adrak) now operated in, had an area that was over ran with *Ròuzhì de Shīzi-bǐng*. To reduce the size of the *Ròuzhì de Shīzi-bǐng Prides*, the government sponsored annual *Ròuzhì de Shīzi-bǐng* hunting seasons.

Licensed hunters would bag their allotment of *Ròuzhì de Shīzi-bǐng* and these were very large animals some reaching 7 feet in length and 500 pounds. Just one *Ròuzhì de Shīzi*-bǐng would be sufficient for a tourist train trip. The meat on the shanks was by far the best cut, and with the proper marinade and tenderizer, the entrées were quite delicious. Martilene and Karli were soon enjoying the taste and the aroma of their servings.

Since Ròuzhì de Shīzi-bǐng hunting season was now in full swing, Geskar marveled at the freshness of the meat and was unaware, this *Ròuzhì de Shīzi-bǐng* meat had been butchered just the day before the train left Praxiskrowtious. The secret marinade sauce the Chef created from his personal cookbook, made the entrée taste better than any farm raised stock.

The fact there was no chit chat going on while Geskar and the two women engorged themselves on the *Ròuzhì de Shīzi-bǐng* entrées was an indication of how great the food tasted.

Halfway through the meal the bottle of Khrustal'ny Zverinets Wine was empty, and the waiter dutifully approached the table asking: "Sir, would you like another bottle of Khrustal'ny Zverinets Wine?"

"Absolutely, yes please. It really helps nicely to was down the *Ròuzhì de Shīzi-bǐng*."

Moments later the waiter refilled the three wine glasses feeling good the passengers were quite pleased and smiling as they carved into nice large servings of *Ròuzhì de Shīzi- bǐng*.

As soon as Artificial Intelligence analyzed the three sitting at table number five appeared to have finished their Entrée's, the waiter approached and asked, "Is anyone ready for dessert?"

"What is available?" Karli asked.

"We have ice cream, *Qiǎokèlì-piàn* (pronounced: Chow-ka-lee Pe-Ann) cookies [chocolate chip cookies], cake, and fruit pies," the waiter answered.

"I'll have the *Qiǎokèlì-piàn* cookies with ice cream." Karli said.

"I'll have what she's having," Martilene requested.

"And you sir?" The waiter asked Geskar.

"I'll have a slice of Píngguǒ pie (pronounced: Ping-gwo) with a scoop of ice cream on top," Geskar responded.

In due time deserts were finished and the three were walking back towards their private rooms.

"I think I need to go freshen up a bit, I'll catch up with you two tomorrow when the train stops at *Jǎmbǒdià Càrǔzǒ.*" Karli said.

"We'll meet you on the train platform at the station after it stops," Geskar said.

"Have a nice rest," Martilene said and Geskar nodded.

"Alright, see you then," Karli said and entered her private room and shut the door.

Martilene and Geskar's private room was in the next car and when they arrived the tourist train staff had made up their beds for the night.

"Go ahead and freshen up, I'll wait until you are done," Geskar said as the perfect gentleman.

"Thank you dear," Martilene said and took her turn first.

In due course they were both ready for bed and the lights went out via artificial intelligence when it determined the two passengers were sleeping.

* * *

In the morning, Geskar awakened before Martilene and carefully left the bed and went into the bathroom where he could do his morning routine. It was kind of early, so Geskar didn't expect Martilene to awaken any time soon, therefore he took care of all his personal requirements, then a quick shower, dried off and exited the bathroom.

Shortly after he entered back into the open area of the private car, Martilene stirred and saw Geskar with a towel wrapped around himself, obviously just finished taking a shower.

"I'm going to get up now and use the bathroom," Martilene said. Martilene then stood up looking a little unhappy Geskar thought.

The truth of the matter, Martilene was thinking about getting some big-A before she cleaned herself up, but as it turned out, it worked out for the best because as soon as she sat down on the toilet, she was quickly grateful there was no action yet allowing her to take her time freshening up.

Martilene knew that Geskar had just exited the toilet so there was no rush on her part since he already took care of business. But in an emergency, in the lower level of the passenger car was a public toilet and shower for the larger private rooms that could have as many as 6 or 7 people staying in those rooms located at the ends of each passenger car.

If Geskar suddenly needed toilet accommodations he knew the toilet located on the lower level was available because he saw them as they entered on the lower level and had to climb stairs to get up to the upper level which was the main corridor throughout the train.

Since Martilene was busy in the bathroom, Geskar checked his personal communicator to see approximately when they would be arriving at *Jămbŏdià Càrŭzŏ*.

Geskar pulled his communicator out of his left front pocket clicked on the *Map Tracker Function* APP icon.

Artificial intelligence then started combining all the attributes of data available to them and immediately showed a scale model train resembling the exact one they were on traveling on the railroad tracks in a five-mile scale.

Geskar then clicked on the landmarks icon and changed the scale to 10 miles. The landmark Geskar was wanting to locate, *Jămbŏdià Càrŭzŏ* now shown on the map and artificial intelligence gave statistics of based on current train speed.

They would arrive at *Jămbŏdià Càrŭzŏ* that gave them time to eat breakfast on the train, then come back to their private room and freshen up and be ready to go enjoy the sights including a terrain follower ride.

Martilene finished her activities in the bathroom including applying new makeup, then exited it to find out what was in store for the day.

No sooner than she was with Geskar in the private room, the intercom gave the announcement:

"Ladies and Gentlemen, breakfast is now being served in the dining car."

Just like the day before, the dining car was only sparsely seated, and three quarters of the tables were empty and available. Geskar quickly chose a table in the middle of the car and Martilene sat down. Next to him.

Soon after the waiter took their drink orders, the illustrious Karli Pauli arrived in the dining car and saw the table that Geskar sat with Martilene could easily seat six passengers, walked over and asked:

"Would it be possible for me to join you?" Karli asked.

"Yes, please sit down with us," Martilene answered swiftly knowing Geskar would have said the same.

The waiter knowing a Celebrity just sat down at the table was curious how the other two that he had seen a couple times before knew Karli Pauli. He approached the table and took Karli's drink order then gave them a rundown of what was being served that morning.

The tourist train tried to have different types of breakfasts each morning so that passengers did not get bored with the food selection.

Geskar waited until the ladies made their choices that turned out to be pastries to go with their morning caffeinated drink. Geskar chose Kratchen Eggs and Styrolean Sausages with toast and white blended butter, most likely produced from nearby farms.

The women were chatting away and Geskar semi-ignored them simply playing along as if he cared what they were saying. Women live in a different universe and their conversations were diabolically different than men. One might think they had a pragmatic approach to life, but the truth is with these two women is that they adapted well to whatever circumstances that were bestowed upon them.

Geskar slowly developed a liking for Martilene, but he understood the dangers of allowing himself to be emotionally tangled with her in view of this mission and what might occur. The little run in with the five criminals back at Potryasayushche Krasivo was a subtle reminder unexpected situation may occur out of his control and the fewer amounts of interpersonal entanglements, the better he would likely avoid the pitfalls that may manifest.

Nevertheless, in the current posture of Geskar's mission this was a development he needed to build to give the appearance of a long bona fide relationship to cement the appearance of he was a local.

Karli was somewhat fixated by the couple, Martilene and Geskar. These were normal people with no big flair for singing Divas and celebrities. To be able to observe them close up in a unobtrusive fashion was quite pleasing to her, no matter if they had any bad traits.

If Karli saw something that wasn't cool to her, she simply withheld her comment and her bias. Afterall she was a guest to their inner circle.

When Karli saw Geskar dipping his toast into the Kratchen egg yolks, if it were another place and time with others, she would say something to the tune: "How disgusting."

But here Karli was with this sweet couple who were gracious and non-assuming, and she was more than willing to overlook the Kratchen egg yolks and ignore it because of all the other tangible positives the two exhibited.

Karli of course was glad when breakfast was over, and they could go back to their private rooms as she was looking forward to her adventure on the terrain followers.

Geskar over time figured out Karli had security with her. A couple men Geskar determined were private dicks hired to look after Karli always showed up wherever she went including breakfast this morning. Geskar figured out readily they were marginal performers to have blown their cover so easily.

It's going to be a comedy show when we get on the terrain followers, Geskar thought.

After freshening up a bit and relaxing they didn't have much time to get it on the way Martilene wanted because Geskar knew Karli and her two closely followed bodyguards would be waiting for them at the train station platform.

Geskar was of course curious how the men would cover their tracks and not be totally humiliated by being discovered what they were doing.

Geskar was certainly way above their pay grade in capability. When they finally split apart at their destination, City of Clamagore they would not know, nor would they ever believe they were amid a galactic level spy.

In a while the train came to a stop and the intercom announced, "Ladies and Gentlemen, we will be stopping here at *Jămbŏdià Càrŭzŏ* for three hours to give you a chance to explore the community. There are lots of shops and things to do in three hours plus there are numerous Terrain Follower rides you can purchase to be able to see some of the hidden illustrious landscape that has no roads or access. You can book those Terrain Follower excursions at the train station.

"The reason why we recommend you do that is the Terrain Follower companies work in conjunction with this tourist railroad and the conductor can radio contact them if you are late getting back to the train, so we do not leave you behind. Usually, the Terrain Follower pilots are punctual and will get you back to the train station in time so as to not miss the train and have to spend the night in a local hotel.

"Have a safe time in *Jămbŏdià Càrŭzŏ* and be sure to be back here in three hours. Lunch will be served as the train leaves the station, but you certainly may want to try the local cuisine."

"Shall we go?" Geskar asked.

"Are you in a hurry because you want to see Karli?" Martilene asked as if she was having a stint of jealousy.

"Actually, no. Karli is a celebrity. I'm a nobody. She has her movie actress domain and as you can tell, she's a very lonely woman, because that's how it is. They are very protected and Karli's contact with us is probably the most exposure to people she's had all year. I actually pity her."

"Is that so?" Martilene asked.

"Yes, you are a normal person with the opportunity to socialize with whomever you wish when you want. You have what I think Karli sorely misses. Feel lucky you are not caught up in her business. I'm sure in due time you would realize it's not you piece of cake."

Martilene suddenly had a deep appreciation for Geskar who had so much common sense and blended in well. But one issue she could not fully resolve was: *those angry criminals that were coming fast at them. What the hell did Geskar do because he walked away from it as if there was no big effort he had to put forth.*

In a way, Martilene wished she wasn't such a big coward and stuck around to see just how Geskar handled it. This mystery caused her some bad dreams last night!

Martilene had no idea how lucky she was because had she seen Geskar's calvary appear coming out of the Inter Dimensional Portals, she likely would have been abducted and taken away and not seen her home again until after the war was over. Martilene put all those thoughts away and was curious to see how Geskar interrelated with Karli.

Geskar led Martilene off the tourist train and waited on the platform for Karli. As expected, Karli soon appeared and the two keystone cops trailed behind her trying to not look conspicuous.

Geskar would ignore the two security men for now because he knew he would get a laugh as the terrain follower they secured would be chasing behind them in attempts to not lose line of sight to their protectorate.

Just like the tourist train announcement made, Geskar led the women to the kiosks at the train station that sold the terrain follower rides.

The passengers were told to wait near their kiosks because the terrain followers would drive up adjacent to them and call their names to make sure prompt contact was made.

They had 3 hours to have fun, but Geskar, being prudent, only purchased an hour ride for the three of them on a terrain follower that would accommodate all of them.

Just like the announcement, soon Geskar's name was called out as several Terrain Followers converged on the pickup location next to the Kiosks.

"Mr. Geskar are you here?"

"Yes, that's me."

"Got your two other riders with you?"

"Yes, here they are."

Geskar led Martilene and Karli to the terrain follower where the pilot had shouted out his name.

The pilot helped everyone strap in to ensure their safety. Then he gave some simple instructions like the seat was their flotation device. What he didn't tell them was that *the water was so cold they would die from hypothermia long before rescuers could get there. No reason for spoiling the fun with critical information.*

With the headphones on to hear the tour and the goggles on the passenger to prevent bugs from hitting them in the eyes, the terrain follower pulled away from the curb and followed the pack over to the launch zone which was a very long concrete slab that was long enough to land on in case they had to abort the takeoff. At the end of the concrete slap a safety observer had an observation post near the end of it to prevent pedestrians to get near it and possibly fall off,

All the Terrain Followers were airborne at least 50 feet up in the air before they got near the end of the long launching concrete slab.

There was a flight pattern leaving the launch zone and the herd of Terrain Followers simply followed the leader. The Terrain followers had transponders and computer guidance in the event they lost visibility, the computer would land it safely where it was launched from.

Since the tour scheduled was only one hour long the terrain follower had sufficient fuel to do the tour without stopping to refuel.

They flew upriver and soon found a lake. Thanks to the unique design the Terrain Followers landed on the lake and ran up the coastline in their hovercraft mode. Halfway up the lake in the intercom, the Terrain Follower pilot announced:

"We are coming up on some local Medveds (appear like Brown Bears)."

They got close to the shoreline and where they were at the water depth was 50 feet, so a Medved would have to swim a good distance to them, meaning they were perfectly safe.

They passed about 20 yards from a few Medveds catching fish coming down off a stream.

The pilot announced via the intercom:

"If you look closely at those Medveds, you will discover they can stand almost 18 feet tall, and their heads are two feet wide."

The image of the huge heads on the bears frightened Martilene and Karli.

Geskar could see a lot from the pilot's rear-view mirrors and could see Karli's security detachment were trailing behind keeping their distance.

The Terrain Follower continued up the lake's coastline until it ended. They were going to a dead end with a small waterfall. They flew up over the hillside and discovered a slow running river that dumped into a waterfall down below.

There were many other wild animals to observe. One could not see all this without obtaining a lift from a terrain follower. They were now in the wilderness. There were no homes, cabins, or any sign of people, except those in the line of Terrain Followers kicking up a cacophony of noise it seems the wild animals had gotten used to. This area was off limits to hunters and the wild animals seemed no not have any fear since none of them had ever seen another animal killed by a hunter or molested by a person in any manner.

The Terrain Follower landed on the water converting from a VTOL to a Hovercraft. While they were cruising along the shoreline now and then they could see signs: "Do Not Feed Wild Animals." Also, there were signs, "These Wild Animals Seem Harmless Are Very Dangerous. DO NOT APPROACH WILD ANIMALS."

Karli was feeling grateful this wonderful couple invited her to come along for the ride on the Terrain Follower, otherwise she would not have seen all this nature that uplifted her several notches.

Karli would soon reward Adrak and Martilene with a nice gesture and invite them to the exclusive night club at the top of a tall high rise building where she performs for the super-rich.

The pilot said over the intercom they could hear with the headphones they were wearing:

"We'll not stop, we'll just look. In case you are wondering, people that were dumb enough to get out of their Terrain Followers and approach wild animals were killed."

In the Hovercraft mode the pilot could either use the VTOL thrusters that made a lot of noise and annoyed the passengers during this exceptional part of the tour, or he could shut down the thrusters and stick his tail in the water which was a quiet electric propelled motor and propeller allowing them to cruise along for a while at slow speeds and enjoy the ambience of the nearby forest full of animals and nature.

All the other Terrain Followers that landed on the slow-moving river did the same, whereas those that didn't turned around and went back to the town of *Jămbŏdià Càrŭzŏ* where the passengers were exchanged, and while other tourists shopped for artwork and found great restaurants that featured food that could only be obtained in the wild whether legally or not. Some poachers got away catching some highly illegal wild animals they were not supposed to bag.

There were four legged creatures. Some were a lot like Deer or Tomlars. The other four-legged creatures they spotted looked like bears but were a lot smaller and skinnier out hunting the other four-legged creatures.

They came across other signs now that said:

"This is a protected area. You are not allowed to go ashore here."

Eventually the Terrain Followers came up to an area where rapids fed the slow-moving river. All the Terrain Followers converted to VTOL mode and went airborne at this point and flew above the rapids for a while then turned around gained altitude and flew back to *Jămbŏdià Càrŭzŏ*.

It seemed like the ride on the Terrain Follower was short but, Geskar knew it lasted an hour. This flight of Terrain Followers was a well-choreographed routine the pilots did every day with a new set of customers, rarely seeing the same people again.

Just like the other passengers, when they arrived back at *Jămbŏdià Càrŭzŏ*, Geskar turned into the tour guide and took the women through the town like the Artist village they had been at yesterday.

Women generally like to look over things. A lot of husbands hate to go shopping with their wives for this very reason. But in the case of Geskar, this was all part of the script he was performing in the seduction of Martilene for the mission prop.

Geskar wondered if he would be lectured by the doctor when he returned to the safe house for his unprotected sex. But he rationalized it. Since he would disappear at the conclusion of the mission. Would he really care if Martilene was pregnant? No doubt he would likely kill people during the mission, and he already beat the hell out of some guys. The moral question for a spy has a very short answer if one at all.

Both women purchased items as they walked around as souvenirs. At their last stop before finding a restaurant, the women picked out some medallions which Geskar insisted on purchasing for them.

Geskar would not know this, but after he disappeared, the women would cherish those tokens for the rest of their lives. Martilene had SMERSH visitors after the Sidis aftermath and became quite emotional when the female SMERSH agents informed her that Geskar who was not whom she thought he was had been killed.

The team bugged out and the following day, SMERSH raided Geskar's home which was empty and there was no sign of any activity as plumbers had removed all the spyware the previous day.

Those days of the confrontation and epic struggle were still off to the future, but during the train ride, two women developed feelings for Geskar he was unaware how strong they were which was probably good for him so that he would not have remorse later.

***

At this point in the train ride, Martilene, Karli, and Geskar wound up in a restaurant that specialized in *Sanicar Qudrellas* (Turtle Meat).

As Geskar entered the restaurant recommended by the Terrain Follower pilot, he wondered what does Sanicar Qudrellas taste like?

Even though Sanicar Qudrellas was once an everyday *Jămbŏdià Càrŭzŏ* staple, it joined the ranks of former popular foods. Nevertheless, in many parts of the Tramular worlds, the *Sanicar Qudrellas* protein is still consumed. As a result, one lingering question remains for those who haven't had a chance to *Sanicar Qudrellas* meat: What does it taste like, and how can it be prepared?

Well, *Sanicar Qudrellas*, according to the Terrain Follower pilot, can be depicted as a cross between wild boar and reptiles, which is why the two proteins were used as a substitution in mock *Sanicar Qudrellas* soup. Nonetheless, putting the Terrain Follower's comments aside, they would soon read in pamphlets with the menu's diner's comments that offered a broader descriptive spectrum of *Sanicar Qudrellas* flavors based on how the entrées was prepared.

For instance, a journalist who writes food articles for a major news provider wrote:

"The *Sanicar Qudrellas* is a holy amalgamation of a variety of distinctive, flavorful meats, such as Tomlars, Phasianidae, fish, shrimp, crustaceans, wild boar, and mountain Shānyáng (pronounced: Shain-yan appear like mountain goats)."

None of the three had tried eating *Sanicar Qudrellas* before so they randomly picked three entrées based on the menu pictures to share.

One entrée appeared like fried chicken. Another appeared and tasted like a curry dish right out of India.

And finally, the third dish tasted much like a stew with a very nice flavor. In doing so the three built a *sampler* dish. The fried *Sanicar Qudrellas* went so fast, they ordered a side dish. The two other dishes were good too, but the fried *Sanicar Qudrellas* tasted so great with the spices used, it was a very popular dish.

The restaurant also had some unique elixirs they ordered. Geskar decided he wanted to try *Wúliáng Huāmì* (pronounced: Wu-long Hwa-me [Unscrupulous nectar]) added measurably to the pleasantness. Geskar was pleased he would be back on the train in a while and freshen up and relax with the splendid effects he felt the *Wúliáng Huāmì* seemed to give him. The women tried the elixir out of curiosity also liked the effects.

If there was a time during the journey Geskar was vulnerable, it was now. He struggled to maintain equilibrium as the *Wúliáng Huāmì* was far more potent than he expected.

Geskar wished he had one of his antidote pills with him to overcome the effects, but he prudently took the next best course of action. As soon as the meal was over, he informed the two ladies he needed to go back to the train to freshen up.

Karli and Joanie also had similar ideas and after paying for the meal they walked back to the train that was not too far from the restaurant and boarded it to take care of their business. Since they were going back to the train a little early the two security guys protecting Karli stood out like keystone cops. Geskar could not help but be amused.

About the time they got on the train, Martilene mentioned she too needed a quick trip to the toilet. Geskar being the perfect gentleman suggested she use their private toilet, and he would use the lower-level toilet which should be available since most of the passengers were still of the train walking around *Jămbŏdià Càrŭzŏ*.

Geskar really wasn't in need of the toilet, he just needed an excuse to get back to the train since the elixir had strong effects on him and he made a mistake by not taking an antidote pill before heading out that could have mitigated the intoxication. After urinating he went up to their private room and laid back on the sofa stretching his legs and relaxing.

In due time, Martilene came out of the toilet walked over and positioned herself in his arms wanting some affection which he gracefully gave since it was the obvious pathway to a good nap from the great food and the utter intoxication.

If Geskar ever drank *Wúliáng Huāmì* again, he knew it was a strong elixir and would take appropriate action or drink sparingly. Martilene similarly affected was suddenly very sleepy and the combination of the intoxication and the ambience of Geskar's arms holding her like a splendid lover, quickly put her into a very pleasant nap which she did not awaken from until the train left the station.

There would be another stop the following day in the town of *Sandenslǐng* another artist/tourist stop over. Besides the restaurants and the souvenir shops, was located very close to geothermal vents and geysers that erupted several times per hour. For a modest fee they could take a bus to the viewpoint that was synchronized to the train schedule.

By the time most of the passengers had a chance at a nice restaurant, souvenir shops, and a visit to the geothermal vents to observe the geysers, it was time for the train to leave the station. Today, Geskar took an antidote pill before leaving the train, and thus did not have the same issue as the day before. However, the women had no such protection, and they were soon back in their private rooms napping and purring like kittens.

Chapter Four

The Spy, The Singer, And the View to a Kill

The next day, the train ride was over as it pulled into the station at Klamagore. The three amigos departed the train about the same time. Karlie approached Martilene and said, "Be sure and contact me. I want to invite you and Geskar to watch one of my performances."

"I would be delighted," Martilene responded but privately pouted internally wondering what the hell could she wear to such an event where the audience would likely have well-dressed people.

Geskar and Martilene said goodbye to their new friend Karli and soon were in a Skycar heading to the airport to fly home to Praxiskrowtious.

The following day, Geskar went back to his job, looking refreshed and refreshed after seeing far more of the planet than most Vekkar's ever would see due to the ongoing conflict created by two hostile personalities of the Tyrants in charge of their governments.

Geskar didn't know it, but he was followed on the train by a Vekkar agent, and that's where his problems started because the Agent had been identified by the Tramular's and due to his sloppiness the Tramular's discovered this spy seemed to be tracking Geskar who did not detect his trail.

Geskar was extremely lucky the Vekkar agent wasn't trailing him too closely and had gone into a restaurant to eat and missed the run in with the five criminals. Otherwise, the Tramular's following the Vekkar watcher agent would be closing in on Geskar fast now.

This is where the Tramulite Spy Sidis came into the picture as this Vekkar Agent discovery slowly evolved into a full-scale investigation.

Analysts at the Inter Dimensional Spy Portal Directorate getting various streams of intel were slowly putting together information for Geskar (a.k.a. Adrak) to investigate that might lead them to what they needed to find which would eventually lead to the *Project Geyser* mission.

In the days to come, Geskar (a.k.a. Adrak) would have to do a break-in via a Inter Dimensional Spy Portal to a Tramular Agency responsible for the research center they need to locate to destroy and possibly kill a few scientists leading the research. All that took a while and would not be privy to that information for a couple of weeks.

Meanwhile, Martilene contacted Karli and the date was set for her and Geskar to go see one of her shows that was in the nightclub on the top floor of a luxury hotel. Martilene got right to the point in the conversation.

"Karli, I'm not sure what to wear to your performance. I probably need to go shopping so I think I might like your advice on the wardrobe."

"Martilene, I have a great idea. You and Geskar took really good care of me on the trip and filled me with a lot of joy and happiness in all those activities we did together, so I want to give something back to you, if you will let me."

"Sure, but I don't think we did that much."

"Trust me dear, you did far more for me than you can imagine. I was burned out and lonely. I needed to get away and find salvation somehow before I went nuts. The two of you gave me great companionship when I needed it the most and you treated me like I was one of your personal friends.'

"I felt like you were our friend very quickly because you are such a nice person." Martilene said

"Thank you, that warms my heart." Karli replied.

"You are most welcome."

"Martilene this is what I want to do. Friday evening since you and Geskar do not have to work the next day, I will make reservations for you in this hotel. I always have a fashion designer here with makeup artists to prepare me for the shows. I will inform them I want them to dress you and Geskar, when you check into the hotel. I'll make you look smoking hot so Geskar will never doubt his feelings for you again the rest of his life!"

The two women laughed for a moment, then Martilene responded:

"Alright Karli, I like the way you operate. I'm good with you plan and will do it, but I need to ask Geskar to get his buy in."

"I'm sure Geskar will agree but call me and let me know you two are good for Friday," Karli said.

"I'm going for a walk with Geskar in the morning, like we usually do at the park. I'll discuss your plan with him then and call you as soon as he agrees." Martilene said

"Thank you Martilene. It will be good to see you again, and I promise I will sing my heart out for the two of you," Karli said.

Karli had secret thoughts of having Martilene drugged so she could try out Geskar one time. She put that on her back burner for another day and time. Karli usually got what she wanted, and she had not had a good lover in a while.

During their walk the next day, Martilene brought up the event on Friday:

"Geskar, I talked with Karli yesterday," Martilene said.

"How is Karli doing?" Geskar asked.

"She's very happy, the train ride is what the doctor ordered for her. She was burned out and stressed out and needed some down time." Martilene said.

"That's good to hear," Geskar responded.

"Geskar, Karli has invited us to see her performance on Friday evening,"

Martilene said.

"What time?" Geskar asked.

"I talked to her about how I wasn't sure what I should wear and probably needed to go shopping, and she came up with an idea," Martilene said.

"What's the idea?" Geskar asked.

"She wants us to check into her hotel. The nightclub is on the top floor of the building. She will reserve the room for us and to solve my wardrobe issue, she's going to have a fashion designer and makeup artists fix me up for the evening so I will look extra cute for you." Martilene said.

"Sounds like a great idea. Do I need to wear a suit?" Geskar asked.

"Just wear your normal clothing. She's going to have her fashion designer also dress you and give you a makeover." Martilene said.

"Sound's kind of interesting," Geskar said.

"Do you agree we can do that?" Martilene asked.

"Why not. Be sure and take some pictures of me with her so I can make my co-workers jealous," Geskar said.

"What about me? Am I a dog?" Martilene asked.

"Of course not, I'm sure you will look smoking hot, I would like some pictures of you as well. I'd like to have a picture of you on my desk at work if you will give me permission to show it," Geskar said.

"I would be delighted. That makes me feel special," Martilene said.

"You are special," Geskar said.

Geskar (a.k.a. Adrak) felt a twinge of guilt because he knew he would ultimately break Martilene's heart when he bugged out and it would be sooner rather than later after the intel briefing, he received today from the courier that would help him get to where he needed to finally finish this mission.

A lot of Intel was rolling in and planning was intense. The only reason why Geskar was allowed to go see Karli's show is planners had a few more snags to deal with which changed the schedule for several days. The dead time dove tailed nicely into the scheduled Karli's performance.

By now Geskar (a.k.a. Adrak) had gone through a critique of his train ride and all that occurred. He knew his communicator was significantly modified to allow snooping on him. He had no secrets.

Executive Director *Doctor Oxyuran Lepidotus Taipan* read the transcripts to all the conversations Adrak had on the train trip and they discussed some of it during the critique.

"You will have quite a moral dilemma when this mission is complete," Doctor Oxyuran Lepidotus Taipan said.

"In what way?" Adrak (a.k.a. Geskar) asked.

"I know you are looking at this like a spy, but I fear in years to come you will have some lingering emotions you are building up with Martilene," Doctor Oxyuran Lepidotus Taipan said.

"I must step away from it. This is what espionage is all about," Geskar said.

"What if you discover you got Martilene pregnant?" Doctor Oxyuran Lepidotus Taipan asked.

"How would I know? I'll be long gone."

"Just because you are gone doesn't mean INTEL will lose interest in Martilene. We will know if you impregnate her and I must warn you that by agency policy, we will be required to inform you. How would you think about it then?" Doctor Oxyuran Lepidotus Taipan asked.

"I think it's a little late to ask me to keep my pecker in my pants," Adrak said.

"You need to seriously start thinking about using protection. One of the issues you would face if she got pregnant is the Tramular's will get some markers on your DNA. You need to think about all aspects of this," Doctor Oxyuran Lepidotus Taipan said.

"I've left so much DNA behind in various manners, if they are on to me, they already have samples," Adrak said.

"Perhaps, but I'm just warning you as a concerned supervisor that you need to be careful how you play the espionage game for your own good," Doctor Oxyuran Lepidotus Taipan said.

"The fact my interpersonal relationship with Martilene has evolved to the way it has, it's only natural that my behavior would be the way it is. Nobody would suspect otherwise," Adrak said.

"As supervisor of the critique I must discuss with you all possible side effects of the mission so that you are better prepared to deal with it. I'm not making a moral judgement on your conduct." Doctor Oxyuran Lepidotus Taipan said.

"That's good to know since you already had me kill people in the past," Adrak said.

"That is the regrettable part of war."

"It certainly is." Adrak responded.

"That's all for today, thanks for coming to the critique."

"Getting here via the portal makes it a hell of a lot easier otherwise."

"More reason why we have to deny the enemy from obtaining this technology."

"I agree with you completely.

The next day after work, Geskar, (a.k.a. Adrak) stopped by Martilene's home and picked her up in a Skycar and the two of them headed for the *Emerald Jasmine Resort*. Since Martilene and Geskar had VIP reservations thanks to Karli Pauli, when the Skycar pilot inserted the destination address, a query was made to the names of the passengers and thanks to artificial intelligence, receptionist protocols were issued and the Skycar was vectored to roof top to enter the *Emerald Jasmine Resort* vice entry via the front lobby.

Furthermore, when the two of them arrived at the *Emerald Jasmine Resort*, a representative met them at the Skycar landing zone and escorted them to a Penthouse that Karli provided for them. Another big surprise was that inside the penthouse, besides having a personal maid and butler, the fashion consultant and her team were waiting on the couple to begin the transformation process to turn them into very photogenic guests. The Emerald Jasmine Resort management loved very good-looking people to arrive at *Rumors and Romance* night club.

The fashion designer had briefed the Butler on what they wanted to do before the guests arrived. As such the designer had some powerful additives to spike their drinks with to create psychological transcendence. They wanted the couple to feel cool and emboldened by the attire they would wear to help create the aura the designer wished to impart on them. The designer instantly knew Martilene and Geskar were a good-looking couple and with the right clothing and makeover they would appear spectacular, which would go a long way for her to sell her design to wealthy clients.

Geskar (a.k.a. Adrak) didn't know he was going to be a fashion model tonight. That was never revealed to him. It was rather incredible that one of Tramulite's enemy spies would be one of the top purveyors of fashion design later that evening.

The penthouse had two bedrooms and two bathrooms. Geskar was marched off to one while Martilene to the other with elixirs provided by the butler.

Geskar and Martilene were surprised they would have to bathe again, even though they had cleaned up prior to coming to the resort.

"I just took a bath an hour ago," Geskar said to the fashion designer's assistant.

"Geskar, we need you to soak in a solution that will modify your personality slightly and allow us to shampoo your hair with a special formula so that when the hair designer works on your hair design, it will be prepared for the treatments that will be applied," Fashion Designer's Assistant said.

"Alright then, do what you must," Geskar replied acting not happy about it.

The young female assisted Geskar in getting out of his clothes to efficiently get him into the bathtub now filling with water with additives already dumped in the water to achieve the desired effect.

"Wow you have such an incredible body. It's no wonder why Karli likes you," Fashion Designer's Assistant said.

"She's never seen my body before," Geskar responded wondering why the fashion person made such a statement.

"I'll be sure and tell Karli how magnificent you look." The Fashion Designer's Assistant said.

"Don't bother, Kari and I are just friends." Geskar said.

"How did you build up such a lovely body?" The Fashion Designer's Assistant asked.

"When my wife died in an accident, I didn't have much to do so I worked out a lot," Geskar lied.

"I'm sorry to hear about that, but Martilene is such a beautiful woman, I'm sure she can help you get over the tragedy."

"She has in more ways than one," Geskar said then winked at the young lady.

Geskar was well endowed, and the fashion lady helped him into the tub and said, "If I didn't have so much to accomplish, I would jump in the tub with you just so I could touch your muscles." The Fashion Designer's Assistant said.

"You are kind of cute, I would probably let you." Geskar said.

"Those are dangerous words to say to a woman like me."

"Should I take them back?" Geskar asked.

"You can't, you already said it, so I know the truth already." The Fashion Designer's Assistant said.

"I'll save it for you for another time," Geskar said.

"I do hope we get a chance," The Fashion Designer's Assistant said.

The water was getting to a high mark and shut off automatically thanks to artificial intelligence.

"Geskar, I want you to close your eyes because I'm going to pour some of the water on your hair then put in a special hair solution that will facilitate the hair designer," The Fashion Designer's Assistant said.

"Alright," Geskar said then closed his eyes.

The assistant took a hose like apparatus and started the water flow checking the temperature with her hand and as soon as it was perfect she doused Geskar getting his hair wet, then took a tube of hair application and placed a large amount in her hand and worked it into Geskar's head. There was a unique smell to it like smells you might find in a forest and the feeling was also quite unique and refreshing.

"You will probably like the way this hair treatment feels." The Fashion Designer's Assistant said.

"I do, and the only thing that would feel better is if you were sitting on my lap right now," Geskar teased her.

"Be careful saying those things, you have no idea how bad I want to do that, and I can be a naughty girl," The Fashion Designer's Assistant said.

"Alright, I'll refrain from giving you any more good ideas," Geskar said.

"That's okay, I like good ideas, especially if one day we might meet again." The Fashion Designer's Assistant said.

"Touché" Geskar responded.

The assistant messaged Geskar's scalp reminding him to keep his eyes closed and soon took the hose fixture and applied nice war water to wash away the soapy substance leaving Geskar feeling slightly invigorated and elevated.

In with the bath water was compounds the Fashion Designer's Assistant dumped with a small container while she was washing Geskar's hair. The compounds she put in the bath water contained pleasurizers and other psychoactive substances to give Geskar higher levels of euphoria to help prepare him mentally for the night allowing him a greater degree of calmness and self-assurance.

Part of the fashion game also included molding the personality of the model to achieve the overall best appearance and forbearance with the public.

Geskar was receiving the same treatment they did do everyone they did a makeover. Geskar was asked to relax in the water for a few minutes to give the treatment time to fulfill the ultimate preparation.

Just as if the assistant had a timer, she soon helped Geskar out of the bathtub and dried him off, had him put on a bath robe then escorted him out into the bedroom where a barber's chair was staged just for his hair design.

The barber was waiting for him. She was another attractive woman wearing very

nice clothing and soon had Geskar sitting in the chair where she ran a hair dryer and got the hair fluffy and ready for her handywork. Geskar was then shown a dozen pictures of hair designs from the *Cosmic Swirl* to what the designer called the *Tumultuous Allegro* Design.

Geskar was taken back on all dozen designs and didn't know which one to pick so he asked the hair designer: "Could you pick one for me?"

"Since you will be with two exquisitely beautiful women tonight, you need to take on risk to impress people. Therefore, I highly recommend you let me give you the *Tumultuous Allegro* hair design," the hair designer stated.

"Alright let's do that one," Geskar responded.

Soon the hair designer was going to work just like a famous chef does with his most successful recipes and she formed and shaped his hair that came out looking just like the picture she had shown earlier.

When the designer was all finished and handed Geskar a mirror to look at his hair design, the first thing Geskar thought was: *This image seems like some of the characters in animated holographic movies I've seen.*

"It looks good, but it almost seems surreal," Geskar noted.

"Yes, I knew that would be the result, and that's why I recommended it," the hair designer replied.

"I have to say, I'm duly impressed," Geskar said.

"Thank you for the compliment. It means a lot to me," the hair designer said.

"You are more than welcome. I feel kind of strange looking at it. I'll be honest, I never thought I would look like this in my lifetime," Geskar said.

"I'll be interested to see how that hair style blends in with the apparel the fashion designer has in mind for you," the hair stylist said.

"So will I," Geskar replied.

As if it were on cue suddenly a couple women came into the room pulling a cart like device that was a mobile closet full of men's clothes to pick from.

After a round of discussions and display of the clothing and attire, the fashion designer, Victoria von Strausstenheimer highly suggested: "Geskar I recommend you wear this designer black suit and tie."

"Alright let me try it on," Geskar replied.

In fifteen minutes Geskar was dressed in matching shoes recommended to go with the suit.

"We all done except for one last item," The fashion designer Victoria von Strausstenheimer said.

"And what is that?" Geskar asked.

"Geskar, I've studied the fashion industry quite a lot and attended many fashion shows over the years. We are under a lot of pressure to sell our designs to exclusive clients and as such experience the thrill of victory and the agony of defeat many times over.

"I can imagine you would," Geskar replied.

"Winning in a fashion contest is always a razor thin advantage because my competitors are all very good. I cannot overlook anything. We study it relentlessly and there is one last item we have not yet prepared you with." The fashion designer Victoria von Strausstenheimer said with a smile.

"What is that?" Geskar asked.

"Your scent must match the physical presentation of the image we have created."

"Alright," Geskar replied.

"I have some very special men's cologne which I want to put on you that will have an amazing influence on women," Victoria von Strausstenheimer said.

"If it impresses Karli and Martilene, I'm all for it.

"It's not only Karli and Martilene we want you to impress, but all the women you will come across in the *Rumors and Romance Night Club* tonight. Once they look at you and then smell your cologne, you will leave an indelible mark in their memories for you." The fashion designer Victoria von Strausstenheimer said with an evil grin.

"What if I do not like the scent?" Geskar asked.

"Remember this is not for you, it's for the women who observe you tonight and get close enough to smell your cologne," Victoria von Strausstenheimer said.

"Alright give me a shot of it. I'll see if I can stand it," Geskar said.

The fashion designer Victoria von Strausstenheimer had a black pouch she opened which Geskar could see was full of men's cologne bottles. The fashion designer Victoria von Strausstenheimer grabbed one of the cologne bottles that had a spray applicator on it and approached Geskar then sprayed it on him.

"Turn around a second," Victoria von Strausstenheimer said.

"What for?" Geskar asked.

This is what we do to multiply the effect, I'm going to apply the cologne to your suit jacket," Victoria von Strausstenheimer said.

"I've never done this before," Geskar said.

"Now you know fashion designers develop techniques to allow them to transcend stratospherically above the competition to earn vast rewards in the business."

"I feel sorry for a lot of women. You made me a dangerous man tonight," Geskar said.

"Something tells me you are already a dangerous man."

"Why do you say that?" Geskar asked.

"While you were getting your hair design, my assistant that gave you a bath earlier described your exquisite body. If you and Martilene ever break up, she and I will probably have a cat fight over you," Victoria von Strausstenheimer said.

"I'm not going to forecast my future, because I do not know what will happen. But if I was suddenly lonely and in need of a female companion, I would hope she would be as talented as you are," Geskar said.

"Thank you," Victoria von Strausstenheimer said.

"You are quite welcome."

"Let me go check up on Martilene and see if she's ready."

"One of the reasons why the assistant fashion designer had Geskar remain in the tub longer besides absorbing more pleasurizers in his skin, but to also time it so that he and Martilene would finish their makeovers about the same time, since women tack a little longer because of the makeup.

Moments later, the fashion designer Victoria von Strausstenheimer came into the bedroom and said, let's go out into the outer room and watch your beautiful date arrive.

Geskar followed Victoria von Strausstenheimer into the Penthouse living room and they faced the door to the other bedroom standing quietly for a moment, suddenly the door opened and Geskar had one of those *Oh My God* moments.

Martilene had movie star quality hair style flowing down with a hair color change. She was now blonder than before. Her makeup was exquisite and in the outer corner of her eyes had a makeup applied that on planet Earth would give her a slight Asian look. The combination of eyebrows, eye shadow design, and her lipstick created an almost surreal look. Geskar knew for a fact he would never see a woman like this out in public.

Martilene was wearing an exquisite evening gown that went down to her knees, and part of the coloration was a reddish pink area. Her eyelids were painted with that same pink color and gave her a majestic look. Martilene would receive pictures on her communicator from Victoria von Strausstenheimer and later Karli, and none of her friends would believe it's her. But they would recognize Geskar even though he too was changed quite a bit, and they would marvel at the makeover. It truly was a Cinderella night for Martilene, normally a decent looking woman, suddenly made over to look better than most movie stars.

This whole event was highly choreographed and the butler, a man named Charles entered the living room and said, "Martilene and Geskar, your escort to take you to *Rumors and Romance Night Club* is here to take you there now. The nightclub is currently serving dinner to guests and Karli Pauli will join you there for dinner before she performs later.

Martilene did not know it, but Victoria von Strausstenheimer had not only sent her pictures on her communicator, but at Karli's request, sent her several pictures as well.

Karli responded to Victoria von Strausstenheimer stating: "You have never let me down a single time. Your work is incredible, and I want to thank you for doing such a splendid job on my friend Martilene."

It was moments of experiencing the thrill of victory like tonight that go along way of healing the wounds of past agony of defeats that made Victoria von Strausstenheimer appreciate Karli's comments.

Just like Charles the Butler announced, the escort was there, a well-dressed gentleman who had multiple roles including resort security, a martial arts expert to help protect guests if need be.

The escort took the couple to the elevator with about fifty steps from the Penthouse then a short ride up to the top of the hotel where Rumors and Romance Night Club existed.

There was no waiting for the Maître d' since the escort knew precisely which table to escort them towards that had Karli standing by it waiting for them.

The table was well prepared with candles, flowers, and exquisite place settings for three.

Some of the regular customers were gawking at Karli who was gorgeous as usual and observing her standing by the table for a couple minutes got them thinking that maybe a VIP was arriving.

When Martilene and Geskar suddenly appeared with their escort who led them to the table, bowed to Karli then promptly turned and left, there was a slight rumble of conversations as the regular guests were trying to figure out who the VIP's were. One thing for sure was, they must be important for as good as they looked. Were they film stars?

"You look so wonderful Martilene," Karli said.

"Well, you are very pretty too," Martilene responded.

"Who's this fine-looking Gentleman you are with?" Karli teased.

"He's that wayward traveler just off a train," Martilene responded.

"Could you imagine what a Contessa would feel being in a private room on the train with a man like this?" Karli asked.

"Trust me, you really do not want to know. But I can assure you the Contessa would be filled and stilled." Martilene responded.

"I absolutely know she would be and I'm already jealous of the Contessa." Karli said.

Geskar smiled taking in all the banter and he could see Karli's body language about the time he thought she had smelled his cologne. The material on Karli's dress was completely opaque and would not reveal anything, but it would not do well to hide her arousal which Geskar (a.k.a. Adrak) a trained spy in body language, quickly saw. He also thought she caught him catching a view of her nipples hardening.

But Karli thought, *if I could someday entice him to make a pass at me it's all worth it.* Karli would not steal Martilene's boyfriend in front of her, but a secret rendezvous was not out of the question.

"Please sit down with me," Karli said and Martilene and Geskar quickly complied.

Geskar's sure is a cool cat, Karli thought thinking how Geskar was not phased about the situation he was in. She knew there must be something special about him. Later when Victoria von Strausstenheimer privately talked with Karli who had voyeurism tendencies, she passed on what her assistant said about his body and his tool. Karli had notions of experiencing all that one of these days real soon.

Karli got to where she is today because she knew the female version of Sun Tzu Art of War, when it comes to love and romance, there are no rules, and the agony of defeat is rather depressive when it comes to lovers. And Karli knew on the train, Martilene had more than her fair share of the thrill of victory and probably orgasmic heaven.

The choreographed evening began almost instantly with staff bringing the entrée. They would have 24 dishes, so the servings were small to allow room to sample the works.

Karli couldn't dilly dally around, she had to eat, go to her penthouse, freshen up, get her makeup fixed, if necessary, change her clothes then come back to perform.

Even though Karli was exquisitely clothed, she would come back with the sparkle and glamour and a much shorter dress to work on the little heads of a lot of men in the audience.

There was some small talk, but the constant serving slowed the conversation down quite a bit. Karli didn't care. She just wanted to treat her two friends who brought her great joy and happiness on the train.

But one thing was certain, Karli knew that if she could steal Geskar away from

Martilene, she would waste very little time to begin to pursue Geskar. But Geskar was such a calm and respectful person. Karli figured he would rather not break Martilene's heart than to get a crack at a sex kitten like her. For that she respected him. And other than catching him spotting her slight earlier arousal, there wasn't much about him doing any sort of extracurricular activities.

Karli could read people. She was always around a lot of people because she's a performer. One thing she suspected was Martilene would not tolerate a horn dog fooling around. She also figured out Martilene most likely was waiting to cement the deal and make Geskar a permanent relationship and unification. She would keep in touch with Martilene to see how all that worked out. She was mildly curious as to how that would evolve. *Would they one day have children?*

Karli could not overeat as she had to be ready to perform. Even though her servings were small she only sampled small amounts of them. She didn't want to feel full and bloated when she went up on stage.

Karli had one of her assistants come up to her and give her a reminder of the time which was her segway to leave and go freshen up and change for the show.

"Karli, you need to go up to your penthouse now and change into your performance costume," the assistant said.

"Thanks for the reminder," Karli said then stood up and said, "Martilene and Geskar, there is more food and desserts coming, but I'm running a little late and need to go get changed. I'll see you in a short while when I come back."

"Alright," Martilene answered.

Geskar nodded, giving Karli the recognition and signaled he understood.

An escort was there who took Karli up to her room to freshen up, change, and fix her makeup.

Karli did a psychological enhancement while she was sitting on the toilet, singing. The Butler and Maid were used to it. But it helped her start out the concert with a bang. Just like Karli planned, she went back to Rumors and Romance Night

Club on the top floor of the Emerald Jasmine Resort. She knew she had about five more minutes before the band started playing and instead of going up on the stage to have the same conversation, she did routinely with the band members, she went to Martilene and Geskar's table and sat down in the chair she earlier left.

"Wow what a change," Martilene said.

"Yes, the customers here demand the glamour and the glitz which I gladly give them," Karli said.

They had a very nice and friendly conversation, but when the percussionist gave a couple hits on one of his digital drums, Karli knew they were ready to start.

"I'm sorry, I must go to work now. I'm so pleased you were able to be here tonight, you made my day. I'll try harder tonight singing to show how much I appreciate you being here," Karli said.

"Thank you," Martilene said.

Karli stood up and walked up to the stage that had a series of steps going up it which singers could use to accentuate their delivery and prose.

The music started playing and Karli began singing one of her keystone songs, "Will I Ever See You Again?"

The title and the music/lyrics seemed to transfix Geskar. Martilene thought Geskar's body language was all about the sentiment in the song. Little did she know *Geskar was feeling the moment as she truly enveloped his life.*

Martilene nor Karli had had any idea who Geskar really was or the fact he was a spy doing espionage. If they did, then they would understand his reaction.

Karli, true to her promise, sang her heart out. The regulars could sense something was going on because Karli never came out swinging and hitting homeruns at the beginning of her performances. Karli quite often performed in exquisite gowns, but tonight the dress covered with lots of beautiful gems was the most profound outfit she ever wore. Someone from Earth who watched Liberace or Elvis would appreciate her dress.

Karli's dress was very short. One could almost see her crotch but with her black panties on she could care less. The combination of Karli's dress and showing most of her legs had a profound effect on the men, whereas her singing affected the women. Even though Geskar (a.k.a. Adrak) wouldn't mind tapping that fine example of sheer elegance, he knew it would complicate his mission and his superiors would not appreciate such behavior.

Geskar would have confirmation shortly on Karli's desires because Martilene decided she needed to use the toilet and timing was terrible, she was at the toilet while Karli went on a break and rejoined their table with only Geskar sitting there. Since they had a private moment, Karli let it all out:

"I like you Geskar. I know you think very highly of Martilene, but I also have needs. Come back here some night by yourself, and watch my show and afterwards, I'll reward you in ways I know you would truly enjoy."

"I know you are quite lovely and talented and most likely would have a huge impact on my emotions if I were to let loose, but Karli, you are a super star. We live in different worlds. I might be too plain for you." Geskar said.

"I like plainness. I saw your behavior for several days. I like the way you are." Karli responded.

"I'm not the kind of person that wants to be responsible for breaking a heart,"

Geskar said.

"I see that in you, I can tell. But if one day you want to venture out and explore some surreal satisfaction, I can give you, come to one of my Rumors and Romance Night Club shows by yourself and I'll make sure you will never regret it," Karli laid it on thick.

"I'll take that into consideration, but I can't predict what I will do in the future, so I'm not going to make any promises. But you will remain my wonderful friend indefinitely because I do like you," Geskar stated.

"The feeling is quite mutual," Karli said.

Geskar knew if the situation was different, he would take Karli on a Tour de Cymbidium [the Kama Sutra version of Tour de France].

Karli was calculating and conniving. She never rose to the top being a nice conservative woman. She was a master manipulator especially great at manipulating the little heads of men.

Karli knew as soon as Martilene washed off all the makeup and took off her designer clothes, she would be a plane Jane again, just like she appeared a few times on the train when she had showered and was at breakfast before she put on her warpaint.

A waiter approached Karli knowing the big discussion had just ended he didn't want to interrupt and asked, "Karli, can I get you something to drink?"

Yes, please get me a *Lotos de Solodka* (pronounced Lotus de Sa-lād-ka [Lotus and Licorice]). The greenish gray elixir was known to have sexual stimulant and motivational effects.

Karli wanted a knockout performance tonight since she was dangling the forbidden fruit in front of Geskar and was hoping he would eventually take a bite.

Karli had plenty of credits because she was now a wealthy woman having earned a lot of money and never the time to spend it.

What Karli didn't have was male companionship with a normal person she could trust. The more Geskar resisted her the more she wanted him and the more she knew he would be a reliable lover if she could steal him away from Martilene.

But Karli was also patient and knew how to snare a rabbit, or in this case hopefully a man who wanted to breed as often as rabbits. She knew how to seduce Geskar and would take her time. She would soon have her private detectives learn all about him, where he lived, worked, and played. If he didn't show up to one of her performances alone, after she received the report from her private dicks, she would ring his doorbell if she had to.

Geskar (a.k.a. Adrak) was flirting with a fatal attraction, a true Latrodectus, and was lucky to be leaving soon as the mission finished. The very last thing he would do before that mission ended would be to touch the lovely Latrodectus now staring into his eyes probing him and wanting him.

As a social engineer, Geskar read Karli like a book, in detail with great precision and fully understood her desires. He also knew when powerful women didn't get what they wanted they would go nuts. He would be long gone before Kari reached that point. *Too bad I can't take her with me*, Geskar (a.k.a. Adrak) thought.

Geskar was soon saved by Martilene who arrived moments later. What took her so long to simply use the bathroom, she didn't wish to go in a public toilet adjacent to the restaurant that was probably well traveled and went instead up to the Penthouse where she would be comfortable and get the job done so she would not feel bloated.

As Martilene was walking out of the restaurant one her way to the penthouse, one of the security men approached her and asked, "Martilene, may I ask you where you are going?"

"I want to go back to the penthouse to use the toilet. I don't desire to use the public bathroom."

"Alright, I'm assigned for your security, I will escort you there and back to the restaurant," the security man stated.

"Thank you."

Because of that lengthy evolution, Karli got in quite a few more swings at the bat with Martilene's absence. Her drink, *Lotos de Solodka* emboldened her and made her more provocative as the night went on.

This long departure of Martilene gave Geskar some worries as to what happened to her. If she didn't show up soon, he would have to excuse himself and go find out where she went and why.

There was nothing out of the ordinary that seemed like a trip wire to Geskar, but the longer Martilene stayed away the deeper and more methodically Karli probed and added to her lust for Geskar, because he was very sophisticated and responded to her in ways few other men could.

Karli was mentally sizing him up Geskar. She could tell by the way he wore the designer suit he had a great body and if what the fashion designer's assistant commented about his body and his tool, she wanted a test drive more and more and the moments went on. At one point she thought she should lay her cards on the table and just be blunt and explain exactly what she wanted. *But would I scare him off?*

Karli could tell Geskar was a man's man and the type of man who always wanted to make the first move. Karli, being a smart social engineer herself, knew not to violate the rules of engagement, and allow things to naturally develop so Geskar would make the first move.

Any thoughts of Karli being more direct suddenly ended as Martilene returned with all smiles with no more bloated feeling as she did a fantastic job of unloading her money's worth.

Martilene saw Karli was drinking a fresh drink assuming she just started taking a break but didn't know she was near the end of her break after working over Geskar with the finest poise a woman with needs could demonstrate.

Karli knew by Geskar's past behavior and his gentlemanly stature, he would likely not divulge to Martilene anything about the discussion they just had. She knew that based on his body language; he was well along his way to explore the splendid euphoria he knew Karli could create for him as she did her own Tour de Cymbidium methods on his little head.

Karli was like a magician; she could switch her discourse at the turn of a hat. She quickly morphed from a horny seductress to a woman's best friend.

Geskar (a.k.a. Adrak) was quite impressed with Karli's acting skills. The women quickly transcended into a female chitchat with trivial discussion of nothing with substance.

Suddenly the percussionist tapped softly on his digital drums to give the signal *the show must go on.*

"I'm so sorry but I need to go back to work now," Karli stated then stood up and walked back to the stage.

Geskar (a.k.a. Adrak) was getting a lot of people observing him, which he knew to expect since he was sitting with the star performer Karli Pauli.

What Geskar didn't know was two men in the audience had great interest in him that was slowly developing. One was the Tramular SMERSH Operative Sidis, and the other was the Vekkar watcher Sidis was following.

SMERSH had already started their operation, *Clover*. They were intently interested in the Vekkar watcher agent and anyone he met or followed around.

It was about this time Sidis was making the connection the Vekkar spy had some kind of interest in the man named Geskar.

SMERSH had good relational databases and a lot of information about each citizen. SMERSH had an ongoing program that operated similar to Project Prism ran by the NSA on planet Earth spying on anyone deemed dangerous based on the Patriot Act after 9/11.

Tramular SMERSH Agents would never go to a Judge to get permission to do a roving wiretap because most of the government had no idea they existed or what they did. Hence permissions were not part of SMERSH's modus operendus.

True Intel operators never get involved in the criminal justice system because it's just a distraction and could expose sensitive sources and methods. Even if they knew nefarious activities were going on such as human trafficking, drug smuggling, arms dealing, money laundering, etc., they would ignore it since it would be a distraction and possibly blow covers if they partnered with law enforcement to deal with a matter.

Geskar was probably unwise to come to this night club tonight. He only did so because it was a huge priority for Martilene who seemed to be having a great time being the friend of a superstar and being exposed to the public.

When Martilene was freshening up in the Penthouse and had the chance to look herself over in the mirror before going back to Rumors and Romance Night Club on the top floor of the Emerald Jasmine Resort. She was astonished how beautiful she looked. She knew never in her life she had ever looked this great.

Before Martilene left the Penthouse she asked the Butler Charles, "Would you mind taking a couple pictures of me, I love this dress and want to send a picture to my mother."

I would be most delighted to do so, Martilene," Charles responded and took her communicator from her and took several pictures and asked Martilene to verify them.

"These are fantastic. Thank you very much." Martilene responded then went to the elevator with her escort who was patiently waiting. While in the elevator Martilene sent a couple pictures to her mother and to her coworker and good friends.

After Karli left the table and began singing again, Martilene felt the buzzer of her communicator and pulled it out of the communicator pocket well hidden in her dress.

First it was her mother who responded how beautiful she looked. Then she was given text messages from her best friend:

"Wow, you look so beautiful. What the hell happened to you?" The best friend text message stated.

With all that going on and Geskar catching some of it, he could see Martilene was in a pleasant mood as her evening was turning out to be wonderful being the guest of a celebrity and a makeover that made her look like a beautiful seductive woman. She was looking movie star quality tonight and two men in the audience did not miss that for a minute.

The SMERSH agent Sidis was in a booth with one of his co-workers a female to make it look legitimate reading Geskar's SMERSH files on their secure computational services and communications database he could review out in the field for in-situ situations that could manifest.

Nothing looked out of the ordinary and they had plenty of information on Geskar, but the fact he was here tonight with one of the top performers, and a spectacular looking woman he was with, obviously showing a romantic connection, gave Sidis a lot to think about, especially with a Vekkar agent bird dogging Geskar who didn't have a sensitive job. So, what was so special about Geskar to warrant a top spy from the enemy to follow him around?

Operation Clover, which started out as another boring counterintelligence operation, was starting to get more interesting.

Watching Geskar communicate with the singer while the other lady was gone created even more interest because the body language exposed something going on there as well.

After a few inquiries to the database data science analysts who worked around the clock, a few more facts started pouring in. Geskar was recently on a five-day tourist train trip and shared a private room with a woman named Martilene. Looking at Martilene, Sidis compared the pictures surveillance cameras made as they drilled down in the data there Martilene was, and even though she had a makeover and looked stunningly beautiful tonight, Sidis could tell the person Geskar was with was Martilene tonight.

Moments later after asking the data scientist about Karli Pauli, she was also identified on the same train trip, and eventually they found surveillance video of the three walking around together. The plot thickened.

Sidis was a smart guy. He was one of SMERSH's top operatives. He could see the physical reaction and was soon advised about Karli's arousal before she changed her clothes for the performance.

So that's what this is about. Karli has the hots for a normal guy Geskar who has a girlfriend Martilene she wants to steal him from, Sidis analyzed most accurately.

Now Sidis was drilling down on Geskar:

He's an ordinary guy whose wife died in an accident a while back and now he's banging her best friend. What a guy! Sidis thought.

There was nothing Geskar's company did that would be of value to Vekkar's, so why are they following him around?

Another aspect to this, Geskar has never looked or spotted the man following him around which means he doesn't know he's being followed. Sidis was thinking.

Sidis knew there were two fundamental possibilities. *The Vekkar spy was either a watcher, or he was planning on doing some nefarious activity that involved Geskar. Just exactly what would that be?*

Sidis was trained by some of the best spies in the business. One of the rules of thumb was: *If you think the person is a watcher, that means the person he is watching is a spy.*

SMERSH was not interested in Geskar now who had never done anything yet to raise a red flag. But the Vekkar agent was a concern to the point the Vekkar watcher triggered Project Clover.

Sidis biggest problem now is he could not approach Geskar without the watcher discovering the surveillance which meant a rapid "bug out" before they could apprehend him.

Around midnight, Geskar decided he had enough for the night and was getting sleepy and during Karli's next break informed her after he previously confirmed with Martilene who also wanted to get in bed, feeling sleepy from the drinks:

"Karli, thank you for inviting us. We are getting sleepy, and we are going back to the Penthouse to rest." Geskar said.

"Thank you for coming tonight, I really appreciate you being here to watch me sing." Karli replied.

Karli then gave Marilene a hug and Geskar a kiss on the cheek which Martilene did not miss for one second.

Moments later their escort safely delivered them to the Penthouse where they had a nightcap, and the Butler Charles refused to go along with Karli's machinations to drug Martilene so she could visit Geskar in the 2nd bedroom and do the boom-boom. When Karli contacted Charles to check up on the status later, Charles said, "They are both sound to sleep. I screwed up and gave Geskar the drugs in the nightcap instead of

Martilene. So, they are both out solid."

Karli was disappointed and wondered if Charles did the screwup on purpose.

Meanwhile Sidis was now fully engaged in checking out Geskar because he wanted to know why a Vekkar agent was following him around. His gut feeling was, *he's a watcher which means Geskar is a spy working for the Vekkar's.* This would not be the first time Sidis was a loose cannon and played *Cowboy*. But it could have been his last if he wasn't careful.

Chapter Five

Break-in

The stage was set. INTEL had discovered some leads and now Geskar was going to do what he was sent to do. Discover the location of the research center they needed to take out to prevent the Tramulite's from developing their own Inter Dimensional Portal Technology.

Several days after the excursion to the Emerald Jasmine Resort and the extracurricular activities at the Rumors and Romance Night Club on the top floor of the Resort to enjoy the lovely singer Karli Pauli, Geskar (a.k.a. Adrak) was being sent via an Inter Dimensional Portal to the office of Doctor Thurston Valery Gergar, who was thought to be the main architect of their efforts. To get to Doctor Gergar's office by normal means entering the building was deemed impossible. The security was ultra tight, and the campus was locked down tight day and night.

One of the security shortfalls was offices within the Tramular research compound had windows and Dr. Gergar's office was one of those seen from a distance via photonics, usually the last to leave late at night. After a long study, the timing from the time his office lights went out to seeing him leaving the building were very consistent. No other offices had light dynamics that matched Dr. Gergar's departure late at night. And few others worked as late and as hard as the brilliant Interdimensional Portal Designer.

This research building had once before been used for general office space assigned to no spectacular researchers. As such Vekkar spies were able to come up with some blueprints for the building which could be used to design an interdimensional portal coordinate to deposit Geskar. There were likely intruder detection devices and as soon as Geskar arrived his sensors and toys would delay them long enough to search and find the secret location to the research center they needed to destroy.

Geskar received a physical checkup and was issued all the appropriate devices he needed to take with him. He was also admonished by the "Doc" for his reckless behavior he conducted with Martilene who seemed to do a good job of taking her antipregnancy pills when she got home.

The stage was set. Geskar was positioned into a room in the safe house set up for the inter dimensional portal that formed. Geskar walked into it and disappeared. Instantaneously he arrived in Doctor Gergar's office. He had on heads-up display glasses that gave him situational awareness from the incredible circuitry in the backpack he was wearing. It also had a tamperproof on it and if the enemy tried to open it up, they would be blown to smithereens.

Upon arrival Geskar knew not to move until his circuitry in the toys he brought with him checked the security measures in the office and proceeded to temporarily deactivate them. All in all, there were fifteen such devices. As soon as he received the "all clear" signal he could move about. He did not turn on the lights and wore an infrared headlamp that instead of shining visible light spectrum used an infrared and the glasses Geskar (a.k.a. Adrak wore) were infrared frequency shifter to convert the infrared spectrum to the light spectrum allowing Geskar to see. With the special high-tech glasses, it appeared almost as lights were on in the room but an outsider looking into the window would only see darkness.

Part of the infrared imaging system included real time recording. Everything Geskar observed was automatically recorded, thus he did not have to take pictures.

Geskar looked over Dr. Gergar's desk and didn't see anything obvious that would be a clue. The desk drawers had sophisticated locks on them the doctor could open with a device like an automobile car lock mechanism. Within moments, the toys Geskar had with him detected the lock system and easily detected the manufacturer and the process the system used to operate the lock including an encrypted code easily broken in a minute.

Within several minutes of arrival, Dr. Gergar's desk drawers were accessible and Geskar started checking all the documents he found in files in one of the drawers. In a brief amount of time Geskar found a file that pertained to the research center on the planet *Drusyltania.*

This is rather clever, this is the very last place we would have looked for it, Geskar said to himself.

He could not take the file because the Tramular's would figure out there was a break- in and the results would be to protect the research center better making it far harder to destroy.

This file was indeed the treasure trove of what they were looking for.

Like all good bureaucrats, Dr. Gergar's file had maps of the base layout, building numbers etc. Within the various maps and pictures, the building where the researchers worked on the Inter Dimensional Portal design was clearly identified.

Dr. Gergar also had attached to the map a couple sheets of papers of contact information, room numbers where they had their offices, their communicator numbers and their intergalactic neutrino high side network communications address to send research papers back and forth at such long distance in incredibly fast means via neutrinos.

Geskar now had what was considered the information sought for this mission.

After viewing the contents of the file, he put it back in the desk drawer and closed it. It was now time to bug out. He then transmitted the bug out code. A couple minutes later as expected the interdimensional portal opened and he walked through it and immediately found himself at the safe house where he handed the backpack and glasses to one of the staff members who would now start processing the information.

Geskar was not going to leave the safehouse for a few more days until headquarters went through all the information he obtained, in case he missed something they needed to send him back to get. He sure as hell hoped that didn't happen in the event the Tramular's had detected him and would be waiting for his second visit.

Sidis was on a hot trail of Geskar. Geskar knew he was going to be departing soon, and got a wild notion to go visit Karli by himself. When Martilene contacted him, he said he had a terrible headache and took some medicine and was going to bed to rest and fall asleep.

Geskar (a.k.a. Adrak) was advised not to go back to the nightclub, but he saw nothing wrong with it. The doc knew the truth, Adrak was a horn dog and wanted a crack at Karli who was indeed an exceptional woman in many ways.

The stage was set for a rendezvous with passions on a theme from Paganini as Geskar was formulating in his mind how delightful Karli was, and since he would soon disappear, it really didn't matter what the outcome was.

Geskar was dressed for success, but not nearly as debonair he had been with the fantastic makeover with the fashion designers. But he knew he looked dignified and attractive.

To not draw too much attention, instead of taking a Skycar Taxi, he took his own and traveled to the Emerald Jasmine Resort ready to commence the extracurricular activities at the Rumors and Romance Night Club on the top floor of the Resort. Geskar arrived fairly early as he thought he would take in a meal since this would be one of his last nights here to enjoy such extravagant resort quality food.

Surprisingly, Geskar obtained a good location for the table he was seated by the Maître d' who remembered he was a special friend of Karli.

Geskar had his elixir and ordered dinner before the entertainment started. Timing was perfect; as the elixir set his personal psychology to a good notch above complete satisfaction, and the food choice was rather astute as the meal added volumes to ambience of the evening.

Geskar was happy because this mission was just about over. He had some notable experiences, but after you operate under cover behind enemy lines, in due time you want to go home because you know the chances of being turned multiply daily.

Geskar would rather be safe than sorry and hoped the data reduction people tomorrow gave him the green light to go home so he could leave this adventure and all the dangers behind and take a rest and relax for a while, plus work on his physical fitness he knew he was lacking.

Karli didn't expect Geskar to show up. He was the last person in the world she thought would be in the audience tonight. The dinner hour was lingering on, but a lot of tables were cleaned off and the dining crowd was slowly being replaced by the night club crowd waiting to experience the entertainment.

Geskar was situated at a table so that when Karli walked on stage, she would most likely detect his presence. He wondered: *what Karli's reaction might be?*

This was another dull evening for Karli. She was disappointed Charles let her down and suspected he screwed up Martilene's drugging on purpose to deny a trip to ecstasy with Geskar. So, Karli was predisposed to be in a sour mood and hoped to snap out of it.

Karlie arrived at the Rumors and Romance Night Club about five minutes before the band was due to start performing. This was typical of her evenings.

As Karli walked through Rumors and Romance Night Club, as she approached the stage, she spotted Geskar sitting by himself with a single place serving set up just finishing his meal. She thus knew the plane Jane Martilene was not with him, and her whole evening seemed suddenly brighter.

The musicians in the band assumed she would come up to them to talk for a few minutes even though their song choices and sequence was already laid out for tonight's festivities. They were surprised she suddenly diverted her path and walked over to one of the customers and sat down with him.

"I'm so delighted you came back tonight, Geskar."

"Karli, I enjoyed your singing so much last night I decided I wanted to come back and hear you sing again." Geskar said.

"You sure there isn't more to your motive?" Karli asked.

"They're possibly may be, we'll have to explore that during your break."

"I do not think I need to explore your motive. I already know what you want, and do you know that I might just want the same?" Karli asked.

"I've learned a long time ago to never assume." Geskar responded.

"Smart boy. You don't need to assume; I'll guide you through it so you will know for certain." Karli sail.

"I'm a willing student." Geskar said.

"I doubt I could teach you much, I'm quite confident after talking with Martilene, you could show me a good Tour de Cymbidium [Tour de France]. Karli said with a wicked grin.

"I strive for perfection; I want to be really good at whatever I do," Geskar advertised.

"The best way to become the best is with a lot of experience, perhaps you would allow me to give you time to practice?" Karli asked.

"The thought never crossed my mind, but you do make a valid point." Geskar replied.

"Stick around, and later I'll give you a Tour de Penthouse." Karli said.

"I would be most happy to *stick* around." Geskar said.

Karli then stood up and walked up to the band for a moment before they started performing. Just like the night before, the band noticed Karli's performance was way above average. They observed her with the stranger and made a connection that person was somehow motivating her.

Sidis had slipped in because the person he now assumed was a watcher led him to the Rumors and Romance Night Club where he soon got to see *Loverboy* Geskar make a connection with the illustrious singer Karli.

Tonight, the surveillance grip of Geskar would tighten. Sidis didn't telegraph his plans to his superiors because he was going to single handedly take this spy down and teach a few people why they need to stop dilly dallying around and deal with the obvious threats.

The night wore on, Geskar remaining fully alert in all respects, did not detect surveillance from two fronts like he should have. Unfortunately, Geskar was temporarily blinded by the lust he exhibited for Karli and spent too much time thinking about after hours with her instead of clearing his baffles like he should have.

If the distraction of Karli wasn't present, in a short amount of time, Geskar would have detected the surveillance. The watcher was now starting to put a picture together which he would soon send off as he realized he was being watched but also the person he was watching was also being watched.

After the last song, Karli approached Geskar and said, "Please come with me, I'm going to take you up to my Penthouse."

The two soon departed and Geskar was now in a major situation he had no idea he had gotten himself into.

The night with Karli was as expected. She wanted to receive the splendid euphoria that she knew Geskar could give to her and when he undressed and she saw his muscles, Karli knew the fashion designer assistant was not embellishing a thing.

Geskar would be classified by women in her circles as a *stud muffin*. And soon Geskar proved he had all the proper credentials as he took Karli on the Tour de Cymbidium that eventually led to her passing out in sheer ecstasy and feeling the splendid euphoria she sought.

Hearing Karli snore passed out gave Geskar the notion to leave. He got up and put on his clothes and bid the butler good night. Like all the butlers, his name was also Charles.

Sidis then decided right then and there to *Cowboy it up* and confront Geskar in the underground parking lot of the hotel.

When a bruiser approaches you in an underground parking lot, rule of thumb, its not going to be a pleasant event. Sidis was overconfident to the point he was going to physically beat up the smaller man when he should have pulled out his laser in stun mode.

But Sidis realized that if Geskar was a real spy he might have a weapon as well and it would be a closeup laser battle where they both got killed.

Sidis went from walking to attack mode and landed some good martial arts punches and kicks that Geskar (a.k.a. Adrak) was not able to block.

Security cameras that caught the event showed an epic battle.

One spy was fighting for glory (Sidis). The other spy was fighting for his life (Adrak). Because of the realization of what Adrak faced, even though he was beat the hell up rapidly, he didn't give up and waited for an opportunistic attack. Faking in fighting is sometimes a valid method. Leaning against the wall acting like he was not capable of defending himself, Adrak gave Sidis the notion it was time to finish it with a knockout blow and came in to administer the Coup de Grâce.

The next move Adrak performed he had mastered and had it wrote to memory. His body was against the was able to facilitate a kick with his heel to Sidis knee. The kick has a longer range than a punch so when Sidis came in for the punch, Adrak destroyed one of his knees that did two things. It created immense pain, and it also caused Sidis to fall over onto the ground in a vulnerable position.

Adrak was a master heel kicker and soon landed a powerful kick to the middle of Sidis back that immediately took away his motor functions below the damage to his spine that was also quite painful and caused Sidis to start shaking like he was in a spastic trauma.

Instead of Sidis who planned to administer the Coup de Grâce, it was Adrak who applied a heel kick to Sidis head, instantly breaking his neck and killing him.

The interdimensional spy Adrak whose identity was so secret, was known only as 000050428A62315. His past was buried and no longer existed. Geskar (a.k.a. Adrak) put the body of the Tramular spy Sidis into the Skycar and propped up his body giving the appearance of a passenger the Tramular's were chasing thinking it was 000050428A62315 (a.k.a. Adrak) it.

With help from the Artificial Intelligence APP *Spĕctrāl de Dòngtài* on his communicator (cell phone) who could operate the Skycar, and make it appear the VIA spy was escaping. The Skycar was soon on its way heading towards the wilderness beyond the city limits.

Tramular SMERSH agents wanted to apprehend this spy who was just about to get away and make it a hard-to-reach-area and escape.

The Skycar now being flown via remote control with the dead man Sidis inside. When 000050428A62315 (a.k.a. Adrak) failed to heed the demands of the Tramular Planetary Defense Force, he was not going to be allowed to escape alive. Even if he was dead and not able to give them information after they shot down 000050428A62315's (a.k.a. Adrak) Skycar, as a dead spy he would not be a threat to them in the future.

However, their agent Sidis was now missing and presumed to have been a captive abducted traveling in the Skycar where the enemy would coerce secrets out of him. Since they couldn't rescue their agent Sidis, it was decided they would be better off if he was dead along with the enemy and not in a position to compromise some of their deep dark secrets.

Right at the last minute the order was given.

Tramulite planetary security cruisers, which were significantly enhanced Skycars, launched a couple plasma vortex weapons. These hypersonic weapons took only a moment to cover the distance and detonate next to the Skycar with proximity detector in its seeker.

By the time the weapon launch transient signatures were detected by Vekkar agents using sophisticated detectors, the interdimensional Spy 000050428A62315's (a.k.a. Adrak) was transported to safety

The plasma inferno created by the plasma vortex melted the Skycar and the occupant with severe heat which added tremendously to the expected explosion.

Just like a fireworks display, once the sparkling plasma subsided, there was nothing left. The Tramular's thought agent 000050428A62315 (a.k.a. Adrak) was now ashes floating down to the surface of the planet with all the other charred debris that used to be part of a Skycar. Case closed, agent 000050428A62315 was dead.

Due to the heat and substantial plasma created by the plasma vortex weapons there would be no bodies to get DNA from to confirm identities.

Tramulite Planetary Defense Force Commander, General Ptolemy Soter, was satisfied that even though they had to sacrifice their spy Sidis, the ample surveillance video showing the fight before 000050428A62315's (a.k.a. Adrak) which lasted 15 minutes before Sidis was made unconscious and dragged into the sky car.

Tramulite Planetary Defense Force Skycars immediately chased Adrak within seconds after on-site Tramular Planetary Defense Force personnel observed the end of the fight and Adrak who was fully exposed and identified by facial recognition, drag Sidis limp body into the Skycar. From that moment until the Skycar was blown up it was under constant surveillance. General Ptolemy Soter knew when 000050428A62315's (a.k.a. Adrak) was killed in the blast the data breach eliminated.

Sidis lost his life because he was another rouge macho Spy who thought he was smarter than the rest and more capable with special weapons and methods could easily take down this one Vekkar agent.

But Sidis, who was ultra intelligent and often conducted independent operations because he was a glory hound and never waited for the Calvary to show up to assist as he felt he had no need for the neophytes, finally met his match and consequently lost his life with the help of SMERSH.

It was none other than Cleitus Beroea of SMERSH 3rd Main Directorate who convinced Tramulite Planetary Defense Force Commander, General Ptolemy Soter, that Sidis was expendable and killing the interdimensional Spy 000050428A62315's (a.k.a. Adrak) they discovered was far more important than sparing Sidis. Plus, Cleitus Beroea explained they didn't know how badly Sidis was wounded. He might have been near death anyway and the interdimensional Spy 000050428A62315 was just using him as a human shield to get away.

SMERSH didn't know for sure, but Cleitus Beroea thought the interdimensional Spy 000050428A62315 needed to get somewhere a portal device existed to leave this dimension for another.

Why was interdimensional spy 000050428A62315 here in the first place?

That is the most important question because it meant they might expect another Spy like 000050428A62315 to show up and continue where the first spy left off. SMERSH would have to maintain eternal vigilance because there was no telling when or if that replacement would arrive.

The huge mistake Sidis made in this *Operation Clover* when he decided to handle the matter by himself without backup is that he was the only living person who knew 000050428A62315's (a.k.a. Adrak) identity, the alias Geskar and where Geskar's home was located.

Geskar's home was a safe house with a watcher staged in a home across the street and neither the safe house staff nor the watcher across the street detected any Tramular Planetary Defense Force surveillance. Their location remained safe, and they monitored the situation with multiple staff until all safe signals were given.

Adrak was doing some soul searching now. He came really close to getting killed.

Sidis did a great job in beating the crap out of him before he was able to prevail and salvage the situation and his life. Adrak was covered with lots of bruises and in serious pain with a busted lip, a black eye, broken nose, pain in his groin, and elsewhere.

Under any other circumstance he would be evacuated and given immediate medical treatment, but the mission was nowhere near completion.

Adrak thought he would be meeting Martilene Chares later that evening, but under the circumstances with his disfigured face could consider such a venture. Plus, Adrak wasn't sure whether Martilene Chares was the person who betrayed him.

Adrak needed to discover if Martilene Chares betrayed him. Martilene Chares would soon have a lot of surveillance to detect whether she had contacts with Tramular Planetary Defense Force or worse yet was she working for Cleitus Beroea of the Tramular SMERSH 3rd Main Directorate.

One thing that would make Adrak very sad would be to discover Martilene Chares was somehow involved in all this.

Adrak had developed some emotional bond to Martilene Chares. The Achillies heel of any Spy seems to always be a female that creates scenarios that become untenable.

But spies in deep cover operations that go away for a long time get lonely, and they must also manipulate and use people in the conduct of their activity.

One way to throw off surveillance is to be seen with a local female in public. A constant loner raises speculation about who the person is and what he's doing.

A person with a good cover story with a local woman creates imagery that confuses potential trackers and investigators. The trick is finding a quiet woman without a big mouth who lives alone and leads a semiprivate life.

Martilene Chares fit the mold. She knew Geskar's wife Mildrayd quite well and they were best friends, but Geskar never made any advances towards Martilene Chares after Mildrayd's death who assumed Geskar was simply undergoing the commiserating of the loss of his wonderful wife and never sought to bring another female in his life.

Adrak had no need outside the performance of his mission to seek a woman, but as he learned all about Geskar's life and everyone who knew him also knew the basis of the relationship, the interdimensional spy Adrak concluded Martilene Chares would be an outstanding prop.

Adrak knew basic behavior would place Martilene Chares sympathetic and possibly vulnerable to a seduction to create the imagery he was a simple person that lived a frugal and quite life since Mildrayd's death.

By the time Adrak arrived to replace Geskar who would be transported via a portal to a Vekkar Interdimensional Transport Directorate facility. Geskar would continue living undergoing extensive interrogations to glean any useful information about his life to allow data mining and imposter creation who would then have unobstructed travel around enemy Tramulite territory allowing significant nefarious operations.

Unknown to the Tramulars, the inter-dimensional portal was right in Geskar's home. As soon as Adrak passed through the portal into the room, one of the safe house attendants was there knowing an arrival was coming and it should be Adrak.

Adrak appearance easily showed he had gone though some serious trauma, and the safe house assistant was also a team medic looked Adrak over and made the obvious comment:

"You look in rough shape," the female team medic said.

"Yes, this is how you look when a galactic class spy beats the hell out of you," Adrak responded.

"Let me put some medications on some of those wounds," the team medic said.

"I have a better idea, give me a strong elixir and I'm going to take a long warm bath and soak my sore body," Adrak responded.

"Sure, no problem. Strip down in the bedroom so I can look you over and do a modified medical triage," the lovely female team medic said.

"You sure you don't want to just look at my tool?" Adrak asked.

"000050428A62315, you have no idea how many bodies I've looked at when I worked in an emergency room at the Space Force Hospital in Leaperring Valentina." The female team medic replied.

"Alright, but I want to start filling the water in the tub before I take my clothes off. I think I will feel a hell of a lot better resting in the bath after you give me a great elixir," Adrak said.

"Not to worry, I'll put some interesting medications in your elixir that will take a lot of your pain away. But I must warn you it will put a damper on your sex life." The female medic responded.

"As bad as I feel now, sex is the last thing in the world I want." Adrak replied.

Adrak observed the Medic go into the attached bathroom and quickly heard the water filling as he started undressing. In short order he was nude only because he wanted to be in the bath as soon as possible and was looking forward to experiencing the elixir the *Doc* had for him.

Shortly after the *Doc* came back from the bathroom, 000050428A62315 (a.k.a. Adrak) was stripped down nude.

The "Doc" knew 000050428A62315's body was beat to hell and more than likely the patient was in terrible pain, but he wasn't a wimp and wasn't going to broadcast it which will make her triage tougher to accomplish.

The swelling black eye and broken nose were easy to figure out. It was all those other terrible bruises all over the patient's body that would be a challenge to figure out. Hopefully 000050428A62315 wasn't damaged to the point he would have to be evacuated, meaning the mission would be a bust and months of preparations wasted at a time they could ill afford to back down.

The *doc* did a thorough investigation and made some quick notes of some areas she needed to focus on for a few days and after the patient took a bath and rested, and sleeping with the help of sedatives, get some blood work done to check for drugging, poisoning, and chemicals that might indicate organ damage or something serious.

"I've seen what I need to look at for now. Go ahead and get in the bath, I've dumped some ingredients in it that are pain killers that will help. I'm going to get you your elixir and some medications to put on your eye and your nose," the *Doc* said.

Adrak crawled into the Tub that had a seat in it allowing the water to come up to his neckline with a back rest he could lean back on and soak and rest. Shortly after, Adrak had the water jets running and was slowly feeling better already.

In a short while the *Doc* came back in with a drink someone from Earth would say tasted like a "screwdriver," orange juice with Vodka. But this Elixier had ferments in it and medications that acted as a healing expediter with vitamins and enzymes that had remarkable effects and were designed to treat war wounds.

"Here you go. I hope you like the taste." The Doc said then handed the metallic drink container to Adrak who quickly took a taste.

"This doesn't taste too bad. What if I want a second helping," Adrak asked.

"Not a problem. You can't overdose on that drink; you will just urinate the excess out. But I must warn you it will help make you sleepy so you can sleep off some of your wounds," the Doc stated with a serious look.

"Alright, thanks" Adrak replied.

"I'm going to my room so I can send a report about your injuries, and I may need to take some pictures later. I'll do that while you are sleeping."

The Doc went into her room and started creating her report for her patient 000050428A62315. She didn't need any pictures because artificial intelligence had already captured all the images required and appended them to her report and put in all the appropriate comments just as if the doctor herself had typed them up.

The Doc's medical report on patient 000050428A62315 only took five minutes then it was zapped into space via a neutrino secret transmitter located on the other side of the planet the Tramulite's could never attribute to this home or patient 000050428A62315 who they thought they had killed.

While Adrak was relaxing and reclining in the bath enjoying his elixir he was having a lot of thoughts about Martilene Chares and Karli Pauli.

Adrak didn't have to wait much longer for his departure. In the morning upon reviewing what happened, the decision was made to send Adrak back to headquarters immediately for a critique on what happened with Sidis.

The staff at the safe house immediately disassembled the support equipment and sent it all back via a portal, then they too departed one by one in a portal and the last person leaving initiated the timer for the self-destruct mechanism as the house would momentarily be on fire with phosphorous canisters synchronized lighting in every room and a major natural gas leak initiated via remote control.

Five minutes after the last Vekkar support staff member left, the house was engulfed in a tremendous flame no fire department was going to put out quickly and by the time the fire department arrived, the roof had already collapsed, and the contents thoroughly destroyed. Any evidence of extra wiring or sensors were melted and burned to ashes with the super-hot fire provided by the phosphorous and the abundance of natural gas feeding the flame. The only benefit of the fire department arriving was to shut off the natural gas by the sidewalk next to the street as well as electricity and water.

After SMERSH stood down from the investigation, because they had killed the agent and his support staff had torched his home to eliminate any evidence, Martilene drove past the home and saw the charred ruins that was mostly laying on the ground in heaps of burned material and ashes. She assumed SMERSH was leaving her alone because Geskar was dead and she would miss him dearly, because no man before him and taken her for such a fantastic ride.

Karli Pauli would always wonder what happened to Geskar and her private investigators informed her his home had burned to the ground and he probably perished in the nasty fire.

The government was not ever going to release the news they had killed the spy who foiled their plans and slipped away. For now, the Tramular government thought Geskar portrayed by the spy was killed in the missile attack on his Skycar where Sidis also died.

SMERSH investigated Sidis' death and security camera video revealed what got him killed, attempting to *Cowboy it up* and grab the glory by taking down a major Vekkar spy by himself.

The security video did show Sidis was beating the hell out of the enemy spy until the spy did some surprising martial arts movements even though he was in terrible shape that temporarily disabled Sidis so the spy could get into position to kill Sidis.

While Sidis was laying in an exposed position, semi-unconscious and struggling to regain his composure, the spy 000050428A62315 struck Sidis in the neck with a heel kick. That's what killed Sidis, but the Tramular's were unaware Sidis was dead afterwards when the spy placed him in his Skycar and drove off where authorities were quickly on the chase and made the fateful decision to attack the Skycar before it would have evaded them in the wilderness area of mountain forests.

The watcher who had an overly tight surveillance on Geskar who was trying to discredit Adrak over professional jealousy, got *snapped up*.

In spy trade *snapped up* means the watcher was captured.

An interdimensional Spy was sent via a portal to rescue the watcher. That person managed to get the spy rescued and sent back to headquarters via an inter dimensional portal, but unfortunately the person that rescued him, a gentleman named Cajarington, was shot with a stun gun before he could walk into the portal and escape. Cajarington was lying on the floor merely 5 feet away from the portal and freedom, unconscious.

Cajarington woke up in a prison infirmary, not a POW but an *enemy spy* that usually meant execution as soon as they got everything out of him they needed.

The watcher had also been watched by a watcher's-watcher and instead of the watcher issuing a pejorative report on Adrak, he was suddenly the focus of acts and omissions and inexcusable behavior. The watcher's-watcher had a report that elucidated two problems.

First, the fact Adrak never detected the watcher as well as Sidis doing reconnaissance on him painted a negative picture that Adrak was distracted by the sensational experiences of two women.

In the case of Martilene it was somewhat unavoidable because she was a prop he had to develop as part of his disguise. But in the case of Karli Pauli, Adrak should have had enough common sense to focus less on Karli and more on in-situ awareness and possible counter espionage efforts against him.

***

Chapter Six

Rescue

Adrak was soon being prepared to rescue the captured spy Cajarington. They didn't have much time. They knew where Cajarington was now located but as soon as the Tramulite's found the tracking device it was destroyed, and he would be moved soon and lost.

Adrak had to be sent in and get him out of there before Cajarington was relocated and presumably tortured and killed. There was also the worry that while being severely tortured, he might reveal some sensitive sources and methods. Time was critical.

There was no rest and recreation for Adrak that he thought he was entitled to after delivering a treasure trove of information on the secret Tramulite interdimensional portal research center.

The only reason why Cajarington hadn't been moved is the overzealous SMERSH agents had the stun gun setting halfway between stun and kill. Cajarington came as close as a person did to being killed by the weapon that had dual purpose stun and kill.

As such Cajarington on life support had not fully come to. When pressed for details the doctors informed the SMERSH agents, it could take him a week or longer to snap out of it. Since Cajarington's room was guarded around the clock by SMERSH agents that timeline did not pose a huge problem for them.

SMERSH certainly wanted the enemy agent fully awake and alert when they started to interrogate him first with soft and simple approaches with psychological exploitation.

But knowing the enemy spy was probably well trained and hardened against such methods, they would swing into more brutal methods that were so inhumane that some SMERSH agents could not stomach what went on and refused to participate. They would however have no qualms about shooting and killing the spy.

As part of the preparations, Adrak carried with him a psychological inducer that would likely wake up Cajarington and give him a huge adrenaline rush to facilitate the escape.

The Interdimensional Spy Portal would be taxed to its maximum capability. They rarely wanted to transport two people at once because of the possibility of disassociation and serious consequences of two bodies brought back together as one. But if Cajarington was incapacitated, they both had to leave together. The plan in that case would be to throw Cajarington into the portal and immediately walk into it. Adrak was directed to count to three after he threw Cajarington into the portal to prevent the disassociation issue.

Adrak was going to take a huge risk because he had to make 2 stops. First, he had to go to security in the building and shut off all the alarms and subdue everyone located there to prevent his next move. Use of deadly force was authorized so if Adrak had to kill a few Tramular's to break Cajarington out, so be it.

Then he would go via portal to the room they had Cajarington hooked up to life support. Even if it meant he might kill Cajarington disconnecting the life support, they would rather have him dead than giving their enemies secrets. They would have doctors standing by to deal with Cajarington when he arrived via Portal. Hopefully Cajarington responded to the wakeup drugs and would be immediately mobile.

Adrak was only about a quarter way through the critiques and dealing with the watcher and watcher's-watcher testimonies, but this critical assignment put all that on hold.

In the middle of the night, Adrak was led to the launch room and one last check of all his equipment was done then it was time to send him to the security room. The portal opened and he stepped in knowing he would be fighting in just a minute.

What saved Adrak's life upon arrival, the two security men staffing the center had never seen a portal before and were utterly stunned which delayed their actions. Adrak was ready for action and stunned both security officers. Adrak's communicator had the Spĕctrāl de Dòngtài artificial intelligence APP and the computational genius immediately scanned the room and moments later informed Adrak, "All Alarms have been disabled for five minutes."

That's all they needed. Adrak then gave a signal via the communicator and a new portal opened and he was soon in Cajarington's infirmary room with two SMERSH agents. The gun battle was fast and furious as Adrak knew he would be shot at immediately and planned for it with a tactical movement as he was trained to jump and shoot making him a harder target to hit while he nailed the two stationary targets with maximum stun disabling them.

Adrak landed on his side and flipped over pointing his weapon in the direction of the two SMERSH agents who were now laying on the floor seemingly unconscious. Adrak didn't want to take any chances so he stunned them again which came close to killing both, but they would survive and feel crappy for a couple days.

Cajarington had steel restraints attached to his arms and legs that would normally prevent Adrak from removing him. There were a couple ways he could handle it but he thought the two SMERSH agents probably had keys to the devices and quickly checked them and found the keys and unlocked all of Cajarington's restraints. He then placed the device up to Cajarington's neck and the blue beam shot into him and Cajarington immediately opened his eyes and saw Adrak who was a friendly.

"We need to leave right now." Adrak said as he disconnected all the life support connections and helped Cajarington up on his feet and walked him over to a portal that opened and shoved him inside. He counted to three and stepped in the portal about the time another SMERSH agent entered the room because the life support instruments were giving off alarms indicating the patient was dying.

Just as the SMERSH agent was pulling up his blaster to shoot Adrak, he saw Adrak waving to him and disappear. THE PATIENT WAS GONE!

As promised, doctors with a wheelchair and gurney were waiting for Cajarington who was wearing a hospital gown and had several hoses and cables attached to his body. Because Cajarington was standing, they had him sit down in the wheelchair that was pointing in the direction of the portal which Adrak soon stepped out of smiling.

There was history between these two prima-donnas. They didn't like each other and often wanted to kick the other's ass.

This was going to be a bad day for Cajarington because he was rescued by Adrak. To him it was like a curse. The one person in the agency that he would not want to be rescued by and be able to remind him of in the future was Adrak. It was a bitter pill to swallow.

In some ways psychologically it was almost as bad as being tortured by the Tramular's.

It did not fail for the Executive Director *Doctor Oxyuran Lepidotus Taipan* to see such animosity to the point Cajarington didn't even thank the man for saving his life. And then *Doctor Oxyuran Lepidotus Taipan* smiled because he had a mission for the two of them that would facilitate them bonding and counting on each other.

***

Chapter Seven

New Mission

The morning started out in seemingly a strange atmosphere as 000050428A62315 (a.k.a. Adrak) found himself sitting across from the Executive Director of Vekkar Interdimensional Transport Directorate, *Doctor Oxyuran Lepidotus Taipan.*

Agent Cajarington, his former rival, was also there sitting on the other side of the conference table.

Before Agent 000040972A48795 (a.k.a. Cajarington) was captured by Tramulite Planetary Defense Force's *Task Force Bagheera*, he never had many good things to say about Adrak. To say he often stabbed Adrak in the back and denigrated him often is an understatement.

It's kind of interesting to observe the transformation of someone living in fear, expecting serious consequences from a brutal enemy, to have a change of heart when the rival saves them from such a fate.

Executive Director *Doctor Oxyuran Lepidotus Taipan* wasn't quite sure that 000040972A48795 (a.k.a. Cajarington) had fully buried the AXE between them. But he was going to soon find out.

The next priority mission listed in the top 10 priorities, would require two Inter Dimensional Portal Spies to achieve the requirements of mission. It would be highly dangerous, filled full of uncertainty and shaky intelligence. Cooperation between the two of them, which included serious physical labor associated with the task, would be necessary or there would be a good possibility neither of them would make it back alive.

One element of the mission would test their fate beyond anything ever attempted before. They would have to carry explosives with them. That was one of the key reasons for the need for two men as the weight of the precision shaped explosives was far more than one man could rapidly carry to the target area with the lift capability of the stealth drone.

When researchers tested carrying explosives via Inter Dimensional Spy Portals, they could not get any volunteers. Smart men thought it would be like taking dynamite and placing it in a microwave oven and cooking it at high power.

The agency experimented with animals sent with explosives to a test location with small amounts in the beginning.

Executive Director Doctor Oxyuran Lepidotus Taipan, the brains behind the Inter Dimensional Spy Portal said that the portal worked there would absolutely no chance of the explosives igniting.

This was an event that added to the animosity between the two portal spies.

Executive Director Doctor Oxyuran Lepidotus Taipan asked for volunteers and got only one, Adrak who traveled to a location with the Director's pet dog: Logan. The two were sent Inter Dimensionally via a Portal to a nearby Agency Building where "Doc" was waiting to provide lifesaving medical help in case Adrak was injured in the portal.

Adrak, the dog Logan and fifty pounds of GVXT explosives arrived intact as planned.

The current mission planning was still some time off and during that time, Cajarington seemed to step up the level of animosity and while in the locker room one day changing after they were in martial arts and Physical Training, when the typical ruse between them lit off, just before a couple other agents had to step in front of them, right after Cajarington made a crass statement,

Cajarington said, "Adrak you got your ass beat good today during martial arts training."

Adrak reminded Cajarington:

"Hey Cajarington, don't forget you pussy'd out on volunteering for the explosives check."

The Tramular's are not nice guys in how they treat captured spies. Besides the neurotic rods causing great pain, and atmospheric pressure changes in a tank over a period of time, Cajarington was about to experience all that reach the point of wishing death to end the pain, had Adrak not saved him. This is one event that extended hostile feelings in Cajarington.

Then to Cajarington's biggest surprise of his life he woke up from almost a coma when, Adrak appeared from a portal and with a very sophisticated plan broke him out of the prison where they each were able to walk through a portal to safety about 30 seconds before a SMERSH agent might have foiled the escape.

Doctor Oxyuran Lepidotus Taipan had no choice but to destroy the Tramulite Secret Inter Dimensional Portal Development Center that would one day soon provide the ability for SMERSH the Tramular elite Spy Agency to send spies via portals meaning, there would be no way of detecting them and preventing their espionage.

The two would travel in a novel manner to fulfill the requirements of the mission that included destroying the well protected buildings and be in position to do post bomb damage assessment to make sure enough of it was destroyed and ensure they set the program back several years. The explosions would have to happen during daylight hours to take out as many of the Tramulite scientists as possible.

How to get bombs into the heavily guarded Tramulite Research Campus during daylight hours was problematic. Staging them during the night then sending them in during broad daylight when security monitors would detect them, and bomb disposal could eliminate the bombs and protect the scientists was just some of the issues.

Going in via Interdimensional Transport was not feasible because the transport Aura is easily observable, and a shootout would begin as soon as the glaring exposure occurred.

Planners at the Inter Dimensional Spy Portal Directorate studied the problem from many angles and the security apparatus at the Tramulite Research Campus was simply too powerful. Eventually some Studies and Observation Group (SOG) guys from the good ole *Cowboy days* came up with a daring plan and the more they thought about it, they came to realize this may be their only option for such a short notice.

Doctor Oxyuran Lepidotus Taipan now laid out the outline for the plan to give his two alpha males time to think about it as he pressed them for their voluntary participation:

Gentlemen, I'm glad your last mission worked out so well. The fact you worked together so succinctly gave me a notion to offer the two of you a chance to go out and do a high priority mission that will no doubt lay the foundations for your future promotions.

"I've heard this song before, how about just tell us what you have in mind," Adrak responded.

Director, *Doctor Oxyuran Lepidotus Taipan* felt some irritation from Adrak's comment, but because of what's he's been through the last two missions had changed him quite a bit. Near death experiences has a way with people. But he also knew Adrak unwittingly gave him a segway into his next comments that would likely challenge Adrak's sensibilities unlike anything he experienced in the recent past.

Alright Adrak, since the two of you know each other's real identity and we are in a private and secret meeting in a *cleared* room, I'm going to inform you about your next mission, *Project Geyser*. Consider this conversation covered under Interdimensional Transport Special Compartmentalization Procedures," *Doctor Oxyuran Lepidotus Taipan* said.

'I'm ready for the mission *Project Geyser*, sir," Adrak responded. Cajarington remained coy and listened without revealing any of his thoughts.

"As you know Adrak from one of your recent missions, the Tramular's moved their Inter Dimensional Portal Research Center to their planet *Drusyltania* where they think they can prevent us from getting there and disrupting their plans," *Doctor Oxyuran Lepidotus Taipan* said.

"That's a nice place for scientists to be. All the green skin women come onto the plain skinners like us. The attraction is strong," Adrak said.

"You probably humped your fair share of green skinners," Cajarington slammed

Adrak with a great comment just like in the good ole days in the past when they were at each other's throats, day in day out.

"Perhaps if you spent more time with the green skinner females, and less time with guys, you might not be so twisted," Adrak replied almost wishing Cajarington would start it so he could finish it.

"That's enough of that crap," *Doctor Oxyuran Lepidotus Taipan* responded now wondering if he was making a prudent decision.

"I was just responding to Cajarington's comments. Obviously, Cajarington doesn't appreciate me busting him out of that flea ridden prison infirmary," Adrak commented.

"This is precisely why you two wise guys are going on this mission together. You will have to help and support each other or it's likely neither of you will come back alive," *Doctor Oxyuran Lepidotus Taipan* elucidated.

"I will do my part," Cajarington said.

"Good, that's all I ask of you," *Doctor Oxyuran Lepidotus Taipan* replied.

"How will we get there?" Adrak asked.

"This will be a mission where we can't use the Inter Dimensional Portal to get you there because you would be sitting ducks arriving and most likely killed on the spot." *Doctor Oxyuran Lepidotus Taipan* replied.

"If that's the case, why are you using Inter Dimensional Portal personnel for this *Project Geyser* mission?" Adrak asked.

"As I explain how this mission has been planned you will understand," *Doctor Oxyuran Lepidotus Taipan* replied.

"I want to hear this," Cajarington said.

"*Project Geyser* requires you two to travel to planet *Drusyltania* via a black marketer ship. Just before you enter the space registration and pre-orbit, you will deploy off the black marketer in a two-man space glider that will take you to a landing zone. A few minutes before you get near the landing zone, a transponder one of our spies delivered and will be gone out of the area, will give your glider vectors you will fly towards and eventually land. The glider is one time use and as you are leaving the planet via other means it will self- destruct," *Doctor Oxyuran Lepidotus Taipan* said.

The two men looked on with great interest as the briefing was now starting to paint a complex picture.

"You will arrive near a river that has a lot of trees and foliage, I'm going to put up a map now on a holograph," *Doctor Oxyuran Lepidotus Taipan* said.

The map was a standard military campaign style map that showed the river, the landing zone, and the campus they would attack. Elevations were shown on the map and there were nearby hills and valleys and off to the distance mountain ranges.

The course to the research campus was straight forward. The landing zone was very near the river and there was a lot of foliage. The two men would have a rig to manually tow the glider to the foliage to hide it for the following day's activity. The men would travel North on the opposite side of the river until they were close to the research campus. Now the realization for two men set in.

"You will fly on drones to the rooftop of the main research building in broad daylight. One drone could not haul all the weight of the explosives needed. Hence 2 drones and two men," *Doctor Oxyuran Lepidotus Taipan* said.

"Alright, we get there, place the bombs, fly the hell out of there with the drones with the possibility of getting shot down, what's next?" Adrak asked.

"The two of you will fly back across the river, get out of the drones and walk a few feet with your transponders activated at that time. We will have another ship that will come in high speed towards the planet that is equipped with an Inter Dimensional Portal that will lock onto you and recover you and then scoot out of the area in high speed," *Doctor Oxyuran Lepidotus Taipan* said.

So, the recovery is the reason why you need to have cleared Inter Dimensional Portal personnel?" Adrak asked?

"That's correct." *Doctor Oxyuran Lepidotus Taipan* said.

"Why must I go with such an unreliable agent?" Cajarington asked.

"Cajarington, this will help you figure out how you can better work with Adrak and at the same time, it's all up to you to help improve his reliability. If the mission fails, you will likely become a prisoner again or die. You already know what will happen to you if you get captured," Doctor Oxyuran Lepidotus Taipan said.

"That's true, but if we get captured if nothing else, I will have moments of joy watching the Tramulite's give Adrak the workover they did to me," Cajarington replied with an evil grin.

"Are we going to get training on the glider and the drones before we go on the mission?" Adrak asked.

"Yes, in fact you two will leave here after the briefing and be transported to an undisclosed location for a couple weeks where you will have all the training associated with planning for this mission," Doctor Oxyuran Lepidotus Taipan said.

"I think I need a few days to take care of some personal matters," Adrak said.

"The reason why we have a support staff to handle the affairs of Inter Dimensional Agents such as yourself is you may need to be called away at any moment for a priority assignment. Your support staff will handle all matters you deem necessary in your absence," Doctor Oxyuran Lepidotus Taipan said.

"Does that include taking care of my female friend?" Adrak asked. Cajarington busted out laughing though he knew it was a touchy subject.

"Adrak, from the reports I've received, you received plenty of action on the road, hence there is no need for you to be concerned about a female friend. You spent more time with Martilene Chares than any other woman in recent years, so your question has no merit," Doctor Oxyuran Lepidotus Taipan said.

Adrak realized Doctor Oxyuran Lepidotus Taipan had a good accounting and it all figured out so there was no point in arguing.

The briefing continued and Doctor Oxyuran Lepidotus Taipan described the building they were going to hit and the best place to put the shaped charges to ensure they damaged the research model and as many scientists as possible developing it. A lot of details were discussed, but this was just the beginning of the briefings. More would happen during their training.

Just as Adrak was wondering how soon they would be transferred to the training facility, Doctor Oxyuran Lepidotus Taipan said, "That will be all for the preliminary briefing for now. You will receive more information during your training over the next few weeks."

About that time two men entered the room who definitely appeared like spooks and people neither Adrak nor Cajarington knew.

"These men will escort you to the Skycar and to the training facility," Doctor Oxyuran Lepidotus Taipan said.

"Have I been there before?" Adrak asked.

"No, this is a new location you did not know existed," Doctor Oxyuran Lepidotus Taipan replied.

"Definitely smells compartmentalized," Cajarington said.

In a brief period, the two bruisers had Adrak and Cajarington up on the rooftop and were led to a Skycar that took them away to the training campus. Today was an interesting ride. The Vekkar Interdimensional Transport Directorate Skycar was automatically flown from computers in underground protected cells and give priority to ascend to the upper transit lane.

Up high like this the Skycar could almost approach the sound barrier. No Skycars would ever exceed the speed of sound and create a sonic boom as the speeds were restricted to prevent such annoyances over the city. At almost the speed of sound the Skycar covered a good distance quickly. They flew over a desert, a short mountain range and soon into a sparsely populated area next to a river.

Adrak could see from the Skycar next to the river appeared to be a facility that oddly looked like the Tramular Research Campus they observed in the briefing.

The Skycar was now in an empty sky lane with no other transport around and pitched downward flying close to the speed of sound into what appeared to be a military airbase. But the place seemed semi abandoned.

In a short period of time the Skycar landed, and the men exited it and met several military people there waiting on them. One of the escorts introduced them.

General Maunoury, let me introduce you to agents 000040972A48795 (a.k.a. Cajarington) and 000050428A62315 (a.k.a. Adrak)," The escort said.

"I doubt I will ever remember their numbers, how about we just call them "Four" and "Five," General Maunoury replied.

"Works for me," Adrak replied.

"Gentlemen, this is Major Divico, he'll be supervising your training. That includes your space operations, deployment of explosives, and familiarization with the new drones." General Maunoury said.

"I'm curious as to how the drone operates," Cajarington said.

"It's basically a backpack with folding wings," Major Divico said.

"Interesting." Cajarington replied.

"What's the purpose of the backpack?" Adrak asked.

"They contain the power storage for the powered folding wings," Major Divico replied.

"Alright, I'm ready got going," Adrak said.

"Major Divico will escort you to your Barracks. You will discover armed guards outside your barracks rooms. They are not there to keep you inside. They are to prevent anyone from approaching you," General Maunoury said.

The Skycar landed close to the barracks where Adrak and Cajarington would be staying. The men were led to their perspective new homes and just like previously announced there were guards outside waiting for them.

General Maunoury and the two escorts soon departed and Adrak was alone with Major Divico and Cajarington.

"We can't have you exposed to the base population so you will be eating in your barracks room. Everything will be delivered. Your support staff is cleared for *Project Geyser.*"

Adrak immediately knew what that meant, the staff were all spooks. "Can you give us an idea about our schedule?" Adrak asked.

"Your mission is half at night and half during the day. Your training schedule is set up for a similar timeline. In the middle of the night, you will be awakened and taken to your training area and then you will return to your barracks around noon to rest and get ready for the next day of training. Therefore, I suggest you go into your barracks room and prepare to rest, and you will be taken away around mid-night to start your first day of training."

"It's kind of hard to start sleeping in the middle of the day," Adrak stated.

"We knew that to be a factor therefore medical staff will be arriving shortly to give you sedatives that will put you out for quite a few hours until we wake you up. Your workout clothes will be laid out for you. You will be wearing exactly what you will wear on the mission. The shoes and the clothes, everything is planned for you."

"Alright, shoot me up so I can get some sleep and I'm ready to train," Adrak responded.

In a brief period, the two spies were sedated, and the rooms had black shades making the rooms dark. They were also acoustically dampened so very little noise existed, and the two men slept well.

Right around midnight with both spies fully sedated, medical and security staff entered their rooms. These spies are trained killers and if you wake them up the wrong way, they may kill you. With restraints in place so they don't jump out of bed and kill someone, the anesthesiologist trained to systematically wake up spies from a drug induced rest period placed the mask over each one separately in their living quarters. They would soon be breathing a mixture of air that would reverse the effects of the drugs administered them earlier to ensure they slept well.

"He will start responding in about a minute," the anesthesiologist said as he stood back.

True to the anesthesiologist word, Adrak started stirring and quickly found himself restrained with hand and leg cuffs wondering WTF.

The anesthesiologist walked over and took off the breathing mask and asked, "000050428A62315 are you awake now?"

"Yes, I'm awake now. Why am I being restrained?" Adrak asked.

"We are going to take off the restraints now. We just wanted to make sure you didn't kill someone when we woke you up," the anesthesiologist responded.

"If you promptly get these restraints off me, I promise not to kill anyone." Adrak responded.

The anesthesiologist nodded to the security people who undid the restraints.

"We are going to let you take care of your personal business in the bathroom, then we will have a meal delivered here for you to eat before Major Divico's men take you on your first training session," the anesthesiologist said.

Adrak got out of bed and stood up and asked, "Which way to the bathroom?"

"Right over here, sir," one of the security men said then walked over and opened the door to the bathroom.

"Okay, thanks." Adrak said.

"There are plenty of towels if you want to take a shower and your training uniform is laid out on a tabletop in the bathroom. Your training footwear are by that chair over there where you can put those on with special socks to wear to protect your feet," a medical person said.

Nothing was left to chance. The whole operation was choreographed by experts.

Adrak took care of his business, took a Hollywood shower, and dressed in his training clothes he would soon learn he would deploy in. He came out of the bathroom and there was only a security man and one other person now in the room with a table and place settings for a meal. He walked over to the chair put on the special socks and workout shoes and was informed:

"Sir, your meal was ready," the support staff administrative aide said.

"Thanks." 000050428A62315 (a.k.a. Adrak) responded.

Adrak sat down at the portable table and discovered he had a high protein meal with a special tasting drink he first thought was Blue Bǎixiāng Guǒzhī (pronounced Bye-shung Gwo-chee).

When the support staff administrative aide observed Adrak tasting the drink with a question on his face, he immediately volunteered: "Sir that is Blue Bǎixiāng Guǒzhī with a special additive that slightly alters the taste."

"May I ask what the additive does?" 000050428A62315 (a.k.a. Adrak) asked.

"Sir, in case you are wondering, that additive does two things. It gives you a slight amount of invisibility syndrome plus vigilance enhancement," the support staff administrative aide replied.

"All I need is a good night sleep, and that does that for me," 000050428A62315 (a.k.a. Adrak) said.

"Sir, I've been informed your actual mission could have complications requiring you to be awake for extended periods. You will be given the same invincibility and vigilance enhancement serum just before you deploy in the glider on your mission," the support staff administrative aide replied.

"I can see that, but why during training?" 000050428A62315 (a.k.a. Adrak) asked.

"Major Divico has determined; he wants everything exercised during your training just like you will experience on your mission, including the psychoactive drugs you are being administered," the support staff administrative aide replied.

That sort of makes sense, however if this is good stuff I hope it does not embolden Carrington to decide to show us who's the better of the two men," 000050428A62315 (a.k.a. Adrak) said.

"000050428A62315 (a.k.a. Adrak) I know you two Inter Dimensional Portals Spies are cocky like the rest, but you will quickly discover Major Divico has very little patience for trainees who do not always conduct themselves professionally. Sometimes he gives people with such behavior enhanced training," the support staff administrative aide replied.

"What would enhanced training be?" Adrak asked.

"Something like a week deployment to the front lines at the insectoid planet, Mercurypraximus," the aide replied.

"I would prefer to never be around those blood suckers, I will conduct myself professionally, but I can't speak for 000040972A48795 (a.k.a. Cajarington)," Adrak replied.

"Just remember 000050428A62315 (a.k.a. Adrak), it takes two to tangle. Save your pent-up emotions for when you get back to the Vekkar Interdimensional Transport Directorate, where I'm sure there is adaquate martial arts events the two of you can socialize at," the aide said.

"I have something else to tame my future partner with." Adrak said.

"What's that if I may ask?" the aide asked.

"If he gets out of line, I'll let him know I'm not going to rescue him from another Tramular prison if he wants to be a jerk," Adrak said.

"That's probably something I shouldn't know about," the aide responded.

"Probably not," Adrak replied.

Adrak finished his meal and the drink and was starting to feel a nice buzz. His alertness seemed to be enhanced, and he knew the psychoactive drugs were affecting him just like they would on the mission.

"Alright, I'm ready to go do the training," Adrak announced.

"Would you like to take a few minutes to visit the toilet and freshen up before we transport you to your training activity?" the Aide asked.

"Yea give me about five minutes. Adrak stood up and suddenly he felt the need to visit the toilet and take care of his personal business. The drugs influenced Adrak's digestive system, to where it almost was as good as a laxative.

Adrak was suddenly delighted the Aide made the astute call otherwise he might have had to immediately come back into his barracks room to take care of business.

The same scenario unfolded for Cajarington who simultaneously was prepared in a similar manner.

The two Inter Dimensional Portal Spy's were escorted to a Skycar and then flown for a few minutes and the Skycar flew into an aircraft hangar and the doors immediately shut behind it, preventing outsiders from viewing the goings on.

Major Divico was inside the hanger waiting with a few other men.

"I hope you all had a good rest," Major Divico said.

"Slept like a baby," Cajarington responded.

"Just like others will know you as #4 and #5, your two trainers here, are #1 and #2. For tonight's training they will split up with each of you and take you through an extensive course on flying the personal drone," Major Divico said.

"Alright," Adrak responded and Cajarington nodded his head.

"As you look around, we have set up an obstacle course inside the hanger you will fly around gaining expertise on handling the drone," Major Divico said.

"What do you expect us to accomplish here?" Cajarington asked.

"We expect that by morning the two of you will be sufficient at piloting your personal drones, and we will have you flown to the simulated Tramulite building and place your simulated bombs, then fly back to your base camp and prepare to be transported via portal to a mother ship," Major Divico said.

"Will we go to that mother ship in the morning?" Adrak (a.k.a. #5) asked.

"No #5, that will complete today's training requirements. After your next rest period, you will become acquainted with the mother ship and the glider," Major Divico said.

"Alright," Adrak (a.k.a. #5) said.

Major Divico didn't need to be there, but due to the importance of the mission, he stayed to observe some of the training.

#1 gave a briefing to #4 (Cajarington) and #5 (Adrak) on the personal drone.

"The drone can be flown via manual control or via networked computer link via the mother ship that would send calibrated lat-long vectors to place you two Inter Dimensional Portal Spies to the precise location on the building we want the charges placed to destroy the prototype and kill as many scientists as possible." Drone Trainer #1 said.

"Sounds good to me," Cajarington said.

"But in case the remote-control signals are jammed or malfunctioned via unknown reasons, you two spies can control your personal drones in manual flight control," Drone Trainer #1 said.

"I like that option," #5 (a.k.a. Adrak) responded.

There were two large backpacks hanging from their storage racks. Drone Trainer #1 walked over and grabbed one of them.

"Here's your personal drone. It looks like a large backpack with two side segments. You put it on like a normal backpack that has a front securing latch that holds the two straps together to ensure it stays on you in all flight conditions," Drone Trainer #1 said.

As soon as the drone trainer #1 put the drone backpack on and latched the strap holding the two backpack straps together nice and firm, then continued with the training.

"These straps have pressure transducers and strain gauge sensors mounted in them. The microprocessor in the drone management system firmware gets automatically activated with any kind of movement. The microprocessor will remain active for 30 minutes unless you shut it off and I will soon show you how you do that," Drone Trainer #1 said.

"Interesting," Adrak said.

"You don't have to jerk too hard but pull down on the two backpack straps three times like this while saying: one thousand one, one thousand two, one thousand three," Drone Trainer #1 said.

The men now saw the two side sections on the backpack suddenly unfold into a short flying wing with a series of shrouded fans along the length of both. Neither Adrak nor Carrington had seen the personal drone before. This was another one of those clandestine toys only used for special operations and required the need to know to be exposed to them.

The personal drone is ready to fly and carry me somewhere. By simply pulling down or up on the straps you will accelerate vertically or decelerate and reduce altitude. If you pull up on the straps four times that tells the computer to transition to flying mode and it will change your pitch more horizontally and increase speed," Drone Trainer #1 said.

"How fast can it go?" Cajarington (#4) asked.

"We have tested it going off tall hills and mountains down into a valley and with a special flying suit and helmet we've achieved in excess of 400 miles per hour," Drone Trainer #1 said.

"Don't get any wild ideas," Adrak (#5) said.

"Maybe one of these days, I'll have a chance to take one of these on a mission and have some real fun," Cajarington (#4) said.

"You will be flown to the Tramulite research building in autopilot. In our numerous tests to create the best flight profile, the test pilots went as fast as 60 miles per hour because the distances are short. Remember we don't want you airborne that long. That's why the glider's landing zone is on the opposite side of the river from the research building," Drone Trainer #1 said.

In due time Adrak and Cajarington were wearing their personal drone backpacks and systematically taken over the obstacle course in auto pilot. Because the training period was significantly longer than the actual mission profile after a couple hours they were landed, and the instructors changed out the battery packs with recharged energy packs to allow further training.

The obstacle course had a real glider like they would use, a simulated river, simulated trees and a building top to land on.

For two hours they were simply passengers as the personal drone microprocessor controlled their flight profile taking them through all the objectives of the obstacle course. After the repetitive processes, Adrak became aware of the highly accurate navigation being performed with the computer mounted in the drone controller in the backpack.

In the morning when the sunlight started showing they left the hangers with their restowed backpacks and batteries changed out with a new set recharged.

They were put aboard a military Skycar that was essentially a flying jeep that had 4 wheels, and it could travel on road networks if required. The *Skyjeep* flew north to an obscure area of the large base reserved for training. No personnel were allowed in this area unless they were part of a scheduled training exercise and there were security personnel around the perimeter of the area to ensure nobody went into the area uninvited.

The Skyjeep landed next to a two-man glider, precisely the model they would fly in the next day.

Drone Trainer #1 instructed:

"I'm going to show you how to stow your personal drone backpacks in the glider. Then I'm going to have you strap into the glider just like you would on the mission. In the cargo bay of the glider are two additional containers that look like backpacks. If you wondered why the backpacks have the hook latch at the bottom of them, that's because the two additional packages that look like backpacks are explosive satchels that will be full of explosives during your mission will clip on to your backpack then you will deploy to the building rooftop structure and place those explosive satchels then leave and fly back here."

"Sounds simple enough," Adrak replied.

"Those explosive satchels in the cargo hold weight the same exact amount of the ones you will deliver during your mission." Drone Trainer #2 said.

"The personal Drone can handle the additional weight?" Adrak asked.

"These personal drones have very powerful lifters on them. When you were training at the obstacle course you were only using less than half of the lift available. When you carry the explosive satchels to the building it will use almost max power. That means the power drain on the power source will be twice as fast. The storage level on the drone power system has enough energy to accommodate you for more than four times the range you need to fly. Plus, when you fly back to the glider which is your pickup zone you will expend considerably less energy than you did flying to the building," Trainer #2 said.

"Now for the procedure. We train just like we fight and how we will conduct the mission. By doing so, everyone knows their assignment." Trainer #1 said.

"Sounds reasonable to me," Adrak responded.

"Unless one of you gets critically wounded and unable to carry out the procedure as we will now disclose to you, we expect it to be done this way," Drone Trainer #1 said.

"Understand." Cajarington replied. Trainer #1 explained the procedure:

"You will get out of the glider, get your drone backpacks and the explosive satchels out of the cargo hold. You will put on the backpacks, then each one of you will click the explosive satchel onto the other person's backpack confirming its secured," Drone Trainer #1 said.

"You will then launch to the building under autopilot navigation to the spot on the building where we want you to place the charges. You will notice the red circle on the explosive satchels. The red circle is to be pointed downwards because it's a shaped charge. You will place the two explosive satchels next to each other. They are synchronized to an atomic clock that can only lose one second in a 100 billion years," Drone Trainer #1 said.

"During your flight from the glider to the building, your prospective personal drone computers will arm the satchel charges and based on its measurements on its Navigational Vectors that will deliver you to the building roof, you will hear through the earpiece you'll wear from the drone computer, *the satchel is armed*," Drone Trainer #1 said.

Both satchels have proximity detectors to the drones and after you are a safe distance away from the satchels, if someone attempts to tamper with them, the telltale device will alert the other satchel, and they will immediately detonate even if the timer has not reached its detonation delay.

"What's the purpose of the delay?" Cajarington asked.

"We want the explosions to occur coinciding with the Inter Dimensional Portal recovery of you as a distraction so they will not be shooting at you." Drone Trainer #2 said.

Trainer #1 continued with the briefing:

"Assuming the plan works the way we designed it, you two will fly back to the glider and when you land its proximity detectors will detect you and start the countdown for the self-destruct."

"The glider has some powerful explosives in it for this purpose. Place the drone backpacks in the cargo hold where you obtained them earlier and we will then recover you via Inter Dimensional Portal. Five seconds after the proximity detector no longer registers your presence and can determine if you vanished in the portal, it will self-destruct."

"What happens if the portals do not appear, and we are stuck there?" Adrak asked.

"In case the plan falls apart and we are not able to extract you, there is a self destruct button on the glider. Press it and run away from it as fast as possible. While you are running count to ten then stop and lay down flat. Most likely the shrapnel will all fly over the top of you." ," Drone Trainer #2 said.

"Which means we'll quickly become prisoners to some pissed off people," Cajarington said.

"If you do not want to suffer through such expected interrogations which we know you have already experienced, the option you have is to sit in the glider while it explodes, and you will perish very quickly. If you don't want to feel the pain associated with the explosion, in the back of each seat are fast acting pills to bite into and swallow. You will immediately become unconscious and not feel a thing ," Drone Trainer #1 said.

"I'm having second thoughts about this," Cajarington said.

"When you agreed to go on this mission the director informed you it was voluntary, is that correct?" Trainer #2 asked.

"Yes, he did," Cajarington quickly responded.

"If you chose at this time, you do not want to go on the mission, for mission security, you will be sequestered in your barracks room until mission specialists return from the mission." Trainer #1 said.

"I'll go but that doesn't mean I have to like it," Cajarington said.

"Nobody likes this business unless they are nuts," Trainer #2 said.

"That's #5 for you, he loves this shit, so he must be nuts," Cajarington said.

"Thank God we have a few nuts like #5 to carry out these scary missions," Trainer #1 replied.

Adrak and Cajarington got into the glider. The canopy shut to simulate just arriving. Then it opened with the trainers observing.

Adrak and Cajarington are intelligent fast learners and enacted the plan exactly like the trainers laid out for them.

Shortly without a lot of fanfare, they had their personal drone backpacks on and the simulated explosives satchel clicked onto the bottom of the backpack.

"Here we go," Adrak said as he lifted on the backpack straps launching and then reorienting to the horizontal flying mode all under control of the internal computer. Once launched it was hands off flying for both *new bird men.*

The trip to the top of the simulated research building was a lot quicker than Adrak expected, and they landed precisely where the satchels were to be placed. Shortly after placing the satchels when the explosive satchels indicated armed and ready, the two personal drones lifted the men off and they flew across the river back to the glider, put their drone backpacks into the glider then stepped back.

Now for their next big shock they were not planning, they were looking at each other and discovered their bodies disassociating in the portal as they were being beamed up to the Black Marketer ship with a portal machine. Then their second big surprise is they were sent via portal to their barracks rooms. Inside each room was a drone trainer (#1 and #2) who was sent there first.

"We are going back to the glider now, to do it again," drone trainer #1 said.

"I'm ready when you are," Adrak replied.

Shortly they were back in the Skyjeep heading back to the same location.

Drone Trainer #1 checked the power levels on the backpacks and stated, "The drone backpacks have 75% of their power remaining. That's enough for two more simulations and we'll be done for the day."

Adrak could see the drone had been serviced and the cargo bays had two explosive satchels in them and assumed they were brought back by the team.

They conducted the next two simulations with the same precision as the first and remained in their Barracks room for the rest of the day until they had a meal and were sedated again and put to sleep.

The next day, the training took on a new element. This time they were transported via Interdimensional Portal up to the Black Marketer ship. They were soon given a training course on the two-man glider.

"This training course will be very simple. The glider is fully automated. There are no manual flight controls. Either it works or it doesn't and if that's the case you will be dead, so it doesn't matter," Drone Trainer #1 said.

"Let's get the show on the road," Adrak said knowing the sooner they finished this done training the quicker the day would come to an end.

"The simulated satchel charges are in the cargo bay of the glider with your personal drone backpacks. All you need to do is get inside the glider, we'll shut the hatch and, in a few minutes, launch you." Drone Trainer #1 said.

"Alright, I'm ready," Cajarington said.

When all conditions were ready, the two-man glider was deployed out of the *Glider Bay* of the souped-up Black-Market Ship.

The time was shortly after midnight. They were landing in the dark. Under such circumstances a person must have great faith in technology. But Adrak knew he was in some dangerous business, and it was only a matter of time before me met his demise. Adrak wasn't going to fret over it.

But Adrak's lessons learned is a person in his position must enjoy the breadcrumbs of life when they become available, such on his last mission when he enjoyed a lovely woman, who probably had a broken heart when he disappeared.

Going into the atmosphere was a noisy event, but they had ear plugs that were also mission ear buds that had some noise cancelation, so it was bearable. Without the noise cancelation it would have been terrible for them.

Coming down on the dark side of the planet they could see city lights and the runway lighting of the base, so spatially they could have some cognitive reality of where they were approaching the landing zone. The glider vectors were highly calculated, and it leveled off at 1000 feet just below supersonic speeds so as to not leave a sonic boom and used calculated distance to bleed off the speed.

The glider also had battery powered thrusters for landing. Instruments put aboard to give the two spies ideas of where they were in the landing could see the speed and altitude start to drop off. Soon they were down to twenty feet paralleling the riverbed approaching the landing zone. When the speed finally reached the point, the craft would become unstable, the battery powered lifters kicked in and kept it on an even keel as it slowly sank down to the surface to a marginally soft landing.

With the battery powered lifters, there were no exhaust plumes to give the glider position away. It probably wasn't necessary, but nothing was left to chance as the two passengers were informed, "It is now safe to exit the glider."

The canopy opened to let them out. The cargo bay hatch automatically opened. Adrak and Cajarington grabbed their personal drone backpacks and put them on they then helped click each other's satchel charge. Sunup was just about to occur as they took off and flew to the building to lay the satchel charges. After depositing their presents to the unsuspecting (simulated), they flew back to the glider and went through the full process and were soon deposited back aboard the Black Marketer ship.

While they were on the black marketer ship waiting for another mission practice, a large VTOL craft flew over to the glider, attached lifting lines to lifting pads crew members installed and flew the glider over to the special projects hanger they practiced flying in and the glider battery was changed out. Others brought the simulated satchel charges to the hanger where they were reinstalled.

The backpack personal drones' batteries were also replaced since that could be done in parallel with the automated health checks being performed on the glider to make sure it was No Faults Detected (NFD) for the next flight. Once the flight supervisor digitally signed concurrence, the glider was loaded on a space shuttle and flown out into space and met up with the Black Marketer.

The space shuttle flew up parallel and close to the black marketer. Personnel on both spaceships were involved in the space transfer. Black Marketers with space suits on, opened the hatches for the glider bay that was currently empty. The shuttle opened its cargo doors and with the help of a large robotic arm, the glider was moved from the shuttle to the Black Marketer spacecraft.

After the transfer was completed, the shuttle retracted the robotic arm, closed the hatches, and then flew off and away from the black marketer and waited at a safe distance while technicians did another series of health checks on the glider and as soon as they received NFD status on all the health checks, the shuttle was allowed to return to the planet to wait for its next assignment.

There were two more simulated missions to the simulated Tramulite research building.

The delay in the mission related to getting reports back from Vekkar spies about the disposition of the research building and determining the most opportune moment to do the attack.

Training evolved during the wait period. They maintained two sorties per day simulated attack on the research facility. The days then allotted time for physical training and martial arts training. Per direction from Executive Director of Vekkar Interdimensional Transport Directorate, *Doctor Oxyuran Lepidotus Taipan,* #4 and #5 (Cajarington and Adrak were not allowed to do any martial arts training and attacks on each other because he knew just one little spark could ignite an inferno and either one or both would be seriously injured to the point, they could not do the mission.

Trainer #1 could tell by the body language at times the way they acted each of them wanted the opportunity to beat the crap out of the other. After the mission if they still felt that way, they would schedule a fight, and several people would line up to see it with plenty of bets placed.

Almost the exact same way Adrak escaped getting killed by Sidis, the Vekkar spy with critical intel on the mission, arrived safely with the update they needed to launch the operation.

Suddenly training was curtailed, and the two men were readied for their journey behind enemy territory.

Nobody knew for sure what happened, either the mission was compromised, or the enemy just got lucky and discovered the two spies on top of the building. Autopilot came in handy this time.

The two spies managed to get the two satchel charges deployed and were getting ready to bug out when the shooting started.

Adrak got away clean with no injuries, but Cajarington received some life-threatening wounds as they were leaving and flying back to the glider.

During the flight back to the glider Cajarington became unconscious and was going to bleed to death if he didn't get help fast.

Adrak got Cajarington out of his backpack and laid him down and got his own there as well. He knew he had to stand Cajarington up or he would not be transported via the Portal to the Black marketer About one second before the Portal opened, Adrak received his one nasty wound and was about to drop Cajarington but they both managed to be transported just in time. The bombs blew up and damaged the building like they predicted and killed a swarm of researchers, but security personnel who were just about onto the two spies made it to the glider just in time to capture it. They didn't know it was too late to stop self-destruction and when it blew it cut down a dozen Tramulite security forces.

Medical personnel aboard the Black Marketer could only stop the bleeding and sedate the two spies. Per the plan the Black Marketer made a mad dash out into deep space and met up with a Vekkar fast frigate and transferred the terribly wounded spies which the Frigate departed with. The Black Marketer got away as well since the Tramular's did not connect the sabotage with a space operation and the men who came upon the glider were instantly killed before they could report some type of space craft.

A few days later, Cajarington woke up and saw he was in a hospital bed next to Adrak who was still in bad shape after undergoing several lifesaving operations.

Nobody knew for sure what all happened because Adrak had not regained consciousness, but Cajarington was informed when they arrived back at the Black Marketer, Adrak was holding him up then he collapsed, and the two bodies plunged to the floor.

Cajarington woke up because he was feeling a lot of pain which the doctors soon took care of with more sedatives and pain killers. Before he went under again, he had the story that Adrak had carried him to his survival. Suddenly Cajarington was having mixed feelings. He hated Adrak with a passion but now that Adrak had saved his life twice he started soul searching and questioning his own behavior.

Jealousy and envy were now suddenly feeling distasteful to Cajarington because, getting his life saved twice from his rival seemed suddenly more important than petty jealousy over anger from assignments he thought he should have been given instead of Adrak.

The next day, Cajarington woke again, with a little less pain, but was hungry and needed to take a serious bowel movement. It hurt like hell going into the bathroom and sitting down on the throne, but he preferred that to a bed pan that would be the next option and he sure as hell didn't want another guy wiping his rear end.

After fantastic relief he hit the buzzer, and the orderlies came into the bathroom and helped him back to his bed and before long a nice meal was served.

He looked over at Adrak who was still under and while Adrak was sleeping during the night, they wheeled Adrak into the operating room and did another surgery, hopefully this time would stop all his internal bleeding. Adrak was on a bed pan and being fed through his veins.

After Carrington finished his meal, he was asked to take a bath and helped to the tub that soon filled with pleasing warm water that had pain killers and pressurizers mixed into the water. He purposely stayed there for thirty minutes because it felt so good. After the bath he was dressed in a clean hospital gown and back in his hospital bed raised slightly at his request. He was then notified he had a visitor who would be there momentarily.

Minutes later, Executive Director of Vekkar Interdimensional Transport Directorate, *Doctor Oxyuran Lepidotus Taipan* walked into the room and up to the side of Cajarington's bed that had a guest chair.

"You don't mind if I sit down, I'm kind of tired," Doctor Oxyuran Lepidotus Taipan said.

"Not at all sir, please sit down," Cajarington replied.

"I'm glad the two of you made it back alive," Doctor Oxyuran Lepidotus Taipan said.

"Is it okay if I use his name?" Cajarington asked.

"Sure, we are alone." Doctor Oxyuran Lepidotus Taipan answered.

"Sir, Adrak has not come back to consciousness yet. I'm worried about him." Cajarington said.

"Cajarington, I talked to Adrak's doctors a little while ago. He's had a rough time, but he'll pull through. They are keeping him heavily sedated because his extensive injuries would cause him great pain if he was awake. They will reduce the sedatives over the next few days when they think they will be able to better administer pain management." Doctor Oxyuran Lepidotus Taipan said.

"That's good to know." Cajarington replied.

"I'll come back and see him when he comes around." Doctor Oxyuran Lepidotus Taipan answered.

"Sir, we obviously could not stick around to see what happened because they were on to us and shooting at us. I think I was unconscious at the time; I don't remember much." Cajarington said.

"Cajarington, your two-man team provided excellent results. Everything that happened with the Satchel Charges fit well into the expected outcome," Doctor Oxyuran Lepidotus Taipan answered.

"That's good to know," Cajarington replied.

"You two will be going on some convalescent leave for a while. Then you will go through some rehabilitation and the doctors will figure out if you're deployable again." Doctor Oxyuran Lepidotus Taipan explained.

"What if I'm not deployable again?" Carrington asked.

"You have some rather interesting experiences. Few people have ever experienced what you have. We need to have cadres and experienced personnel of your stature to train the next generation of Inter Dimensional Portal Spies," Doctor Oxyuran Lepidotus Taipan said.

"Sounds interesting Doctor." Cajarington said.

"With some of your experience you might be helpful in counterintelligence," Doctor Oxyuran Lepidotus Taipan offered.

"I do not know if I have the patience to do that sort of work. Spy catching requires a huge amount of time and effort," Carrington Responded.

"Yes, it does. We'll find a spot for you that is most suitable for your experience. But let's hope you become physically fit again, because I have some missions in mind for you," Doctor Oxyuran Lepidotus Taipan announced.

"That sounds more to my liking. I know if I work hard enough, I can get back into shape to do other missions," Cajarington said.

"Alright Carrington, I wanted to personally thank you for your efforts on this mission. It required two men to lift the number of explosives we needed to get the job done. Your willingness to place yourself in a harmful way, and the fact you received some major wounds, speaks heavily to your commitment to our mission. I've placed a special citation in your service record. We can't state what you did for security reasons, but it does state you went above and beyond the call of duty," Doctor Oxyuran Lepidotus Taipan explained.

"I appreciate that, sir," Cajarington responded.

"When the doctors contact me and inform me Adrak has regained consciousness, I'll be back to see the two of you," Doctor Oxyuran Lepidotus Taipan explained.

"Thank you, sir, we appreciate it," Cajarington replied.

Chapter Eight

Submarine Adventure

The calm before the storm gave Adrak and Cajarington a mistaken sense of reality. The rehabilitation was supervised by top medical researchers to enhance the healing and move the timeline forward to when these premier spies would be deployable again.

Adrak didn't say anything, but he noticed a sharp change in Cajarington. He didn't know why but thought maybe his near-death experience on the last mission might have cooled off his cockiness and rude manners.

Adrak learned a valuable lesson. Just when you think the mission is going smoothly and you are about to bug out, just might be when you'll take that magic bullet. The truth of the matter is the Tramulite gunners were aiming at Cajarington but due to the poor marksmanship hit Adrak. Had the gunner shot just another inch or two off from where he hit Adrak, the bullet would have entered Cajarington's head and killed him instantly.

Right after the two spies disappeared in the portal and vanished, the gunner and his comrades unwisely approached the glider and were near proximity to it when the telltale circuitry got a trigger from the proximity sensor and detonated the explosives on the glider, killing the shooter and his comrades. The explosion was so powerful, there were only pieces of their charred bodies to pick up.

The director knew better than to have the two spies convalesce together. They were never destined to be best friends or travel and socialize in the circles each of them orbited.

Adrak enjoyed his time at a tropical paradise and experienced numerous sessions of pain and pain management during the restoration process.

As soon as the doctors deemed the two spies ready to resume the full rigor of training, they were transported to a location neither of them had ever seen before or even knew about. This demonstrated to Adrak there was a lot going on in the spook business he had no idea existed, which further explained to him just how large and how broad the Vekkar Intelligence Agency (VIA) really was.

There was a lot more to Vekkar Intelligence Agencies than the Inter Dimensional Spy Portals that would take Adrak to Unknown Intrigue and Tragedies. One of those tragedies was becoming somewhat emotionally attached to Martilene Chares whom he could never see again the rest of his life.

The next mission deemed so secret, Adrak and Cajarington were not informed of the location of the target until the week before the deployment because at that time the trainers had to get into the specificity of the operational orders.

Again because of the nature of the location and the vast surveillance that protected the site, they could not be inserted via an Interdimensional Portal. This was a hard target and the only way it could be approached was by sea. Due to the Naval Presence in the Area, the only method of penetration by sea was via a two-man submarine.

The days started out with high energy meals, physical training, and martial arts training. By director's orders, the two spies were not to practice martial arts with each other for fear of resurfacing former rivalry. Hence the training community had to provide all the opponents for the spies to exercise their martial arts skills.

In some cases, prisoners were brought in and informed if they killed the spy, they would be set free. Cajarington and Adrak knew the offer the prisoners had and knew they would be fighting for their lives. When you know, the other man will attempt to kill you, it takes on an entirely different dimension to the training. It makes it more realistic and savage.

These prisoners were very bad guys and would never see freedom again for the rest of their lives. Their only way out of confinement would be to kill one of these two spies. That set the tempo for the event.

If for some reason the prisoner was able to knock Adrak or Cajarington unconscious, trainers would jump in and subdue the prisoner and stop the prisoner from administering the Coup de Grâce.

In many cases the prisoners preferred to snap the neck and kill the opponent which would have happened if the trainers were not immediately next to the criminal to prevent further injury.

Cajarington and Adrak knocked out their opponents most of the time, but they themselves also took a beating and needed medical attention. Each one of them was knocked out at least once.

After the spy was removed and taken to the infirmary for medical treatment, the prisoner was cleaned and dressed up and in front of all the other prisoners, led out of the facility as a free man and put in a sky car, where he was transported to freedom. In some cases, the VIA immediately recruited them for nefarious purposes, but some of them were deemed so dangerous they were taken to another destination where they discovered they really didn't earn their freedom and bad things happened to them.

After a month of martial arts training, Adrak and Cajarington got quite good at defending themselves and the prisoners usually had similar types of attacks they could predict and mitigate. At that point, there was nothing more to be gained by this method. But it did harden and improve their skills in defending themselves if they were unarmed.

The other half of the day, they were given extensive training on the two-man submarine. The submarine was divided in half, a wet side and a dry side. The pilot would remain in the dry side and the passenger would be in the wet side that during insertion would open and the chosen one would swim ashore and do his espionage and sabotage, then hustle back to the waterfront and swim out to the rendezvous zone.

The submarine had a "clicker" receiver. The onboard sensors would localize the source of the clicker then approach it which would be the diver who energized the clicker by pressing 4 times on his diver belt that had sensors and activated the algorithms the computer built into the belt would operate. The diver's belt that looked innocuous had diver's weights to make the diver neutral buoyant making it easier to swim longer distances.

Neither Adrak nor Cajarington knew who the pilot was and who the passenger would be. They would not be informed of the decision until they were on the black marketer ship taking an attached glider that had the submarine piggy backed on it.

The glider, just like the previous one they used was disposable. It's only purpose in life was to help get the submarine down on the ocean sixty miles offshore where the two men would submerge in it and travel to the designated infiltration area.

The diver would remain dry until his compartment flooded down, and the hatch opened to allow him to swim out with his backpack full of mission requirements.

The submarine would be sitting on the bottom in fifty feet of water offshore when all this transpired. Once the diver departed for his mission, the hatch would be shut, water pumped out of the passenger compartment giving the submarine added buoyancy. The submarine would then slowly depart the area very quietly hugging the bottom until it got near the 100-fathom curve, and it would continue on at a prescribed depth and its miniature nuclear power plant could easily get it around 60 miles offshore where the submarine would the rise to periscope depth, copy broadcasts which would determine its next move.

There was no time they could specify for the spy to return to the waterfront because it was unknown when he would finish his acts.

Besides the information gathering and espionage capturing communications and other sources of intelligence, before the spy departed and went back into the ocean, a bomb would be placed in critical infrastructure. From space the black marketer ship would observe the explosion on the planet and if necessary, a burst transmission from the spy that he was bugging out. The submarine would then be notified via secure communications sent via a disposable probe that operated like a space buoy but near the surface of the planet in the area the submarine would be loitering and expecting broadcasts at specific times of which it would be at periscope depth to receive the notification or further instructions.

Since it was unknown which of the two would be the pilot, the two spies, Adrak and Cajarington were trained and certified as both pilot and swimmer/spy.

That meant they also had extensive swimming exercises with professional divers and swimmers to build up their stamina and ability to swim long distances. The swimmer would be injected with invincibility serum before he departed the Black

Marketer Space Craft. Neither person would be sleeping for 72 hours in a drugged state.

Between classroom training and actual at-sea operations, the two spies became well trained in submarine's operation as well as swimmer certifications. They were now combat swimmers trained as well as UDT and Clandestine Frogmen.

The submarine had a training mode where at the side of the pier a cable was ran over to a trailer driven onto the pier that had experts and simulation software. The entire submarine was placed in simulator mode where it would act as if it were to sea and the pilots would go through various scenarios to get infinitely versed on its operations. Once they were well acquainted with operations, they would take the sub out and submerge it for real.

The back seater was a trainer not the passenger who had a portable device that gave him full observation on displays and virtual submarine gauges and instruments. Every indicator was on glass, there were no actual gauges. The main display and backup display all wireless for the pilot and the trainer allowed effective situational awareness of what the pilot trainee was doing. Once both Cajarington and Adrak were deemed ready for the next phase, they were taken out in space and one at a time would ride the glider to the ocean and deploy.

The glider was essentially a flying wing with great computer controls powered by a small nuclear fusion reactor that was replaceable as easily as changing batteries.

One pilot at a time went down to the surface. The submarine in the belly of the space craft allowed ease of pilot and passenger entry. Once they were inside the submarine and hatches closed and sealed. The deployment hatch would open by the two halves sliding sideways. The submarine slung from the overhead was then lowered to the cradle of the flying wing that had electromagnetic grabbers securing the submarine that would experience some turbulence coming through the atmosphere.

A heat shield positioned on the front of the cradle protected the submarine for the most part. When all systems were "GO," the flying wing deployed from a mockup of the actual Black Marketer's ship and via a few retro rockets and trajectory initiated by the Back Marketer's ship deploying the flying wing in a trajectory heading for the ozone layer, it was on its way to the surface of the planet traveling at about 18,000 miles per hour.

The flying wing had turbulence for about two minutes entering the atmosphere and as it got closer to the planet's surface bled off speed in a spiral down to the planet. Just like the previous glider, it was well programmed, and its flight vectors were well established to get the flying wing to a specific spot in the ocean. As it got near the surface of the water using the ground effect to slow it down further, the wing slowed to a point where it was about to become unstable when the electric motors on the wing kicked in the vertical lift and stabilizer controls.

The flying wing used in the mission was disposable and would not be coming back and after it sank to the bottom, the high explosives detonated blowing it into a million pieces long after the submarine finished its mission and similarly self-destructed after the pilot and passenger were safely teleported via Inter Dimensional Portal back to the Black Marketer ship that immediately left the area.

On the first few training drops, the back seater was there with his own set of controls and displays making sure everything worked out per plan. For the pilot's it was deemed to be all in autopilot hands off landing on the ocean. After the submarine deployed from the flying wing after it submerged slowly, the pilot then had control of the submarine if necessary. But for the first few trips the submarine remained in autopilot.

The training flying wings were reused. Upon deploying the submarine these flying wings had special compartments with inflatable buoys that would raise the flying wing to the surface and a large VTOL would come out and pick it up with diver's assistance who hooked the lifting cables to the lifting pads on the flying wing then raised it up in the air and flew it back to land. They would not wait for the flying wing's refurbishment. Another wing was ready to go so as not to delay training.

After each pilot did several sorties, and the autopilot modes were well certified, the passenger came down on subsequent deployments.

Once the training phase demonstrated the two spies could get the submarine to the ocean on the planet, they shifted into the next phase of submerged transit to the target area and subsequently deployment of the passenger on his mission delivering explosives to damage infrastructure, as well as pick up INTEL via his ISR equipment built into his communicator.

Every aspect of the mission was exercised until either spy could be the pilot or passenger.

The director sent out his special assistant on the Black Marketer flight to inform the two men which one would be the pilot. Knowing the sensitivity that Cajarington might have been a former prisoner as well as severely wounded on a mission, the director had already made the decision. Cajarington would be the pilot and Adrak would be the passenger.

Cajarington did not display any outward jubilation with the realization he would not step foot on land, was very happy with the decision.

Adrak who was a semi-fatalist knowing his number could be up at any time just wanted to get the show on the road because if he was killed on the mission there would never be any more fretting about when he might meet his end.

The flight to the planet and subsequent deployment reeked of quietness. There was nothing to discuss. It was showtime. At the proper coordinates the pilot and passenger were directed to climb down into the submarine and prepare for launch.

Once the computers indicated all interlocks were closed and ready to launch, the sequence began. Just like they had practiced many times before, the submarine was lowered into the cradle and the electromagnetic grabbers deployed securing the submarine. Those grabbers could experience significant stress and still hold the submarine. That part of the design was robust.

As the launch sequence reached the standby [STBY] condition with the indicator lit. The launch controller was given permission by the pilot to launch the flying wing.

The launch controller pressed the [STBY] button that lit up green, then he pressed the [LAUNCH] button that turned green indicating successful launch. Sensors on the Black Marketer ship as well as inside the submarine indicated a successful launch was in progress.

Cajarington and Adrak could feel the effects of the retrorockets that reorientated the flying wing heading it into a flight profile they experienced many times before training going to the planet.

The flying wing and the submarine were coated with radar absorbent materials and unless an operator was on his toes, would not detect the arrival.

The flying wing slowly moved down towards the ocean's surface. From space the continent was easily observable. But as the got closer to water, the landfall slowly slid off the display leaving only the ocean image.

Cajarington had not touched any controls or did anything. He preferred the automation do it all so there would be less chance of a screwup.

Just like they trained the flying wing was able to softly land on the water surface with the electric motors operating the very powerful VTOL lifters.

The landing was in the middle of the night with poor visibility. There was little chance the enemy spotted the penetration.

In due course the submarine deployed off the flying wing that slowly sank to the bottom of the ocean in that area where it would self-destruct at the delay specified as to not expose the spies by creating an explosion before the bombs were planted.

There was no chit chat on the way to the passenger deployment area. The two men were professionals and knew the gravity of the situation, they were expendable and on a very dangerous mission.

They did have communications via wireless until Adrak swam away. Just before Adrak opened the hatch to swim away, he heard in his earbud via wireless Cajarington's remark:

"Good luck Adrak, I hope you make it back. I'll be waiting for you."

Adrak was almost dumbfounded. Within just the past 48 hours they wanted to kick each other's asses. *What brought this on? Adrak asked himself.*

Adrak had no idea the level to which Cajarington was happy that Adrak was swimming to shore and not him. Cajarington secretly knew he probably wasn't emotionally and psychologically prepared to do what Adrak now set out to do.

Adrak swam to a peaceful uninhabited beach. This beach close to the Tramulite base did not allow civilians to live in the vicinity and it was closed off and patrolled intermittently as the Tramulite's had plenty of firepower at the base and didn't believe any spy would have the balls to swim up on this beach and deploy from here. The Tramulite's were seriously caught up in their complacency. Today was Adrak's lucky day, the security check of this beach area and beyond was blown off by the Tramulite security force as another wasted adventure. They had more important things to do such as training, keeping the base spick and span, waiting for an inspection, and the other myriads of events that happen on a large base where the left hand seldomly knows what the right hand is doing.

In a dense brush area, Adrak took off his wet suit and put on Tramulite military clothes. This was a very dangerous event because if he was caught with Tramulite military uniform on, he would be immediately treated as a spy with a bullet to the back of the head after they tortured him to get as much information out of him as they could.

Unfortunately for the Tramulite's Adrak had a special pill surgically attached in his mouth and if he was captured, he could bite it and swallow it and be dead in ten minutes, so there wasn't much they were going to get out of him.

With the uniform on and nothing indicating he was a saboteur as his backpack contained innocuous consumer items necessary for a soldier to survive on a base like toothpaste, deodorant, mouthwash, a couple novels, pens, pencils, stationary, etc.

Some of the buildings were fenced in because they had operational centers and command centers. But there were also important buildings that were innocuous that outsiders and most of the base personnel did not know the purpose of and seldom were they visited. These buildings contained communication hubs, electrical switches for the underground power grids and a few other important infrastructures.

Adrak had his choice of 3 buildings to destroy. He would go after the lowest hanging fruit. Incredible as it was, the building with no windows was not fenced in or manned. It was the communications hub for the base.

Walking around the base with a lot of people coming and going in multiple directions going about their business, Adrak simply appeared like most of them. At this point none of them would believe Adrak was a spy. Adrak had credits, fake I.D. etc. He could go into base comfort areas that had drinks, entertainment, and reading rooms. Nobody would consider it odd for Adrak to hang out there for several hours and taking a nap at one of the foot message booths.

Adrak could also get a body message and for an additional amount the special message which corrupt officials overlooked because they got a cut of the action.

The building Adrak chose was in a darker area of the base with very little pedestrian traffic and only intermittent vehicular traffic. All he had to do is activate the backpack throw it up on the roof with the delay set and tamperproof sensors. If someone attempted to pick up the backpack it would immediately blow killing the person and demolishing the building.

Just after dark Adrak approached the building, did his reconnaissance and looked around and after one of the intermittent vehicles passed by and turned down the way going in its own direction to its destination, after one last look around, Adrak threw the backpack up on the building all set to explode. He then retraced his steps back to the lonely beach and got down into the brush and cover and waited for a while checking to make sure no beach patrols were coming.

Tonight was Adrak's unlucky night it seemed. A beach patrol vehicle did come by. Adrak knew to let time run its course but had to be cognizant of the timer on the bomb or an early detonation caused by the tamperproof circuitry. The car was loitering on the beach because a male and female were copulating in the vehicle knowing nobody would suspect what they were doing.

With his earbuds and his acoustic pickup, Adrak quickly determined what the couple were doing. Adrak then silently and carefully got back into his wet suit waiting for the love birds to finish up their action. He also knew he was up against the clock because he was running out of time before the package detonated and when the base discovered their communications hub had just been wiped out, there would be a massive search for saboteurs.

Adrak was ready to go. He had to move soon. Listening very carefully, he keyed in on the love making and when it sounded like the dude was about a minute or two away from launching his rockets, Adrak double clicked out onto the beach and into the water carefully listening on the way to determine if there was any possibility of detects.

Just as Adrak hit the surf and was quickly heading out into deeper water a set of lights came up from behind the car. It was likely a supervisor wondering what the delay was in the security patrol getting back filing their reports suspecting he knew what they were up to and wanted to catch them in the act.

For a brief moment the supervisor thought he saw something move into the water but he was so intense on catching the lovebirds, he didn't pursue his image as he thought he must have been seeing something that disappeared as Adrak fully submerged swimming out from shore.

Adrak was so scared he didn't activate his clicker code for quite a few minutes and as he was swimming, he saw lighted water overhead which told him someone had a searchlight looking out in this direction. Adrak was smart, he knew better than go to the surface to look because they would then spot him for sure and the chase would be on.

The searchlights were not for Adrak. It was the supervisor giving the two love birds a wakeup call laughing his ass off while he did so. Eventually the lighted surface ended which meant to Adrak the Tramulite's had given up looking for him thinking it might be a false call.

A few moments later, Adrak initiated his clicker codes which Cajarington immediately detected and had already slowly started moving towards the shoreline expecting the clicker codes about now.

The clicker receivers started processing and automatically turned the submarine to perform target motion analysis to find the range to the clicker code source.

The submarine slowly headed towards the beach in a zigzag course that slowly built- up coefficients to fair in the range to the clicker code. The closer they arrived, the better range coefficients were produced and the estimated range to the clicker code was now within a ball bark figure of plus or minus 50 yards.

The submarine could not point the swimmer for fear of running over him and possibly killing him with the propeller. Once the submarine was 100 calculated yards from the swimmer, the liquid lens system started providing higher resolution and an acoustic image of the diver that was easily observable on the display. Once the submarine was within thirty feet of the swimmer random fast flashes from an LED driven visual beacon gave Adrak precise direction of the submarine he swam to.

Once the liquid lens showed the swimmer was coming towards, the submarine all propulsion stopped, and the passenger compartment started flooding down which sank the submarine slowly to the bottom. Because of his arousal and fear of detection, Adrak swam hard to the submarine and reached it about the time the passenger compartment was equalized to sea pressure so the hatch could be opened.

Adrak soon settled down inside the passenger compartment and shut the hatch manually and locked it. Once Cajarington saw the hatched closed, he turned on the low light so he could see into the passenger compartment and knew Adrak was there, and he started pumping the water out and bleeding in air to equalize it to approximately 15 psi.

When most of the water was pumped out of the passenger compartment of the submarine, it lightened up and the buoyancy control system moved it off the seabed, then Cajarington initiated the maneuver to head them back to the wing.

The two would soon be in another dangerous position as they would have to surface the submarine to be extracted via a portal.

Utilizing the inertial navigation in the slow quiet transit back to the wing they were soon in position to complete this phase of the mission. The submarine went up to periscope depth and from a distance almost over the horizon they could see a lit-up beach area where the two cars were shining their search lights as if they might have seen something. They would probably see the portal open when Cajarington and Adrak departed, but there would not be anything they could do about it since they were well beyond their weapons range.

Cajarington surfaced the submarine and set the dead man timer that would sink the submarine down near the wing where they would both self-destruct after the two spies were long gone.

Just like they planned the portal opened and the two men were gone. They were observed from the beach and shortly after the spies were on the Black Marketer heading high speed away from the planet, the satchel charge on top of the communications hub blew that disrupted the base communications and also sent chills up the security supervisor because he knew he had observed the saboteur and had he not been so hell bent on screwing around with the two love birds, he might have been able to call out a warning to put the base on alert.

Unfortunately, due to the way the explosives were organized with a tamper proof system, he wasn't going to stop the loss of the communications hub. Just like they planned the submarine exploded at the same time as the wing creating an explosion and shock waves the Tramular's would be investigating for months not aware there were submarine and glider fragments strewn all over the ocean bottom in that area.

The black marketer spacecraft left the area, and eventually they made it back to friendly forces, then Adrak received the remainder of his previous critiques and was sent to a camp where he would go through more training and re-education to better mold standards of conduct in him so that he would be less likely to be involved with women during his next assignment.

Chapter Nine

Intergalactic Dreadnaught Carrier

Adrak always lucked out because some serious issue came up that often interrupted critiques and retraining and indoctrination.

Vekkar Intelligence was like a 100-armed octopus that was always looking for trouble. Just when Adrak was slowly starting to feel disenfranchised at his apparent punishment because he had the audacity to think outside the box, serious requirements unfolded.

Mobilizing forces can take on numerous dimensions especially when your government gets caught with its pants down.

The Tramular's were master ship builders. They built some of the best spacecraft in the galaxy and that's one of the reasons the Vekkar's were now in a stalemate with them.

The people living under the control of both governments didn't want another 100- year war. They wanted the dispute over neutral planets finished and the fighting stopped.

The neutral planets didn't desire to become part of either empire, but the military planners all thought on both sides, whoever possessed the string of neutral star systems and planets that separated them, they would be better able to fence off their territory and prevent future military adventurism.

Just about the time Vekkar leadership was feeling comfortable after destroying the research center, a new surprise suddenly unfolded.

Vekkar's Intelligence had a few opportunistic spies behind enemy lines. They were deemed unreliable because they were never available when they were needed the most. But now and then one of them surfaced and sent in a secret report because they were running low on Credits₿ and were accustomed to living well without having to work too hard. They lived below the radar, didn't do extravagant spending to create attention.

Such reports were unexpected, and they could arrive at any time covering everything in the kitchen sink. A special team existed to be on the lookout for the wayward spies to receive their reports, analyze them and evaluate the information.

It was via one of those unexpected reports *that upset the apple cart so to speak.*

The critiques were painful especially when you have a couple backstabbing office warriors who want to denigrate you for their own personal gain.

Adrak wasn't too terribly concerned because the facts showed he rescued a spy twice and helped take out one of the top enemy research centers getting severely wounded in the process. He chose not to respond to the diatribe uttered by office warriors who never put their skin in the game.

Plus, Adrak smugly knew one other thing. Sidis the Tramulite SMERSH agent would have killed those men who were bad mouthing him. Adrak got his ass beat up but in the end of the fight Sidis was dead and soon incinerated with the Tramulite's thought they were killing agent 000050428A62315 (a.k.a. Adrak).

The following day there were going to be charges leveled against Adrak for his reckless behavior that manifested some of these emergency extractions.

Vekkar Interdimensional Transport Directorate, *Doctor Oxyuran Lepidotus Taipan* warned Adrak these were well founded and powerful charges against him that could result in his dismissal. Adrak's response was, "I'll find something else to do with my life."

The next morning was going to be a big showdown.

The charges were going to be adjudicated and Adrak would learn his fate and his possible dismissal.

Unemployment didn't sound too bad. Adrak had saved up a lot of credits thanks to being fed on missions by the government. In the past two years, thanks to his operational tempo, Adrak banked most of his earnings. He now had enough money to exist for another 20 to 30 years without the need to find a job. What would he do with his time?

Just when Adrak's adversaries were jubilant they had taken out the person who aggravated them the most and they bitterly disdained, the critique and adjudication was put on hold indefinitely.

Nobody could predict this coming up but *Doctor Oxyuran Lepidotus Taipan* superiors who were notified by the most secret section of Vekkar intelligence that Inter Dimensional Portals Directorate, would be called upon to do an urgent mission and they wanted the best spy he had available to do it. They wanted the name of his best agent, and he reported: 000050428A62315 (a.k.a. Adrak) is my best spy but he's probably not going to be available."

"This is one of our most important missions, you need to shift him off his assignments to support this operation." *Doctor Oxyuran Lepidotus Taipan* superior said.

"He's in a critique right now and has some serious allegations against him from his peers that hate his guts and are trying to undermine him."

"End the critique and tell his peers to shut their mouths, because we do not have time for that crap now. " *Doctor Oxyuran Lepidotus Taipan* superior ordered.

"I would be most happy to do so, but you need to notify my boss about this urgent requirement." *Doctor Oxyuran Lepidotus Taipan* said.

"Not a problem, he's standing right next to me listening in on this conversation."

"*Doctor Oxyuran Lepidotus Taipan,* assign 000050428A62315 (a.k.a. Adrak) to this mission, code name KOBRA SPEKTR.

"Alright consider him assigned," *Doctor Oxyuran Lepidotus Taipan* replied happy that such an event circumvented an adverse action proceeding he knew was outright BS. What the malcontents didn't know is that by pulling this stunt to get Adrak who they despised, they also burned their bridges with *Doctor Oxyuran Lepidotus Taipan* who knew they were chickenshits and never put any skin into the game.

"Good. Because this is a rush job, we are sending over escorts that should be there in about a half an hour to take 000050428A62315 (a.k.a. Adrak) to a KOBRA SPEKTR facility to begin his briefings and preparations for the assignment."

"I'll let him know, I was scheduled to meet with him in about five minutes to give him an update on the findings in his personal case, and then brief his accusers."

"Tell his accusers any story you want, then put the case in the circular file."

"Understand sir, consider it in the circular file. He'll be waiting in my office when the escorts arrive." *Doctor Oxyuran Lepidotus Taipan* said.

"Thank you for your assistance in this matter. It is quite serious."

"Glad my man can be of assistance to you." *Doctor Oxyuran Lepidotus Taipan* said.

The conversation ended and *Doctor Oxyuran Lepidotus Taipan's* secretary announced via interoffice intercom, "*Doctor Oxyuran Lepidotus Taipan,* agent 000050428A62315 (a.k.a. Adrak) is here as requested."

"Good show him in and be advised I will have some visitors in about half an hour who are escorts."

"Understand sir."

Momentarily, Adrak walked into *Doctor Oxyuran Lepidotus Taipan's* office, expecting to be fired in a few minutes. He didn't care if that happened. The bullet wounds from his last mission were painful, so if he was leaving now, so be it.

After Adrak was in the Doctor's office his secretary shut the door so they would have privacy in this secure room bug-checked several times a day.

"Please have a seat, Adrak." *Doctor Oxyuran Lepidotus Taipan* said.

"Thank you." Adrak replied

After Adrak was sitting down and comfortably, the director began the conversation.

"You were lucky this time," *Doctor Oxyuran Lepidotus Taipan's* said.

"In what way?" Adrak asked.

"The three amigos came close to nailing you with their administrative complaints, but all that has now been overcome by events." *Doctor Oxyuran Lepidotus Taipan's* said.

"Really?" Adrak asked.

"As per direction from my boss the case is closed and sent to the circular file." *Doctor Oxyuran Lepidotus Taipan's* said.

"What brought this on?" Adrak asked.

"Something has happened which I've not been informed about, but Vekkar Intel needs a superior person of your caliber for a special mission."

"When is this going to happen?" Adrak asked.

"I hope you do not have any major plans." *Doctor Oxyuran Lepidotus Taipan's* said.

"Actually, I do not. I was waiting for the outcome of the critique before I made any plans."

"That's good because within 30 minutes, escorts are going to be here to take you to your new assignment." *Doctor Oxyuran Lepidotus Taipan's* said.

"What's the assignment?" Adrak asked.

"I honestly do not have any details at all or know anything about what this is." *Doctor Oxyuran Lepidotus Taipan's* said.

"No idea what I will be doing?" Adrak asked.

"For your purposes, you have been assigned to a task force called KOBRA SPEKTR." *Doctor Oxyuran Lepidotus Taipan's* said.

"What's that all about?" Adrak asked.

"That is a compartmentalized activity, nobody in this office is cleared to know KOBRA SPEKTR exits nor are you authorized to divulge that code word to anyone." *Doctor Oxyuran Lepidotus Taipan's* said.

"You do not know anything about KOBRA SPEKTR?" Adrak asked.

"I have no clue what KOBRA SPEKTR is about, nor have I been briefed in any manner. All I can tell you is VIA asked for my best spy, and I gave them your name because I have more faith in you than all your peers. You have never let me down and I appreciate all that you have done for me." *Doctor Oxyuran Lepidotus Taipan's* said.

"May I ask you a question?" Adrak asked.

"Sure." *Doctor Oxyuran Lepidotus Taipan's* said.

"If that's the case, why was I subjected to this bullshit critique?" Adrak asked.

"That's all part of administrative controls. I have no say in the matter. Once it gets triggered by malcontents, we must let it run its course to make them feel that we took their complaints seriously and dealt with you appropriately." *Doctor Oxyuran Lepidotus Taipan's* said.

"What are you going to tell these Bozo's with my departure?" Adrak asked.

"They will simply be told you have been reassigned and will not be here. As such the critique is finished and go about their normal business." *Doctor Oxyuran Lepidotus Taipan's* said.

"Just like that?" Adrak asked.

"Yes, just like that." *Doctor Oxyuran Lepidotus Taipan's* said.

"I suppose under the circumstances, this is beneficial to me to not have to face them any time soon." Adrak said.

"In their twisted minds, they will have temporal euphoria thinking they got you. I'm not going to spoil their illusions and will simply inform them, now that you are no longer here, I do not have any reason to discuss you with them." *Doctor Oxyuran Lepidotus Taipan's* said.

"I see, it makes it easier for everyone." Adrak said. "Sure does." *Doctor Oxyuran Lepidotus Taipan's* said.

"After the mission will I come back here?" Adrak asked.

"Sure, with some nice awards your enemies will be jealous of." *Doctor Oxyuran Lepidotus Taipan's* said.

"Anything I can do to piss them off if fine by me." Adrak said.

"You have big things coming up and those peep squeaks really are not material in your life now. My recommendation is you forget everything that happened up to this moment and focus on your future. The fact they wanted my best man and put your complaints into the circular file show how important KOBRA SPEKTR is. That will consume all your mental powers and likely tax you just as hard as your mission resulting in serious injuries." *Doctor Oxyuran Lepidotus Taipan's* said.

As the small talk continued for a few minutes, the secretary soon notified *Doctor Oxyuran Lepidotus Taipan,* "Doctor, we have a couple of Agency escorts here that are to meet with agent 000050428A62315 (a.k.a. Adrak).

"Yes, I'm expecting them, please bring them into my office."

Moments later the secretary led in two men that looked too slick to figure out just what the hell they were. They were people couriers, delivering VIPs in a manner they are protected and no issues going through any security barrier they may cross or dealing with any agency that thinks they have jurisdiction.

The two escorts appeared to be mean SOB's, and they were. They would twist the head off a kitten if it was required to get their escorted person safely to the destination.

There are officials in high places who wished they were protected by guys like this, well-armed, well intentioned, and had their fair share of shootouts in the past.

They already knew how agent 000050428A62315 (a.k.a. Adrak) appeared because they were given recently updated photos via surveillance system. They also knew *Doctor Oxyuran Lepidotus Taipan's* appearance.

"Agent 000050428A62315 (a.k.a. Adrak) are you ready to depart with us?" One escort asked.

"Since you guys are getting me out of this critique, I'm very happy to depart with you." Adrak replied.

"*Doctor Oxyuran Lepidotus Taipan,* we obviously can't predict our timeline now because it's still being formed so we can't promise how soon Agent 000050428A62315 (a.k.a. Adrak) will return when the mission is completed."

"Understand," *Doctor Oxyuran Lepidotus Taipan,* said not happy he was losing his best operative for a while, but he was happy Adrak's departure meant the BS critique is over and now the three hombres would get to deal with him.

Doctor Oxyuran Lepidotus Taipan was hoping that real soon he would have a terrible shithole to send the three amigos to for rewarding their conduct towards Adrak that was not only disingenuous, but outright nonsense.

One of the escorts then informed Adrak, "Your official designation of 000050428A62315 remains for emergency use, but from now until the mission is over your alias will be Boone Whitaker. Here is a change of clothes and a new communicator you will now use. During your transit to your training and indoctrination center, you will be required to watch a video on your new communicator which is the real-life history of Boone Whitaker." The escort stated.

"Alright," Adrak responded.

"After you change your clothes now, put everything you have on you now including your personal communicator in the same packaging and director *Doctor*

Oxyuran Lepidotus Taipan is tasked with putting it in safe storage. At the completion of your mission, you will be bought back here to change back in those clothes and retrieve all your personal items."

"Understand." Adrak replied then started changing into new garments delivered.

Adrak changed into a change of clothing and put on new attire. He then folded up his clothes previously worn, along with his communicator and other possessions and put them in the packaging and handed it to *Doctor Oxyuran Lepidotus Taipan.*

Doctor Oxyuran Lepidotus Taipan gladly received Adrak's personal possessions and took custody, knowing Adrak was now going to have his life put in serious jeopardy on a high priority mission. Few men before him ever endured such an op tempo or the level of danger now presented Adrak who took it in stride.

Adrak was more than willing to suffer some serious fatigue and possible wounds to get away from the interoffice inquisition spawned by office warriors bucking for promotion who he felt deep down in his heart didn't do jack shit worth mentioning.

As Adrak left the offices, the secretary looked at him with a strange look. She knew where the two escorts came from, and this was about as serious as it gets. She didn't know what Adrak would be doing but she hoped he would come back alive.

Doctor Oxyuran Lepidotus Taipan's secretary was mildly shocked to learn he was going on a Vekkar Intel mission and barely recovered from his terrible wounds in the recent mission. From this day forward she would have special feelings for Adrak because she knew what he had been through and with minimal recovery time was going again with some very special characters.

The Vekkar Intelligence Agency (VIA) escorts whisked Adrak up to the rooftop Skycar parking where they all got into the escort's Skycar that briefly departed and was vectored up to the priority high speed sky lane reserved for emergency and VIP transports.

Up in the upper sky lanes the Skycars would travel up to below the speed of sound to prevent sonic booms that irritate the public. In a short period, the three landed inside the space port which only government Skycars would be permitted to do. The VIA Skycar landed a short distance from an intergalactic transport destined for planet *Heuronvale.*

The two escorts would not be traveling with Adrak. After they climbed the stairs of the crew access port of the intergalactic transport, the two escorts introduced Adrak to a male and female VIA agent dressed in intergalactic transport crew uniforms. The introduction was made.

"Boone Whitaker, this is Corgrelius and Joanie who work for us, are part of the flight crew to be part of your eyes and ears to make sure you arrive safely at *Heuronvale."* Escort number one said.

"What's going to happen when I get to *Heuronvale*?" Adrak asked.

"Corgrelius and Joanie personally know the escorts that will be taking you to your training camp on *Heuronvale* who will also be dressed up as flight crew members to take you from the Intergalactic Transport to the training center." Escort number one said.

"Sounds like I'm being babied around," Adrak said."

"Until you are situated in your upcoming mission VIA personnel will always be with you safeguarding you and making sure you arrive unmolested wherever you are sent." Escort number one said.

"Thanks, I feel safe now. How ever just because I got good guys around me doesn't mean I'm going to let my guard down," Arak responded.

"Nor would we expect you to,' Escort number one said.

"This way Boone, let me show you to your private bunk then escort you to your seat for takeoff," Joanie said.

Adrak bowed to Escort number one, and said, "Thanks for the ride." "No problem," Escort number one said.

"Please show me the way," Adrak said to Joanie.

"This way please," Joanie said, then opened the crew access door and took Adrak into the intergalactic transport and to his private bunk that had a hard security shield that once locked, no other passengers could interfere with him in any manner.

"Boone, the access code to allow opening your bunk access is the last four digits of your assignment code (000050428A62315). The craft has AI observing all passenger areas and if anyone other than you attempt entering those 4 digits an alarm will be given off and that person will be promptly apprehended and put in suspended animation for the duration of the flight and handed over to authorities when we arrive." Joanie said.

"Good, I feel safer already," Adrak responded in an almost satire manner.

"We never know what may happen on a long flight like this and sometimes the enemy manages to get operatives aboard our Intergalactic Transports." Joanie said.

"Yes, I understand that." Adrak responded.

"In the event I need to have a private meeting with you and approach you in the passenger lounge, if you see me do two winks with my left eye, that means come find me back around the toilets and showers. Do not say anything if anyone else is around."

"Understand," Adrak replied.

"Boone, I'm going to escort you to your seat for takeoff." Joanie said.

"I would rather be in my bunk during takeoff," Adrak said.

"The transport company does not allow people in bunks during takeoff to prevent stowaways," Joanie said.

"Alright." Boone (a.k.a.) Adrak responded.

"When you are approaching your seat, in the overhead you will see a small green light lit up that verifies the seat next to you is your assigned seat. You are in the back row by the isle, which is closest to the galley and passenger lounge," Joanie explained.

As the three approached Boone (a.k.a. Adrak's seat he saw the green light it up by AI facial recognition. Easy location to remember, the green light was redundant.

The intergalactic transport was a large craft that would take several days to get to *Heuronvale.*

To get such a huge spacecraft launched from the surface of the planet utilized a flying wing. The spacecraft was latched to the flying wing via electromechanical latches until launch at high altitude.

The eight turbofan engines on the flying wing were injected with LOX and kerosene enabling them to have sufficient thrust up to 100,000 feet where they would obtain supersonic velocity high enough up in the sky to not give sonic booms to annoy the public.

As soon as the Intergalactic Transport riding on the wing lifter was given clearance, it was towed away from the terminal with an electric tug. They would not waste precious fuel or create pollution by ground operations of the flying wing engines.

To assist in takeoff, the flying wing had an electric catapult that worked like maglev to accelerate the large mass up to above 400 miles per hour at takeoff. Once the flying wing reached near the end of the runway, the maglev was switched off and the flying wing was released allowing it to gain altitude promptly.

The lift was amazing, and the passengers were exposed to two G forces continuously until they reached the launch point.

When the flying wing reached 100,000 feet the space craft rocket engines running in idle during the takeoff process slowly increased throttle settings. At the same time the flying wing deactivated the holding mechanism in the cradle that held the spacecraft allowing it to separate.

The separation process worked off inertia. In essence the Spacecraft had substantial supersonic velocity with retro rockets for maneuvering away from the flying wing upon separation. The two craft separated seamlessly and went in opposite directions, The spacecraft went up vertical towards space and the flying wing back towards the space port for landing.

This process saved an incredible amount of fuel required for the spacecraft now accelerating with rocket engines powering up in autothrottles now taking it out into space.

With all the fuel savings of the flying wing deployment, enough fuel remained allowing the intergalactic transport to continue acceleration all the way up to light speed. What used to take centuries was now completed in just a few days.

The acceleration continued and when the spacecraft was one thousand miles above the planet heading out into deep space, the captain came on with the announcement over the intercom:

"Ladies and Gentlemen, thank you for choosing Quasar Space Travel today. We are now outside the planet's main gravity and therefore can energize artificial gravity which is based on the ship's keel and centerline."

Adrak thought the captain's voice sounded familiar. *Is it Captain Buck?*

"You will only have more than one half of normal gravity you are used to on the planet, but enough to allow you to move around and have liquids in containers."

Adrak was almost certain now that Captain's voice was someone he knew, Captain Buck from a couple previous missions.

"If for some reason, we lose artificial gravity there will be an alarm. I'm going to now initiate the alarm so that all of you know it. If you hear this alarm grab on to whatever you can, and the crew will assist you to your assigned seat."

"We do not expect that to happen, but in case it does, you now know we have a plan to deal with it. I will now activate the loss of artificial gravity for five seconds so that you will be aware of the sound."

Any former crew member that had served on nuclear missile submarines would think they were hearing a missile emergency alarm which is slightly unnerving.

After the alarm the Intergalactic Transport captain then announced via the intercom: "Ladies and gentlemen, you are now free to move about the space cabin. There will be a flight attendant in the passenger lounge for a while to answer any questions you might have. I hope you enjoy your flight."

Adrak sat there for a while watching all the passengers and took the time to look over everyone, he could see to spot possible spies or assassins. If one was aboard now this would not be the first or last time such an attempt was made during this conflict with the Tramular's.

Adrak went to his bunk and got in and shut the security panel, put in his ear buds and started listening to his Boone Whitaker indoctrination. He knew he needed to know as much as possible for his cover story in case he met someone on the Intergalactic Transport. After he felt he got the jest of his cover story he went back to his seat in the cabin and did personal surveillance of the passengers in case there was someone there who might be trouble for him.

Elixirs are free on Intergalactic Transports, but unbeknown to the public, many of them were spiked with sleep inducers. The more passengers sleeping during a transit reduced oxygen intake and strain on system resources.

Adrak waited about an hour and as the cabin slowly emptied out with people going to the passenger lounge eating snacks and drinking spiked elixirs or going to their bunks to sleep. Adrak followed suit. He arrived in the passenger lounge and obtained a snack and an elixir. The flight attendant stationed in the lounge to answer a myriad of questions from the passengers was none other than Joanie.

Adrak got to see Joanie in action. She played the role well and didn't seem phased interacting with all the passengers asking dumb questions for the most part.

In a few instances, Joanie had to escort the passengers to their bunks to assist them. Over half of the passengers had never traveled on an intergalactic transport before and were like fish out of water, desperately needing help. But since the intergalactic transport was so comfortable, everyone seemed to adapt quickly.

Thanks to approximately sixty percent artificial gravity, toilets worked normally and so did the showers. It did not matter if a person took a Hollywood shower, the reverse osmosis system quickly reclaimed the water, and other residuals like poop made their way to the nuclear rocket engines and was injected with high pressure into the slip stream of the Firey Nuclear rocket inferno supplying such majestic accelerations.

By the time the intergalactic transport landed, all the sanitaries would be flamed in the nuclear rocket engines mixed with LOX and hydrogen to create the tremendous thrust. The toroid shaped nuclear reactors superheated the hydrogen and the sanitaries injected under high pressure that were a small portion of the fuel into the plasma supplying substantial thrust.

While Boone (a.k.a. Adrak) was eating his snack and drinking an elixir he knew was probably saturated with sleeping compounds was suddenly facing a beautiful blonde who introduced herself named Karoline Morganthau.

Adrak did not know it at the time, but Karoline Morganthau was actually an enemy Tramular SMERSH agent, and Adrak was her target. Karoline had an alias as a medical doctor treating war wounded. Her clairvoyance was second to none.

Karoline Morganthau was the consummate SMERSH agent spy who would make the famous Russian spy Margarita Konenkova who seduced Einstein proud.

Karoline Morganthau was a PhD in spy tradecraft. She was one of the best Tramular's had.

Unfortunately, due to betrayal by some of Adrak's office warrior visceral enemies, the Tramular's now knew 000050428A62315 (a.k.a. Adrak) was not dead as they previously thought and did not die with Sidis when they destroyed the Skycar Adrak was escaping taking an unconscious Sidis with him.

Karoline Morganthau had previously been a well planted spy in intergalactic banking consortiums. With her special handlers she was able to work her way up to the top of the bankers on her backside as she was beautiful and a seductress. After 24 beautification facial surgeries and 3D biological printing, made Karoline Morganthau extremely beautiful.

Karoline Morganthau could easily have killed Adrak on this flight, but that was not her purpose. Her purpose was to find out why he was being sent to *Heuronvale*. Karoline was informed Adrak would be accompanied by VIA agents and to assume there were several onboard and not to do anything that would raise their suspicions.

Karoline used the new disguise as a Medical Doctor which is much easier to implement. Though she experienced penetrating bankers "little heads" was no challenge.

Leaving behind Karli and Martilene left a huge hole in the fabric of Adrak's life. Few men ever experienced just one woman like the two of them in their lifetimes. But when a man can feel the excitement of ethereal transcendence with a fabulous singer like Karli, their psyche is woven forever. Nothing can ever match the evocative nature of making love to a fabulous singer after watching her performance, especially such a beautiful and effervescent woman like Karli Pauli.

As a spy Adrak knew he could never see Karli or Martilene again for the rest of his life because he knew deep in his heart this conflict with the Tramulite's would not end for many years if not decades. It was bitter-sweet in the memories of these two women that transfixed him and lingered. Adrak knew as a spy, he had to properly compartmentalize his emotions. *Is it even possible with women like this?*

And here Adrak was suddenly sitting across the table from an illustrious woman Karoline Morganthau who was something totally new in a different line of work, in the medical profession.

"So, Doctor Morgenthau, what is your specialty?" Boone (a.k.a. Adrak) asked.

"Please call me Karoline by my first name since I'm not at work now."

"Alright Karoline," Adrak said.

"Thank you, Boone. I'm an orthopedic surgeon."

"All right." Boone (a.k.a. Adrak) replied.

Karoline would now tease Adrak slightly knowing whatever he said was contrived.

"Tell me Boone, what do you do for a living?" Karoline asked.

"I'm a consultant in Artificial Intelligence and Machine Learning," Adrak said which was his cover story for Boone Whitaker who did that in real life until he had an identity change when he started working for the VIA.

Karoline knew this information was all part of the ruse because she had the real story but had to play along to get more involved with Adrak to discover the essence of his mission.

Karoline's discovery of Boone's real name Adrak was the biggest betrayal of Inter Dimensional Portal Directorate history. Adrak was such a highly sought target that Karoline would have gladly killed him, but what Adrak was sent to do was a much greater secret her superiors would prefer he stay alive to lead her to the discovery of what SMERSH wanted to discover possibly heading off another disaster like the Intergalactic communications center Karoline now knew Adrak blew up.

Karolin Morgenthau would discover: *what is Adrak's current mission and where he is being sent and why*? This mission Karoline was doing was created because the Mole that betrayed Adrak had no details of why he was being sent somewhere for training. Adrak's mission was compartmentalized, and he left no breadcrumbs when he suddenly deployed.

Thanks to the betrayal from Adrak's own office, SMERSH now knew Adrak had something to do with their Tramulite Inter Dimensional Spy Portal Research Center destruction and Adrak was terribly wounded during the exit.

SMERSH also knew Sidis beat the crap out of Adrak before Adrak got one final lucky shot to survive and overcome and kill Sidis. Karoline Morgenthau knew the jest of most of this so when she was sitting across from Boone Whitaker looking into his eyes doing her utmost honey pot scheme, she understood she was facing a deadly spy.

Karoline Morgenthau also knew that if Adrak knew she was a spy he would have no remorse in killing her especially if it made certain of his own survival.

Adrak was of course watched during this flight and anyone coming onto him was equally watched. Karoline Morgenthau immediately hit VIA trip wires. Joanie, was nearby in the passenger lounge observed Karoline in pursuit while Adrak was simply casually responding to her, not really giving an impression Karoline was motivating his little head.

Karoline's approach would have worked on anyone else, but Adrak was now suffering from an emotional decline he brought onto himself by his interactions with Karli Pauli and Martilene Chares.

Since Adrak wasn't responding in the fashion Karoline Morgenthau worked, she doubled down her efforts which went a long way towards crossing over VIA tripwires.

Nothing would be suspicious of Joanie leaving the crew's lounge for a while to walk through the cabin. Joanie went back to the passenger cabin where she found Corgrelius and asked him to follow her into the passenger berthing area up to by the public toilets and showers where they could talk privately.

"There is a woman in the lounge toying with Boone who is attempting to seduce him," Joanie said.

"Which passenger is it? Corgrelius asked.

"Let me pull her image up on my communicator," Joanie said.

Joanie then gave the Spĕctrāl de Dòngtài-Joanie AI APP on her cell phone the command: "Pull up the image and identity of the woman sitting across from Boone Whitaker in the passenger lounge."

The APP which had access to the Intergalactic Transport surveillance system pulled up the image of Karoline Morganthau and showed her and her registered passenger name. Joanie then showed Corgrelius who said, "Send me a link to that report. I'm going to go up to the communicator's cabin where I can do some long-distance neutrino duplex transmission and find out what I can about the lovely Karoline Morganthau." Corgrelius said.

Spĕctrāl de Dòngtài-Joanie monitoring the conversation complied as the two spies knew it would and quickly informed Corgrelius: "The report is available to you in the Communicator's Cabin."

"Alright, I'm going back to the lounge, let's meet back here in an hour if you discover something." Joanie said.

Corgrelius walked to the lounge and through it and saw Boone (a.k.a. Adrak) talking to a nicely dressed woman who appeared the same as what he had just viewed on Joanie's communicator. It was clear the woman was stringing Boone along.

Corgrelius went forward through the door to crews berthing, which had AI door locks and passengers were not permitted in this area. Once Corgrelius was in the crew's berthing, he walked through it, through another door also AI controlled that would only allow flight crew members associated with Controls and Communications to pass. That meant Pilots, Copilot, Navigator, and Communicator were the only people allowed past this AI checkpoint, except for three VIA reps onboard as part of the escort mission or someone the VIA reps escorted.

The reason for several sets of pilots was the cockpit was occupied with flight crew around the clock. They were not allowed to fly through space in pilotless autopilot. They also had extra flight attendant's, male and female that worked in shifts after launch.

The VIA members also had unrestricted access to the communicator's cabin which had all the special equipment for long distance duplex neutrino communication, and for this trip, there was carry on equipment VIA personnel promptly installed to allow them to have real time VIA neutrino encrypted communications. Corgrelius immediately put together a SITREP that went only to a strictly controlled VIA communication hub and transferred encapsulated in an encrypted VIA slot to the designated party who had the decryption algorithms capable of reading it.

As expected withing five minutes Corgrelius got the report back from his VIA supervisor, *"The woman you inquired about real name is Agnes Renceladus, a top SMERSH agent."*

There were a few duplex communications that now occurred. Questions and answered provided Corgrelius a couple of insights:

"First of all, it's been decided here that if Karoline Morganthau, a.k.a. Agnes Renceladus made a beeline to 000050428A62315 (a.k.a. Adrak) that means he is the reason why she's aboard the Intergalactic Transport. It also means his mission has been compromised.

"Secondly, only three other VIA reps knew about the mission and that Adrak had any involvement. These three VIA reps are fully vetted and will undergo enhanced interrogation via a neurotic probe to verify the leak did not come from them.

"That probably narrows the leak down to someone who works for Interdimensional Transport Directorate, Doctor Oxyuran Lepidotus Taipan."

"Moments ago, Doctor Oxyuran Lepidotus Taipan was notified he's coming to headquarters for a special briefing. We now believe the source of the leak and betrayal is one of Doctor Oxyuran Lepidotus Taipan's agents. Counterintelligence is now working on that end of the issue.

"Your new mission is to keep Karoline Morganthau, a.k.a. Agnes Renceladus away from 000050428A62315 (a.k.a. Adrak).

"Secondly, we do not believe Karoline Morganthau, a.k.a. Agnes Renceladus traveled by herself. Assume there is another enemy Tramular SMERSH agent aboard the Intergalactic Transporter. During the flight we may have the opportunity to identify the second enemy spy now aboard the Intergalactic Transporter. Send us incremental surveillance video once every six hours and our AI and Electro-Correlator/Clarifier Applications will be used to discover semaphores or other methods of signaling to the second covert Tramular party who we think is aboard the Intergalactic Transport.

"The head pilot for this Intergalactic Transport flight today is Captain Buck. Adrak personally knows Captain Buck from past missions. As part of the ruse to get Adrak to the communicator's cabin, have him request permission to visit Captain Buck. Bring him to the communicator's cabin and have him read the attached briefing file and there is an acknowledgement macro attached he is to activate when he understands everything in the briefing.

"Adrak needs to be fully aware he is now in jeopardy and to spend most of his time away from other passengers. Captain Buck will initiate a tracker on Adrak's bunk including monitoring anyone getting near it that will trigger alerts in your earpieces to intervene as necessary. Deadly Force is authorized.

"If you must take down Karoline Morganthau or her accomplice attempt to do it out of the view of other passengers. Place the body in an empty bunk that is not in

use due to the Intergalactic Transport departed without a full manifest. Your flight manifest will show available bunks to hide the body."

Corgrelius thought VIA was overkill escorting an accomplished spy to the mission training facility. Now suddenly with the latest unfolding events Corgrelius suddenly had a different outlook as it seemed as if someone in high places predicted something like this would happen.

One thing is quite evident. The Counterintelligence Division (CIVIA) never discusses their cases and methods with anyone. They learned their lesson the hard way.

All the politically correct guidance from above that implied everyone was in such a cooperative modus operendus was a total myth. CIVIA were ruthless bastards, and they were always blamed for enemy penetration. Hence, they took their kid gloves off a long time ago and were deemed untouchable. One thing Corgrelius knew quite well, never piss off a CIVIA agent because your life will suck immediately. *Was this all fostered by CIVIA?*

Corgrelius logged off the terminal and departed the communicator's cabin and walked aft towards the passenger lounge through crew's berthing. He then walked up past Joanie and gave her a designated signal, pulling his communicator out of his pocket in front of her, which is not unexpected by flight crews who use them to track various in-flight requirements. He put his communicator back in his pocket and continued walking aft without looking at anyone or giving anyone any possible notion he was signaling.

Corgrelius then walked all the way aft to the public toilets and showers and patiently waited for Joanie to join him for a discussion.

Corgrelius looked at his special APP on his communicator which was a ship wide surveillance video. On the APP display, passenger Karoline Morganthau had a tracker marker on a locator graph and when Corgrelius drilled down to lower echelon graphics Karoline Morganthau had a digital tracker on her. Karoline Morganthau was now a person of interest and if she made any movements outside the norm of a passenger, security would be all over her.

Besides the VIA agents on board for this flight, also the Intergalactic Transport Company had six of their own agents who doubled as pilots and flight attendants as their secondary role. Their primary role was security, and they had their protocols. All six of the transport company security members had a similar ship wide surveillance video APP that showed people of interest with trackers on them. Thus quite a few onboard agents will know Karoline is an enemy SMERSH agent, and as soon as Boone was informed there would be the 10th.

Joanie had to delay five minutes to give the appearance she was responding to a customer as in the lounge they could hear a customer request chime. Joanie stood up when the chime happened that was triggered by Corgrelius and walked aft. Normally she would see an overhead blue light at the seat of the customer or at their bunk needing assistance.

Joanie already knew from Corgrelius semaphore, this was not a customer request and went to the toilet shower area in the far aft portion of the passenger cabin to meet him.

"We have a serious problem. The woman sitting with Boone is a SMERSH agent. I've been in contact with headquarters. The captain on the flight deck is Captain Buck. Boone personally knows captain Buck." Corgrelius said.

"That's good to know but what about it?" Joanie asked.

"The next time you are able to get near Boone without anyone around inform him to request permission to visit Captain buck up on the Flight Deck." Corgrelius said.

"Alright." Joanie replied.

"After you get Boone through crews berthing before you take him up to the Flight Deck, pull him into the Communicator's Cabin and let him know there is a communique waiting for him to read." Corgrelius said.

"Alright, what then?" Joanie asked.

"After Boone finishes reading the communique, ask him to activate the Macro that will be attached to the file to let headquarters know he understands the briefing sent to him." Corgrelius said.

"Then what?" Joanie asked.

"Take him up to the flight deck so he can socialize with Captain Buck for a while. They are old buddies."

"Does Captain Buck know what's going on?" Joanie asked.

"He's received a text message notifying his friend Boone with his picture is aboard and to read the message in the Communicator's Cabin when he gets off watch." Corgrelius said.

"Is Captain Buck aware of Boone's stature?" Joanie asked.

"Captain Buck has flown clandestine missions for VIA in the past. Some of those missions included a passenger Boone with a different name. When he saw the picture of Boone in the text message, he received a short while ago, he responded with a understand all semaphore." Corgrelius said.

"I'll meet up with Boone in a short time and deliver the message. Do me a favor and send a passenger request in five minutes to make it easy for me to do the transaction." Joanie said.

"Sure," Corgrelius responded.

Joanie walked forward back to the passenger lounge and sat back down at her station waiting for more customers to ask for help or ask a lot of dumb questions they normally did.

In the lounge only Boone and the illustrious Karoline Morganthau were present. Boone, being a smart spy picked a table at the forward end of the passenger lounge, so nobody was sitting behind him. This made it more difficult for Karoline Morgenthau, who could not position her accomplice behind Boone to provide 360-degree surveillance.

This was one of the times Karoline and her partner screwed up because it gave Joanie the opportunity to do the two winks without being observed by anyone, a clean semaphore signal without detection.

Joanie knew Boone was watching her and the entire room. He was not a rookie. She gave the two winks just moments before Corgrelius gave the passenger request signal and chime. Joanie stood up and almost bumped into Karoline's accomplice who was coming into the lounge doing a surveillance check.

"Pardon me," Joanie said to the man then turned and walked aft.

The man got a snack and a drink and sat down at a table diagonally away from where Boone and Karoline were sitting facing forward. He could see whatever transpired between Karoline and Boone.

Boone gave it about five minutes to provide enough separation in time to not make it look suspicious as the conversation flowed. He then said, Karoline, please excuse me for a minute. Nature calls. I'll be right back.

In case he was being followed, Boone walked back to the toilets and went inside. He faked urinating then did the flush which outsiders could hear just like on an airliner.

Meanwhile, Joanie had cleared his baffles and made sure nobody was following and looked at her surveillance APP on her communicator and observed Karoline sitting in the Crews Lounge with another person there. At this point the other person was innocuous and unrelated to the case but in the semi privacy of the passenger lounge, he screwed up and communicated with Karoline in a cryptic manner.

Artificial Intelligence did not miss it and recorded all the conversation and immediately analyzed it. Based on the AI analysis, the man was suddenly identified with a tracker signal as a possible threat and portions of the conversation that was heavily analyzed easily determined the Tramular SMERSH agents had no idea the enhanced level of security on this flight.

When VIA plumbers come into an Intergalactic Transport dressed up as ground personnel preparing it for departure, they have numerous ways to install their bugs and remote video. Everywhere Boone was expected to be saturated with sensors and remote video.

The Tramulite SMERSH agent was obviously overconfident, and his OP SEC was deplorable. Karoline Morganthau did not react negatively, but you could tell by the surveillance video she was uncomfortable with the man speaking in the manner he did. Karoline appeared agitated based on thermal and pulse measurements. Anyone observing the surveillance video would know Karoline Morganthau wanted to tell her accomplice to *stop the conversation* but doing that would also expose her in a very serious manner.

The man didn't say anything else. He didn't have to since he already gave it away. His identity was now pegged and soon VIA would sift through archives to attempt to find a match. After several hours they finally matched the man. His name was Boris Clevenger.

Boris Clevenger had been very successful against VIA agents in the past and killed his fair share. Perhaps that's why he felt so invincible and cocky and this meeting in the passenger lounge that exposed all that also tagged him in ways he would regret.

Since Boris Clevenger didn't have diplomatic immunity, he would enjoy receiving some of the same treatment he gave to VIA spies in the past. His only hope would be a spy trade in the future.

The next question was: Is there just two spies aboard or is there another such as a watcher or a watcher's watcher?

Since AI had trackers on the two Tramulite spies, anyone they purposely came in contact with or had conversations with Boris or Karoline would be fully investigated. If there were a third spy onboard, they would soon know unless the person was the classical watcher who never came in direct contact with the person they are watching.

After receiving his special instructions in the toilet via text message, Boone went back to the passenger lounge and poured himself another elixir drink and continued socializing with the illustrious and beautiful Karoline he now knew was a SMERSH agent.

Just before Boone arrived back at the passenger lounge, Karoline informed Boris Clevenger: "Don't you think you need to get some rest?" This was a code word for your big mouth may have just got us into trouble, leave me immediately. Karoline's facial expressions conveyed, "You are *one dumb son of a bitch.*"

Borris Clevenger didn't know why Karoline was reacting the way she was and could only think, *she must be experiencing the bitch of the month club syndrome now, which was attributed to her monthly period.*

A couple of the elixirs Borris drank quickly hit the spot and he was sleepy and glad to accommodate Karoline whom he thought was overreacting.

Karoline wasn't overreacting. In fact, she was far more attuned to the spy business than Borris Clevenger who was living on borrowed time.

Karoline was well schooled in betrayal and double spies. Some of her missions she could never disclose to Borris were manifested by simple remarks like Borris made thinking they were in a safe zone to speak freely.

When Karoline returned to the facility, she worked out of in Praxiskrowtious, she would take this matter to her superior and ask that she never get assigned on a serious mission with the goofball Borris Clevenger who severely lacked respect for potential bugs and surveillance equipment.

Soon after Boone got a new drink and sat down across from Karoline the discussions continued and Karoline's honey pot scheme was fully activated pouring on the Charm and dishing out suggestive phrases that people who are not in the spy business would start to think was genuine flirting and signaling the desire for transcendence to new situation on a theme from Paganini when neophytes would throw caution to the wind and eagerly seek gratification.

Karoline knew she was dealing with a deadly spy, and he might not be gullible to engage in what she dished out.

During the Karoline and Adrak conversation, the flight attendant Joanie arrived and sat back down in her seat. She wanted to give Boone a segway into the conversation about Captain buck and since it was now only Boone and Karoline in the room she asked, "How is everyone doing today?"

"Doing just fine," Boone answered.

Karoline smiled at Joanie without saying anything.

"Earlier today when the captain made the announcement after takeoff, he sounded like one of my friends I know and flown with in the past," Boone said.

"Who is your captain friend," Joanie asked.

"Captain Buck." Boone responded.

"Isn't it amazing, Captain Buck just so happens to be the senior officer on the flight deck now," Joanie replied.

"Could you do me a favor and inform Captain Buck his old buddy from way back, Boone Whitaker is onboard?" Boone asked.

"I would be most delighted to do so," Joanie responded.

Joanie stood up and walked forward towards the bow of the spaceship through the crew's berthing, past the communicator's cabin and to the flight deck. Looking around to make sure nobody was with her, she made the statement, "Request permission to enter the flight deck."

Captain Buck looked at an adjacent flat screen left of his pilot's console and saw the flight attendant, one of the VIA spooks aboard, and heard her voice. Artificial

Intelligence read Joanie's statement and prompted Captain Buck with a prompt on the auxiliary flatscreen: "Do you want to allow the flight crew member to access the flight deck?" In his headphones he heard the notification chime, and on the touch sensitive flatscreen touched the prompt: [Allow].

Captain Buck was briefed in preflight about many things including the special passenger onboard named Boone Whitaker.

Joanie was what the flight crew would call, "eye candy." She was a good-looking woman and built like what captain Buck would say: *A brick shithouse*, a colloquialism from the past.

"Captain Buck, we have a passenger on board who says he knows you by the name of Boone Whitaker and wanted me to inform you he's onboard this flight with you," Joanie reported.

"Well-well-well, if it isn't Boone Whitaker of all people. Could you do me a favor Joanie?"

"Sure Captain Buck."

"Could you ask Boone Whitaker if he wouldn't mind coming up to the flight deck for a visit and tell my copilot some of his old stale jokes, he gave us on some previous flights?"

"I would be most happy to do so sir." Joanie said.

"Thank you." Captain Buck replied.

Joanie left the cockpit and walked through crews berthing and to the passenger lounge and stood by Boone Whitaker and said, "Boone, Captain Buck sends you his regards and asked me to request you go with me up to the flight deck where you can tell his co-pilot some of those stale jokes you had from previous trips."

"It would be my great pleasure," Boone replied.

Boone looked at the cunning spy that was throwing on the charm and said to her, "Excuse me Karoline, Captain Buck and I are old friends, and I want to go visit with him for a while. I'll catch up with you later."

"Sure, no problem," Karoline Morganthau said.

Boone then stood and followed Joanie through crews berthing and past the second door that went through a space that had the Communicator's cabin, plus navigation center, and the electronics suite rooms.

As soon as the door shut behind them going to crews berthing, Joanie said, Boone, you need to first go into the Communicator's cabin and read a file sent to you about your current mission and things they want you to know about."

"Certainly."

Joanie walked to the Communicator's Cabin door and AI verified her credentials and opened the door. She was authorized to escort people into the Communicator's Cabin for issues like this, so the door remained open until Boone (a.k.a. Adrak) entered.

Have a seat, Joanie gestured towards the communications console and then said, "Bring up the communication for Boone Whitaker to read."

AI confirmed Boone Whitaker was present and he had a communique sent to him to read. This would never happen with a regular passenger. AI had already discerned Boone Whitaker was the government agent 000050428A62315 and this high priority communication was sent for his requirements.

Boone read the message and easily understood Karoline Morganthau was a SMERSH agent by the real name of *Agnes Renceladus.* After reading the file, he pressed the icon for the macro that notified headquarters he understood the situation he was in with enemy spies on board. He waited for the confirmation before he logged out of the communications APP queued up for him and instantly got another notification.

There is a second spy onboard working with *Karoline Morganthau, a.k.a. Agnes Renceladus,* by the name of Boris Clevenger. His picture taken in the passenger lounge was then displayed.

"That's good to know," Boone replied, clicked on the macro icon that informed headquarters he had been briefed on the second spy.

"Looks like they knew I was coming." Boone said.

"Yes, it appears there has been a security breach. Counterintelligence is handling the matter."

"Where did the breach happen?" Boone asked.

"The preliminary findings indicate the security breach came from your office. Your boss *Doctor Oxyuran Lepidotus Taipan* is on his way to a special briefing and no doubt will be talking to counterintelligence CIVIP reps in a short while."

"Whoever it is I hope CIVIP finds them."

"I know some of the CIVIP people that will likely be called into investigate. Don't be surprised if they offer you the opportunity to administer the Coup de Grâce."

"I can think of a few fun things to do to a traitor, but I would be inclined to just shove him or her out of an airlock in space."

After the communications terminal was slicked and shut down, Joanie escorted Boone up to the flight deck where he entered. At the present time there were just two officers there, Captain Buck and his co-pilot.

"Captain Buck I'm going to leave Boone with you guys for now. Page me when he's ready to leave and I'll come back and get him."

"Not a problem," Captain Buck said.

As Joanie was leaving the flight deck, she heard Captain Buck ask, "Boone, do you have any new jokes or you going to tell us some of your old stale ones?"

Joanie kind of thought she might want to hear the answer, but then started thinking perhaps she shouldn't as it might indicate some disgusting things and promptly departed.

As soon as Joanie was gone, the banter started. It was just like old times. "Tell me Boone, have you met any pretty girls on the flight?"

"Actually, I did, and I think she would be an eager beaver, but I'm holding off on women for a while."

"Why is that?"

"You may not believe this, but I recently had a gorgeous woman on a train trip for five days, but I had to leave her behind."

"You were always sort of an unsavory character."

"It goes with the territory of a road warrior. Never know when we will meet our end so we might as well enjoy it while we can."

"So, this woman you had on the train is stopping you from progressing with the woman on our Intergalactic Transport?"

"Actually, there was a second woman that makes all the rest taste rather plane." "What was special about her?"

"Besides her looks she was an incredible singer."

"Wow."

"I would show you a picture of her, but my communicator had an issue before this trip, and I could not bring it along."

"Maybe next time."

"Definitely."

"How did you meet this singer?"

"I met the singer on the same train trip. The lady I was with, and I became friends with her."

"Did you get to first base with her?"

"Actually, I hit a bases loaded home run."

"Did you do that on the train?"

"Hell no. She invited us to the nightclub where she performed and while my girlfriend was using the toilet and took too long because she went up to our hotel room to do it because she didn't want to use the public toilet by the nightclub, I had plenty of time alone with the singer. She gave me her business card and asked me to come back another night without my girlfriend so we could have some fun."

"And you did?"

"Yea now my mind is ruined after being with a woman like that, I'll never feel frisky again."

"She did a number on you?"

"Yes, she's an incredible lover and I seriously doubt I will ever meet another woman like her again."

"Do me a favor Boone."

"What's that?"

"Give me all your rejects and I'll never have to go looking again for it."

Captain Buck, I think the discovery process and finding them, is part of the luster of the game. I would never diminish you by giving you my former girlfriends. I don't want you to miss out on the discovery and the chase.

"What about the woman you met on this flight?"

"She's more than I can handle. Plus, I've not gotten over the two women I recently left. If it was possible I would go back to one of them."

"Why isn't that possible?"

"Loose lips sink ships."

"Ah, operational convenience left behind."

"Captain Buck, you of all people know we can't bring back all the women we meet, plus I only experienced them for a short while. I'm not sure how that relationship would be if I were with them for several years."

"Want a hint?" Captain asked.

"Sure." Boone replied.

"After a while they seem stale like old bread and you are stuck with them."

"Yea I sort of figured that. I know the entertainer has her own world. The best we would have would be an artificial relationship."

"What about the other woman you mentioned?"

"I don't wish to get into the ugly details, but I burned my bridges there. No chance of ever going back."

"If you could, would you want to go back to her?"

"Yes and no." Boone answered.

"Why is that?" Captain Buck asked.

"To be honest there was an element of deception and I used her. I know it was selfish of me, but what's a road warrior to do? We get lonely too."

"That's true," Captain Buck said.

"The way I departed I seriously doubt she ever expects to see me again."

"One of those here today and gone tomorrow sort of things."

"Yes. If things were different, I could see unifying with her in a permanent relationship, but that's not ever going to happen."

"No chances of reconciling the relationship?"

"None whatsoever. That relationship is permanently dead."

"What if this woman on this ship gives you an offer you cannot refuse?"

"I'm sure she would like to, but I'm not ready to cultivate any new romances. The singer I recently left behind bewitched me and destroyed any desire to find another romance."

"She was that good?"

"Here are the basic facts. She's a fantastic singer, as good as any of them. She is very physically attractive. Since she's always performing, she doesn't have much time for a social life and the few breadcrumbs of life she gets, she cherishes.

"You gave her some of those crumbs of life?"

"Yes, I put on a pretty good show. When I took her through Tour de Cymbidium, I uttered total fabrications to make her feel the moment."

"Did she respond to what you did?"

"Yes, when I uttered the magical words softly in her ears when I could feel her orgasm starting, she started bucking me like a wild horse. When I finished, she was sobbing because she lost control. She knew I had pierced her heart with impecable timing. I'm sure she had never experienced something like this before and it left an indelible mark on her."

"So, no chance of ever hooking up with the singer?" Captain Buck asked.

"I recently came close to getting fired because of some malcontents in my office who are my visceral enemies. Had I got fired I would have thought seriously about going back to the singer," Adrak said.

"What would you do for a living to support yourself if you did that?"

"Captain Buck, you have seen me over many years, right?"

"Sure have."

"I was the only person in the office who routinely volunteered for high pressure tasks. I was always gone on travel, doing those tasks and living off what was provided to me. I never had to buy groceries, or buy fuel for my Skycar, or a lot of expenses. Hence, I banked all that extra money and invested it. I've multiplied my wealth and no longer worry about future income. I would just take it easy."

"A lot of people wish they were in your shoes." Captain Buck said.

"If they had the scars I have they may not desire what it took to get it." Adrak said.

"You have a lot of physical scars?" Captain Buck asked.

"Sure, a lot more you can imagine." Adrak said.

"Show me one of your scars," Captain Buck said.

"Alright but never reveal this to anyone."

"You know my lips are sealed."

Boone stood up, unbuttoned his shirt and pulled up the back side where the scars from the bullet wounds were quite severe.

"How the hell could those women stand to see you with those scars?"

"I got those scars after the love affairs."

Boone buttoned up his shirt and sat down.

"You know Boone, I always knew you were into some heavy shit, but those scars are far more than I can ever imagine. I bet that hurt like hell."

"I received a lot of pain killer medications. I didn't feel any pain until the rehabilitation started."

"Boone, I know you do a lot, and I do not allow too many visitors up here. You earned your visit a long time ago."

"Thanks, I appreciate that." Boone said.

Suddenly Boone Whitaker felt the non-ringing vibrator annunciator signaling him on his communicator. He pulled the communicator out of his left front pocket where he always carried it out of habit and keys and other devices in his right front pocket and billfold in his rear right pocket.

He pulled up his communicator and it was a text message from Joanie with an attachment:

"Your Tramulite Spy Friend is hanging out in the passenger lounge. We intercepted communications between her and the accomplice Boris Clevenger. It's going to be too difficult dealing with two spies, so we are setting up to drug Boris with a suspended animation drug and tuck him away in his bunk."

Boone Whitaker texted back, "Do you need assistance in handling Boris Clevenger?"

"No, we have a role for you to play. When we find the opportunity to take him down, we want you to be in the passenger lounge where we think *Karoline Morganthau, a.k.a. Agnes Renceladus,* will attempt to seduce you in a honey pot scheme."

"Sounds like I should let her seduce me so I can find out if she's any good." Boone Whitaker (a.k.a. Adrak) texted back.

"The attachment I sent you has a tracker APP on it. I want you to open up the APP and look at the tracker information updating in real time." Joanie texted.

"Looking at it now in a sub window." Boone said.

The tracker APP had a map of the Intergalactic Transport in three dimensions showed at a perception angle of 45 degrees above centerline and 45 degrees forward perpendicular. There were two trackers shown with boxes around a miniature display of the animated people they were tracking. AI utilized recent surveillance video to create the image of Karoline Morgenthau inside a blue tracker box. It also had a similarly created image of Boris Clevenger in a red tracker box showing his location and disposition. Boris Clevenger was working at getting into his bunk and resting while Karoline was doing her tricks up in the passenger lounge.

While Borris Clevenger was climbing into his bunk he was at the most vulnerable, that's when he got hit and would soon not be aware of reality as his body shut down slowly into suspended animation. When he woke up later would not remember much of what happened because the compounds in the drugs were extremely powerful and had a side effect of erasing a person's short-term memory. He was then positioned into his bunk by the two VIA agents lying on his side. His security enclosure was then shut, and he would be sleeping for most of the remainder of the trip. Eventually after the suspended animation drugs wore off, he would come awake and have to urinate and possibly have a bowel movement.

Karoline Morganthau in due time would become severely agitated because Boris Clevenger did not answer any of her texts asking him where the hell he was.

Karoline Morganthau would also be drugged with compounds that would make her sleepy. She would think she's going to take a nap and get up and bird dog Boone Whitaker (a.k.a. Adrak) but she would discover she didn't wake up until they were almost due to arrive, and Boone Whitaker was long gone, and she would not see him again the rest of the flight.

Boone Whitaker's final hours aboard the Intergalactic Transport would be first with Captain Buck saying goodbye and then in the communicator's cabin where he had an employee uniform to wear and a mask to change his identity.

Per instructions from Joanie, Boone Whitaker would remain in the communicator's cabin until landing, then Joanie would escort him out of the Intergalactic Transport through the crew's access and into an employee van that would drive them into cargo reception area where they would be inserted into a cargo shipping container and loaded on a freight delivery flatbed and driven out of the airport heading for a warehouse across the city.

Once inside the warehouse in a sealed off area, Joanie and Boone left it in a change of clothes and change of masks and hopped into a Skycar that was waiting for them next to the cargo container. Within twenty minutes, Boone was delivered to his training center.

Karoline and Boris had their own reception committee and were accusing each other of blowing the mission and losing track of Boone Whitaker. They were purposely left unmolested nor were they arrested and detained as to give the appearance Boone who is a quite capable spy flew the coop, and they didn't catch his slick exit.

They were free to roam around Heuronvale to make them and their handlers think they had penetrated the spacecraft and arrived at Heuronvale without being detected as enemy spies.

Chapter Ten

It's All About Training

It was now dark and other than city lights, Boone Whitaker (a.k.a. Adrak) had no idea where they were going. Flying in the upper echelon traffic reserved for military, law enforcement, and VIP's the Skycar was moving along more than 400 miles per hour and covered distance quickly. Looking out the windows the city lights thinned out and in another 10 minutes it was pitch black with no signs of life down below. Soon off in the distance there were just a few lights. The real surveillance was infrared lights to light up the area. The white lights were to keep outsiders guessing.

The Skycar landed and immediately drove into a camouflage parking structure and a door closed behind them. Suddenly another large door in front of them opened. Inside this area it was well lit up and exposed a large hidden facility.

This Heuronvale special forces training facility was well hidden including hidden physical fitness areas that included a quarter mile track to run around and in the middle of the track was a padded area

The radar reflecting camouflaged cover over the facility designed to withstand hurricane strength winds was nothing more than a high-tech tent. But from the air it looked like part of the forest. Several strategically located trees were allowed to remain and their lower branches were cut off and adjustable straps held planks in a vertical position the structure used as support beams with enough overhead clearance to allow trailers and other mobile structures inside.

Those vertical support beams were fastened to steel I-beams that ran in several concentric circles creating what appeared to be a small hill as the trees were trimmed accordingly. Underground piping allowed installation of potable water, sewage hookups, and buried electrical and communications cables.

The thick black canvas that created the foundation for the camouflaged cover prevented light from escaping and the double doors allowed entry without exposing the well-lit inside structure. Air conditioning was provided by refrigerant units that had heat exchangers that had a closed loop pure water loop to a nearby lake that had a cabin to conceal the exchange coils and were a guard house for the nearby facility to keep out uninvited guests.

Should a forest fire get going nearby there were sprinkler heads that came up that sprayed water at 100 PSI into the air surrounding the facility that had sufficient water from the nearby lake to put up quite a water barrier to protect it.

When Joanie and Boone Whitaker (a.k.a. Adrak) got out of the Skycar they were met by a couple VIA men wearing agency *field attire* and a couple military, a male and female in camouflaged uniforms.

"Boone, this is VIA agents Astor and Sorge," Joanie said.

"Please to meet you," Boone bowed since there were four.

"Two military experts that will be part of your training are Colonel Suzan Marklar, and Lt. Col. Tom Atractaspidi," Agent Astor said.

The VIA field attire was a modified uniform that included stretch pants and a polo style shirt, and combat boots.

"What's in store for today?" Joanie asked.

"We are going to show you to your trailer you will call home for a while, let you rest up until in the morning. Then we will start your classroom training mixed in with physical training." Agent Astor said.

"Alright lead the way." Joanie said.

The VIA wanted to isolate Joanie and Boone from the rest of the camp as much as possible. They found a guard outside the trailer they would share that had bedrooms on each end and a community center in the middle that had an entertainment center and a kitchen table to eat meals.

They arrived with virtually nothing.

"Everything you need will be provided and your meals will be delivered to the trailer," Astor said.

"Alright," Boone (a.k.a. Adrak) said.

"While you are away from the trailer during the day maids will come in do the cleanup and then depart. Security people would then arrive afterwards with bug sniffers to make sure nothing got planted."

"We have a guard outside our door?" Joanie asked.

"Yes, their purpose is to always keep base personnel away from you. Your interactions with people here are on a need-to-know basis. Nobody knows who you are or what you will be doing. For your safety as well as the successful completion of the mission, very few people other than who you just met, will be in contact with you before you deploy."

"That's fine with me," Boone said having experienced getting his ass beat to one inch of his life recently because of some type of compromise or disclosure. The two were shown inside the trailer and the bedrooms at each end were identical. But the doorway into the bedrooms had their names on them.

"I find it odd our names are on a placard above the door," Boone said.

"We randomly selected the rooms for you two, but we put a name above each door so that if we have to send someone in to wake you up, or the maids bring in clean uniforms for the next day's training, they know which size to bring to which room." Astor said.

"Check out your rooms. You will notice telephones in each one of them hooked up via a land line," Astor said.

"Alright." Joanie responded.

Astor followed Joanie over to her room while she looked inside and saw there wasn't much in the room, not that she needed much but she did see the phone next to her bed.

"When you pick up the phone to call about a complaint or a need, a staff member will automatically answer you and deal with the situation." Astor said.

"Okay." Joanie replied.

"In case the two of you are in the communal room eating or watching entertainment, each room has a different dial tone. I'm going to call Joanie's room now so she can hear the chimes and dial tone." Astor said then called the room and they the chimes indicating someone is trying to reach Joanie.

"I'm sure I'll remember those chimes," Joanie said.

"Now I'm calling Boone's room," Astor said, and the sound was quite a bit different.

They walked back to the center of the trailer which had a communal room for entertainment and lounging.

"This room is monitored by artificial intelligence. If you need help with an entertainment device you can ask questions on how to operate a device such as the holographic display for entertainment, and AI or sometimes referred to as AL will assist. If AL cannot help you, it will contact someone to come assist. In a few minutes doctors will arrive and give each of you a physical exam, then your food will be served for your evening meal. Recommend getting some sleep afterwards so you will be ready for tomorrow." Astor said.

No sooner than Astor finished his statement, a guest arrival doorbell rang, and Astor walked over and opened the door and medical staff came in. The staff knew who each of them were and had looked at their sanitized copies of their medical records which had several pictures created by AI, showed side and front views.

One of the doctors said, "Joanie, please go with me to your bedroom."

Joanie said, "Okay," and the two went in and closed the door.

The other doctor a female said, "Boone, please come with me."

The two spies were checked over quite well. The reason why the female doctor went with Boone was to look over the scars on his back and see how well the skin grafts were holding up from post-surgery of his last mission.

While examining the doctor said, "They did a good job on your wounds. You are lucky to be alive."

"Yea, I know, my bad luck, I got hit about a second or two before I would have left the target area with no injuries," Boone said.

"You will have some strenuous workouts during your training. Because of your recent surgery, I need to look you over really good after training each day."

"Sure," Adrak replied.

In about two weeks, I've scheduled you for a series of X-rays to verify all your internals are holding up well," the doctor said with great appreciation for this spy.

"Alright," Boone said.

The doctor got to see firsthand what Adrak suffered in the line of duty. The fact he was willing to come back for more resonated with her. Adrak truly was a remarkable man from what she was observing, and she didn't know the half of it.

"After you finish dressing, we'll go out to the communal area and your meal should be arriving soon. You have a special diet that is designed to support vigorous training and restorative properties," the doctor said.

Moments later the two walked into the communal area and found Joanie was already complete with her examination, then the medical staff departed just as couriers were bringing in their sealed meal containers. Nothing was left to chance. Everything they were about to eat was in tamper proof containers. The outer cover was like a balloon inflated so if someone poked it to drug or poison them, the balloon would deflate. It had warning stickers on it: DO NOT EAT IF THE CONTAINER IS DEFLATED.

Boone had meals like this before. Joanie had not and thought it was a novel idea.

They were now left alone as all the staff had departed.

"I was skeptical at first at how I was escorted here, but now that we all know what has transpired, I'm sure glad you got me here safely." Boone said.

"It was a team effort," Joanie responded.

The two were unaware their meals were spiked with sleep inducers and shortly after eating their late dinner they found themselves in their beds sleeping well.

The two each had their own private bathrooms attached to their bedrooms and AL was omni present and when Boone woke up in the middle of the night needing to use the bathroom, as soon as he stood up AL turned on the soft light slowly. Boone remembering AL was everywhere asked, "Which way to the bathroom?"

AL replied, "I'm shining a bright light on the bathroom door for you now."

"Thanks."

Boone walked over to the well-lit door and opened it to the bathroom where he went inside and did his business. When he finished, he asked:

"AL, how much more time do I have left to sleep?"

"Boone you will be woken up in four hours."

"Thank you, AL."

"You are welcome, Boone."

Boone went back to bed and discovered thanks to his Space-lag, he was sleepy and quickly passed back out into dreamland.

Boone had a lot to dream about, good and bad. One thing Boone learned after some horrible episodes in his life where his dreams came true and he was shot, to steer his dream. One of the psychiatrists explained to him he can do that whenever he wants, and he is in control of his dreams.

Tonight was no exception, Adrak's dream ventured into some terrifying scenarios, and then he steered it to Karli Pauli a beautiful woman with a golden voice and a great lover. He would never go after her and ask her to defect and come with him because he admired her artistic talent so much, he didn't in any way wish to interrupt that and change her lifeline.

Martilene was another factor, he wouldn't mind altering her timeline, but he also knew she had relatives and if she defected, she could never see them again. Family is important, especially an aging mother in the works. As a decent person Boone would not want to screw that up either.

Would he ever meet a desirable woman that wasn't behind enemy lines he could pursue? Boone's fundamental problem was that due to his profession, it would be highly unlikely for him to meet a suitable woman. If he ever wanted to entertain a normal life with a spouse and children, he would have to divorce the Inter Dimensional Spy Portal business. Then he started thinking, even that might not be possible. Would they allow me to leave?

In his mental state Boone knew he had to shift his thoughts; it was time to steer his dream to another destination.

Boone did a lot of reading in the past. He had many Novels and books in his head that had far more pleasant aspects to them. Some of the holographic entertainment content also had very pleasing scenarios in them.

Boone (a.k.a. Adrak) had to latch on to one of those dreams and continue feeling good for the rest of his four-hour sleep time. He didn't know when or how it manifested but suddenly four hours later he was awakened. The room telephone acted like an alarm clock wakeup call. It rang for about 10 rings that forced Boone out of his pleasant dream into reality and as he started stirring, the artificial intelligence personality AL said:

"Boone, it's time for you to get up and get ready for today's events. I suggest you take a shower. The negative ions you will breathe in during your shower will invigorate you and give you a stronger awareness."

"Alright," Boone said then swung his feet around and stood up. AL knew the probability was Boone would need to use the bathroom, so he lit up the bathroom door with higher concentrations of light allowing Boone to see the door to approach.

Boone did his S/S/S and as he came out of the bathroom AL said, "Boone your workout shoes and clothes are in the closet for you to wear to training."

"Alright, thanks," Boone responded.

Boone dressed and the clothes fit perfectly. Of course, VIA knew his sizes and much about Boone. He then walked out into the trailer's communal area and found Joanie sitting there. AL had an APP that communicated with the VIA training staff which notified them of all of Boone's activities and they knew he was up and dressed and ready for his breakfast.

The guest arriving doorbell rang and suddenly a couple staffers entered carrying those inflated food delivery devices. Aside from keeping the food secure from poisoning or drugging, the compressed hot air kept the food warm. Drinks with secure twist off tops were also provided and the staffer made the comment:

"Your drinks are enriched with compounds that will enhance your training. Please enjoy."

The meal was modest but powerful. The drink went down rather smoothly, and Boone could feel the effects. It was like an elixir he drank once before that was designed to give more endurance with his girlfriend.

The two finished their meals and went their separate ways to their private bathrooms to freshen up and clean their teeth with provided dental care equipment and pastes plus a fantastic mouthwash, like Boone never had before.

Boone made it out to the communal area several minutes before Joanie and was wondering why she was here and what her role would be. Her main reason is a couple are easier to walk around together than two males without picking any suspicion. Over the next few days Boone would discover Joanie was his right-hand person and she could be one heck of a mean bitch in a fist fight as displayed with her martial arts training.

About a minute after Joanie walked out of her bedroom into the communal area, the guest arriving doorbell rang and in walked Astor all smiles.

"I hope everyone had a good sleep?" Astor asked.

"I slept like a Tommy (an animal like gazelle found on Vekkar worlds), Boone replied.

"Good. Will the two of you please follow me." Astor said and led them outside.

An electric cart was waiting for them.

VIA rep (Vekkar Intelligence Agency rep) Sorge, and Vekkar military training experts Colonel Suzan Marklar, and Lt. Colonel Tom Atractaspidi were waiting in the electric cart that could easily haul eight people plus gear in a rear open area. One might think it was a super stretch golf cart.

Boone was wondering why they needed to ride an electric cart. He soon discovered why. The cart went along an internal road network inside this monster size tent, then into a tunnel. The tunnel well-lit was a mile long or more, Boone estimated. At the end of the tunnel, they came into what appeared to be a parking garage full of electric carts.

"We get out here," VIA rep Astor said.

Boone and Joanie got out of the cart with the rest of them and they went through a door that led them into an underground facility. They came upon a security checkpoint manned with armed guards who looked serious and attentive. These two security men had AI backup who monitored them and everything they did as well as warn them when carts were approaching, or people were exiting the facility.

AI informed the security men the six people were cleared to enter and one of them went to the second door and opened it up for the visitors and held the door open until they all passed, then took his seat looking at a display with security scan images cycling with AI generated reports such as identifying who is in the picture. The guard could say freeze the image so he could look longer at it.

Inside the facility they came to an elevator. After they were inside AI asked, "What floor do you wish to go to Mr. Astor?"

"Take us to KOBRA SPEKTR enclave," Astor said. "Yes sir," the security guard replied.

Boone (a.k.a. Adrak could feel the elevator drop as the G forces went negative. Momentarily they slowed down and stopped, and the door opened to a small lobby with a security member behind a bullet proof glass enclosure with computer screens advising him these people were cleared for Project KOBRA SPEKTR.

Astor walked over and placed his hand on the palm reader and put his face up to the retina scan platform that automatically adjusted to his height and the robotic detector scanned his retina. A moment later they could hear solenoids activating and the door slid sideways with compressed air which the six passed through. As soon as the last person Joanie entered the door slid shut behind her.

The group walked through a very clean and sterile hallway which Astor knew his way around and led them into a conference room and asked them all to be seated. He took his position at the end of the conference room table since he oversaw the operation.

Since breakfast was just served, there was no need for snacks or drinks and the meeting commenced. Astor started the meeting with the comments:

"In a short while we are going to begin your training. I felt we had to tell you a little about the agenda at the beginning of your training so that you would know how serious this is and why we pulled in an Inter Dimensional Spy to participate in this."

"There may come a time and place due to circumstances out of our control we'll need an Inter Dimensional Spy Portal as a last-ditch effort to accomplish what we must. That option will be a last option as we think we'll have to approach this in more conventional manner."

"000050428A62315 (a.k.a. Adrak), you have been trained in a lot of the things you will be doing, but like anyone else you need proficiency training. Because of your recent missions and wounds, you suffered, you were not able to train with the aptitude and vigor as you have in the past. Physical training will help you peak up again and be physically ready for the stresses of the deployment." Astor commented.

Adrak nodded his head at Astor giving a visual affirmative.

"Certain things you will be doing such as high-altitude insertion Wing glider suits training will happen for both of you since neither of you are proficient at using Wing Suits yet."

"Can you take a moment and tell us what a high-altitude insertion glider suit is like?" Boone (a.k.a. Adrak) asked.

"Certainly. It's like a jump suit. But with a helmet that provides oxygen so you can breathe at jump altitudes up to 60,000 feet," Astor responded.

"Is this glider like one I just went on in my recent mission?" Boone asked

"No, you will wear a Wingsuit that gives you glider ability. I'm going to show you a video of it now. We are jumping ahead a little, but since you will be training in it soon, you might as well look at it.

Possibly The Best Wingsuit Flying Ever Captured On Video | HeliBASE 74 ep. 4 (youtube.com)

Artificial Intelligence (AI) was always listening to the room.

"Play the Glider Wingsuit training video." Astor stated knowing AI would comply.

"Glider Wingsuit training video will now commence," AI voice in the background said.

The video started playing on a projection screen opposite where Astor was sitting about ten feet away in view of the six people in the room.

The video did a little introduction of the glider Wingsuit then showed cuts of people launched out of aircraft at high altitudes wearing a helmet. The video narrator said:

"These Wing suit Jumpers can obtain supersonic speeds very quickly that would be dangerous, so a drag chute drogué will be attached to the glider parachutist upon exiting the aircraft."

Adrak watched the video and looked rather intrigued.

"The drogué would be unlatched and let go around 5,000 feet as velocity will then be dropping off with thicker atmosphere and drag from horizontal flight," the narrator said.

"The landing zone is planned out well in advance and thanks to AI assistance when the flyer gets near the landing zone, a parachute deploys which the person guides down to the bull's mark," The narrator said for the video as the action happened.

Astor then continued with his statements after the video ended:

"Boone (a.k.a. Adrak) was selected for the mission because Executive Director of Vekkar Interdimensional Transport Directorate, *Doctor Oxyuran Lepidotus Taipan* viewed him as one of his most capable agents and the most trustworthy," Astor recapitulated.

Adrak nodded feeling uplifted discovering his supervisor's assessment of him was not only quite positive, but also broadcasted to higher ups in the VIA.

"Joanie was picked for the mission because we need a female to make Boone and Joanie appear as a couple to reduce the possibility SMERSH would think a loving couple are engaged in espionage and sabotage."

Joanie knew immediately what that meant. She and Boone would soon be instructed they would have to sleep together in hotel rooms to put on an act to foil any surveillance.

Joanie would soon be visited by psychiatrists to tell her some spies must use all their tools and where they were going, they might come under severe surveillance and might even have to do coitus to give the appearance they were a real couple.

Joanie shocked the psychiatrists when she said, "I can handle it, but I don't want Boone falling in love with me because it's just an act."

That's when the VIA started realizing the depth of intrigue Joanie would go. She had the psychology to be a very dangerous spy. She knew her body was a tool of spy craft and manipulation of little heads was just as important as manipulating the big heads.

But she also knew this would be one of those rare moments in the history of the VIA where she used her body on friendly forces to give the enemy a false impression.

Boone (a.k.a. Adrak) would learn through this mission he had no other loyal partner that came close to Joanies expertise, dedication, and capability.

With the video presentation of the glider Wingsuits was over, Astor directed their attention to why they would be using some extraordinary measures to get into the target area:

"Before we go any further into sources and methods, I want to get back on the agenda and now I'm going to tell you what you will be doing and why only six of us are in this room."

Everyone had their eyes on Astor. This was the moment they were all waiting for: *the what and not the why*. All of them had experienced surprises in their lifetimes. Certainly Boone (a.k.a. Adrak), had a lot of recent surprises that only Astor knew the extent of.

The mission you will be going on will be to steal the building plans to the Tramular's new *Intergalactic Dreadnaught Carrier*.

"Play the video of the Tramular *Intergalactic Dreadnaught Carrier*." Astor said.

The Tramulite *Intergalactic Dreadnaught Carrier* video will now start," AI said in the background.

The narrated video showed a series of artist conceptions as well as pictures taken from space of hull sections moving into the building ways.

Some of the animation using artist conceptions and implied realization formulated by artificial intelligence to give it a real look like one would expect at a movie theater showed a mock operation of the Tramular's new *Intergalactic Dreadnaught Carrier* launching space capable fighter bombers.

"Each *Intergalactic Dreadnaught Carrier* can carry 120 Zygov fighter bombers, but the Tramulars's are testing a *Spratz Prototype Fighter Bombers* about half the size with just as lethal a punch The new *Intergalactic Dreadnaught Carrier* can deploy with 240 *Spratz Prototype Fighter Bombers* onboard," the narrator stated.

For several minutes there were videos of Zygov fighter bombers used in fighting against the Vekkar's followed by stolen videos of Spratz prototype fighter bombers.

The narrator stated: "The reason for smaller Spratz prototype fighter bombers is their conventional warheads on the air to surface and air to air missiles use Krypton (U36) and Tabastanite (U115) to create a much greater explosion with one fourth the amount of mass. Also, the new hypersonic missiles utilize a new type of solid fuel aluminum oxidizer mixed with a solid metallic hydrogen and ammonium perchlorate."

"These new missiles have double the range with the weight less than one half the weight of existing weapons. Trübsal-Anwende (pronounced Trubsal Anvend) is the codeword for the new Tramulite missiles with new rocket engines and warhead," Narrator stated.

"To project power of multiple squadrons of Spratz fighter bombers requires a platform such as the Intergalactic Dreadnaught Carrier. Without the Intergalactic Dreadnaught Carrier, those Spratz fighter bombers can only be brought to the battles piecemeal in other classes of ships, and it would be impossible to deploy them from a large cargo hauler," Narrator continued.

The Empire Security Council has determined if we can stop the Tramular's *Intergalactic Dreadnaught Carrier* from deployment, that will spare our front-line troops from Spratz fighter bombers launching Trübsal-Anwende weapons," Narrator continued.

The video ended with the VIA logo in the middle of the screen.

VIA

"I know that's a lot to dump on you all at once, but now you know how important your mission is and the implications of failure to prevent the new *Intergalactic Dreadnaught Carrier* from deploying will save a lot of Vekkar lives," Astor stated.

Astor was a smart man, he had read 000050428A62315 (a.k.a. Adrak) portfolio provided by the Inter Dimensional Spy Directorate three times. He wasn't going to leave anything to chance. It was now crystal clear to him why Executive Director of Vekkar Interdimensional Transport Directorate, *Doctor Oxyuran Lepidotus Taipan* thought so highly of Adrak to recommend him for this mission.

Astor was working on borrowed time. While Joanie and Boone (a.k.a. Adrak) were sleeping, Astor spent over four hours talking directly to the *Oxyuran Lepidotus Taipan* himself. As soon as this briefing was over the two spies would go about their training and Astor would go to his private office that had a cot in it to take a serious nap.

Chapter Eleven

The Mole

Doctor Oxyuran Lepidotus Taipan was spending time with counterintelligence agents who now were doing deep surveillance on the three amigos who were likely the source of the Betrayal that resulted in a top Tramulite SMERSH agent like Karoline Morganthau to be sent after 000050428A62315 (a.k.a. Adrak). That also implied SMERSH now knew 000050428A62315 is Adrak and was going by the alias Boone Whitaker.

Since VIA didn't know the depth of betrayal yet, Joanie and Boone would likely have new identities before they were sent to Tramular worlds to do their operation.

The other change would be *Doctor Oxyuran Lepidotus Taipan's* office would be cut off from any involvement or communications associated with Project KOBRA SPEKTR compartmentalized and if KOBRA SPEKTR needed an INTER DIMENSIONAL SPY Portal the three amigos would be put on ice during the time to make sure they had no knowledge of it occurring. *Doctor Oxyuran Lepidotus Taipan* and Astor had a plan in how the three Amigos would be put on ice.

Two of the three would suffer because they would have to be sequestered with the traitor until the KOBRA SPEKTR mission was completed. Hopefully they would identify the Mole before it was necessary to do this, but just in case the contingency was put in place.

It was now critical to find out which of the three was the traitor. Once they identified him, he would become a double spy for a while, and like most traitors would learn the hard way what happens to them when they get caught.

In the spy business, they never prosecute traitors. It gets too messy, and the legal system does not know how to protect sensitive sources and methods despite all the assurances they may state.

With a war going on its easy to explain a death even if the story is fabricated. One of those three men will go on a mission soon, and his family will be spoon fed he made the supreme sacrifice for the empire. This of course would happen after this mission while they use him as a double spy as soon as they figure out who it is.

The problem with a traitor is that they know what their own office is doing, but since they have a complete disconnect from counterintelligence, they have no idea what's going on in such an investigation. Nobody in the office would be informed of what transpires.

Counterintelligence could not allow *Doctor Oxyuran Lepidotus Taipan* to divulge anything to his office now or ever because it could possibly compromise sensitive methods and procedures.

As far as the office would know the spy simply was killed on a mission which happens. Nobody except *Doctor Oxyuran Lepidotus Taipan* would know who the mole is. Since the mole will probably die behind enemy lines, they would never be able to find his remains especially if they were fed to a hog farm which people in the office knew the Tramulars's did with spies as well as putting them in incinerators alive. The incinerator deaths were filmed to show future spies they captured what would happen to them if they did not divulge everything they knew about their operations and who was involved.

As far as the counterintelligence agents are concerned, getting it down to three makes it easy. They will spoon feed all three and watch where the breadcrumbs go. Nobody inside the organization knew counterintelligence operations were in effect except for *Doctor Oxyuran Lepidotus Taipan* who had no mercy for the spy because by betraying Adrak for whatever reason, he was also betraying the empire and the Director himself.

Counterintelligence was very happy *Doctor Oxyuran Lepidotus Taipan* agreed to whatever they wanted to do. They had Carte Blanche. That would speed up the time to discover the mole.

There is nothing sacred in the counterintelligence business. They are not law enforcement required to conform to laws, rules, and regulations, since none of their actions would ever end up in court. They didn't get permission to do anything. They just did it. In some ways they were worse than the Tramular's. A sophisticated manager like *Doctor Oxyuran Lepidotus Taipan* had been around the block and knew what to expect. He himself would be the source of some disinformation to the three Amigos.

Chapter Twelve

Uncommon Training

There would be briefings of some type almost every day. The security people would soon discover Boone and Joanie were routine visitors to project KOBRA SPEKTR and the conference room.

Today, however, they would soon leave and end up at an Air Base. They left KOBRA SPEKTR and went to the elevator and went upwards. They did not stop at the floor they arrived at. The ride in the elevator stopped and they were led outside a tunnel that had security guards inside it looking out with several hidden sensors around the camouflaged tunnel entrance they stepped out on a flat surface that had an image painted on it. From the air it simply looked like terrain.

Moments after exiting the tunnel a Skycar came down and landed and the doors opened for four people that would be going with them. Astor then went back to the elevator with agent Sorge and went to their offices. Sorge had things to do immediately, whereas Astor was going to take a long nap because he was suffering from sleep deprivation dealing with Interdimensional Transport Directorate, *Doctor Oxyuran Lepidotus Taipan* and that mess.

Colonel Suzan Marklar, and Lt. Colonel Tom Atractaspidi would be spending a lot of time with Boone and Joanie.

When they arrived at the Vekkar Air Base, the Skycar which belonged to Colonel Suzan Marklar special forces detachment was vectored down to the building complex parking structure adjacent to her group's offices.

They were soon out of the Skycar and promptly walked into Colonel Suzan Marklar's offices where they met with a flight surgeon who took them aside and did a quick medical exam, blood pressure, eyesight, and general medical conditions and informed Colonel Suzan Marklar, they were ready for flight operations.

Colonel Suzan Marklar took them to a ready room that had lockers and a set of military flight coveralls. To change into and put the clothes they had been wearing in lockers. A couple parachute technicians came in with parachutes for both.

"According to your records you both have had previous parachute training," Colonel Suzan Marklar said.

"That's correct for me," Boone (a.k.a. Adrak said).

"Me too," Joanie responded.

Good, I don't have to waste a lot of time taking you through parachute school. Let me know if you feel like you are not ready to go for a jump right now," Colonel Suzan Marklar said.

"I'm ready to jump," Joanie responded. "I'm good to go too," Boone replied.

"Go ahead and strap into your parachutes and put on your helmets. You will not need the oxygen because today you are only going to jump from 12,000 feet."

"Alright," Boone replied.

"According to your records you are both certified in the MX-501Y Steerable parachute that you are now wearing."

The two spies acknowledged, yes.

"Okay follow me. We have a landing pad on top of the building and a VTOL is arriving to pick us up. I'm going up with you to watch you jump. Your helmet has altitude reporting. When you get down to 4000 feet deploy your parachutes. That will give us time to rescue you in case you have a parachute failure."

The two spies and the two officers went up to the rooftop landing pad and soon enough a military VTOL came down and landed on the landing pad. The rear ramp dropped down. Joanie and Boone had been on this type of VTOL before and understood to just follow Colonel Suzan Marklar up the ramp. Lt. Colonel Tom Atractaspidi followed them up as he was the last person and as soon as he was aboard the VTOL took off and went vertical.

There was another person on the VTOL wearing a parachute. Lt. Colonel Tom Atractaspidi announced:

"This is Toland, he's jumping with you as your safety observer. He has a more capable parachute and if necessary, had a lanyard to hook onto your parachute pack to safely drop you down to the surface to prevent injury.

"That's nice to know," Joanie said.

"You are not going to parachute over the airbase. We have a designated jump zone to take you not far away," Lt. Colonel Tom Atractaspidi said.

"Alright," Boone said, then sat down on one of the numerous empty seats and Joanie followed suit and naturally hooked up at seat belt which gave Boone the notion he should strap in as well.

"As soon as we get over the drop zone, I want the two of you to do a last look at each other's parachute to look for packing flaws or anything that could be an issue," Lt. Colonel Tom Atractaspidi stated.

In less than 10 minutes they were at 12,000 feet directly over the drop zone. "We are over the drop zone, prepare to jump," the Pilot said over the intercom.

Toland stood up and walked over to the rear door/ramp and lowered it so they could just walk off it together and freefall for a while.

Boone and Joanie stood up. Boone said, "Go ahead and check my parachute, then I'll check yours."

"Alright," Joanie said as Boone turned his back to her to make it easier for Joanie to do an inspection. Joanie was thorough and soon said, "It all looks good."

Boone then checked Joanie's parachute and said the same thing. "We are ready." Boone said.

"I want us to all step off the VTOL together at the same time so I can observe both of you up close," Toland said.

The three walked to the rear and on a count of three stepped off the ramp together at the same time and began their freefall.

Toland understood they had each attended parachute school and did numerous jumps in the past for proficiency training as well as actual mission insertions. Toland expected Boone and Joanie to be able to control their freefall and avoid going into a tumble.

Joanie and Boone came down just like professional jumpers and at the 4000foot level deployed their MX-501Y Steerable parachute and could see the designated landing zone below Joanie deployed her parachute first so when Boone opened his he was down below her when he opened his and Toland opened his about the same time.

Boone corkscrewed the steerable parachute down and Joanie, who was good at steering her parachute followed him down almost in formation. Toland maneuvered and using his expertise in controlling the parachute ended up above the two spies watching them come down and videotaping them with his bodycam to replay later to evaluate and critique if necessary. It made Toland feel good watching the two spies land on the bull's eye in the landing zone on their first jump.

The VTOL was not far behind.

"Go ahead and roll up your parachutes and carry them back on the VTOL. We have another set of parachutes staged for your next jump. This time you will be using the oxygen from your helmet, and we are dropping you at 30,000 feet. When you jump out of the VTOL you will have a drogue line attached with a small parachute to keep you from going supersonic and keep you stable. When you deploy your chute the drogue line will pull the chute out.

When they walked up the ramp to the VTOL, they noticed everyone onboard was wearing a helmet with oxygen source.

"When we get ready to open the rear door of the VTOL, everyone will turn on their oxygen and, on the heads, up display of the helmet your oxygen status will be shown. We will not open the rear door until all crew members verify their oxygen status indicates no faults detected. On this jump you will deploy the chutes at 5,000 feet," Lt. Colonel Tom Atractaspidi said.

"Alright," Boone replied.

The spiral up to 30,000 feet took a little longer than to get up to 12,000 feet. Thanks to autopilot and satellite navigation the VTOL was stationary directly above the landing zone. From 30,000 feet it looked a lot smaller. Boone (a.k.a. Adrak) could see a long distance out the window and it was apparent this was a sparsely populated area.

The trainers took nothing to chance. Toland walked up to Boone and Joani and said, turn on the oxygen enable switch inside the service access on the side of your helmet."

"These helmets were wider than most because they had small oxygen tanks and rechargeable battery powered circuitry. In front of Boone and Joanie, he opened up his own service access and flipped the oxygen enable switch which the two spies immediately copied, and everyone put on their helmets. Everyone else was ready to go.

Toland then stated in his helmet microphone:

"Crew report status of your helmets." Pilot: Oxygen enabled; no faults detected.

Copilot: Oxygen enabled; no faults detected.

Crew chief: Oxygen enabled; no faults detected.

Colonel Suzan Marklar: Oxygen enabled; no faults detected.

Lt. Colonel Tom Atractaspidi: Oxygen enabled; no faults detected.

Chief Trainer Toland: Oxygen enabled; no faults detected.

Boone: Oxygen enabled; no faults detected.

Joanie: Oxygen enabled; no faults detected.

Toland said, "Alright Boone and Joanie, check each other's parachute.

After they each took turns checking the other's parachute, they reported all sat.

Moments later, the cabin was depressurized, and the rear door opened. Toland and the two spies stepped out to the rear ramp to begin their freefall.

Toland said to them they could hear in their helmet communications, "Count to five before you let loose on the drogué line."

The end of the drogué had stabilizing fins that channeled air onto turban like shrouded propeller blades that made them more efficient due to maximizing air flow.

As they sped up and started going faster the propeller generated a lot of electricity powering a small generator that spread speed breaks at the end of the drogue to reduce the velocity and prevent them going supersonic. The crew chief noted the three had jumped and closed the VTOL rear ramp door and the pilots began cork screwing downwards spiral to observe the three parachutists.

Before they reached thicker air their velocities approached supersonic, but the drogue slowed them down breaking and as the air thickened the breaking action was very efficient. By the time they reached 15,000 feet their need for oxygen lessoned and the helmet began an environmental analysis that soon turned off the oxygen with the message, "*normal air sufficient for breathing, oxygen shutting off.*"

Boone and Joanie observed Toland's hand movements as he steered on the way down quite satisfactorily. They copied his actions and the three were soon flying in a great formation as if it was planned.

When they reached 5,000 feet Toland gave them the slight reminder to deploy their chutes in the event he had to intervene. Thanks to the drogué, the chutes deployed far more efficiently and the three then glided down in formation to a perfect arrival on the landing zone. Moments later the VTOL arrived and the crew chief along with Colonel Suzan Marklar, and Lt. Colonel Tom Atractaspidi walked down the rear ramp and assisted them wrapping up their parachutes.

"That's it for your jumps for today," Colonel Suzan Marklar said.

"What's next?" Boone asked.

"You will now go back to the air base with us and change then we'll take you back to the facility, have a meal and a rest period, then you will do some physical training and martial arts proficiency workouts." Lt. Colonel Tom Atractaspidi announced.

They went back to where they came from in the same manner eventually pulling up to their trailer in the electric carts.

"Your meals will arrive soon. We'll see you in a couple hours, "Lt. Colonel Tom Atractaspidi said.

Joanie and Boone walked up into their trailer and with the efficiency they had come accustomed to, within minutes their meals arrived.

They each received a high protein meal and a special endurance drink. The food was delicious, and filling and it was good they were given a two-hour break because Boone felt the need to take a nap. After he finished, he went to his bedroom and laid down. Joanie figured that's what he would be doing and thought it was a great idea herself.

Meanwhile, during a working lunch, Lt. Colonel Tom Atractaspidi, Colonel Suzan Marklar, and Toland held a critique on the parachute jumps the two spies just performed.

Colonel Suzan Marklar was brilliant, but she was also quite experienced and had deployed with special forces and had plenty of her own lessons learned. These two spies would not be the first nor the last they would prepare for missions.

Because of those lessons learned Colonel Suzan Marklar had an agenda sheet along with checkoffs they needed to complete during the critique. Every aspect was covered. These were somewhat proficient parachutists from past experiences and not neophytes or amateurs.

Some of the checkoffs included characteristics observed such as fear, reluctance, or apprehension observed.

As they went through Colonel Suzan Marklar's checkoff sheet, the scorecards were annotated. At the completion of the critique in two hours which is why they gave the two spies a two-hour break, they had a complete picture of where these two students were in the overall scheme of things and what they knew they could expect out of them.

"Any final comments before we get the two students and take them to their physical training?"

"I seriously doubt we will ever have two students like these again," Toland said.

"That's quite apparent and now you know why they each came highly recommended. It's going to be interesting to see how they perform with the rest of the training," Colonel Suzan Marklar said.

"From the doctor's report on Boone Whitaker, I'd say he's been to hell and back and knows how important the efficacy of his training is, especially now that he knows a little about what he's going to be doing," Lt. Colonel Tom Atractaspidi added.

The staff gave the two spies a wakeup call and informed them their Physical Training clothes were set out for them to change into including a different type of shoe designed for running.

Without much fanfare the two spies changed into their physical training clothes and when they arrived at the communal room a staff member said, "An electric cart is outside to take you to your physical training."

Joanie and Boone walked outside the trailer and Toland was in the electric cart by himself. Colonel Suzan Marklar, and Lt. Colonel Tom Atractaspidi would be engaged in other activities and Toland would supervise the physical training.

The two got in the electric cart and it drove to the tunnel again and when it reached the facility, they visited earlier they did not stop. The tunnel went on a way further and they came into a parking zone for a few electric carts and got out and walked out of a guarded access out onto a small dirt road that went around this portion of the lake. As they were standing there for a few minutes with Toland waiting for something obviously, he said:

"We are going for a run around part of the lake. See directly across from us? That's where we'll be running as soon as our escort shows up."

Moments later they heard a strange sound. It came closer and it was a drone. "This drone is our escort," Toland said then added, "Let's go."

They took off at a good pace. Boone (a.k.a. Adrak) had done some running in rehab but had not fully recovered back to his original stamina before his casualties he received during the attack on the Tramulite research center mission.

Toland knew all this and knew he may not be 100% and go easy on Boone as they needed to build him up slowly without breaking him.

Joanie on the other hand was in perfect physical condition. She was what they called in the business, *a spy's spy*. Psychiatrists didn't really know what drove Joanie, but they knew she was going to apply 100%.

Joanie knew her trainers knew what they were doing and whatever they had her do was all part of the big plan and the better she did it the likelihood is she would come back alive. Her destiny was in her own hands, and she knew these trainers would do their best to prepare her. Therefore, all she had to do was put forth one hundred percent effort and she would strive to get to where they wanted her to be when she was launched in the mission.

Joanie ran seemingly effortlessly as if she was a star runner in a marathon.

Boone on the other hand was running in pain. His injuries were not 100% recovered. He had to suck it up and do it with sheer determination. He also knew this workout would help make him stronger and continue with the recovery. It was mind over matter or mind over pain. The drink they had with their lunch had exotic chemicals in it that would facilitate this run. He would only make it halfway otherwise.

The drone also had audio it could communicate with them if it had too, as a repeater from a monitor somewhere within the compound. The drone's other purpose was to video record the entire event sending the video via telemetry to the monitoring center and drone pilot real time.

Toland was mindful of Boone's recovery and kept the pace down to six miles per hour. Before he picked up the two spies, he directed the drone pilot to run it at six miles per hour so that he could use it as a pace setter. The drone was flying at about twenty feet and about thirty feet in front of them for easy observation with one camera on the runners and the other camera ahead for navigation backup even though the drone was being flown on a digital map inside the drone's computer memory calibrated via satellite navigation precisely to go in the middle of the road.

At about the one-hour mark, which was around six miles, Boone (a.k.a. Adrak) was feeling a lot of pain. He then did some soul searching and employed some meditation techniques previously taught him to endure torture if he was caught as a spy. He simply kept his running synchronized with Toland in front of him while he did the meditation which split his thoughts. Half of his thoughts were somewhere else which went a long way to obscure the pain. In about fifteen minutes this process he used developed what he wanted to achieve, to continue running and be able to not register the pain in his thoughts in any way. Later as the next critique unfolded analysts poured over the running minute by minute and could tell by infrared and ultraviolet imagery the point at which both runners were starting to experience stress.

It was expected that Boone would likely be the first to give the telltale signatures on the ultraviolet imagery and predictably just like someone looking at him with night vision goggles, his aura brightened up, he was now sweating profusely, and his facial images showed excruciating pain. Then suddenly the infrared and the ultraviolet became quite blurry on Boone but not on Joanie. This surprised the analysts and because two other people running, Toland and Joanie didn't have the blurriness in the infrared and ultraviolet, they knew this was a singularity with Boone.

The pace was held in congruency, as a lock step formation and trackers put on the runners highlighting their bodies in colored squares each had data boxes on multiple screens showing precise measurements of velocity. The drone velocity was very easy to control quite precisely with onboard microprocessors that could manipulate flight controls just as efficiently as a modern transport aircraft.

The fuzziness on Boone's spectral imagery remained until they finished at the 12-mile mark.

Now the training has taken on a new dimension. This is what it was all about. Toland said in a very astute manner, "The possibility exists you may have been running for safety and your lives depend on you swimming across a river or a lake. See that small boat approaching now?

"Yes." Joanie responded.

"We are now going to get in the water. It will be cold for a while until your body adjusts and that boat will act like the drone as our pacemaker, and we will follow it across the lake. The shoes you have on are designed for running and swimming. Follow me into the water and let's go."

The boat had a couple people on board who were lifeguards in case one of the swimmers got into trouble. And after a two-hour run that could be easy.

It felt strange swimming in the shoes, but at least they didn't have to worry about stepping on sharp rocks or seashells.

The cold water helped them get over their run quickly. Toland knew that based on a lot of testing they did, their students, many of them could swim six miles per hour if they were fresh. But these two had just ran 12 miles. The boat which was under microprocessor control and a GPS like system would set a pace at 3 miles per hour. They would slowly raise that speed after the two students got into better shape.

It was only one mile across the lake that was oval in shape. As expected, they swam up to the other shoreline in about twenty minutes, completely exhausted. They had no energy left. This was it. A staff member drove up in a cart because they knew Toland was probably too tired to drive and gave each of them a nice thermal towel to wrap around themselves and they all got into the electric cart and went to project KOBRA SPEKTR offices where Boone and Joanie each met privately with doctors who provided them a change of clothes and shoes to change into then had them lay down on an examination table and took a lot of measurements.

Boone had the same female doctor who examined him before. She was mildly astonished at how his muscles now looked after he stressed them up quite a bit.

"I know your muscles are tight, do you feel like you might cramp up?" the doctor asked.

"Yes, I feel tight it could happen."

"I have all the measurements I need. Lay here for a few minutes while I get an assistant to take you in a wheelchair to a room where you will get a message and a hot bath," the doctor stated.

"Sounds good." Boone replied.

"I'm going to give you an injection now that will help you recover quicker and the message and bath will take care of the rest of it," the doctor said.

"Thanks." Boone replied.

The injection was a new type of invincibility drug laced with muscle relaxers. Boone was feeling immediately better, and an orderly arrived with a wheelchair and took him down the hallway to a room that had a bath and a massage table with an eager beaver ready to work over Boone.

Boone's muscles were now nice and tight, and he feared he could cramp up at any moment. The orderly and the massage therapist undressed Boone and helped him into the warm tub with water jets and chemicals added that are muscle relaxers.

Joanie received similar treatment, but she was not in such dire need as she was in much better physical condition having not gone through physical therapy and recovery recently like Boone did.

The water jets and the muscle relaxers alone were doing a good job of making Boone feel better, but the invincibility drug the doctor gave him added greatly to his psychological transcendence.

After about ten minutes, the massage therapist asked Boone:

"Do you think you can get out of the hot tub by yourself?"

"I think I can," Boone answered.

The massage therapist helped dry off Boone with nice soft towels and walked him over to her therapy table and proceeded to give him what is best described a NURU message.

The beautiful massage therapist was utterly amazed how hard Boone's muscles felt and when she saw all the scars on his back and knew he was a spook, she wondered *what terrible traumas he must have experienced.* The massage therapist also knew *military members with those kinds of scars would have been given a medical discharge and retired. But for this man to undergo the intensive training he is doing underscored how important he is.*

The massage therapists, one of the best in the business, was a contractor because Project KOBRA SPEKTR did unusual things and needed unusual talent. If it were not for the fact, this message therapist knew the room was bugged and filmed, she would have rewarded Boone with a little kiss on his little head to get him some gratification he truly deserved.

Since the massage therapist could not reward Boone in that manner, she did the next best thing with a NURU like message that loosened up his muscles and made him feel great.

After getting herself all oiled up doing Boone's massage she said, "You need to now get back in the bath to get all that oil off and I need to hop in with you because I'm drenched in it too. Soon they were in the tub together nude getting the oil off and went through a wash and rinse cycle.

When they finished the nice-looking massage technician whispered in Boone's ear:

"You have no idea how badly I wanted to hop on your lap and have you insert your manliness into me, but I can't because we are watched."

"You are very sweet. Thank you I feel so much better now." Boone replied.

Boone was soon dressed as well as the massage technician, and just like everything else that went on a staff member came into the room and informed Boone, "I will take you to the conference room where you will be given training."

"Thanks."

Chapter Thirteen

Cancel the Watcher

Soon Boone was in the conference room with Joanie and Astor going over some of the target area information and how they would arrive and later egress."

There was a lot to learn, and Astor knew they could only spoon feed it so fast. The benefit of the physical training was it would allow them to space the classroom training out and not overwhelm them with details they may forget by learning it too fast.

Part of this training was interactive, and the fact was the best laid plans were often subject to failure unless one improvised. Even though Adrak had been heavily criticized for his conduct and the adverse critiques manifested, he knew so did Astor and Interdimensional Transport Directorate, *Doctor Oxyuran Lepidotus Taipan,* Sidis was one of SMERSH's best agents and the plan wasn't all that great to begin with.

The SMERSH agent Sidis sure as hell figured it out without much effort and part of it was collateral damage from a watcher poorly executed activities and the Mole who betrayed Adrak.

Doctor Oxyuran Lepidotus Taipan also knew the three amigos were Adrak's biggest antagonists and the worst one of the three is who he privately theorized was the mole.

Whatever grudge the mole had against Adrak would be far less to him in the future than what the counterintelligence boys would do to him when they confirmed he's the traitor.

Part of the interactive discussion with Astor and Joanie, had a rather significant change to the planning and timing.

Planners who came up with the strategies were not recently laying in a hospital bed with a bunch of bullet holes. No matter how noble their cause was and how sophisticated they felt the plan seemed, Astor, Joanie, and Boone (a.k.a. Adrak) tweaked it and in some cases based on some of Boone's comments and requests, those subtle changes would not be presented to the planners.

When Boone requested the strict confidentiality between the three of them and Astor was extremely curious why, Boone [000050428A62315 (a.k.a. Adrak)] offered:

I was beaten and almost killed by one of SMERSH's best agent's because the planners didn't consider compromise by a watcher who probably should not have been assigned because his actions led the enemy to me.

That led to another incredible discussion. Boone said:

"Since my life is on the line, I do not want another watcher around me. I will be looking for him and if I find one, I will personally kill him."

"If you do that, we will have to prosecute you," Astor said.

"My advice is informing the planners to terminate the watcher aspect of the mission because he's a dead man. No doubt he will be a slug like the one who got me identified by SMERSH, so he will be easily discovered, and I will kill him before he can betray me by his presence."

"I can't tell the planners that, but I have an idea," Astor said. "What's that?" Boone asked.

"It's my responsibility to deliver you, Joanie, and the watcher to the target area. It will be very easy for me to have him drugged and get very sick so we must evacuate him and by the time you are on the planet, and move to your undisclosed location, it will be impossible for us to insert another watcher."

I appreciate this and from my perspective, and I don't want to denigrate the VIA in any manner, but I honestly do not believe the VIA does not respect SMERSH as much as they should. I know that Sidis is dead because I personally killed him, but there are other SMERSH agents as good as him.

"Yes, like Karoline Morganthau, a.k.a. Agnes Renceladus," Joanie commented.

"Good point. She's done a great job of escaping VIA surveillance," Astor noted.

"Karoline Morganthau would have picked up that watcher just as quickly as Sidis did at Praxiskrowtious," Boone stated.

"He wouldn't be the first man she cut his dick off," Joanie said and winked at Boone.

"Alright consider this an executive session. Everything we said today, will not be revealed to anyone else, since it discloses some of our vulnerabilities."

"Any chance we can round up Karoline Morganthau before we go on this mission?" Boone asked.

"Would you volunteer for a reverse honey pot scheme?" Astor asked.

"I might need some special training by Joanie," Boone said as a slight joke.

"I would be more than willing to train you on what you need to do rope her in," Joanie responded.

"I would only consider such a mission if I knew I got Joanie as a backup," Boone said.

"Perhaps we do need to do such a mission as a confidence builder in both of you," Astor said.

"I already have plenty of confidence in Joanie," Boone said.

"She may not have enough confidence in you yet," Astor replied.

The executive session soon ended.

Boon and Joanie were taken back to their trailer where dinner was soon served.

While they were eating, the critique on their running and swimming concluded.

The result of the critique led Colonel Suzan Marklar to decide to bring in some top Vekkar scientists to look at this drone training video and give their take on it. Colonel Suzan Marklar was utterly astonished and soon so would be the scientists who could not explain the blur on the infrared and ultra-violet composite on just one of the three runners.

The food was great and the elixirs very powerful. The two spies needed some restful sleep. As soon as they finished their meals, they were asked to page the staff to remove all the tableware and dishes brought in for their meals. Just as soon as the common area was cleaned up, and the last staffer was leaving, two doctors arrived and took each spy to their private bedrooms and did some checks such as blood pressure, eyes, heartbeat, lungs etc.

"Boone, you will have another tough day tomorrow. You and your partner need a good night's rest. I want to give you an injection that will put you to sleep for about twelve hours," the female doctor said.

"Sure, I want a good night's sleep," Boone (a.k.a. Adrak) responded.

The doctor asked Adrak: "Please lie down in the bed like he would if he was going to sleep."

Boone complied and the doctor gave him the injection. Boone was asleep before the Doctor left the room.

Joanie received similar treatment and like Adrak was sound asleep when the two doctors left the trailer, and the guard locked the door to the trailer after the doctors left in an electric cart.

In about twelve hours the telephone chimes began, and artificial intelligence roused Adrak and informed him it was time to get up and start his day.

Adrak did his normal routine then went to the communal area and soon met Joanie who was almost in the same mental situation as he was.

They again had a power breakfast and as soon as the staff started removing the dishes and the two freshened up, Toland was there to take them to the day's events.

This time when they went to the Air Base they arrived in another area. And were taken inside a large building. They were led down a long hallway and into a large room and the door shut behind them. What they now observed was a large transparent vertical cylinder. On the side of the cylinder was an access door.

Toland said, "This is a vertical wind tunnel to teach people how to glide with the Wingsuit on. Keep in mind that even with a glider Wingsuit you will still land with a parachute. On a wall adjacent to the vertical wind tunnel there were some glider Wingsuits for you to put on for your training."

"Okay," Boone responded.

"Okay I'm going to put one of these gliders Wingsuits on with a dummy parachute and demonstrate how you will use this for ground training before we take you up into the air," Toland said.

"This should be interesting," Joanie said.

A couple staffers came into the room and adjacent to the other side of the wind tunnel was an instrument panel that controlled everything. After Toland was dressed he informed the staffers, "I'm ready."

Toland walked through the door into the wind tunnel,

As soon as Toland was in the center in the wind tunnel, the technicians started the wind tunnel operation and everyone could hear the sudden shift of pitch and the loud rumble caused by the wind generator.

Very quickly the two spies could see the glider Wingsuit start flapping. Toland had a lot of experience in the wind tunnel teaching students, both military Calvary Units that do force recon, but also spies that got inserted this way. After about a minute the sound was almost leveling off at its operational pitch and Toland spread his arms slowly and started lifting into the air.

When Toland spread his arms fully he started rising to the top of the wind tunnel, then he pulled his arms closer to his body and his body started sinking towards the floor of the wind tunnel which was an automated net. Should Toland start tumbling and falling the automated net would be the bottom as the floor below it lowered like an elevator to make sure he had a soft landing.

The wind tunnel was all computer controlled because the trainers learned from practicality, human operators may not catch the fall quick enough. Toland went up and down a few times and then pulled his arms close to his body when he got near the floor and landed. The technicians who had observed Toland do lots of demonstrations knew when he put his arms next to his body to shut down the wind tunnel. The pitch changed as the wind generator turbines wound down and breaks on the shaft slowed it down and stopped it within a minute.

Toland then walked through the access door and approached his two students.

"Which one of you wants to be next?" Toland asked.

Neither volunteered as Boone didn't want to upstage Joanie.

"Boone will you go first?" Toland asked.

"Sure, if that's what you want." Boone replied.

Joanie remained quiet and was interested in watching the process first.

Boone put on the glider Wingsuit, Helmet, and the fake parachute pack and Toland checked everything to make sure it was put on correct.

"Okay now, just spread your arms out a few times and look at how your Wingsuit changes," Toland directed Boone.

After spreading them a few times and looking at the dynamics of the artificial wings, Boone said, "Alright I think I'm ready to try it."

"Since this is your first time, as soon as you are airborne, we are going to expose the net so you will psychologically feel safer. If you drop you will fall in the net and be perfectly safe," Toland said.

"Sure, let's do it," Boone said and walked over to the door and as soon as he reached for the handle, he heard a solenoid shift which the technician was unlocking for him.

Boone went inside and the door closed automatically as we walked to the center of the vertical wind tunnel.

"Are you ready sir?" One of the technicians asked via the intercom.

Boone gave a thumbs up and the technician started up the wind tunnel.

The airflow started immediately along with the sound and vibration.

Boone (a.k.a. Adrak) held his arms against his body as the wind increased. Just like he observed Toland doing he slowly separated his arms from his body that immediately affected the fabric of the Wingsuit which caught an air pocket and Boone could feel some lift force.

The air flow increased as the wind tunnel turbines increased velocity. The impression the wind tunnel gave Boone was what he felt walking outdoors once during a Hurricane. The air flow increased and the force on Boone's arms also increased.

Suddenly Boone felt like he was being lifted off the meshed floor and indeed he was rising very slowly, but at the same time the floor was going down and he could now see the net that would protect him from a hard landing.

Boone spread his arms a little wider and he saw his vertical velocity increase. He also played with his arms pulling one in to see how it allowed him to turn if required.

In due time Boone was 30 feet up in the air and he slowly pulled his arms together and started sinking towards the net below him. He allowed himself to sink all the way down to the net then he opened his arms up more abruptly the next time and moved vertically a lot quicker then pulled his arms together to slow the ascent.

Boone made another four ascents, then pulled his hands closer to his body coming near the net. Toland directed the technicians to raise the floor back up into position and stop the wind tunnel which Boone could hear in the intercom despite the noise thanks to his helmet. About the time the floor was back in place the wind tunnel turbos were slowing and breaking and the wind was decreasing fast.

As soon as the wind stopped Boone walked to the exit and Joanie was now suited up and ready to try it. Joanie was a fast learner and observing Boone and Toland she had a firm understanding of what she needed to do and just like Boone went up for or five times.

As soon as Joanie was finished doing four ups and downs, she too left the wind tunnel.

"I'm now going to do a demonstration which I believe in a couple weeks you will be able to perform," Toland said, and the technicians knew what he was about to do as he did this demonstration with other students to motivate them.

Once the wind tunnel was back and running with full wind, Toland started doing stunts. He was doing what appeared to be back flips and other movements a person would do on a trampoline. After a couple triple somersaults, Toland gave the signal, and the technicians shut down the wind tunnel.

After Toland exited the wind tunnel he approached Joanie and Boone and said, "Take off those parachutes and leave them here, but keep on your Wingsuit. We are now going up on the roof top to get in a VTOL and do a parachute jump from 12,000 feet. Today you will open your parachutes at 5,000 feet."

"What's the purpose of this jump," Boone asked.

"What I want you to get out of your exercise today is to practice gliding down to the parachute deployment area," Toland said.

"Alright," Boone replied.

Soon everyone was out of the simulated parachute packs that were color coded orange to make sure nobody accidentally went up to do a jump in one of them.

Toland escorted them up to the roof of the building where a VTOL landing zone existed. A VTOL was there waiting for them in full anticipation.

The three walked up the rear ramp of the VTOL which raised halfway after the crew chief saw the three were onboard and taking seats and fastening their seatbelts.

The crew chief notified the pilot, "Passengers are onboard, ready for takeoff." The pilot did a modified repeat back, "Passengers on board, taking off."

The VTOL was soon at the drop zone soon at 12,000 feet and hovering.

Everyone put on their parachutes that were going to jump and just like before, Boone and Joanie checked each other to make sure there were no issues.

"Since we are doing a low altitude parachute, we will not use the drogue's today," Toland said.

Toland nodded at the crew chief who lowered the ramp down and the three approached the ramp to jump at the same time.

"Don't forget. Today we will deploy the chutes at 5,000 feet," Toland said.

"Understand," Joanie replied.

"At 5,000 feet," Boone responded and nodded.

Soon the three were free falling and testing their flying suit. Boone and Joanie immediately discovered they did not drop straight down like when they parachuted.

They could glide with this special suit, and they could feel it when they were about to stall so they pulled their hands closer to their bodies and quickly gained velocity. Toland was watching them very carefully and VTOL craft was in hot pursuit also filming them.

Boone and Joanie are intrinsically far more intelligent than the general population, which helps them excel as spies. The same mental aptitude that sets them ahead of their peers also played into today's events as they were really mastering the glide suit very quickly. By the time they reached 5,000 feet to deploy their parachutes, they had truly learned to glide on their first attempt. Toland was amazed.

Landing in the bull's eye was expected and they did.

Shortly the VTOL landed near them and Toland asked, "Want to do another glide?"

"Sure," Joanie said first, and Boone followed.

"Alright, we'll go up to 20,000 feet the next jump. You will have to use your oxygen. Since the air is thinner at 20,000 feet, you will find control is not as good as when you jumped at 12,000 feet. But when you get below 15,000 feet you will feel far more control. During your mission, do not bother attempting to glide unless you reach a critical velocity or get down lower."

"What altitude do you think we'll be able to glide?" Boone asked.

"We've not done any high-speed drops yet," but since you will be approaching supersonic with the drogué attached, at 20,000 feet you will be able to glide nicely due to your velocity."

"How far do you think we'll be able to go on the horizontal during the mission?" Boone asked.

"At the 50,000-to-60,000-foot level which is your probable drop altitudes, you will not have a lot of control, but you will have some. Based on tests we have done we think you can obtain a 45-degree descent angle and have decent control down to 20,000 feet. At 20,000 feet since you will be going fast you will be able to maintain a 30 degree down angle.

"That should be fun," Boone replied.

"The other factor is wind direction. We will not launch you into the wind. You will come down with the wind to your back to give you the added push to the touchdown area. At the time of year of your mission, we believe that with the combination of wind and gliding you can easily go 30 miles horizontally from your launch point.

"Can we be tracked by radar?" Joanie asked.

"The glide Wingsuit is radar absorbing. It has very little reflective properties. Your helmet is coated with a radar absorbent as well as your combat boots."

Soon they were at 20,000 feet hovering above the target area. With new parachutes and helmets fully charged with oxygen, they stepped out the back and began their next Wingsuit ride down to the target's bullseye.

This time around with 8000 more feet of maneuvering, Boone and Joanie were able to work on their gliding skills. From the 20,000-foot level down to the parachute deployment they had a lot more time to experiment with controlling their flight and gliding.

The two spies did not know it yet, but mission plans will have them open the parachute at 2000 feet to make sure they more accurately reached their target and had less time vulnerable in the air. They would not practice 2,000-foot parachute deployment until after they did 50,000- and 60,000-foot jumps. The reason for two options on the drop zone depended on wind direction and speed. They preferred the 50,000-foot drops but if the wind was not cooperating with their plans, they would have no choice but to do it at 60,000 feet to give them the added glide range to get them closer to the target before parachute deployment.

Using robots for testing, they were trying to determine if they could suspend the use of a parachute if they landed on a body of water. The benefit of landing on water, if it was close to land, such as in a lake or large river, the parachute and other things with small weights would sink to the bottom making it easier to hide any artifacts the enemy might find. Since that research would not conclude prior to the mission the two would each be equipped with a small shovel to bury the helmet, parachute, and the Wingsuit.

After the 20,000-foot jump Toland saw he had some slack in the schedule and asked the two spies: "Do you want to try 30,000 feet today?" "Might as well," Boone said.

Joanie didn't want to appear as a wimp even though she was mildly scared and didn't say anything.

Up they went again. They had more than sufficient oxygen in their helmets and with a new parachute, they were ready to jump. After the crew and the jumpers had their helmets on and oxygen flowing, the cabin was depressurized, and the rear ramp lowered then the three jumped.

Just like before, the crew chief shut the rear ramp and started pressurizing the cabin as the pilot started chasing the jumpers down in a corkscrew trajectory keeping an eye on them and filming.

The two students felt the difference as they had far less control, but they did have a drogué this time. In the heads-up display, Boone could see the altitude and velocity. He was pointing straight down and obtained 500 miles per hour. He would have gone supersonic without the drogué. When they reached 20,000 feet the drogué was doing a much better job of slowing and the speed was dropping off. At this altitude Boone announced to the two other parachutists, "I'm going to start gliding now."

Joanie watched closely what Boone was doing and she copied his actions so that she flew with him in a reasonable fashion as they were now gliding together.

Toland, who was a much better Wingsuit jumper since he had substantial experience maneuvered and got into their 6:00 O'clock and followed them down filming them with his body cam. His instrument package would make a playback quite accurate as the microprocessor in the helmet recorded pitch, role, velocity, heading, altitude, and relative track calculated.

With all that the post flight replay and critique could show the glide ratio and other aspects of the descent based on how the students were handling their Wingsuits since Toland followed them down, their trajectory matched his.

They were not flying straight horizontal flight like they would in future drops and on the mission, but with all the instrumentation they could stretch out the corkscrew into actual miles traveled.

By the time they landed they had extended the distance from deployment to target by fifteen miles, which for a 30,000-foot drop was considered impressive.

Toland knew the obvious, Joanie was following the leader Boone. She needed to learn how to direct her own flight path so in subsequent drops to develop her capabilities, she would jump first, then Toland, then after a delay, Boone who would start out far behind.

This was the last drop of the day as they would go out and do the run and the swim like they did the day before.

The researcher's looking into the blurry infrared and ultraviolet image emanating from Boone's image, was in the drone pilots' room where all the telemetry arrived and preliminary information was available, long before the start of the next critique.

These were brilliant scientists who had a hand in creating portals. Nothing would surprise them. Their minds were open far more than the public. They would try to make heads or tails of what was happening with Boone, but what they discerned almost immediately was the determination as to what caused it was not going to come quickly.

When a person does hard exercise in the fashion Boone was doing, his endurance improves. In today's run, he was almost at the seven-mile distance when he was fatigued to the point he had to start the meditation. Up until this point the combined infrared and ultraviolet composite imagery looked the same as the other two without any significant or major difference.

Colonel Suzan Marklar suddenly was not feeling good about flying these researchers here for a wild goose chase that was probably just a technical problem with their instruments. At the seven-mile point Boone was starting to sweat profusely which was an expected trait and all three runners exhibited such body fluids. Then as Boone was starting to meditate because he was now feeling the pain suddenly the composite infrared and ultraviolet imagery started blurring again. The researchers were stunned. Today for the special investigation, they had a lead drone, but they also now had a chase drone a little further back, two independent sources of the imagery. The chase drone started showing the blurring on the composite precisely the same time as the lead drone's cameras with special wavelength capability.

One of the researchers said, "We must confirm what we are seeing. This is one of the most astonishing things I've ever seen, and it deserves a lot more investigation. We need to do this again tomorrow with a third drone digitizing and transmitting it via different telemetry receivers."

Colonel Suzan Marklar was starting to feel considerably better now that these distinguished professors had observed a simultaneous image via the second trailing drone source.

Colonel Suzan Marklar turned to Astor and said, "Whatever you had planned for them tomorrow will have to be changed to make sure we can carry out the scientists' measurements they just requested."

"I was going to give them a rest period tomorrow and do more glide drops. But in lieu of this situation, we'll have them run at the same time again tomorrow."

"How soon can we talk to Boone," one of the researchers asked.

"Boone will be almost crippled when he finishes the swim. We'll take him to see the doctor again, he'll get some injections and a massage. You will not be able to see him for at least two hours after he finishes the swim." Astor said.

"Not a problem, I'm more than willing to wait for a few hours as I've never seen anything like this before in my life. In fact, it gives me the willies." The Chief Scientist said.

"What do you mean by the willies," Astor asked."

"That's a colloquialism for someone that just saw a ghost." the Chief Scientist said. "I can attest to that," Astor replied.

"Alright, I think we'll grab a bite to eat, then come back here in two hours and see what the projected timeline is. We would like to interview him alone." the Chief Scientist said.

"Where do you want to interview him?" Astor asked.

"We could interview Boone in your conference room, but I think here is better because all the recordings are here that we can do the playback on when we talk to Boone." the Chief Scientist said.

"I'll have to have one of these technicians stay to operate the equipment for you," Astor said.

"That's fine. We'll take him to dinner with us and feed him some good food to make up for his lost time," the Chief Scientist said.

"I'm sure he wouldn't mind that, but can you please do me a favor?" Astor asked. "Sure, what would you like?" the Chief Scientist asked.

"You guys have a habit of recruiting my personnel. Promise me you will not recruit him to go work for you?" Astor asked.

"Of course, I'll swear to *Vekkar the Great's* Honor not to recruit him," the Chief Scientist said with a peculiar smile.

The scientists took the drone operator and video technician to a restaurant for a nice meal.

Boone and Joanie received their doctor's visits and a bath. Boone received the NURU massage, but Joanie only received a traditional massage.

Boone's muscles were hard as a brick. The massage therapist knew she was getting Boone excited in the bath where she climbed in and sat on his lap messaging his arms, shoulders and abdomen. The masseuse had removed her clothing and could feel Boones erection and rubbed against it rhythmically as she massaged Boone who felt invigorated and would have inserted it in her if she requested.

But even without going to the extra course they both were feeling mounting arousal and Boone quickly forgot about his aches and pain thanks to the injection the doctor gave him, and the chemicals dumped into the bath water that had muscle relaxers and pleasurizers.

After about ten minutes the massage therapist stood up and stepped out of the tub and dried off. She didn't bother putting her clothes on because the NURU message was coming next, and the masseuse would be climbing on Boone using her body to message him in ways he never experienced before.

The special oil the masseuse used today was the same substance organized crime used in their NURU massage parlors creating erotic sensations during complete body contact while both the masseur or masseuse and client are nude and coated with the oil, traditionally made from seaweed with the illegal compounds added.

Because the masseuse now made full body contact with Boone giving the massage hoped to give him a "happy ending."

NURU massage falls under legal prohibitions against prostitution and organized crime brothels in many Vekkar cities. VIA didn't care what technique the masseuse used if it was effective.

The beautiful masseuse didn't need penetration to give herself an orgasm nor did Boone. The way she rubbed against him created unusual pleasure that eventually caused an explosive release of pleasure for both as they each succumbed to the NURU now creating norepinephrine, serotonin, oxytocin, vasopressin, nitric oxide (NO), and the hormone prolactin releases in Boone's pleasure center in his brain that triggered Boone's massive ejaculation.

At the exact same time, the masseuse also had ejaculation gushing or squirting a clear fluid produced by the masseuse Skene's glands (paraurethral glands). They didn't need to perform the normal coitus to produce the wonderful feeling the two now had that invigorated both. All the oil on their bodies blended in well with their excrement's, thus if it was being filmed, nobody would know the difference.

In due time the two were in the bathtub again getting all the NURU oil off their bodies and redressed. Boone was feeling satisfied and suddenly realized he didn't know the remarkable woman's name.

"I'm sorry, I should have asked you sooner what your name is, but I've been conditioned not to do that in my line of business," Boone said.

"That's quite alright, we are indoctrinated not to give out our real names to patients. Let me tell you something in a whisper."

"Alright." Boone answered.

The masseuse approached Boone and whispered in his ear:

"My secret name is Zhēnabscoto (pronounced Gin-ab-scoto). The next time I see you I will tell you what it means."

The masseuse pulled away and soon the two smiled at each other as they both had more, they wanted to learn about the other.

Like all the multitudes of arranged events, an escort was immediately there to take the two spies back to their trailer who were feeling slight hunger knowing it was about their mealtime.

Chapter Fourteen

Adrak's Aura

Before Boone could walk up into the trailer Astor and a well-dressed stranger pulled up in an electric cart.

Astor and the researcher got out of the electric cart and approached Boone.

"Hello Boone, let me introduce you to Doctor Svirepy Drakon, who is the lead researcher in Portal Technology and other matters," Astor said.

"Pleased to meet you Doctor Svirepy Drakon," Boone (a.k.a. Adrak) said.

"Boone, I want to talk to you about something we are looking into, and I need your help in order for me to figure out how we need to investigate a scientific matter," Doctor Svirepy Drakon said.

"Sure, if I can be of assistance," Boone replied.

"Boone, I know it's almost your dinner time, but we need to go somewhere to look over some videos together and your input would help us realize some aspects of what we want to investigate," Doctor Svirepy Drakon said.

"Dinner can wait, I'm not all that hungry," Boone said, wondering WTF this was all about.

"Boone let's get in the cart and drive Doctor Svirepy Drakon over to Project KOBRA SPEKTR offices where we can have proper security for the discussions," Astor said.

"Sure," Boone replied and hopped in the cart.

A security guard opened the door for Joanie, to give her the unspoken message, this was none of her business, and she went inside where in a short while she was served her dinner wondering what Boone was involved in.

The cart retraced its way back to Project KOBRA SPEKTR offices where they all got out and Astor led the men through security and to the Drone Controller and Command Center.

Boone was a spy and had been in similar facilities and the electronics and displays did not faze him too much. But he did recognize there was a substantial installation in this room and thus knew to expect some interesting revelations.

Boone was introduced to Doctor Svirepy Drakon's associates and then they walked over to the replay displays the drone pilot had set up for the dog and pony show. The Drone Controller was spooked about as much as the rest of them because what they observed qualified as a paranormal event.

People like to know basic physics surrounding their environment and personal situations and this event caused them to think beyond their world and what may exist they never encountered before. The Portals that Doctor Svirepy Drakon developed was considered the spookiest event in galactic history and its implications were huge as the under rated Vekkar's were not only standing up well against the Tramular's, but they have inflicted some major disasters, especially the one's Boone (a.k.a. Adrak) personally was involved.

Doctor Svirepy Drakon directed the drone pilot to do the replay starting at about two minutes before video mark "A" which is where the infrared and ultraviolet fuzziness first started.

The video started playing and this was the run on the previous day. They watched it for a minute with nothing unusual or out of the ordinary showing other than three people running at about six miles per hour at a good pace.

"We are coming up on the first instance of what we want to talk about," Doctor Svirepy Drakon announced.

There was total silence in the room as everyone present had some emotions about what they were interpreting.

The drone pilot announced, "5 seconds to *Video Mark A*." Five seconds later it started showing the fuzziness.

Doctor Svirepy Drakon now said, "We are looking at a stitched infrared and ultraviolet video. Your trainers use these wavelengths to derive things such as body temperature, blood circulation, respiratory activity, and other physiological phenomena."

"Alright," Boone responded.

"Boone, I'm sure you see that Toland and Joanie do not have fuzziness on their images that are crisp and well defined," Doctor Svirepy Drakon said.

"Yes, I can see that." Boone responded.

"This is at the halfway point around mile post six, can you relate to us anything unusual you were thinking or doing at the time this fuzziness started?" Doctor Svirepy Drakon asked.

"Around the halfway point, I wasn't sure I could continue. I had a lot of pain from my injuries that are not fully recovered, and I knew I had to push myself and enhance my physical condition knowing I'm going on a dangerous mission behind enemy lines," Boone said.

"What kind of injuries did you have?" Doctor Svirepy Drakon asked.

"Look at my back and you will see all the bullet holes," Boone said and lifted his shirt showing the multiple scars.

Doctor Svirepy Drakon, looking at Boone's scar tissue on his back, knew he had experienced some incredible trauma and was lucky to be alive. Without his Kevlar body armor, he would be dead because the high-powered rounds would have torn through his body and his organs and killed him.

Astor then gave Doctor Svirepy Drakon a quick report on how long he was laid up and his surgeries and convalescence period.

"Can you tell me, is there anything special you did to push yourself to overcome your injuries?" Doctor Svirepy Drakon asked.

"This is about when I was meditating," Boone replied.

"You can meditate while you run?" Doctor Svirepy Drakon asked.

"Yes, as part of my training to deploy behind enemy lines, Interdimensional Transport Directorate, *Doctor Oxyuran Lepidotus Taipan* decided to send me to the *Vekkar Meditatsiya Institute* to learn advanced meditation techniques. One of them is silent meditation so that while I'm being beaten by the enemy if they captured me, I could use silent meditation for pain management."

"Interesting," Doctor Svirepy Drakon said. Then he asked, "Were you able to employ that meditation while running?"

"Yes, the *Vekkar Meditatsiya Institute* developed a method for me to perform meditation under extremely stressful events such as running away from an enemy or while engaged in a gun battle.

"You are absolutely sure this is when you started meditating?" Doctor Svirepy Drakon.

"If you back up the video a couple minutes, you will see we are curving around the end of the lake and run over a small bridge the stream flows into the lake and when we reach the center of the curve dead ahead is a rock clearing that has a pyramid shaped rock structure on the hillside. *Vekkar Meditatsiya Institute* trainers taught me to capture an image and put that in my mind and make it the center of my thoughts as I silently meditated while running."

They could not see that structure until they did the replay with the second drone flying behind them. Doctor Svirepy Drakon saw the little bridge and soon enough the pyramid shaped rock structure was dead ahead exactly at the time the image started blurring.

It was a somber moment in the drone control room as there were no answers, just a lot more questions with no idea how to proceed in investigating it.

"Perhaps the only events in Boone's life that are unusual from practically anyone else is the fact he had traveled through portals. *Was Portal travel part of it?"* Astor asked.

They went through videos of both days and Boone (a.k.a. Adrak) was almost astonished as Doctor Svirepy Drakon.

All of them knew one thing this would not be resolved any time soon. Another thing that came up shortly was Astor became extremely agitated because Doctor Svirepy Drakon knew people at the very top of the government and wanted Boone removed from the mission because he felt it would be in better national interest if they found out what Boone was creating while he was meditating, and his gut feeling was this somehow might be connected as a portal traveler.

That resulted in a major showdown a few days later with Colonel Suzan Marklar regretting she called in experts to investigate this phenomenon.

They were all in the Project KOBRA SPEKTR conference room with all interested parties including Boone, and a rep resentative from the leader of the Vekkar empire who had earned the reputation as the "Gopher." To say the room wasn't full of a lot of tense people was an understatement.

It all came down to what the head of the government decided, and his rep was there to announce the decision.

"Alright gentlemen, these are my instructions from our fearless leader. He understands the scientific significance of this investigation, which is perhaps the most remarkable event since our first Portal operation," Gopher stated.

Astor knew the pressure was on because planning and timing for the event were crucial. INTEL wanted this badly.

"And what precisely is those instructions sir, if you don't mind me asking," Astor responded.

"The decision will be made by 000050428A62315 (a.k.a. Adrak)," Gopher said. Everyone in the room knew Boone was an alias, but the number designator was valid.

All eyes were on Boone now as he responded:

"I kind of would like to know what's going on when I do this process as much as the rest of you. But first and foremost, I'm a Patriot and I know Astor is up against a clock."

Astor was looking directly at Boone intensely studying every word he uttered.

"We have some serious challenges ahead. I know this phenomenon of seemingly my aura is a novelty for the scientific community, because we have never experienced something like this before."

Astor looked at Boone and knew at that moment how important his decision was. After a short delay appearing like Boone was gathering his wits, he continued:

"I think the mission is more important than me finding out the cause of the anomaly I experience while meditating."

Astor knew right then and there Boone would make the supreme sacrifice if necessary. He was one of the most unusual spies ever ran before. He had been through more than almost all of them and endured bloody backstabbing from his peers. But even with all the diversity in his life and the sidebars of his personal life, he was still a soldier ready to march ahead smartly.

Doctor Svirepy Drakon was not happy this opportunity was slipping out of his hands and knew vividly talking to planners they expected Boone to have a 50% probability of coming back alive.

"If Boone is killed in this next mission, we will never have the chance to find out why all this was happening with his meditation," Doctor Svirepy Drakon said

But being a realist and a scientist, Doctor Svirepy Drakon knew the obvious, when it came to the INTEL boys, you were not going to win a fight especially with Boone siding with Astor.

Doctor Svirepy Drakon knew that Boone was aware he could easily back out of this mission and have years of research ahead of him where he would probably never have to endure dangerous missions for the rest of his life.

On one hand there was disappointment, but on the other hand there was appreciation for the fact they had such a noble person in the mix who gave their utmost. For that at least, Doctor Svirepy Drakon could be happy to have spent time with this rather incredible person who was unlike anyone he ever met in his lifetime.

"Alright, I understand all," Doctor Svirepy Drakon said. Then he asked, "When Boone comes back after his mission, would it be possible to borrow him to conduct the investigation I wish to do?"

"When Boone comes back from the mission, he will probably have to spend some time here for the debriefing and critiques. At that time, we'll invite you back to pick up where you left off with Boone and I'm sure he'll want to assist you," Astor said.

"Any chance I can have incremental access to Boone while he's training?" Doctor Svirepy Drakon asked.

Astor chimed right in now feeling slightly agitated knowing such a request might be granted by politically correct superiors:

"Due to the urgency of the mission, since Boone has chosen to continue training for it, we are now going to remove any further distractions so that he can concentrate on preparing for his mission."

Colonel Suzan Marklar intuitively thought those remarks were directed at her and she was absolutely correct because the very next day she was relieved and another Colonel "Blackjack" Langardo arrived to relieve Colonel Suzan Marklar.

Colonel "Blackjack" Langardo had a reputation in special forces and higher ups knew he would not be distracted and stay attuned to the task at hand.

Colonel Suzan Marklar was a great officer and tactician thus had redeeming qualities and because of her leadership skills and great proficiency at unconventional tactics was transferred to fighting units where her talents would best be served.

This worked out well for Colonel Suzan Marklar because she truly wanted to be with the troops in combat and not stuck in a training command. Plus, Colonel Suzan Marklar didn't mind getting away from the VIA and all their prima donna's.

To make sure Colonel Suzan Marklar received no undue punishment, her transfer was written in such a way to appear she was being rushed to a battle where the commander of a group of special forces was killed in a battle, which in fact was partially true.

Hence, nobody but Colonel Suzan Marklar, Astor, and few others knew the truth that was covered up and buried. Colonel Suzan Marklar left project KOBRA SPEKTR in flying colors and high regards. It irritated her for being relieved but at the same time she knew Astor looked out for her in the way he cleaned up the paper trail to obscure the true reason of her departure.

The next training day, they got a breather. The running and swimming were curtailed under the guise of classroom training and mission requirements.

Boone had a sore body and was pleased to get a breather to let his body heal some.

Joanie had some more psychological indoctrination with the psychiatrist who was overly concerned how she would feel victimized for her departure in the mission from her living standards when she was required to play the role of part of a couple and sleep with Boone possibly engaging in coitus to leave no doubt, they were a couple and not spies faking it.

That night Joanie decided she would end the psychiatrist overly concern who was not really used to dealing with deadly female spies who fully understood what all their weapons were.

After dinner and relaxation Joanie and Boone went to their bedrooms to rest like they normally would, but to Boones utter surprise Joanie knocked on his bedroom door and asked, "Boone, may I come in and talk to you for a while."

"Sure, come in," Boone answered.

Joanie was an attractive woman. She didn't need makeup, nor did she have any with her as it wasn't deemed necessary for this time with her training. Even without makeup she had a luster and cuteness that would motivate most men.

Boone was already lying in bed relaxing and thinking about sleep and would have gone to sleep in a short while until Joanie brought up the subject.

"The psychiatrist is over doing it with her concern about my role in the mission and how I have to sleep with you to give the appearance we are a couple."

"Is that so?" Boone asked.

"I need your help?" Joanie asked

"In what way?" Boone responded.

"I want to have sex with you now so tomorrow I can tell her we had sex and I enjoyed it and there is nothing to worry about," Joanie announce.

"Are you for real?" Boone asked.

Joanie had been sitting on the side of the bed, had a sleeping gown on, stood up dropped it to the floor showing she had on no undergarments exposing her womanhood, and crawled in bed with Boone and said:

"Don't fall in love with me. I do not love you; I just need to use you like a cheap whore to demonstrate this part of the mission is already well prepared and get that psychiatrist away from me."

"Alright I'll try to help; you be the conductor and tell me what to do."

Joanie pulled Boones undergarments down exposing his manliness. Perhaps he was in the state of shock, he had no erection that a man seeing the body of a beautiful woman might otherwise have.

Joanie knew Boone was probably in a state of bewilderment, not expecting such a radical event. As a trained seductress to perform honey pot schemes, if necessary, Joanie went down and started performing fellatio on Boone who responded very quickly.

As soon as Joanie had Boone rock hard, she mounted him and put his manliness inside her and began copulating in a fashion she knew would create a quick path to an orgasm for Boone. She had great vaginal muscles she practiced with her sex coach to get them strong for such an event if she had to do it.

Joanie knew the psychological aspect of it and how to induce orgasms a lot quicker than men think they can do it. Part of that psychological exploitation was her next statement:

"Go ahead and shoot your rocks inside me. I've already taken an anti-pregnancy pill, you are safe."

Just like she predicted the combination of squeezing Boone's penis with the strength of her vaginal muscles and the statement for psychological reasons short circuited Boone's pathway to orgasm and suddenly prolactin was flooding into the pleasure center of Boone's brain and the neuro-electrical process started his fantastic orgasm.

Boone (a.k.a. Adrak) knew he was shooting a lot of rocks into Joanie and was enjoying the transcendental effects immensely. Boone also loved the way she said, "Don't fall in love with me this is just training."

Soon they succumbed to their physical exhibition and Boone was laying there reflecting in a post orgasmic fog that was adding to the sleepiness he was feeling from the drugs put into his food for a restful sleep.

This was all business for Joanie who got up, went into Boone's bathroom, and took a washcloth and got it wet with nice warm water and went back to the bed and cleaned up Boone who awoke and felt appreciative of what she was doing, but she explained:

"I don't want you to smell funny in the morning when you wake up. Just forget this happened, it was just training, and you should be confident I will portray a person that is part of a loving couple. Don't get the words I say on the mission as reality. I don't love you; this is all mission related.

"Understand," Boone said. But at the same time, he enjoyed what Joanie did to him.

"Now close your eyes and go to sleep. All is well," Joanie said as she got up, walked to the bathroom and deposited the washcloth then went to her own bedroom where she took a Q-Tip took vaginal samples, put them in a plastic bag to hand to the psychiatrist in the morning to tell her not to get worked up about what she was going to be doing.

The next morning started out as normal, doctor visits and the psychiatrist came to deal with Joanies emotional fragility and then got the surprise of her life.

"This plastic bag has QTIPs that have Boones DNA on them from his sperm and are my vaginal samples." Joanie said then handed the psychiatrist the plastic bag.

Right then and there the psychiatrist started realizing *Joanie was a pathological spy. Joanie's whole being was first and foremost a spy, a deadly killer, and having sex for a mission was another small task that a good female spy would do in using all her weapons to defeat the enemy.*

The psychiatrist didn't know why she asked it, perhaps it was out of curiosity since Joanie had already completely shocked her with the revelation and samples to prove it that she copulated unemotionally with Boone, enticed her to ask the question:

"May I ask you a question Joanie?" The psychiatrist asked.

"Sure." Joanie replied.

"Have you ever killed someone?" The psychiatrist asked.

"Yes." Joanie replied.

"Was it work related?" The psychiatrist asked.

"In a spy's life sometimes, it is kill or be killed. I knew the other spy was going to kill me and self-preservation has a lot of incentives." Joanie replied.

The psychiatrist knew right then and there, Joanie was a spy, a cold-blooded murderer if necessary, and had been around the block.

The psychiatrist was wasting her time preparing Joanie for something that might happen on the mission when Joanie proved a head of time, it was expected and that's what being a spy is all about.

The psychiatrist then received another comment by Joanie that made her wish Joanie was not one of her assignments.

"All that matters in espionage and sabotage is success. What it takes to get it done doesn't really matter," Joanie said as she rationalized her activities.

"How so?" The psychiatrist asked.

"In some of my missions where I had to kill an enemy spy, both male and females I knew would save countless lives, which certainly was far more crucial than my modesty.

The psychiatrist's naivety was now utterly shattered beyond belief.

And Joanie then informed the psychiatrist the next shocker and reduced the future number of visits significantly:

"If Boone thinks that was a one-night stand, he's wrong. I will go back to him between now and deployment for proficiency training," Joanie advised.

"Why would Boone need proficiency training? He's probably as good as any other horny guy who wants to copulate in sex for sex?" The psychiatrist asked.

"When we do it during the mission, it must appear as if we are very acquainted with each other's mannerisms otherwise a good spy catcher might think we are faking it," Joanie said.

"You are something else," the Psychiatrist said.

"That's true. I'm a successful spy, otherwise I would not have been chosen for this mission."

"I would assume so," the psychiatrist replied.

"Here's something you need to know, and Astor will probably corroborate it if you ask him, I've already helped save Boone's life once already in support of the mission. Without my help an enemy spy who is very good at what she does, would have killed Boone."

"Thank you for telling and showing all this to me. It clarifies a lot, and it clearly tells me I was going about it with the wrong approach," the psychiatrist replied.

"You're welcome," Joanie replied.

"You are certainly far more advanced than I understood in the beginning. Your expertise and your awareness as well as your conduct advances your preparation for this mission to a great extent that I thought I was going to have to prepare you for, which to be honest I felt was a dirty task I didn't like doing."

"Now you know, preparation is not required, I'm teaching Boone all my mannerisms," Joanie said.

"You clarified a lot and thus have saved me a significant amount of time I would have otherwise wasted," the psychiatrist said.

"I know you wanted to help me. You are a nice person. I know what I need to do to prepare for this mission. I know it's very dangerous and we probably have a 50% chance of coming back alive."

"My whole approach will now change because you have gone way past the point of what I was hoping to accomplish thanks in part to your past training and expertise."

"Alright Doctor." Joanie said.

"I do want to visit with you now and then to see how you are holding up and I'll be available to assist you in any way I can," the psychiatrist said.

"Thank you I appreciate that and one thing you can help me with is I probably need some more anti-pregnancy pills so that I can work well at my proficiency training for Boone and choreography I need to design and teach him to perfection."

"I certainly will get you what you need," the psychiatrist said then stood up and held out her hand which Joanie took, and they exchanged a thank you type handshake, then the psychiatrist left with a lot of troubling thoughts.

The psychiatrist could not leave anything to chance. Sometimes patients are diabolical, and you get false information that distorts the reality of the situation. The psychiatrist did two things to confirm today's discussions with Joanie including lab tests on the vaginal swabs which confirmed the presence of Boone's DNA and anecdotal results of the copulation.

The psychiatrist also had a private meeting with Astor to confirm Joanie helped save Boone's life which was confirmed. The psychiatrist now knew Joanie's information was pure and accurate as would be the case with a very successful spy.

Wondering how Joanie killed both men and women did send chills down the psychiatrist's spine. Some of it was likely very dirty business like she had seen in holographic movies. The Psychiatrist was not too far off the mark because in one case when the large male spy was choking her to death, she had no choice but to do a reverse thumb punch into the assailant's eye socket. Since Joanie was unarmed as soon as she disorientated the enemy spy, she shoved two fingers in his eye sockets and wiggled them around like she was taught killing the guy.

What Joanie did to a female spy would make the psychiatrist puke and not to ever be around her again. It was best she didn't know, otherwise she would have nightmares for a long time.

The next day they had a jump at 50,000 feet which was highly successful, and the distance extended was twenty miles with the glide suits. Then more mission classroom training.

***

The day's training incorporated a new method of jumping. They jumped at 50,000 feet and continued in a straight like using the heads up display to fly towards a specific destination which happened to be the bull's eye they had jumped to many times.

This was the ultimate test in that it did not require calculations as their trackers would provide detailed placement recorded with lat-long markers on the results map. This digital map was a 3D real time image of their track and positioning from the time they left the VTOL until landing.

There was a road that went past the Bulls Eye that continued for several miles. Their instruction was to keep flying above that road until they hit 5000 feet then parachute down.

Thanks to the tail wind, Joanie and Boone achieved 30 miles on the horizontal flying with their Wingsuits. Planners were hoping they would obtain 30 miles during the mission without having to drop from 60,000 feet. But if there was no wind that day, they had no choice and would have to do the 60,000-foot drop.

The next day, they dropped from 60,000 feet with only a slight tailwind and traveled thirty-two miles along the dirt road that went past the bullseye.

Later that night, Joanie also decided she needed to give Boone more proficiency training in their sexual choreography and when doing it she explained to Boone why they had to act very familiar with each other's sexual performance to give the appearance of legitimacy. Of the two, Joanie was the better provocateur and choreographer.

By the time they deployed, Boone and Joanie would go at it as if they had been very familiar with each other for a while like a couple normally would.

There was a possibility the two would have to be rescued via portals, so Joanie was introduced to Inter Dimensional Portal transportation. She did several portals to get a feel for it and learn.

Colonel "Blackjack" Langardo and Astor were both happy that after Joanie's Interdimensional Portal experiences, her infrared/ultraviolet images did not get fuzzy like Boone.

Otherwise, Doctor Svirepy Drakon, who was still doing surveillance on Boone could use that as an excuse to jerk Boone off the mission or delay things to allow him to investigate this paranormal event as a side effect of Interdimensional Portal events.

Boone (a.k.a. Adrak) enjoyed getting his rocks off under the veil of mission requirements, and he knew the likelihood existed that after this mission was completed, he might never see Joanie again.

Adrak knew vividly Joanie's a spy living on borrowed time. So, if Boone (a.k.a. Adrak) were to let his emotions go beyond the usefulness of faking out the enemy, his world could be turned upside down if something happened to Joanie. It's one thing to feel bad about your co-worker getting killed. But it's another thing to know your lover was killed and would be far harder to cope with her death.

Boone (a.k.a. Adrak) already felt the remorse of leaving behind Martilene and Karli, two magnificent women. He could imagine the severity of a psychological trauma he would feel if he allowed himself to be in love with Joanie and she was captured or killed.

Boone also got his taste in psychoanalysts who probed him deeply to determine if any psychological attachment had manifested with Joanie. Being great analysts, they knew a few examples of what they were dealing with.

The analysts had a secret video of Boone and Joanie doing the *horizonal tango*. "You have no special feelings for Joanie?" the psychiatrist asked.

"No." Boone replied.

"Your love making you say things that tell us otherwise," the psychiatrist said.

"And how do you know that?" Boone asked, toying with the psychiatrist knowing damn well their rooms were probably bugged and secretly videoed.

"I'm sorry I can't reveal sensitive sources and methods," the psychiatrist responded.

"Listen, I'm a spy and a big boy. You don't think I have a clue?" Boone asked toying with the female strawberry blonde psychiatrist with aqua-blue marine eyes.

"I'm sorry I'm not going to discuss with you how we discover information," the woman said feeling slightly agitated.

"You have a flaw in your data acquisition system," Boone said.

"Why do you say that?" the female psychiatrist asked.

"You obviously did not record it all," Boone responded.

"What did we miss?" the Psychiatrist asked now, getting more agitated about to end the session.

"You understand I'm a spy and Joanie is a spy as well," Boone stated.

"Yes, I'm fully aware," the Psychiatrist said.

"Alright this is the part you missed because Joanie and I are not always near your microphones and video monitors. We were acting."

"What do you mean by that?

"We know when we go behind enemy lines where they are very clever and also do a lot of monitoring, we have to be convincing."

"Yes, I get that."

"Joanie knows we have to act like we are very familiar with each other, as a real couple would be, does that make sense to you?"

"Yes, it does."

"In our private discussions, we articulate how we are going to act to be convincing. The questions you posed me are evidence we were successful in our acting because you started believing I have some kind of emotional attachment to Joanie because of what we say to each other in the bedroom."

"It does portray you are real lovers in spite of what you might say."

"Go ahead and say that to Joanie and she will laugh at you."

"I just might do that."

"I'm going to tell you something about Joanie that will make your blood curl. She's a cold-blooded murderer and has killed and will kill again. She's first and foremost a spy. She's not interested in romance or relationships because she's like me, she knows we are living on borrowed time. We could be dead on the very next mission."

"I understand all that, Boone."

"I screwed up with Martilene and Karli. I allowed myself to obtain some level of emotional attachment to them which was very foolish because I will never see them again the rest of my life."

"You appear to have fully recovered from that romantic entanglement."

"Yes, I have, but I now know better to guard my emotions because the next woman will be more or the same, a temporal menagerie that I will never experience again the rest of my life."

"It's good that you understand it," the psychiatrist said.

"You may not realize, that even if Joanie and I survive this mission, we will likely go in different directions in the future, and it will unlikely be that she and I will ever work together again," Boone said.

"That would not surprise me," the psychiatrist said.

"As soon as we get back and she finishes her R&R she will start training for another mission and be assigned to go do something. She's a VIA spy. Her missions are standard spy protocols where they go about it in a legacy manner."

"What does that have to do with you?"

"I'm an Inter Dimensional Portal Spy. I seriously doubt Interdimensional Transport Directorate, *Doctor Oxyuran Lepidotus Taipan* will be willing to share me with VIA INTEL operations again after this."

"What makes you think that?"

"We have our own tasks that we must do, and he will not be able to spare me. Joanie and I will likely never see each other again."

"I'll believe it when I see it."

"You see it the way Joanie and I faked you out."

"I think you are telling me a fairy tale about this is all play acting and you are not emotionally touched to Joanie in any manner."

"This may not seem logical to you because what Joanie and I are doing is something that is rarely experienced in life by people. She could care less about my emotions when we are practicing our act to convince the Tramular's we are a couple."

"I'm not going to argue with you Boone. But when you get your heart shattered feel free to contact me so I can help you get over it."

"Doctor, I know you are probably good at what you do with normal people, and if I ever encounter a situation, I need help to get over it, I will contact you," Boone said with a hint of emotion.

"Boone, I've had briefings. I know you are going in harm's way and one or both of you might not make it back alive. I think when you finish the mission, if something goes wrong and you come back by yourself, you will not need to call me. I will know and I will find you," the psychiatrist said.

"Thank you, Doctor. I know you said that in all sincerity."

"You are welcome, Boone. And thank you for clarifying a lot of things for me. I must admit you and Joanie had me convinced you were lovers to the point I was going to recommend you not deploy together."

"Thanks for the affirmative backup that Joanie the choreographer did a great job in bringing us up to the level we could convince you. Because if we can convince a psychiatrist, we can probably convince a neophyte who is focused on the inherent aspects of a couple. That analyst will not know we are good actors."

Each day Boone grew steadily stronger, and the trainers knew it because the blurry image was happening later in his run when he was approaching the ten-mile mark before he started meditation.

Boone was also feeling better, less pain, more focused on the mission as briefings and the planning slowly unfurled his thoughts into the trepidation he knew would soon unfold. But training is done to minimize that.

When Colonel "Blackjack" Langardo received reports from Toland he felt Boone and Joanie had mastered the 50,000- and 60,000-foot lateral drops, he said the obvious which Toland expected:

"We are going to shift to night training now."

The insertion would be at night. They could not do it with an Interdimensional Portal because that operation might be detected and become a wasted effort.

The last thing the Tramular's would ever expect is a couple spies coming down to the planet in Wingsuits.

The night drops began in baby steps just like they did in daylight. The first drop was at 12,000 feet over the usual bullseye target.

The visors on their helmets had a night vision projection system just like a heads-up display, but the image was put on a curved surface recalibrated for spatial orientation like they were looking at the same imagery in daylight.

Night operations were significantly different, but it was not difficult. Just like before there were three jumpers. Toland went with them to rescue one of them if he had too and they opened the parachute at 5,000 feet to give him adaquate time to stop their fall.

Toland was trained for parachute rescue operations for such events. He had live guinea pigs to practice with, but if he didn't have them rescued by 4,000 feet, they would pull their own parachute. So, there was no risk.

After a week they did the longitudinal 50,000- and 60,000-foot drops and hoped for wind on the day of the insertion to avoid a 60,000-foot drop.

Then it was time for the big test. This was the moment when Toland had the most stress of his life.

When they went into the mission area, they had no choice but to deploy the

parachutes at 2000 feet to avoid observation. 5000 feet was unsatisfactory.

During the following days they went nice and slow starting at 5,000-foot openings then down to 4,000 feet, then 3,000 and finally 2,000 feet.

The 2,000-foot parachute deployments were a rush and great for a risk taker.

If one of the two were killed in the drop, the survivor would immediately be recalled with the carcass of the other via an Inter Dimensional Portal and the mission aborted.

Colonel "Blackjack" Langardo was hated by a lot of his men in the past. He was considered one of the most ruthless special forces commanders that ever existed. He seemed heartless and cruel. But he understood the paradigm of life, there is no substitute for success. Either succeed or you deserve to die. Failure cannot be tolerated.

Anyone who thought they would do one drop with parachute deployment at 2,000 feet and put a checkmark on the objective sheet was a fool.

Colonel "Blackjack" Langardo was a realist. He knew for a fact they could not predict the weather for a random selection of deployment date. To prevent spies from warning when they would deploy the two spies were prepared to deploy every day along with the entire support infrastructure.

They would report in and determine if they had the "GO" signal.

Just like SUMO wrestlers, they do not go at it until they damn well feel it's the moment. They will wait out the other guy stand up and come back 3 or 4 times, get their opponent as we as the referee and the crowd pissed off.

Astor, Sorge, Toland, and Lt. Colonel Tom Atractaspidi would meet in the morning and because of protocol, the chief trainer Colonel "Blackjack" Langardo had the final say on mission "GO."

Colonel "Blackjack" Langardo was not required to state his rationale for his decisions. It was all part of the game, and they knew it. They also knew never to *fuck with* Colonel "Blackjack" Langardo, because when you piss off the bull you might just get the horn.

Colonel "Blackjack" Langardo was in fact one of the most successful special forces leaders in history. One reason why he was successful was random deployments. The enemy could never predict when he was coming.

Colonel "Blackjack" Langardo had a simple trick for picking the day. He had his favorite book, and he would randomly open pages and if the page number turned out to be a perfect totient number he would deploy.

Note:

In number theory, a perfect totient number is an integer that is equal to the sum of its iterated totients. That is, one applies the totient function to a number n, apply it again to the resulting totient, and so on, until the number 1 is reached, and adds together the resulting sequence of numbers; if the sum equals n, then n is a perfect totient number. Number 111 is a perfect totient number.

If after seven days, if Colonel "Blackjack" Langardo was unable to obtain a random perfect totient number, he flipped a coin. Oddly he usually obtained the totient number within 3 or 4 days because he had an area in the book, he knew likely had the number.

When asked why, he would say, they need to do some more 2000-foot parachute openings from 50,000 and 60,000 feet.

To some extent Joanie and Boone were happy with the delays because they developed more confidence in their 2000-foot parachute openings. As much as the planners thought they had covered all the bases, there was additional classroom training going over the mission and more familiarity grew in each session.

Astor was starting to feel anxious because it seemed like there was no end in sight and he was about ready to ask for a private meeting with Colonel "Blackjack" Langardo to discuss the continual delay. He was going to ask for that meeting this morning right after the decision was stated.

Everyone required to be there including Joanie and Boone were there today at the request of Colonel "Blackjack" Langardo wearing his poker face.

All faces were on Colonel "Blackjack" Langardo as the moment of truth now came about. Everyone including the two spies were feeling anxious and dreading doing more jumps and running.

"It's a GO," Colonel "Blackjack" Langardo stated very calmly as if it was no big deal.

Astor sat there astonished wondering and asking himself WTF?

The GO signal set off a series of activities. All the chess pieces had to be moved now and quite frankly a lot of people were not ready. Spies could not get off the warning quick enough.

Chapter Fifteen

Karoline Morganthau

Karoline Morganthau, a.k.a. Agnes Renceladus slowly making inroads into discovery was out of position and didn't know 000050428A62315 (a.k.a. Adrak) had deployed for several days. Nor did she know where he was heading.

Another *Feint* built into the plans were the target planet. Only Colonel "Blackjack" Langardo, Astor, and Sorge knew the true destination. To pull off the *Feint*, Sorge had to ride with the spies in the deployment craft, a black marketer spaceship. It would launch a shuttle that would go as low as 50,000 feet and the two spies would jump from there. The shuttle would then go back up to the black marketer and fly to safety.

The *Feint* had the black marketer fly to planet *Drusyltania*. Go into orbit for a short period of time then leave. Tramulite's, who thought this was the target area, would then go on a massive search for Boone and Joanie.

Then the black marketer would fly a circuitous route to the real target, the planet of Fŏrlāgér. Using stolen identifications, they would arrive near the tourist town of Kōrāll where they would operate as tourists in an artist town like *Jămbŏdià Càrŭzŏ*.

People would get off at the train station and besides artists and restaurants there were *You-Tell-No-Tell-Motels* (YTNTM) where people on honeymoons or flings would check into.

The various YTNTM were used to having train passengers arrive without reservations traveling incognito cheating on their spouses or preventing people from knowing a romance was going on between two adults who were not prepared to disclose to their parents they were already sleeping together as couple's.

Through neutral countries VIA could send contractors in doing surveys for the tourist industry. They had no idea they were working for the VIA because the front company was so successful and supported numerous operations.

VIA thus had a great reconnaissance of the tourist town of Kōrāll at planet Fŏrlāgér deep inside the Tramulite empire. Using stolen identifications, Boone and Joanie would arrive near the town of Kōrāll during the night, then on a preplanned walk after they buried all their arrival gear wearing backpacks with clothes and domestic items take a short and obscure walk to a park that was near a train station.

By the time they arrived at the park it was sunup and morning people were out exercising and the couple blended in. This location was picked because it was close to the train station. They would wait for the first tourist train to arrive and then as it pulled away, they would walk from the train station to a hotel and check in, as expected from many couples wanting to utilize a YTNTM for their flings and affairs.

Based on the contractors providing a complete rundown of the tourist hotels in Kōrāll the couple planned to check into the Nètsòn de Plàtinā Resort which was probably operated by organized crime and thus assume all conversations are monitored. Hence Joanie and Boone knew they had to act like lovers right away because what is the first thing people do when they arrive at a Nètsòn de Plàtinā Resort for a fling? Big-A, right? Certainly, they were not there to investigate butterfly collections.

For this mission the two were given the opportunity to select names they had used in the past unassociated with missions against Tramulite's.

Sometimes the VIA had to spy on neutral worlds. When Joanie and Boone arrived at Kōrāll they checked into the Nètsòn de Plàtinā Resort under the alias of the stolen identities, Alexis Tegaro and Sabastian Rollie.

Just in case they were under surveillance, they planned on doing the horizontal tango on a theme from Paganini right away that would give the appearance of a typical fling in paradise.

Joanie was getting used to having sexual gratification in their choregraphed training they did together and regretted that one day soon the mission would be concluded, and she would no longer have her *boy toy* there to accommodate her physical needs.

Boone (a.k.a. Adrak) on the other hand knew to enjoy all the free stuff while he got it but realized that eventually all good things come to an end. All throughout this process he convinced himself it was sex for sex and nothing to do with love.

Boone's psychiatrist knew better. She understood vividly that Joanie was staining Boone's heart whether he liked it or not and the day of reconning might be sooner than Boone realized, especially if they ran into trouble during the mission and something bad happened to Joanie.

Nètsòn de Plàtinā Resort was not like a big city resort where people dressed up. They could calmly go to the Nètsòn de Plàtinā Resort restaurant to have their meals, enjoy the entertainment and come as they are. They would dress as ordinary and not stand out.

One of the unique attributes of the tourist town of Kōrāll included regular vehicles and Two-Wheel Terrain Sportster Rentals which all the train passengers that arrived could rent. Skycars were few and far between and none were available to rent. However, there were Skycar sightseeing tours they could purchase: one half hour or full hour rides.

The artificial intelligence APP on each of Alexis Tegaro (a.k.a. Joanie) and Sabastian Rollie (a.k.a. Boone a.k.a. Adrak) communicators was called Spěctrāl de Dòngtài. They operated as cloud applications and linked up to each other.

Spěctrāl de Dòngtài-Joanie was the name of the artificial intelligence on Alexis' communicator and Spěctrāl de Dòngtài-Boone was the name of the artificial intelligence on Boone's communicator.

To save room on the communicator's memory, they did not store the same information except for critical information and encrypted credits. When they spent a credit, it was zapped by a credit removal on the other communicator to prevent them from counterfeiting which would get them in trouble fast.

One communicator spent credits on the top of the index whereas the other communicator spent credits from the bottom of the index which would give them ample time to reconcile the transactions and prevent a counterfeit flag that would immediately send government agents after them.

Once either communicator reached the halfway point in the index no more credits would be disbursed until the other communicator shifted the index line opening more credits to be used.

Sabastian (a.k.a. Adrak) was happy to get right at the sexual activity. It did two things for him. It allowed him first and foremost to get his rocks off which he hadn't for a few days, and secondly to calm down and be at peace with his surroundings and deconflict his emotions surrounding the anticipation of greater events that would soon manifest.

After sex they dressed and decided to go for a walk and see the lay of the land. Thanks to the neutral worlds contractors filming the tourist town and creating a fantastic training document that allowed 3D holographic imagery during the training to make the viewer feel they were in the image, Sabastian Rollie (a.k.a. Adrak) and Alexis Tegaro (a.k.a. Joanie) had psychological conditioning of familiarity just as if they had been here before and knew their way around without looking at maps or asking for directions.

The tourist town was orientated based on a road that ran through town and the railroad and train station which was in the very center of the inner city.

On the outskirts of town were sparsely separate homes build on widely separated properties, a hold over for when farmers and ranchers used to operate until the tourism business slowly took its toll on them as most of them sold out to VIP's who wanted to live in an artist village or people that worked at the military base and could commute to and from work via commuter trains that stopped at a train station in a little town Arapakar next to the Tramulite spacecraft building ways and research center. Further on down the tracks past the military base and construction site, a medium size city existed where most of the base employees and contractors lived.

The two lovers (as they portrayed) walked along all the arts and crafts places and in order to look legitimate, they had to act the role.

Alexis found a few souvenirs along the way she felt the agency would mind her keeping after the mission and just like two lovers on a tryst, Sabastian insisted on buying them for Alexis which she responded in front of the business owner in utter delight just like a woman in a legitimate relationship would act under such circumstances. If there were a watcher or an enemy agent following them, they would conclude this was a legitimate couple out on a lover's tryst at a popular resort town.

After they shopped until they almost dropped, the two of them were feeling some hunger and unanimously determined to go back to the Nètsòn de Plàtinā Resort, deposited their purchases in their hotel room, then check out Nètsòn de Plàtinā Resort's dining facilities.

If they were being watched, the watchers would know they just did the boom boom a few hours before and no need to jump right back into it. Even though Alexis wouldn't mind if Sebastian made the first move and did it again. Alexis had plenty of gas in her tank and had quite a few more miles she could go on this fill up.

Alexis rationalized her situation as being with one of the top spies in the galaxy and a man with a tool and lots of strength to please a woman. She knew vividly most women realizing what and who Adrak was, likely would want to get out of their panties and get it on with him without any remorse.

Alexis (a.k.a. Joanie) felt blessed that role she performed in this spy intrigue afforded her the ability to use the famous spy as her own personal *boy toy* and she was going to get the maximum enjoyment out of it knowing she was living on borrowed time and could be killed any day now. Just getting to the planet in darkness in a Wingsuit jumping from 60,000 feet because the weather didn't cooperate underscored how dangerous this mission was, and they had not yet got to the dangerous portion, breaking into the military base and stealing the plans and possibly sabotaging the ship.

Every day an expendable probe would fly in space a safe distance away from the planet so that if the spies were in trouble they could request immediate evacuation. If that happened the Black Marketer Spaceship would approach the planet and bring them back via the Inter Dimensional Portal. When they were out walking about in a crowd, their two Spĕctrāl de Dòngtài that were equipped with mission timers and qualifiers would synchronize and the master Spĕctrāl de Dòngtài APP which resided in Spĕctrāl de Dòngtài-Boone and would send a scripted very short burst transmission lasting a millisecond that was the encoded message: Situation Normal All Conditions Satisfactory (SNACS).

After 72 hours if the probe did not receive a SNACS message that would mean possible betrayal and mission compromise or a lucky break for the enemy catching the two spies. That would trigger a trip wire. The next probe sent would arrive and send a Report Status Immediately (RSI). God help them if they received and RSI due to negligence or failure to comply with mission milestones. Since the two communicators that had self- awareness and visual capability by hacking into security cameras and their timers set up the basis for the reporting, so RSI should not happen.

The implication of and RSI message is the AI in the communicators were either compromised or damaged in such a way the SNACS message never got transmitted.

Since both spies were wearing conformal ear buds (not visible) they would be

notified the SNACS message was due and getting transmitted.

However, if either spy had reason to believe they were in trouble without permission from the other spy, which might be necessary under certain conditions, they could utter the code word BAT SNAC (Basic Action Terminated – Situation Now Actively Changing). Spĕctrāl de Dòngtài would then inform probe that would subsequently inform VIA and the extraction would commence.

Adrak and Joanie didn't know this at the time, they were only two days ahead of Karoline who discovered where the two spies were going through skullduggery.

The mole had not been stopped yet, but it was coming close as the counterintelligence agents were slowly getting enough information to nail the suspect. Unfortunately, by the time they apprehended the mole, Karoline had been gone for two hours and was on her way to stir things up good at the planet Fŏrlāgér.

In her after-action report Karoline cited her difficulties in dealing with 000050428A62315 (a.k.a. Adrak) stemmed from Boris Clevenger:

"Boris Clevenger's conduct was detrimental to the mission starting from not performing on the Intergalactic Transport and later his actions on planet Fŏrlāgér."

But all was not lost, Karoline had some mixed success that dovetailed nicely into her next mission.

***

Being directed by the two spies' stomachs and not their libido's the lovely couple of Alexis and Sabastian walked by some restaurants that looked promising, and would check out tomorrow, and made their way to the Nètsòn de Plàtinā Resort back to their room and placed todays purchases there.

It was perfect timing because Spĕctrāl de Dòngtài-Boone informed Adrak, "The SNACS message is ready to send."

Unless Otherwise Directed (*You know dear* a.k.a. Unless Otherwise Directed was the type of response) based on protocol, the SNACS message would be sent in about fifteen seconds. Adrak would have to stop it by a statement, or it was going to be broadcasted to the probe. After the fifteen second countdown, Spĕctrāl de Dòngtài-Boone transmitted the SNACS message.

As to not indicate the probe and Spĕctrāl de Dòngtài-Boone were synchronized in any manner, after a five-minute delay padded with random amount of time that could be up to several minutes later, the probe transmitted the receipt acknowledgement.

Spĕctrāl de Dòngtài-Boone received an acknowledgement from the probe indicating it received the receipt acknowledgement to the SNACS message and Adrak was duly informed through his conformal ear bud.

Back at Project KOBRA SPEKTR, Astor and Colonel "Blackjack" Langardo now knew phase one, *insertion*, completed satisfactory.

The two spies had a long way to go to complete the mission, but arrival and insertion was a very dangerous operation. Surviving that and staying viable as two spies with the element of surprise truly represented one small victory. Nevertheless, the battle was still being fought to the bitter end.

Joanie had a sixth sense. In her gut feeling she thought they were being monitored and she was correct. Organized crime was indeed monitoring her and deciding if any of their action deserved to go on the black web in some of the porn sights. What killed that deal from happening, was the couple portrayed themselves as a loving couple and not two sex heathens.

The people who were into voyeurism and porn wanted a sex heathen style act with a lot of verbal and sexual acrobatics. They didn't want plane love and respect style intercourse that two fond lovers very familiar with each other did.

Joanie was the supreme actor. Just before they left to go down to the resort's dining room, she approached Adrak and put her arms around him and hugged him and said, "Thank you darling for taking me on this vacation, it means a lot to me."

"You have always been kind and sweet to me, that's why I wanted to do this," Adrak said after he received three pats on his back from Joanie which was a signal she thought she discovered surveillance. *It's time to act.*

"I'm hungry, let's go check out the restaurant," Alexis (a.k.a. Joanie) said.

"I could use something to eat," Sabastian (a.k.a. Adrak) replied.

The two then left the room and made their way to the dining room.

The lovely Maître d' seated them at a table with a good view of the picturesque countryside that attracted a lot of tourists.

The waitress arrived and asked, "May I get you something to drink?"

"Do you have Trambrosier Elixir?" Alexis (a.k.a. Joanie) asked.

"Yes, we do." The waitress replied.

"That's what I'll have." Alexis responded.

"And you sir?" The waitress asked.

"I'll have what she's having," Sabastian said.

They looked over the menus and quickly came to decisions by the time the waitress appeared with their drinks to take their orders.

"I'll have the baked white fish," Alexis said.

"And you sir?"

"I would like the Baked Phasianidae," Sabastian replied.

"That's a great choice, one of our chef's best dishes," The waitress said.

There was some pleasant dinner music to add to the ambience of their meal. They had to take their time and play like tourists on a vacation and let it all unfold. They were also recorded in the dining hall as the management liked to see the clientele and what they ordered, as a means to make sure the staff was not stealing from them. They knew if a lot of diners ordered Baked Phasianidae an expensive entrée then they should show ample profits that night. Also, the Trambrosier Elixir is an expensive drink. The bean counters looked over the video.

Adrak and Joanie (a.k.a. Alexis Tegaro and Sabastian Rollie) had far more credits than they needed for the mission. The purpose was to bribe someone if they had to.

The meal had some friendly conversations about the day's events, shopping and what they wanted to do tomorrow.

"Maybe we can go on a Skycar Tour tomorrow," Sabastian said.

"I like that idea, honey," Alexis responded.

Sabastian (a.k.a. Adrak) gave Alexis a big smile.

"I would like to go shopping again, I saw some things I liked I want to buy."

Alexis said.

"Maybe we can do that after the Skycar tour. The brochure said they show some of the local mountains that would take too long to drive up and see," Sebastian said.

"During the Skycar Tour do you think they can land somewhere so we can take pictures?"

"I'm sure there are probably Skycar parking in the mountains for couples to take pictures for their memories," Sebastian said.

"That would be great. I know a couple women I want to make jealous by showing them some pictures of our trip," Alexis said.

"I'm sure the Skycar operator would be happy to take pictures for us. I'll give him a nice *picture taking tip* in advance to get his cooperation," Sebastian said.

"I like the way you operate honey." Alexis said.

Their meals were served and soon the comments started.

"This fish tastes so wonderful," Alexis said.

"This Baked Phasianidae melts in my mouth. The Chef knows what he's doing that's for sure," Sebastian said.

The conversations were monitored in the dining hall to sneak feedback to the staff. Little comments like Sebastian's about the Baked Phasianidae were added to the top 20 they would save on today's calendar and the chef would be notified as management liked to give the chef feedback on how he was preparing the food. Secretly obtaining this information was powerful because it was the unfettered truth and given privately without anyone influencing the conversation.

Just like many other couples Alexis and Sebastian were not in a big hurry. Because of management hearing real time the nice comments about the food which pleased them, the waitress was called into the manager's office for a moment.

"Yes sir, what may I help you with?" the waitress asked.

"The lovely couple that is sitting at table #18 had some good things to say about the food. I want you to take this vase and rose to their table and convey to them, we hope they can stay a little longer after their meal to hear our entertainment and the manager would like to come and talk to them about what they thought about the musicians," the manager said.

"Yes sir, I would be delighted to do so," the waitress said and smiled. She suspected that rose and the nice comments to the couple might net her a larger tip. She was not too far off the mark.

The purpose of the rose is so the manager could quickly come into the dining room and spot the table with the rose. It was like a homing beacon, so he didn't have to remember what the customer looked like.

The waitress delivered the rose in a vase to the table and gave the message. By now the Trambrosier Elixir was making them feel good because organized crime spiked it with slightly more narcotics than would normally be served at a restaurant or bar. It was a happy time for the couple.

Dinner time was slowly ending, and tables were cleaned off and new people arrived for entertainment and not dinner. No doubt a lot of Trambrosier Elixir and other such delightful drinks would be flowing.

The singer had not made her appearance yet. The band played dinner music but at the top of the hour it was show time.

The dining hall turned into a night club with a cabaret singer and an area near the band where dancers could enjoy their partners.

The singer appeared elegantly dressed and Sabastian (a.k.a. Adrak) thought this singer looked as good as Karli, who he truly admired. Karli was a class act. The dining hall transcended into a dance hall with fancy lighting for the singer and the lighting for the band operated from a nearby room with surveillance cameras and a lot of AI and robotic control of the lighting to give special effects.

The singer introduced herself as *Rose.*

Isn't that a coincidence, Sebastian thought as he looked suddenly down at the rose and made eye contact with the singer.

This was a routine for the establishment. The rose on the table not only helped the manager quickly find the table, but also the cabaret singer, *Rose*, was schooled to pay particular attention to the table with the rose and vase to percolate more enthusiasm. The ploy always worked.

Rose noticed the woman at the table was uniquely attractive and so was the man. With the attire the male patron wore, Rose could see he was exceptionally built and in great physical condition and not some couch potato that often showed up with a nagging wife.

Rose had an attitude. She thought, *the bimbo with the attractive man thinks she's cute, I'll show her a thing or two.*

Rose decided to hit a home run for the first time at bat. She dug into that first song she sang a thousand times and found ways to improve it some more. Rose had a voice ever as good as Karli and she poured on the charm.

The band could never figure out Rose. Sometimes she had these spurts of incredible talent, and she enthralled the crowd like tonight. If they could figure out how to get her to perform this well every night, they would be the best hit around bar none.

The first song was one of their showcase hits to expose their rarified talents. They usually opened the show with this song, and they had another they always ended with. Everything in the middle was randomly selected. The band played continuously for 45 minutes, and the singer Rose knew what song to sing as the leader of the band on a piano like instrument played the lead in which Rose knew to follow.

The manager had the routine down pat. He knew at after 40 minutes of playing he needed to go to the table with the rose offer them a drink on the house, ask if he could join them for a drink and then during their break Rose would walk around saying hello to the guests, then approach the managers table where he would introduce Rose and ask her to join them for a drink.

Just like he planned Rose arrived at the table and they got through the introductions, and she sat down directly across the table from Sebastian (a.k.a. Adrak).

Up closer Sebastian looked even better and the muscles in his arms and the dimensions quickly exposed to Rose the man was into physical fitness. Sebastian and Alexis had nice suntans from running and swimming doing physical training every day. Sebastian's hair was partially sun bleached that added an aura to him. The manager knew up close and personally this was a beautiful couple.

Looking at the tantalizing Alexis, the manager thought, this dude is *one lucky son of a bitch*. The manager had already observed the secret video taken from Alexis and Sebastian's resort hotel room and had seen Alexis's nude body. He thought he would take Rose into his office later and show her the incredible build on this man. *Maybe that might loosen her up a bit?*

The typical information flowed even though it was scripted and manufactured for the mission. The manager and Rose would never know the information was all fake and because it was simple and nothing spectacular, it was believable.

The Nètsòn de Plàtinā Resort manager and Rose swallowed hook, line, and sinker.

The conversations were friendly then the percussionist made a little noise on his digital drums to signal to the band it was time to start playing the next set.

Alexis was getting a little annoyed at the manager hanging around and the second song Rose sang in the second set was a slow dance. Alexis had never heard it before and didn't care she informed Sabastian, "I love this song, can we go dance?"

"Certainly."

The manager took the hint the couple wanted to enjoy each other, and he departed their table and went back to his office and looked at some more nude video of Alexis.

One thing the resort manager knew the couple made love; they were very familiar with each other meaning they probably had a long relationship.

Looking at the dude's muscles and build the resort manager had rarely seen a man built like this tourist before. Ther was no fat on the man, he was all muscle.

It was a pleasure to observe uncommon people in an uncommon situation. In the days to come when the investigators showed up and the manager discovered he was sitting next to a couple of top enemy spies he reflected. It was an incredible revelation to him. The investigators confiscated all his surveillance videos of the two spies. At least that's what they thought.

The manager was somewhat a pervert and made himself copies of the two and took them home before the investigation, and nobody knew. Those videos in due time would be priceless. He knew he could find buyers because wealthy people wanted videos of spies copulating, especially when they are considered the best in the business.

Sabastian (a.k.a. Adrak) felt good holding Alexis (a.k.a. Joanie) in his arms. Joanie thought Sebastian (she knew as Boone) was doing a great job of acting. But he wasn't acting. He was getting the milk for free, but at the same time, it didn't mean he couldn't appreciate a few breadcrumbs of life coming his way.

Adrak understood quite well after having to relearn it again with Karli and Martilene, not to fall in love with Joanie, for she was here today and gone tomorrow and if their managers knew they crossed over the line and developed and sort of bond and affection, they would go out of their way to separate them and send them in different directions. But in this case, Adrak would soon be sent in exclusive directions that would not have room for Joanie. He knew that and he also knew there was no point in a relationship with Joanie.

The love and feedback Adrak now gave to Joanie was nothing more than a temporal anomaly and he knew that, but if it made her feel better so be it. But, in reality it changed nothing. Adrak thought, *consider it a down payment for rejoicing if we complete the mission alive.*

In the slow dance Joanie could feel Adrak's erection and thought she needed to terminate things before they got out of control and said softly, "The manager is gone now, let's go sit down."

The two love birds rejoined their chairs with an unobstructed view of Rose singing.

Rose was pouring on the charm and was already scheming on how to break Sebastian away from the trollop so she could get her fangs into him.

Alexis had a 6th sense about other women and trained in body language she knew exactly what the singer Rose was up to. She really would not care if Adrak screwed Rose's brains out, but it would possibly interfere with them getting the job done. Alexis's focus was getting the job done and getting the hell out of here because they were in fact living in severe danger because they would not know if they were victims of betrayal until it was too late. Hence the sooner they finished and bugged out was preferable to Alexis (a.k.a. Joanie).

Alexis made a command decision and decided it was time to get the hell out of there before Rose made a bee line to them on her next break and poured on more charm.

"I think I would like to go for a walk and walk off some of this dinner, I stuffed myself," Alexis lied.

"Sure, let me pay and we can go."

Sebastian signaled the waitress who thought they were going to ask for refills and approached the table.

"Yes, sir how may I help you?" the waitress asked.

"I want to pay for the meal because we want to go for a walk."

Not a problem, just need you to hold your communicator and I'll send the funds request.

This was typical for Tramular worlds and thus Sebastian held his communicator that had a proximity detector from the charge device.

He quickly looked at the bill on his communicator and clicked accept and for the tip gave the top listed percentage posted.

When the waitress who immediately saw her tip, she was more than grateful and lavished Sebastian with fine positive comments, and a beautiful happy smile.

Adrak and Joanie (a.k.a. Alexis Tegaro and Sabastian Rollie) stood up and walked out of the Nètsòn de Plàtinā Resort dining hall/night club. Adrak understood Rose got to Joanie and that's why they were leaving. As they were walking away from the table, Adrak looked back at Rose and gave her a wink that Rose could not miss. It almost floored Rose because she felt sad the trollop was leading the man out of the club by his nose just like ancient people led water buffalo.

They went for a walk just a couple blocks and turned back. About that time, Spĕctrāl de Dòngtài notified both spies through their conformal ear buds:

"I confirmed your hotel room is bugged and has secret video. The night club is also bugged, and the manager is a pervert enjoying watching the video of you two copulating."

"I guess it's a good thing I had reconstructive surgery," Joanie said knowing her appearance had been changed and would be changed again after this mission. She then wondered, based on the scars on Boone's (a.k.a. Adrak) back, *did they change his appearance as well?*

"It looks like our training paid off, we are being observed," Boone (a.k.a. Adrak, a.k.a. Sebastian) said.

"I seriously doubt you will be given the opportunity to train with a female like me again," Joanie (a.k.a. Alexis) said.

"It was quite unusual," Adrak (a.k.a. Boone) said. But he wasn't just thinking of bedroom activity, he had a couple other training experiences he never expected in his life such as the Wingsuits and the blurry image he developed when he started meditating to overcome his pain running.

"It's a good time to go to bed and get some sleep," Joanie (a.k.a. Alexis) said.

"I agree. We can get up in the morning and walk around and get some exercise," Adrak (a.k.a. Boone) said.

In twenty minutes, they were back in their room and getting into bed. Mindful of the surveillance, Joanie cuddled up with Adrak who didn't mind because he knew she was the director of bedroom services.

The manager had infrared viewing of the room and when he looked at them cuddling and sleeping, he said to himself, *how sweet.* The manager was mildly disappointed they were not doing the horizontal tango on a theme from Paganini. He turned off his display, then relocated to the manager's bedroom in the Nètsòn de Plàtinā Resort next to his office where he could sleep and be woken up in case something came up that required his attention.

It was another typical night at the Nètsòn de Plàtinā Resort allowing the manager to have a good night's sleep without extraneous actions he might have to take.

Rose on the other hand was not satisfied. She had not been with a man for a while, and she was long overdue. The man she met tonight was the creature she wanted to experience.

Chapter Sixteen

Skycar Tour

The morning arrived too early. The two spies were suffering from Space Lag that could persist for a couple days. They didn't want to get up but Adrak (a.k.a. Sebastian/ Boone) had to get up and drain his lizard before Joanie took command of the bathroom. Once he performed that act, he could sit back, watch some Tramular Comnet News commonly referred to as TCN.

The OPSEC of the nearby Tramular military base was not up for prime time. In a way, the planet Fŏrlāgér was like a lot of other provincial worlds located deep inside Tramular Territory, and they had a Garrison like mentality which the average soldier was pleased not to be near the fighting but on the other hand asked themselves *WTF am I doing here?*

Duty at planet Fŏrlāgér was a dead-end job and a career killer for officers because Garrison mentality flourished here.

If it were not for the fact the Tramular Spacecraft Builder's Consortium was located at planet Fŏrlāgér, there might not be a reason to have a Garrison here in the first place. Nobody ever expected an attack here so no need for excessive defenses was a fore gone conclusion.

To make matters worse the few officers who had some hope of ever getting out of this rat hole and reassigned to a better career path were big on advertising the fact they were overseeing the construction of the Intergalactic Dreadnaught Carrier.

This disclosed information was INTEL at its finest and because Spĕctrāl de Dòngtài successfully hacked into Nètsòn de Plàtinā Resort's computer and computation network they could download the news reports and informed Adrak via his conformal ear bud what the Tramular Space Force is doing.

"That's a big SOB," Adrak said to himself as he watched the news report wondering *how the hell, they would get something so massive out into space?*

Just as Adrak was wondering, the interviewer asked the Tramular Space Force representative that very question.

The Space Force representative explained: "Since the outfitting will be completed out in space with no fighter bombers or weapons onboard and minimum crew of four people necessary to operate the Intergalactic Dreadnaught Carrier reducing critical weight, we just require a partial amount of fuel necessary to launch. Rocket boosters to assist the launch are now being attached to the hard points we normally mount defensive weapons. Scheduled in just a couple more days from now we'll launch the Intergalactic Dreadnaught Carrier to orbit in space allowing completion of outfitting."

Adrak now knew this mission was running out of time; they would have to act very quickly, especially if they had any notion of applying any sabotage.

As soon as Alexis (a.k.a. Joanie was dressed, Sabastian (a.k.a. Adrak) said, "I'm getting kind of hungry let's go find a restaurant and have some breakfast."

"I'm kind of hungry too, honey. Great idea," Alexis said.

The two were soon out the door and the manager was disappointed he would not be treated to some morning boom-boom show on his secret monitoring display.

The couple left the Nètsòn de Plàtinā Resort and walked up the street towards the train station where they knew most of the restaurants were located and saw Skycar rides vehicles lined up they would soon visit. As they were near one particular restaurant they smelled fresh baked bread.

"Let's try this place," Alexis said.

"Why not." Sabastian replied.

They were soon inside and seated as the crowd had not showed up since they were early.

They both requested Cobana Kāfēi, a nice drink laced with caffein.

Alexis was looking at the menu and asked Sabastian to order first while she thought about it.

Sabastian ordered: "I'll have the scrambled Kratchen Eggs covered with Mountain Tommy cheese, and Tommy bacon."

Alexis couldn't decide so she said, "I'll have what he's having."

Soon their meals were delivered since there were not many patrons yet in the restaurant. Coming with the meal was wonderful fresh baked bread that smelled so good along with Mountain Tommy butter. The white butter was soft and utterly delicious.

It did not take long for them to wrap up breakfast and Sabastian being the perfect gentleman asked Alexis: "Would you like to go back to the hotel room and freshen up before we go on the Sky tour?"

"No, I'm good to go, I want to get this done." Alexis replied.

"Alright." Sabastian said then led Alexis across the street to the first Skycar in line to give Sky tours.

"Can I help you sir?"

"Yes, we would like the one-hour Skycar tour."

"Would you mind holding your communicator so I can send you the bill for the fee?"

"Not a problem," Sabastian said as he held out his communicator.

As soon as Sabastian looked at the charge sent to his communicator, he approved the expenditure as well as a generous tip which the Skycar driver immediately recognized and appreciated. The Skycar driver liked people like this who showed their generosity up front. They were usually good people to take.

"Anywhere special you would like to go?" the Skycar driver asked.

"Yes, I would like to follow the train tracks up to the next town to see the sights, then fly over to the mountains." Sabastian said.

"Not a problem sir." The Skycar driver said.

"When we get to the mountains, is there a place you can land where we can take some pictures?" Sabastian asked.

"Absolutely." The Skycar driver said.

The Skycar venues didn't have very many customers because it was still early in the morning. As a result, the two passengers Alexix and Sabastian were sitting up front next to the driver with Alexis in the middle and could see directly ahead. Skycar tours usually flew at 1000 feet above ground, but that also meant 1000 feet above mountains and hills.

Based on Travel Industry experts hired as contractors to scout this area out for a future tour group that would descend upon it, the path along the railroad tracks had some of the most spectacular landscape. It was no coincidence other Skycar tours were going in the general direction.

The Skycar was not traveling very fast but in less than ten minutes they approached the town Arapakar that was situated next to the industrial center and the Tramular Space Force Base existed on the other side of the industrial area where spacecraft were built.

"This is the town of Arapakar we are coming up to, I'll slow down to give you a good view of the town," the Skycar driver said.

"Alright," Joanie replied.

"There wasn't much remarkable about Arapakar, but sightseers enjoyed looking at it from the air," the Skycar driver said.

They then flew around the outskirts of the industrial area.

"We are not allowed to fly directly over the industrial area, but from the side view of it you can see there are some substantial buildings on the site," the Skycar driver said.

"I would think the town would be larger with all that going on," Alexis said.

"A small city exists up the railroad tracks where a lot of workers commute from. A lot of people do not want to live in this small town," the Skycar driver said.

"I can understand why. I grew up in a small town," Alexis said.

Sabastian was waiting to see the Tramular Space Force Base, located North of the industrial area. As they were flying East of the Industrial area, Sabastian's followed the access road that was located East of the Industrial area and the Tramulite Space Force Base.

"What's that up ahead?" Sabastian asked to look natural even though he already knew what it was after watching the Tramulite Comnet News affiliate TCN.

That's a military base where we deploy our military spacecraft.

It looks like some Skycars are passing by it.

"Yes, in fact we will pass by it too on the way to the mountains. We must stay East of that road down below us."

"Are we allowed to take pictures?"

"There are no government officials in this Skycar to tell you no."

They flew less than a mile East from the new Intergalactic Dreadnaught Carrier following the road that went past the base.

Sitting out in the open, the monster size *Intergalactic Dreadnaught Carrier* Spacecraft appeared to be a work of art. Having recalled the Tramular Comnet News affiliate reporter earlier, Sabastian (a.k.a. Adrak) could see preparations. He saw the Tramulite's mounting solid rocket boosters on the hard points and several fuel trucks there ostensibly delivering liquid fuel to the spacecraft for its rocket engines that had fusion nuclear reactors that super-heated the fuel creating phenomenal thrust.

Sabastian (a.k.a. Adrak), not knowing the severe time limits now imposed on him with Karoline on the way, was fortunate he was hustling the problem along and saw the sitting ducks. This mission had two parts: steal the design plans, if you can and sabotage the ship if given the opportunity. Adrak made the command decision, sabotage the ship and then get the hell out of there with a Portal escape. He then thought of a way of doing it.

Adrak took a few pictures of the Intergalactic Dreadnaught Carrier as it flew past on its way to the nearby mountains.

The Skycar followed the terrain of the mountains flying above the road that went over them, but instead of crawling around the mountains in a slow speed like the vehicles down below, the Skycar flew up to the tops of the mountains in a span of time that would take those vehicles all day long.

Just like the Skycar driver knew, there were scenic views spread out along the mountains just for people like Sabastian and Alexis to take pictures against majestic backdrops. Some of these view parking areas had room for fifty Skycars and at times they were almost full of Skycars. But since the couple started out immediately after breakfast, they beat the crowds and were only one of two Skycars that landed at this time up on the viewing area. They exited the Skycar and walked over to a viewing area that had a platform on stilts sticking out 40 feet above the canyon below.

The Skycar driver appreciated the large tip and was very accommodative and asked if he could be of service taking pictures. The couple soon had a dozen pictures to remember their trip. Unfortunately, all those pictures would soon be confiscated by the VIA and sealed for 25 years. After that time if Adrak or Joanie wanted the pictures, they could request them.

If Adrak and Joanie they were both dead because of deaths associated with clandestine activities, then the pictures would go into archives until the government decided there was no purpose in maintaining them and at that time since they were all computer electronic files containing the pictures, the files would simply be sent to the bit- bucket where a digital bleach erased their existence.

One hour after they left on the Skycar tour they were taken back to the area next to the train station. As they were leaving the Skycar saying goodbye, Sebastian (a.k.a. Adrak asked the Skycar driver:

"Do you do night tours? I might want to see the nearby city lit up at night."

"Yes, I do but it costs a lot more."

"Do you have a business card?"

"My contact information is on your bill I sent you earlier for the payment."

"Alright thanks."

"Do you have any friends that do *Terrain Sportster* rentals?"

"In fact, I do, and one of them is up just a half a block from us."

"Could you introduce us?"

"It will be my pleasure."

The Skycar driver drove Sabastian and Alexis to his buddy Rokko's *Terrain Sportster* rentals and introduced them. Sabastian then rented a *Terrain Sportster* that had a second seat for a passenger.

"Have you driven one of these in the past?" Rokko said.

"Yes, I'm very familiar with them," Sebastian (a.k.a. Adrak) said.

"Alright I'll rent one to you, but I must have you drive with me for a few minutes so I can verify you know what you are doing." Rokko said.

"Sure, no problem," Sebastian said.

Rokko walked over to one of his bright shiny Terrain Sportsters and said this is your rental. Do you want your girlfriend to ride with you? Rokko said.

"Yes. She knows how to drive as well."

"Alright put on your helmets and follow me, I'll take you on a short drive and watch you." Rokko said.

"Not a problem." Sebastian said.

Inter Dimensional Portal Spy's and VIA agents were taught how to operate Terrain Sportsters because these modes of transportation were sometimes ideal for carrying out a mission as they can go to many places a vehicle cannot and in much tighter spaces.

Sabastian (a.k.a. Adrak) knew better than hot dogging it, this test drive included demonstrating respect for the law and decent handling.

Rokko led Sabastian on a route and watched him closely. It did not take Rokko long to figure out Sebastian knew how to handle a *Terrain Sportster*. Sabastian purchased the supplemental insurance as part of the rental so if he wrecked the *Terrain Sportster,* Rokko would get a new replacement for one that had a lot less miles on it. Rokko had given Sabastian and Alexis safety helmets and reminded them: "If you lose them, you buy them."

Rokko pulled into the front of his business and dismounted the *Terrain Sportster* he was riding and walked over to Sabastian.

"You look like you know what you are doing. Please treat the *Terrain Sportster* decently," Rokko said.

"I definitely will, and I'm not interested in risking injury," Sebastian replied.

"Too bad more people do not think like you do. Have a safe trip," Rokko said.

"Thank you," Sebastian replied.

Sabastian then drove the *Terrain Sportster* West along the main road, then pulled over to the side of the road and asked Alexis (a.k.a. Joanie), "Do you feel comfortable driving this *Terrain Sportster*?

"Yes, I'm very proficient in driving *Terrain Sportsters.*"

"Put on your throat patch so I can talk to you while we are driving."

"Sure."

The throat patch was a device that stuck to the side of the throat via a suction mechanism until released by verbal command to the communicator. It had good microphone acoustics and was covered with a special fabric that reduced noise from wind or other sources.

As soon as the two were situated, with Alexis as the driver and Sebastian the passenger they drove back out onto the road heading for Arapakar.

When Adrak wanted to talk to his AI Spĕctrāl de Dòngtài on the communicator, he did not say the whole title. He would simply start the sentence out with "Spĕctrāl."

"Spectral, give directions to Alexis for the road that runs East of the Tramulite Military Base we flew over earlier and took the pictures," Sebastian said.

"Route is calculated, Alexis will be given driving directions," Spĕctrāl de Dòngtài- Boone said.

Alexis (a.k.a. Joanie) was wondering what this was all about, but she knew they needed to get somewhere safe to talk about it. Even the *Terrain Sportster* could be bugged.

Sebastian did not preannounce anything. Spĕctrāl gave Alexis the instructions when to turn with advance warnings. They were lucky there was a streetlight at the turn making it safer to negotiate.

"Spĕctrāl, let me know when we are five miles past the Tramulite military base," Sebastian (a.k.a. Adrak) said.

Soon they drove past the base and the view was no better than up in the Skycar. However out in the open and exposed Spĕctrāl should be able to intercept communications signals and perform ISR. He would discover later what they could get.

They drove past the base and a short time later Spĕctrāl announced, "We have traveled five miles past the base."

"Good. Alexis, please pull over someplace safe."

Alexis found a driveway ahead they could pull into and turn around and not be near any traffic for added safety.

"Let's get off the *Terrain Sportster* and walk towards the trees to the right," Sabastian said.

The two were soon 50 feet away from the *Terrain Sportster* where Adrak thought it would be safe to talk.

"What are you thinking?" Joanie (portraying Alexis) asked.

"Let me ask Spĕctrāl some questions then I'll tell you what I'm thinking about planning."

"Alright."

"Spĕctrāl, were you able to breach Tramular fire walls and hack their networks?" Adrak asked.

"Boone (Spĕctrāl did not know Boone is actually Adrak), Tramular's use extensive amounts of wireless communications. I've been able to penetrate their networks and as we passed by the base I could break into their networks as well."

"Any possibility of finding a pathway to archives with the Intergalactic Dreadnaught Carrier design plans?"

"Yes, I have penetrated the archives and am in the process of downloading now. I anticipate download complete in about an hour."

"That's great."

"Spĕctrāl, are you able to hack into the Skycar navigation controls and fly them manually?"

"Boone during your Skycar tour, I hacked the Skycar and actually corrected some of the mistakes the driver made to make your ride safer."

"Great. If I ask you to fly a Skycar and crash, it into one of the fuel trucks parked by the Intergalactic Dreadnaught Carrier, can you accomplish it?"

"Most definitely. Thanks to the pictures you took today, I have the exact Lat Long of the Intergalactic Dreadnaught Carrier and the fuel trucks."

Boone looked at Joanie and said, "I'll tell you now, what I want to do."

After laying out the plan Joanie responded with, "I like that plan, I feel safer doing it this way."

"I know it's not the way Colonel "Blackjack" Langardo wanted us to do it. He wanted us to use brute force where one or both of us could be casualties," Boone said.

"I think we'll have plenty of opportunities in the future to do it the Colonel "Blackjack" Langardo method. I like this way better. I think it's smarter and more effective and we get the hell out of here sooner than later," Joanie said, then the two of them went back and got on the *Terrain Sportster.*

They drove back to the Nètsòn de Plàtinā Resort that had guest parking. When they arrived the parking lot attendant gave them a receipt for the parking and said his booth was near where the *Terrain Sportster* was parked, and he would keep an eye out for it.

They then went up to their room where the master of ceremonies Alexis thought this would likely be the last time she would ever have sex with Boone again and started the activities.

The creepy manager was going to be happy tonight because Alexis put on a show for him. The manager was self-administering his own gratification watching the two go at it. If they went to the restaurant tonight, which he hoped, he would certainly put a rose on their table since they earned it.

Boone now said to Joanie (a.k.a. Sebastian and Alexis) I want you to take your birth prevention pill now. That was the code word for antidote since they would soon go to the restaurant and needed protection from drugging in the elixirs as they needed to perform tonight. When Boone took his turn in the bathroom freshening up with a sprite shower, he too slipped in a pill in a way nobody would notice.

They soon made their way down to the resort dining hall and had their last supper for the mission with last sex completed. The rose was delivered, and the Cabaret Singer Rose arrived and poured on the charm. Tonight Alexis (a.k.a. Joanie) could give a damn how Rose acted since she and Boone were going to be gone soon.

Adrak estimated the time they needed the portals and instead of a SNACS message, a EOM (end of mission) message was sent with approximate time for the Portal to be provided. They would send a second RIE (request immediate evacuation) message eventually which Spĕctrāl would send the actual LAT-LONG to send the portal.

Sebastian had scheduled the night Sky tour and went there by himself. They had disposed of everything. Nothing was left behind. The manager by this time was sound to sleep and did not know the couple had bugged out.

Alexis headed out on the *Terrain Sportster* going to the spot they had turned into earlier in the day when they discussed the mission.

Sabastian got in the Skycar with the gentleman he met earlier and paid 3 times as much for the night Sky Tour and double the tip.

"Where's your girlfriend?" The Sky Tour Driver asked.

"We had great sex and she wanted to stay behind and sleep." Sabastian said.

"Sounds like a smart woman."

"She is."

Sabastian had the plan worked out today when he said the phrase, "I really enjoyed looking at that spaceship today," Spĕctrāl would take control of the Skycar and Adrak would inject the driver with a *night's out drug*. Adrak had Spĕctrāl drive to a park that was abandoned this time of night where he dropped off the driver. He didn't want to needlessly kill him. The Skycar then made its way to the rendezvous point and landed next to where Joanie was waiting.

Spĕctrāl had his instructions. He would control the Skycar following the *Terrain Sportster* carrying Boone and Joanie and veer off to the fueling trucks after they passed the base and pulled over so they could film the destruction. Just like they planned the

Skycar came down and struck the fueling trucks that were still half full of fuel starting a fire, but the battery in the Skycar had megawatts of stored energy that now had a rapid discharge creating a very hot plasma causing both fuel trucks to explode that then made the solid rocket boosters disintegrate.

The lonely gate guard controlling access to where the *Intergalactic Dreadnaught Carrier was* secured for the night, was instantly fried with the inferno so there was now no eyewitness as to what happened. Once the solid rocket boosters blew up the *Intergalactic Dreadnaught Carrier* which also had 400,000 pounds of fuel onboard lit off under pressure blew the Carrier into about 50 pieces some of which came down close to the two spies who were now hauling ass down the road to get on the main hiway and made their way back into town and dropped the sportster off at the rental in perfect condition, not that it really mattered.

The Skycar that wrecked was blown into a million pieces and nobody would ever know it was used because the smart people at the base were doing maintenance on the security system and none of the surveillance systems were operational and the Garrison minded commander knew nothing was going to happen in just 30 minutes, they would be back online in plenty of time for any event.

The couple walked down under a railway bridge near where they buried their glide suits, and Spĕctrāl sent the RIE message.

Several minutes later, two portals appeared, and the two spies departed the planet and were soon outbound on the Black Marketer ship going back to Project KOBRA SPEKTR offices for debrief.

When *Karoline Morganthau, a.k.a. Agnes Renceladus* arrived at Fŏrlāgér the next day, she was immediately sick to her stomach because she knew damn well who did this. She had no idea how, but she sure as hell knew who.

Then the investigations began, and nearby communities were scoured for clues and strangers who arrived within the time frame of the sabotage were investigated and quite often governments turn to organized crime to do their dirty work. They hire organized crime as contractors, and they seek information from all their associates. The manager of Nètsòn de Plàtinā Resort had a gut feeling he knew who the perpetrators were and informed his crime boss.

The next day *Karoline Morganthau, a.k.a. Agnes Renceladus* was in Nètsòn de Plàtinā Resort managers office looking at the videos and confirmed, "Those are our prime suspects." Tramulite agents then arrived and took away all the recorded information.

Karoline's respect for the two spies grew that day and she observed some of their sexual activities in the videos and at one point saw all the scars on Boone's back. That totally confirmed it. She also knew by information provided by the mole when Boone a.k.a. Adrak sustained those wounds. She also knew one other thing. Adrak killed Sidis.

Recalling when they were talking on the Intergalactic Transport a while back, Adrak did not seem like the mean and conniving person that one would expect a spy to be. He seemed gentle and soft, not the wrecker that he really is.

Had the Tramular *Intergalactic Dreadnaught Carrier* made it to space the Vekkar's might have lost over 100 ships trying to destroy it.

Chapter 16 Extra

A Time for Luster
A Time for a Mole

Astor and Colonel "Blackjack" Langardo received a visitor at the Project KOBRA SPEKTR. This man was the Gopher, a special operative for their illustrious leader. This man's official title was Special Assistant for Critical Initiatives. The reason why their leader picked this man to be his personal Gopher is he was clever and always figured out how to accomplish the leader's agenda. In fact, he was the only person in the chain of command the leader fully trusted.

The Special Assistant for Critical Initiatives met privately with Astor and Colonel "Blackjack" Langardo. These two men were also viewed as highly reliable, and the latest success story added greatly to the leader's viewpoint of their dedication and performance.

There was another person with the Special Assistant for Critical Initiatives. A man often considered rouge but nonetheless was known in the inner circles as a true warrior.

The special party the Gopher brought with him had a code name Spraticus.

Spraticus did dirty deeds for counterintelligence. Gopher's only purpose was to introduce Spraticus and state his project was officially sanctioned because their fearless leader had been fully briefed the mole in Interdimensional Transport Directorate came very close to sabotaging the successful mission that saved the lives of 100 spaceship crews plus a lot more damage that could have been done.

The other aspect of the recent successful mission was that because of the remarkable explosion that blew the hell out of the Tramular's future space carrier, it could never be patched up or restored. Any hope for a new carrier required laying a new keel and starting with basic construction.

The Tramular's had additional delays because once Spĕctrāl de Dòngtài finished downloading the design plans archives, he was able to toggle a bit in the memory protect system making the files read and writeable and proceeded to insert a worm that replaced the contents in the archives with random numbers. This was a terrible disaster as the Tramulite's would now have to go back to individual agencies and hoped they retained files to reconstruct the archives, or no space carrier would be built any time soon.

The conference room security system had a lock box. The *Gopher* had a special key he informed Astor he needed to insert. Astor knew quite well what the Gopher was going to insert. It was a deactivation key designed by security protocols and visionaries, that once the Gopher inserted his key which he was entitled by delegation of authority to insert, all sensors in the room were disabled until the key was removed. This was an added security measure to make sure a private meeting remained private.

"Spraticus will now inform you why we are here and what we expect out of you," the Gopher stated.

"Executive Director of Vekkar Interdimensional Transport Directorate, *Doctor Oxyuran Lepidotus Taipan,* was briefed a short while ago about what we are about to do. He was sadly informed we identified the mole in his office who came close to compromising the spectacular mission just completed. We came within 12 hours of that mission being compromised and assets captured or killed in the line of duty." Spraticus said.

"A mole is the responsibility of counterintelligence, why is Project KOBRA SPEKTR involved?" Astor asked.

"You were selected mainly because we have not determined if there are additional moles involved with VIA who Counterintelligence would normally assign what we are going to task you to do." Spraticus said.

"What if we decide we can't do it?" Astor asked.

"We'll quickly change the terminology from *ask* to *direct you to do it.*" Spraticus replied.

"Astor you know I can give you direct orders to do it by special government seal," the Gopher stated.

"Understand you can do that. What will we be doing?" Astor asked.

"Interdimensional Transport Directorate, *Doctor Oxyuran Lepidotus Taipan,* who is working with us to remove the mole is sending him on a mission. The mole does not know we are doing unprecedented surveillance on him. We have already discovered he had informed his Tramular controller about his mission. He thinks he's going there to support 000050428A62315 (a.k.a. Adrak). Unfortunately, Adrak will have to go there to be the bait. A Tramular's SMERSH team plan on capturing Adrak and taking him back to their home worlds and make a show case of they can get our spies who do a lot of damage and teach them a lesson," the Gopher stated.

"The Mole will be brought into a scenario where he gets involved in a shootout protecting and saving Adrak but makes the supreme sacrifice in doing so. Meanwhile we will kill or capture important Tramulite SMERSH agents being sent to be part of this takedown," Spraticus chimed in.

"Alright why did you pick us?" Astor asked.

"It's quite simple. Colonel "Blackjack" Langardo's reputation proceeds him. He's an expert at planning and executing ambushes and making things look the way we want them too."

"What is it we want to project?" Colonel "Blackjack" Langardo asked.

"At the Mole's memorial we'll have in the future, you, Colonel "Blackjack" Langardo, will state the Mole was one of our very best double spies and personally foiled the attempt on agent 000050428A62315 (a.k.a. Adrak), giving his life as the rear guard so that wounded Adrak could be evacuated. When his position was simultaneously attacked by SMERSH agents the gun battle that erupted resulted in all the SMERSH agents killed along with the Mole.

"Will we give out the Mole's name?" Astor asked.

"No because we must protect his family who doesn't know about his treachery.

The memorial will be videotaped for the family who will not be invited to attend for their own safety, and they will be informed because of potential retaliation. He will only be identified by his special designator 000090317A512941," the Gopher said.

"What's Spraticus role in all this?" Colonel "Blackjack" Langardo asked.

"I will be loosely with your team. My specific task is to assassinate the Mole and make sure he does not survive the gun battle."

"If that's the case, why don't you just go kill the Mole and be done with him?"

"We want to take down as many SMERSH agents as possible plus we want to give the appearance the MOLE was a double agent spoon feeding them disinformation. It's all part of a greater strategy," Spraticus said.

"How is 000050428A62315 (a.k.a. Adrak) going to be protected since he's the decoy?"

"I will have a few of my people in place to protect 000050428A62315 (a.k.a. Adrak). As soon as the shooting starts, he will be transported via Inter Dimensional Portal to an orbiting ship and out of harm's way. His only purpose in life is to be the decoy to get SMERSH agents in position for the gunfight," Spraticus said.

"I'm going to have to inform 000050428A62315 (a.k.a. Adrak) about this because he will be in harm's way," Astor said.

"We would assume you did. We in fact planned for it. When we leave here in a short while, 000050428A62315 (a.k.a. Adrak) is coming with us to Counterintelligence and he will be briefed by his boss *Doctor Oxyuran Lepidotus Taipan* who is there now waiting."

"Will 000050428A62315 (a.k.a. Adrak) be informed who the mole is?" Astor asked.

"000050428A62315 (a.k.a. Adrak) knows it's one of three people. With me present *Doctor Oxyuran Lepidotus Taipan* will disclose who the mole is in case something goes awry, he can protect himself and he will be informed by *Doctor Oxyuran Lepidotus Taipan* lethal force is authorized and if the Mole makes any threatening move towards him, he is authorized to use deadly force to protect his own life," Spraticus said.

"We were not quite done with the debrief with 000050428A62315 (a.k.a. Adrak)," Astor said.

"No further debriefing is necessary. We have complete confirmation of the results of the mission. The *Intergalactic Dreadnaught Carrier* was destroyed thanks to the placement of the fuel trucks, partial fueling of the Carrier, and the solid rocket boosters mounted and next to the fuel trucks." Spraticus said.

"We were lucky 000050428A62315 (a.k.a. Adrak) used the Skycar as the weapon because when its battery did the unscheduled rapid discharge, it created a plasma that turned those solid rockets into a larger plasma igniting all the Carrier's fuel under pressure in the fuel tanks multiplying the explosive potential," Astor noted

"Thanks to the EOM (end of mission) message 000050428A62315 (a.k.a. Adrak) estimated the time they needed the approximate time for the Portal to be provided, and ISR probe was sent from a Fast Frigate stationed at a nearby uninhabited planet to provide emergency egress help. The ISR probe was in an excellent position to record the demolition and in the morning after sunrise the debris field created by the former Intergalactic Dreadnaught Carrier. We also have communications intercepts reporting to their leaders what happened to the spaceship, it was a complete loss," The Gopher said.

'Interesting," Astor said.

"We also have data scientists pouring over the archived data and have confirmed most of the design information we obtained. Further debriefings are not necessary for now. If we come across new information that requires clarification, then we can bring the two spies back in for further debriefing." The Gopher added.

"What about mission training?" Astor asked.

"You trained 000050428A62315 (a.k.a. Adrak) so well, he just achieved one of the greatest acts of espionage in VIA history. And many other missions that netted far less results had substantially more training. We think since this was such a fast-paced mission just concluded, 000050428A62315 (a.k.a. Adrak) does not need any more training. Information he will need and weapons he'll be using for his own protection will be provided today," Spraticus replied.

"000050428A62315 (a.k.a. Adrak) is down in his trailer right now having a meal between debriefings," Astor said.

"Send someone to bring him here. We will leave with him in a few minutes by VTOL," the *Gopher* said.

Astor nodded at Colonel "Blackjack" Langardo who knew he was just appointed as the person to bring 000050428A62315 (a.k.a. Adrak) known as Boone to the conference room.

When the security guard opened the trailer door for Colonel "Blackjack" Langardo, Boone (a.k.a. Adrak) was quite surprised and was almost finished with his meal.

"Hello Boone, I need to talk with you for a few minutes."

"Sure." Boone said.

"I hate to be the bearer of bad news, but you are going on another mission right away." Colonel "Blackjack" Langardo said.

"I thought as soon as we finished this debrief, I was going back to the Inter Dimensional Portal Directorate." Boone replied.

"I was sent here by Astor to escort you to Project KOBRA SPEKTR conference room."

"I was just there forty-five minutes ago, why couldn't this be discussed then?"

"Immediately after you left, we had some special visitors." Colonel "Blackjack" Langardo said.

"I see." Boone replied.

"I can't discuss it here, because this trailer is not cleared for this security level."

"No problem I understand." Boone said.

"Are you finished eating?" Colonel "Blackjack" Langardo asked.

"I think I had enough for now. If I'm going on another mission, the rest of the meal doesn't matter." Boone said.

"Good, come with me and you will get briefed in the conference room."

"Sure, no problem." Boone said.

The two men left the trailer and got into the electric cart that made its way to parking at the Project KOBRA SPEKTR facility. They must have been expecting Boone because all the doors were opened for him on his way to the conference room. It was quiet in the elevator and Project KOBRA SPEKTR was not going to reveal anything outside the conference room, not that it mattered to Adrak (a.k.a. Boone).

When Adrak entered the conference room, the Gopher and Spraticus stood up and walked over to him and greeted him.

"It's good to meet you, agent 000050428A62315 (a.k.a. Adrak)," the Gopher said and held out his hand for an official handshake. Normally they only bowed.

"Thank you." Adrak replied.

"I'm the special envoy from our leader and also the person who gave Astor the assignment that you will be part of." The Gopher said

"Alright, glad to help out if I can." Boone said.

With the blinking blue light on, the Gopher turned to Astor and asked, "Is every one of your people cleared to know agent 000050428A62315 (a.k.a. Adrak's) real name?"

"Yes, they are cleared to know his real name and know it," Astor said which completely surprised Adrak.

"Good. Adrak I'm sorry we have to put you in harm's way so soon after your last mission, but this mission will help us deal with the mole who has compromised you."

"Good, I'm all for that," Adrak responded.

"You were twelve hours away from being captured by *Karoline Morganthau, a.k.a. Agnes Renceladus* in your last mission. Thanks in part to your fast thinking and extraordinary timing, you and Joanie pulled off one of the greatest acts of espionage and sabotage in VIA history before she arrived to arrest you." The Gopher said.

"Thanks for the nice comments but I don't think it was that tough." Adrak replied.

"You don't know how tough you really had it because you were not aware that Interdimensional Transport Directorate, *Doctor Oxyuran Lepidotus Taipan* has a mole working for him."

"Is that so?"

"The reason why *Karoline Morganthau, a.k.a. Agnes Renceladus* and her accomplice, a person named Boris Clevenger were on the Transport that brought you to this planet, was to follow you and discover where you would be training, and what it is you were training for, because a mole betrayed you," the Gopher stated.

"Alright." Adrak replied.

"Thanks to delay in the mole providing your mission destination to planet Fŏrlāgér, you arrived there just in time to do the work, and you brainstormed the solution in-situ and accomplished everything we hoped you would."

"To be honest, I wanted to get it done and leave and I figured if we could come up quickly with the results of the desired mission milestones, then it would be in our best interest to get it done and leave," Adrak stated.

Your planning was very providential in that it allowed you to leave Fŏrlāgér 12 hours before *Karoline Morganthau* and her takedown team arrived. She showed up with a substantial force, you would have been trapped and arrested and likely executed had you not engineered such an elaborate egress plan."

"What is my new mission?"

"I know you are not going to like this because you will feel we are putting you into danger, but we need to correct the situation with the mole."

"What's my role?"

"You are the decoy."

The Gopher's statement hit Adrak like a ton of bricks. It meant he was a bait and could easily be killed. Adrak did not respond, waiting to hear more about the mission.

"The blue light is flashing which means this is a guarded discussion and compartmentalized. You can rest assured very few people outside this room know what's going on. Nobody in this room will leak this information, because they are our most trusted people."

"Alright."

"Besides counterintelligence, Interdimensional Transport Directorate, *Doctor Oxyuran Lepidotus Taipan* is the only other person who knows who the mole is, one of your co-workers who has undermined you several times and almost got you killed a few times. He's responsible for those scars on your back. You are lucky you were not killed."

Adrak intensely listened to the Gopher because he now felt some passion.

"If I knew who the mole is I would kill him with my own bear hands as soon as I can get my hands on him." Adrak said with a tinge of emotion.

"You will be meeting in a short while with Interdimensional Transport Directorate, *Doctor Oxyuran Lepidotus Taipan.* He will tell you who the mole is. We want him reveal who the person is so that you have no doubt about the information." The Gopher said.

"Alright."

"We have set up a dummy mission. The mole has already reported it to his Tramulite contact. The SMERSH people are sending in people to kill you including the illustrious *Karoline Morganthau, a.k.a. Agnes Renceladus* and her side kick Boris Clevenger. They have a group of SMERSH agents as part of your takedown team."

"How does the mole fit into all this?" Adrak asked.

"The mole is being sent to provide you affirmative backup. He tried to wiggle his way out of it, but *Doctor Oxyuran Lepidotus Taipan* explained to him he had no option he was going to back you up."

"If it's who I think it is, he always comes up with wife and kid stories and people like me end up taking all his missions. The guy is nothing more than an office warrior."

"Precisely. When the mole said his wife was having issues, *Doctor Oxyuran Lepidotus Taipan* said this mission was so crucial they would have no option but to put her in a mental hospital and his children in a care center until you finished the mission and came back."

"He's never used such strong threats before."

"What this mission is about is taking out several SMERSH agents at the same time we deal with the mole. If he points a weapon at you or is threatening you in any way, you are authorized deadly force. If he becomes a hero protecting you and collateral casualty, then so be it. His wife will be proud of him and enjoy his pension and insurance policy."

"When am I traveling for this mission?"

"We are leaving now, and you are coming with us. You will be escorted with us to our VTOL that should be arriving up on the roof top about now."

"Alright," Adrak said.

Everyone in the room then left and went up to the top of the hill via an elevator where the camouflaged landing pad existed. As soon as the VTOL came close the camouflage cover shifted, the VTOL then landed. Moments later the group boarded the VTOL that took off and went subsonic a good distance to a spaceport where a private intergalactic transport was waiting for them.

It did not take long for the VTOL to arrive at planet *Heuronvale* spaceport. The men were put on an unmarked intergalactic transport mounted on a flying wing. They were soon in the air heading up into space. Once they were in orbit around the planet the next surprise happened. A shuttle came and picked them up and took them to a Vekkar Fast Frigate that subsequently took them to the Vekkar home world.

Adrak smiled because he knew he was not far from Vekkar Interdimensional Transport Directorate. Suddenly the men were shuttled down to a mountain outpost

Adrak thought he knew a lot about this planet but had never seen this place before. Inside the outpost, they were put on a tube train that could travel at fast speeds that soon deposited them to another facility they all entered and were escorted to their destination.

Adrak knew better than to ask questions and followed along and was taken to a secure conference room that had a blue light blinking in it. This was serious business!

The men took their seats at the conference table that had placards telling them where to sit so that counterintelligence people at the meeting would know who they are talking with.

Moments after everyone was seated, except for an empty chair that was not yet occupied, the door suddenly opened and in walked Interdimensional Transport Directorate, *Doctor Oxyuran Lepidotus Taipan,* who was escorted to his seat.

The man sitting at the end of the table who appeared to be running the show suddenly began talking.

Counterintelligence C2 director:

My name is "Q." People in the room knew "Q" was his code name. Just like the rest of them, with 0000xxxxxxxxx designators, his identity could not be revealed.

It appears everyone is here that was requested, we'll start now. Rarely have I seen so many distinguished people together as now. I feel it's an extraordinary privilege since I know what each one of you do. Since some of you do not know where you are, we are inside a counterintelligence facility. As you know we work independently of all of you and from lessons learned in the past, we rarely disclose to you what we are doing for your own good because like today we are dealing with a mole in *Doctor Oxyuran Lepidotus Taipan's office*. He didn't know he had a mole until we informed him."

Agent 000050428A62315 (a.k.a. Adrak) was almost killed and captured a few times because of this mole. Agent 000050428A62315's back is covered with nasty scars from being shot in an ambush perpetrated by the mole.

The reason why some of you were asked to come and participate in a team is we are going to use the mole to capture or kill a group of SMERSH agents that have been deployed to capture or kill agent 000050428A62315 (a.k.a. Adrak).

Doctor Oxyuran Lepidotus Taipan has assigned the mole to travel to planet *Craterus* where a set piece takedown is being staged. The mole thinks he' being sent as affirmative backup to agent 000050428A62315 (a.k.a. Adrak) who is our sacrificial lamb known as a *decoy* in the business.

Since timing and execution is critical and we did not want the mole to tip off his SMERSH handler he was being sent to where agent 000050428A62315 was traveling to planet Craterus. The mole was escorted from *Doctor Oxyuran Lepidotus Taipan's* office directly to the spaceport and departed the planet as soon as *Doctor Oxyuran Lepidotus Taipan* finished the conversation to prevent him from contacting his SMERSH controller that might have triggered a trip wire resulting in SMERSH avoiding the trap.

The whole plan will be discussed with you people on the Fast Frigate that will take you to *Craterus. Doctor Oxyuran Lepidotus Taipan* will not be going with you. His purpose for being at this meeting is to inform 000050428A62315 who betrayed him so that he will know who to protect himself against. He will also now be given permission to use deadly force. *Doctor Oxyuran Lepidotus Taipan*, please provide the information you planned on presenting.

Doctor Oxyuran Lepidotus Taipan looked directly at Adrak who the focus of his discussion was, then he said:

"I'm very sorry about the pain and suffering you went through when you were seriously wounded because of the betrayal. You know his real name but for people in this room they can only be told he is 000090317A512941 (a.k.a. Zmeya Rembert).

Adrak wasn't shocked. Zmeya Rembert was the ringleader of the 3 amigos who were the source of several critiques he went through, which he could have lost his job and his reputation.

"Is there any chance his two buddies are involved?" Adrak asked.

"We are looking into that and if we find evidence, counterintelligence will take care of it quite differently than in this case. Your participation in this operation is because counterintelligence needs you as the decoy. That's the only way we can lead the SMERSH agents into a trap."

"Thanks for the information, I will feel safer now knowing who to protect myself from." Adrak stated.

"You have authorization to use deadly force. 000090317A512941 is a traitor and a dangerous spy. If he makes any dangerous movement towards you, we expect you to protect yourself."

"Understand."

The remaining time explained logistics to the mission. The intricate spy business would be laid out on the Fast Frigate that would take them to *Craterus.*

The Mole 000090317A512941 (a.k.a. Zmeya Rembert) was traveling to Craterus with escorts to make sure he arrived in the set piece ambush. They were none other than Corgrelius and Joanie. They too had their special instructions, if 000090317A512941 (a.k.a. Zmeya Rembert) didn't cooperate, they would sedate him and he would wake up a few feet away from Adrak put in the decoy spot they wanted him to be for *Karoline Morganthau, a.k.a. Agnes Renceladus* to make a play for capture or kill.

Since spies are taught to shoot the laser blasters at the midsection to fry the hearts and kill the person quickly, Adrak would be wearing a special laser protector that could defend him for several laser shots. There would not be enough time to attempt any more shots as the SMERSH agents would be taken down by then.

The meeting soon ended and half the people in the room went back to their offices and the rest went up on the roof top and into a VTOL that took them to the airport got on the same shuttle they arrived in and went back up to the Fast Frigate that would get them to Craterus promptly.

Adrak had a sense of appreciation that Colonel "Blackjack" Langardo would be in the mix. He had no idea or reason to believe the counterintelligence personnel were proficient at what they did, but Adrak damn well knew Colonel "Blackjack" Langardo was one quite capable fighter you would want on your side in a knife fight.

The Mole 000090317A512941 (a.k.a. Zmeya Rembert) felt very uneasy going to Craterus where Adrak was going because he now understood there would likely be a big shootout if these two agents were escorting him there. He also wondered if there were watchers on the plane and indeed there were a couple and if Zmeya Rembert stepped out of line they had their instructions. Sedate him and deposit him where he needed to go.

Zmeya Rembert did not get frisked or checked for weapons, he thought he was getting away with carrying an ultra-secret X-MPQ7775 laser pistol and if necessary, he would kill Adrak and escape with SMERSH who offered Zmeya Rembert a superb pension and retirement after he did a few more devious deeds such as he was doing now. Zmeya Rembert wasn't as great a spy as he thought he was often avoiding missions with the "my wife" story. In fact, he was such a poor spy he didn't catch when he was being drugged.

While Zmeya Rembert was incoherent, his X-MPQ7775 laser pistol was switched out with a modified model that could not kill Adrak. He wasn't wise enough that when the planners went over risk factors and needed to determine what weapons Zmeya Rembert possessed, and they purposely let him carry it on the plane so they could switch it out as part of the setup.

When Zmeya Rembert arrived at Craterus with Corgrelius and Joanie, they were taken to a safe house.

The Mole 000090317A512941 (a.k.a. Zmeya Rembert) knew precisely when the action was going to happen because he advised SMERSH the details on when Adrak was to meet with the enemy spy to with a SMERSH traitor. The SMERSH traitor had a variety of things VIA would like to possess such as a SMERSH NOK list and several encryption keys.

In the safe house the three received their final briefing on what to expect. Nothing seemed out of the ordinary to the Mole 000090317A512941 (a.k.a. Zmeya Rembert).

The following morning, they were transported to where the action was going to happen. Adrak was already in position. The Mole's requirements were to be in the building with Adrak to give him affirmative backup in case it went down wrong. Corgrelius and Joanie were to stay outside under cover performing perimeter protection. The truth of the matter was they were lookouts and there to assist the force that was going to deal with SMERSH agents arriving.

Just like they planned for the set piece event the SMERSH traitor showed up first. Whether he was really a traitor or not they would never know.

When *Karoline Morganthau, a.k.a. Agnes Renceladus* let her team in from the back of the building well scouted, there was no sign of the enemy. She had her getaway well staged everything was set and here he was, the person that caused her a lot of grief when he blew up that Tramular *Intergalactic Dreadnaught Carrier*.

The SMERSH agents walked in boldly and Adrak pulled out his laser weapon, but Karoline Morganthau walked directly up to him brandishing her own weapon and said:

"Well-well-well, if it isn't Adrak himself. You really are something else. First you killed my lover Sidis, you snuck past my trap on the intergalactic transport, then you blew up our *Intergalactic Dreadnaught Carrier* before I could stop you. Adrak, I have a sizeable force here and I'm finally going to apprehend you." Karoline Morganthau said.

"Don't come any closer or I will shoot and kill you." Adrak said.

"Adrak, don't you think you should look at who's pointing a laser at you before you make such bold statements?" Karoline Morganthau said.

Adrak, without looking, knew who it was but had been promised not to worry about it.

"Drop the weapon Adrak." The mole Zmeya Rembert said.

Without them knowing what he was doing, Adrak flipped the blaster to stun. Then he said, "Don't come any closer, I mean it."

On stun it can disable the person but also gave ten times as many shots.

Adrak could feel when Zmeya Rembert started shooting him, but he was protected and this automatically gave the mole an attempted murder rap.

Adrak ignored the annoying low powered laser shot and hit Karoline Morganthau with a stun that made her fall to the floor which shook up the rest of the team then he turned towards the mole Zmeya Rembert and stunned him who was becoming utterly surprised that Adrak didn't respond to his laser hit and when he got stunned, he dropped to the floor then. Suddenly the calvary arrived.

Colonel "Blackjack" Langardo and his crew suddenly arrived out of nowhere and entered the fray and before Karoline Morgenthau's people could shoot at Adrak they were getting hit from multiple directions and it was like shooting ducks in a barrel. One of the Tramular's shot and killed the traitor who was handing over the secrets. In less than a minute, a dozen SMERSH agents were dead and Karoline Morganthau along with Zmeya Rembert were unconscious and immediately taken away in custody. The rest of the SMERSH agents' bodies, who did not have any sort of identification on them because they were spooks, were taken up to space in a shuttle and shoved out of an airlock in space where they would burn up in the atmosphere in a short while.

To the surprise of the other two amigo's Adrak was returned to the Vekkar Interdimensional Transport Directorate as they were wondering *what happened to Zmeya Rembert?*

With the ringleader out of the works, the two others seemed to coward about almost as if they were afraid to attack Adrak since their bully buddy wasn't around to lead them on.

After a while one of them approached Adrak and asked: "Do you know what happened to Zmeya Rembert?"

"I'm not authorized to discuss the mission with anyone. If you have some questions you want to ask, take them to *Doctor Oxyuran Lepidotus Taipan*," Adrak replied.

Adrak could see the fear in their eyes. They knew Zmeya Rembert conspired against Adrak and probably knew he compromised Adrak with SMERSH. Adrak arriving shortly after Zmeya Rembert disappeared added to their consternation. They also knew something else most vividly. As a spy they were subject to neurotic probes if there was less than reasonable doubt.

The two amigos helped Zmeya Rembert set up Adrak for a fall. If management ever came to that conclusion they were in serious trouble. They received annual refresher training on reporting requirements. If they were aware of Zmeya Rembert conspiring with SMERSH they were obligated to report it, otherwise it was a C2 security violation punishable by a lengthy prison sentence.

But they also knew something else. Sometimes VIA foregoes prosecution and the guilty party simply disappears to protect sensitive sources and information. *Did Adrak suddenly come back to help Zmeya Rembert disappear?*

Another event that the two members of the three amigos were quite aware of. Zmeya Rembert made statements to them in private that Adrak would not be coming back as if he knew for sure his departure was predestined just before the sudden assignment that Zmeya Rembert went on.

When Zmeya left the office with the escorts he had a painful look on his face. When Zmeya Rembert didn't come back and his wife didn't contact the office asking about him, they knew something bad happened. They also knew Adrak was carrying around an attitude with him that spoke volumes about he probably got even. Were they next?

The three amigos' worlds started crumbling because Zmeya Rembert acted upon his utter hatred for Adrak who he feared would one day be his boss. Their previous activities were easily hidden because only Vekkar Interdimensional Transport Directorate was involved in the missions. Hence there were no outside agencies involved where a trip wire might be crossed.

When Adrak was picked because he was the most successful spy in the group for the special operation, they didn't count on this being a VIA mission and more so, their special project KOBRA SPEKTR exposed Karoline Morganthau bird dogging Adrak.

Had Boris Clevenger not been so incompetent, they might not have been able to mitigate a top spy like Karoline Morganthau getting to Adrak and discovering precisely what his mission was she could have prevented.

These two amigos would soon pay dearly for their involvement with Zmeya Rembert, and it came a lot sooner than they could imagine.

Chapter Seventeen

A Spy's Spy

Days and weeks passed by. Karoline Morganthau and Zmeya Rembert were almost to the point they wished they were dead.

Counterintelligence interrogators were not boy scouts. They had great knowledge of enhanced interrogations. There was much at stake in the espionage world and the bottom line is you sometimes had to do immoral treatment to prisoners to get the truth out of them.

The neurological probes made ancient lie detectors completely obsolete. As well as Karoline Morganthau was trained to defeat neurological probes, she was unable to because counterintelligence investigators knew that nobody knew what happened to these two people. They simply disappeared off the planet. That gave them time and space to repeat the neurological probes that would make the two prisoners wish they were being waterboarded.

SMERSH suspected Karoline Morganthau was killed or captured. The rest of her team was wiped out. One of the three Amigos closest to Zmeya Rembert was approached by a deep cover SMERSH agent during his daily routines away from work after hours.

The amigo named Cornelius Bragrand met this SMERSH agent once before but thought he was just a friend of Zmeya Rembert.

Hey Cornelius, I've not seen Zmeya around lately. How's he doing? The SMERSH agent knew through intercepts and a few cribs and breadcrumbs Zmeya disappeared exactly at the same time as Karoline Morganthau and was either killed or captured with her.

"He's on assignment, out of town."

"Any idea when he's coming back?"

"I have no idea."

"Do you know where he went?"

"He didn't inform me before he left."

"That seems rather odd."

Counterintelligence had been following Cornelius Bragrand and placed extensive surveillance on him. Counterintelligence knew Cornelius was talking with a SMERSH agent, and the two of them were utterly surprised when the net came crashing down on them and they were hauled away.

The SMERSH agent's watcher reported his capture. To SMERSH that meant it was all likely Karoline Morgenthau was probably still alive and held prisoner somewhere.

***

A good spy like Joanie and her side kick Corgrelius were not going to stay inoperative for long after their post mission R&R for two weeks. They went back to their offices at VIA and were immediately sent on a secret mission to planet *Drusyltania*.

SMERSH is quite capable and anyone that didn't respect them would soon regret the error of their ways. Just because they lost some agents of failed a mission did not mean they were going to give up roll over and play dead. They also had their own visceral leaders on par with Colonel "Blackjack" Langardo.

Joanie and Corgrelius made no mistakes, their spy craft was exemplary, but you can't win them all. When through luck, SMERSH took them down they were both severely wounded and clinging to life. They would have died had it not been for the fact SMERSH wanted them to live to interrogate them.

Their injuries were a blessing in disguise because it's best to torture someone without injuries, so they feel the pain more intensely. Thus, they were spared the torture for a while.

Karoline was one of SMERSH's best agents. That's the only reason why a SPY SWAP was offered. Oddly SMERSH wanted Karoline plus Zmeya Rembert. *How did they know we had the two in custody?* Counterintelligence was now realizing they had more work to do.

The Switzerland like planet Omnicrom Reticulum of this part of the Galaxy was fully neutral and had a sizeable defense force. The small celestial cluster Omnicrom Reticulum had been used in Spy swaps between the Tramular's and the VIA. In recent years there had been less swaps because active combat existed but prior to the launch of the war, spies were traded at Omnicrom Reticulum almost monthly.

Omnicrom Reticulum itself was the major planet that hosted intergalactic bankers, organized crime, human traffickers and just about every type of nefarious activity one could imagine. It was also the playground for the wealthy.

Some of the tourists and businessmen to traveled to Omnicrom Reticulum were restricted on their own worlds and not allowed to partake in some of the activities offered there. Whether it be illegal elixirs, women who may not be of legal age, gambling, narcotics, the total sum of possibilities acted as a magnet to bring them in.

The leaders of Omnicrom Reticulum were able to pay for their strong military by taxing some of this despicable activity. However, to give the appearance that the

Omnicrom Reticulum government was not corrupt, the terminology was changed on the taxation documents. As an example, organized crime that was utilizing underaged prostitutes, was taxed for domestic services management. Organizations that specialized in narcotics were taxed on health supplements, and gambling establishments were taxed on numerology technology development.

Because so many spy swaps had been done here in the past, the Omnicrom Reticulum officials had a very well-organized procedure:

No military spacecraft were allowed to approach Omnicrom Reticulum. Governments representing perspective spies were directed to specific locations on the planet in shuttles only from orbiting transports. From that location Omnicrom officials would take the representatives to the spy swap location after appropriate fees were paid. Spy swaps did not come cheap. Everyone of course was frisked before they arrived at the destination.

Adrak and Colonel "Blackjack" Langardo escorted the two prisoners who had hands and legs shackled.

On the way to planet Omnicrom Reticulum, the Mole 000090317A512941 (a.k.a. Zmeya Rembert) stated, "I do not want to go to the Tramulite worlds because I will never see my family again."

"Zmeya, you have a capital C2 offense which is punishable by death. Your family has already been notified you are dead. You will either go away with Karoline Morganthau, or you will be taken back to the facility you just came from to be executed."

"This is inhumane," Zmeya Rembert said.

Adrak had enough of Zmeya's crap and stood up and took his shirt off and turned his back towards Zmeya and Karoline and asked, "Zmeya how long do you think I was in intensive care and how long do you think it took me to recover from all these wounds you arranged."

Karoline was utterly astonished to see how many bullet holes Adrak received in the ambush and the fact he survived.

Adrak put his shirt on and sat down.

Zmeya started whimpering and it started to make Karoline sick to her stomach.

"Zmeya, I've never seen a weaker man in all my life. You call yourself a spy. You were never a spy; you prove it by crying like a little girl. Stop this now or when I get you home, I will personally beat your ass," Karoline Morganthau said in a terse manner.

"Karoline, I kind of like you, have you ever considered defecting?" Adrak said which kind of startled Karoline.

"Adrak, you can't be serious?" Karoline asked.

"Don't say I didn't offer." Adrak said.

Colonel "Blackjack" Langardo knew Adrak was toying with Karoline, but *what if she suddenly decided she wanted to defect?*

There was one last conversation before the passengers moved to the shuttle and went down to the planet.

"Zmeya, I owe you a lot. In case you decide you want to start working for SMERSH and get back in the business, I want to caution you. For the pain and suffering you caused me, I will gladly come and get you and kill you with my own bare hands," Adrak said.

They were soon on the planet meeting their Omnicrom Reticulum hosts and taken to the prisoner exchange.

Corgrelius and Joanie were in wheelchairs still suffering from severe wounds they suffered during the takedown. They didn't look happy, and Karoline knew that if they reported to the Vekkar's about torture, it would not be good for the next SMERSH agents that were captured.

VIA of course was relieved when Joanie returned to VIA and informed her that it was from their initial wounds during the takedown and gun battle.

The parties were separating when Adrak said, "Karoline, I hope to one day meet you when we are on better terms."

"Adrak, you are one of the best spies that ever lived, I would be proud to meet you when that day comes." Karoline said.

"The feeling is mutual; you were always close at my heels." Adrak said.

"But not close enough, you always slithered away from me before I could capture you. It tells me you had a better plan." Karoline said.

The enemies were soon gone, and the Omnicrom Reticulum's were all smiles because they just received a substantial payment from two warring governments. Once again, they proved, *it pays to be neutral.*

The Vekkar group made it safely home. Joanie and Corgrelius went to a special VIA hospital where they could simultaneously be debriefed and receive the best medical treatment possible.

Adrak and Colonel "Blackjack" Langardo were taken back to Project KOBRA SPEKTR where new things were already on the horizon thanks to fast work by counterintelligence.

Adrak found himself back in training with Project KOBRA SPEKTR and was visited by Interdimensional Transport Directorate, *Doctor Oxyuran Lepidotus Taipan* and was taken to the conference room for a private meeting.

"Adrak something has come up and Project KOBRA SPEKTR needs your services again."

"Alright, I'll help if I can, but may I ask a question?" Adrak asked.

"Sure." *Doctor Oxyuran Lepidotus Taipan* said.

"I've been working really hard for a long time; would it be possible to have some time off when this mission is done?" Adrak asked.

"This is very important as to what you will be doing. I was personally briefed by the Gopher himself. As soon as you finish this mission, I will give you time off, but you must do something to help me give you time off," *Doctor Oxyuran Lepidotus Taipan* said.

"What's that?" Adrak asked.

"You need to immediately leave for some unknown destination for some quality time off before they can snag you for another mission. I will personally take you to the Intergalactic Transport Terminal to help you get away quickly." *Doctor Oxyuran Lepidotus Taipan* said.

"What if they say they need me for some bullshit debriefing?" Adrak asked.

"I will inform them I sent you on a mission, it's compartmentalized because it's super sensitive," *Doctor Oxyuran Lepidotus Taipan* said.

"If Joanie is healed up by then do you think you could arrange for her convalescence leave to go where I'm heading?"

"Before I get in the middle of that, don't you think you need to go visit her in the hospital and see if she would like to spend some time with you?" *Doctor Oxyuran Lepidotus Taipan* asked.

"I would love to go visit Joanie. Is there any way you can help me get to her?" Adrak asked.

"The Gopher owes me a lot for what I've done for him. The reason why our fearless leader likes the Gopher to handle serious matters for him is because I always make him look good."

"Alright Doctor, I appreciate you helping me. I like Joanie." Adrak said.

"You need to keep what you said just now very private and don't let anyone else know otherwise VIA will do everything they can to send you in different directions." *Doctor Oxyuran Lepidotus Taipan* said.

"Doctor you are the only person that knows." Adrak said.

"Adrak, I like you. You never cease to amaze me. Not only are you fast on your feet, but you are also fast in your head. When we are alone, I would appreciate it if you called me *Taipan* instead of Doctor." *Doctor Oxyuran Lepidotus Taipan* said.

"It will be my most distinct honor, *Taipan.* " Adrak said realizing not very many people were on first name basis with the inventor of Inter Dimensional Spy Portals.

The two men left the conference room and made their way down to the electric cart where they were driven to the trailer and Adrak got out there and went into the trailer where he expected his dinner shortly. *Doctor Oxyuran Lepidotus Taipan* continued on his way to the entrance where a Skycar was waiting to take him back to his office.

Adrak received his meal but was not drugged. He didn't know it, but arrangements had been made for him for some other activities.

The same Project KOBRA SPEKTR psychiatrist that dealt with Joanie before her mission with Adrak to blow up the Intergalactic Dreadnaught Carrier and had all the proper clearances was assigned to treat Joanie.

Joanie was suffering not only from the wounds she received during her last mission when she was captured, but also exhibited the condition of post-traumatic stress disorder (PTSD). Joanie had severe wounds but at least her face and breasts were not disfigured.

The psychiatrist was contacted by the chief medical officer for VIA and informed:

"Someone very high up in the food chain has requested permission for someone you are aware of to visit Joanie. Joanie went with him on a successful mission recently you helped her prepare for."

"Is the person requesting 000050428A62315 (a.k.a. Adrak)?" the psychiatrist asked.

"Apparently that is the person." Chief Medical Officer replied.

"Doctor, Joanie is suffering from PTSD. When I debriefed her after that mission, she went with that man she was happy and vibrant. I think 000050428A62315 (a.k.a. Adrak) would provide a positive valance for her to get over some of her anguish and deal better with the trauma she went through that is the source of her PTSD."

"How soon can 000050428A62315 (a.k.a. Adrak) visit Joanie?" Chief Medical Officer asked.

"I would like a couple days to help prepare her for his visit," the psychiatrist said.

"Doctor, I'm sorry but we do not have a couple days. 000050428A62315 (a.k.a. Adrak) is going on a mission very soon. Is there any reason why he can't visit this evening?" Chief Medical Officer asked.

"Well under the circumstances, I suppose I do not have a choice." The psychiatrist said.

"Doctor, 000050428A62315 (a.k.a. Adrak) has paid one hell of a price just like Joanie has. His next mission is extremely dangerous, another one of those 50% chance of survival type missions. This may be his last chance to ever see Joanie again."

"Go ahead and send 000050428A62315 (a.k.a. Adrak) here. I'll go help prepare her now, the best we can," the psychiatrist said.

After the conversation ended, the psychiatrist immediately walked to Joanies private hospital room with an armed guard posted outside. When she went into the room she looked at Joanie who appeared to be very sad, which is understandable for someone suffering from severe PTSD. The psychiatrist went to Joanie's bedside and sat down on the chair facing Joanie who appeared to be ignoring her and appeared to be in a sad state of affairs.

"Joanie, you are going to have a visitor soon, someone who really cares about you." The psychiatrist said.

In what seemed like a half-drugged state Joanie who was a smart spy and quite coherent, just sad asked, "Who is the visitor?" Joanie asked.

"It's Boone." The Psychiatrist said.

Just like a lightning bolt hit her Joanie suddenly sat up in her bed and her whole facial expression changed.

"Oh my God, I know I look terrible, I can't see him now." Joanie said.

"But do you want to see him?" the psychiatrist asked.

"I would love to see him but not looking like an old hag," Joanie said.

"We can tell Boone to come here say in two hours that would give us time to feed you and have some makeup artists come in and make you look adorable," the psychiatrist said.

"If you can do that, I would be so grateful," Joanie said.

"It will be my pleasure. I'm going to send a nurse in to help you take a bath, change your wound dressings, and then get your meal. As soon as you finish your meal, I promise I will have a makeup artist here." The psychiatrist said.

Joanie was in a lot of physical pain, but she moved her body and grabbed the psychiatrist and started hugging her, thanking her profusely.

Moments later as the psychiatrist was leaving the room she had tears coming down the sides of her face. One of the nurses on the ward approached the doctor who knew she had a very difficult patient and was giving her a lot of sedatives asked, "Are you okay doctor?"

"Oh yes, thank you."

"Then why are you crying?"

"I'm sobbing because I just saw the power of love. We have a lot to get done in two hours. We are going to have a visitor, come with me where we can discuss this and I want you to ask the other nurses to help as much as possible because this patient deserves our help, after what she's been through."

"Sure doctor, we will help as much as we can."

The team sprang in action together as soon as the word was passed. And just as the psychiatrist hoped, in two hours when the Vekkar Interdimensional Transport Directorate, *Doctor Oxyuran Lepidotus Taipan* escorted Adrak into the hospital, the psychiatrist who knew who he was waited patiently because she wanted to be available after the visit to help Joanie if required.

The team was watching at the nurse's station as the mystery man came into the ward. The mystery man definitely was a good looker and had a body these women would die to have a chance at. They suddenly knew instantly why Joanie had such an attraction to the handsome man and the security people behind them to protect *Doctor Oxyuran Lepidotus Taipan,* underscored the priority of the patient.

The psychiatrist said, "I will take Boone in to see the patient, you other men must wait outside."

The psychiatrist really didn't need to escort Boone (a.k.a. Adrak) into the room but as part of her clinical work with Joanie she wanted to see her reaction and her body language. The first sight would be the most telling as she would be focused on Joanie.

They entered the room. Joanie, who rarely sat up in her bed because of the pain and her mental anguish, was now sitting up in her hospital gown with fresh bandages and makeup for a princess.

The psychiatrist was so proud of how nicely the makeup artists made Joanie look glamourous even though she was wearing a medical gown.

The psychiatrist could see the happiness flowing out of Joanie. It was like love at first sight type look there was no mistake about it.

"Joanie, look who is here, you have a visitor," the psychiatrist said.

"Oh, thank you very much doctor, you don't know how much I appreciate this."

"I think I do my dear and I'm quite happy. I'll be outside talking with a few men if you need any help just press the buzzer," the psychiatrist said then winked at Joanie and turned around and left the room.

The room was of course under surveillance and VIA technicians were recording all of this. The psychiatrist would review the video later and doubt she would be able to keep a dry eye.

Boone (a.k.a. Adrak) sat down in the chair next to Joanie and said, "It's good to see you."

"I'm very happy you came to see me. I was kind of groggy on the transport and couldn't really speak." Joanie said.

"That's not a problem, you were in a lot of pain," Boone said.

"Boone if I asked you to do something would you?" Joanie asked.

"You know I would do whatever you asked even if it got me in trouble," Boone replied.

"Boone you have no idea how much this means to me, and I'm not shy as you should know by now."

"Yes, I know."

"Boone would you please kiss me?"

"You have no idea how badly I want to."

Boone stood up bent over and gave Joanie a very soft and sensual kiss on her lips. Joanie threw her arms around Boone and held him tightly and started sobbing. In the video recording that had several angles, the psychiatrist could see that emotional outpour. She knew that sometimes a PTSD patient goes through an episode like this when they find closure to their dilemma and often it's a precursor to better mental health and most encouraging. What followed next was further evidence.

Joanie got her emotions under control and let go of Boone and then said, "Boone please sit back down on the chair so I can look at you."

After Boone sat down smiling at Joanie, he then said, "Joanie, I know you gave me some strict orders when you were training me up for our mission, but I'm afraid I can't fully comply with your orders."

"Boone, what are you talking about."

"Joanie, you ordered me not to fall in love with you."

"That I did, and I probably made a mistake in doing so."

"Well, now you know you own a piece of my heart. I willingly give it to you."

"We have to be very careful not to broadcast that because the VIA will try to separate us from each other."

"I'm sure we can work things out."

"We will."

"Joanie I'm very sorry but in a couple days I must go somewhere. I will not be able to see you for a while, but as soon as I can come and see you, I'll be back."

"I understand Boone."

"I want you to get well soon, because I miss running and swimming with you in the mornings."

"Boone, I can't promise you how fast I'll heal, but when you come back, I will be able to walk with you. We'll take it in baby steps."

"Alright, coach, I will try to walk properly for you. Maybe when you feel up to it, we can take ballroom dancing lessons together?"

"Wow you sure are giving me a lot of enthusiasm really quickly," Joanie said.

"The same enthusiasm you gave me."

"You know Boone I must say, I never had so much fun on a mission before. Another thing is I always felt safe with you. I knew you would get us back alive, and you proved it."

"You were a fantastic partner. I could never ask for more."

"Actually, you can, after I heal up."

The medical staff had their orders to remove Boone in 15 minutes, then inject Joanie for pain management and to allow her to get a long period of sleep. The ward nurse who helped orchestrate the event walked into the room and said, "I'm afraid visiting hours are over now. Joanie needs her medications and so sir I'm afraid you must leave now to allow us to give her medications and prepare her for her rest period."

"Understand and thank you for allowing me to visit it means a lot to me." Boone (a.k.a. Adrak) said.

Joanie was all smiles and said, "Boone thank you for coming here tonight, this is one of my best days in a long time."

"Mine too," Boone said, then he stood up, bent over and kissed Joanie on her forehead and said, "I will see you again as soon as I can."

"Thank you. Stay safe Boone stay focused on what you need to do. We'll be together soon enough."

There was a soft touch of the hands and Boone was out the door. The psychiatrist walked with the men out to the elevator and said goodbye then went back to Joanies room and saw the blossom. Joanie was all smiles sitting up in her bed eagerly taking her medications instead of fighting it like before. She was a changed woman. Life wasn't so bad after all.

Chapter Eighteen Project

Anaserdova

The Gopher and Spraticus had just briefed the supreme commander about the *Intergalactic Dreadnaught Carrier* destruction and the spy swap when Vekkar Intelligence Agency (VIA) provided a briefing paper on a new development that required immediate action.

"The Tramular's are developing Zygov Fighter Bomber munitions, and the test phase had just concluded with very good success," the Gopher stated.

"Tell me more," The supreme commander asked.

"This new weapon system that Tramular scientists finalized is the *Quasar-Sonic Stasijar Battlefield Penetrators,*" Spraticus added.

"The *Quasar-Sonic Stasijar Battlefield Penetrators* is the weapon the Tramulite Force Commanders always wanted," the Gopher reiterated.

"*Quasar-Sonic Stasijar Battlefield Penetrators* is a weapon with a small footprint of 40 millimeters in diameter and 45 centimeters long used in a launcher mechanism that can deploy 1000 rounds per minute," Spraticus explained.

"What's so special about these weapons?" the supreme commander asked. Spraticus who had all the details explained:

"Each *Quasar-Sonic Stasijar Battlefield Penetrator* weighs only 20 pounds but has the explosive force of a 1000-pound gravity bomb thanks to a new sophisticated explosive developed using Roentgenium, $_{111}$Rg, in a binary explosive munition.

"A Roentgenium rod encased and encapsulated in a sealed package is inserted into a pipe like projectile with a proximity detector activated via built in microprocessor when launched as part of a mini rocket.

"The outer cylinder-shaped binary component fits over the inner Roentgenium rod was made from a mixture of powdered aluminum and the cylinder shaped RDX sleeve with the rocket body encasing it.

"What's RDX?" the supreme commander asked.

RDX (Research Department Explosive), uses an explosive nitroamine, is bound by a mixture of 5.3% dioctyl sebacate (DOS) or dioctyl adipate (DOA) as the plasticizer (to increase the plasticity of the explosive), thickened with 2.1% polyisobutylene (PIB, a synthetic rubber) as the binder, and 1.6% of a mineral oil manufactured from process oil."

"Sounds like powerful stuff," the supreme commander responded.

"There is more to it. The RDX was impregnated with aluminum powder that adds to the explosive force by the chemical reaction with the Roentgenium, $_{111}$Rg," Spraticus added.

"What's the tactical use of this new weapon? the supreme commander asked.

"A fighter bomber coming down from space cannot dip below 100,000 feet until the anti-air weapons are all destroyed. Thus, used just like it was cluster munitions, many of the *Quasar-Sonic Stasijar Battlefield Penetrators* would be fired immediately achieving 4000 feet per second at terminal Quasar velocity to take out the air defenses," Spraticus explained.

"How does it go so fast?" the supreme commander asked.

"The *Quasar-Sonic* rocket engine is a Tramular state secret and Vekkar VIA has not obtained the physics behind how it works, though our scientists believe the propulsion to be some type of solid rocket fuel propulsion leap frogging ahead of previous propulsion methods."

"We need to find this out, it could be a game changer," the supreme commander said.

"Our scientists know in the fog of war it was only a matter of time before we would obtain an unexploded round to dissect. Once we obtain the unexploded round, robotic disassemblers would separate the rocket engine from the explosive easily seen as a two- part body." Spraticus said.

"What's this mission you want me to approve?" the supreme commander asked.

It's a two-man team to penetrate security at a military warehouse facility at Anaserdova where the first *Quasar-Sonic Stasijar Battlefield Penetrators* shipments via intergalactic transport converted to a freighter would load them up and take them to the front lines air wings where a pitched battles continues."

"How serious is this?" the supreme commander asked.

"If our spies fail in eliminating the stockpile in the warehouse at Anaserdova, the likelihood that over 100,000 Vekkar military personnel could be slaughtered," the Gopher answered prompting the supreme commander.

"Do it." The supreme commander stated.

***

Adrak was somewhat uplifted seeing Joanie mindful that if he had not captured Karoline Morganthau, there never would have been a spy trade and in a few more weeks after recovery when she got most of her strength back, the brutal interrogations would begin.

Joanie was aware how Adrak brought her back from the soon to be dead as spies always died a painful death.

The wounds Joanie received had two significant positive results for her. First, Joanie wasn't healed far enough along for the savage interrogations she soon would have experienced the ordeal.

Secondly Joanies wounds and rehabilitation would require a lot longer than sewing up Adrak's back and removing bullet residue slowed down by his Kevlar vest.

Hence, Joanies injuries would keep her from receiving a medical certification for deployment for a several months and it would be a while before she was discharged out of the hospital.

During Joanies hospital stay the medical staff would work to overcome her injuries assisting her walking and workout with a trainer and therapist followed by swimming and when she was ready to start running.

Plans were afoot to temporarily assign Joanie to Project KOBRA SPEKTR as a planner's assistant after she was restored to the point, she was functional.

Adrak had no idea how the mission was going to unfold or very little about it. The following day, Colonel "Blackjack" Langardo and Toland arrived at Adrak's trailer where he was dressed in his temporary uniform provided that had no specific markings on it exposing rank, name, or military unit.

The security guard opened the door to the trailer as his ear bud informed him via communications, Adrak was sitting in the communal spaces dressed and ready to depart. He said:

"Your ride is here."

"Thanks," Adrak replied.

Adrak walked out to the cart and nodded at the two men and hopped in the back seat, then the cart took off and headed directly to Project KOBRA SPEKTR facilities. In a very brief period, they took the elevator up to the camouflaged landing pad to the VTOL that was waiting for them. The VTOL took them to the Intergalactic Spaceport where a Transport on a flying wing was waiting for them.

As soon as the men were seated in the Intergalactic Transport with no markings on it, the spacecraft latch up with the flying wing headed to the end of the runway via a service ramp and positioned for takeoff.

The pilot of the Transport was a frustrated former fighter jocky and loved it when he was flying an empty plane with just three passengers onboard. Because of the lack of weight with throttles all the way forward for takeoff, the flying wing raised up off the runway in about half the length normally required with a load of passengers. It was almost like ferrying the spacecraft which sometimes happened.

Normally passengers would feel 2G's at the most, today the men had the distinct pleasure of feeling 6G's until the flying wing pitched downwards to almost an even keel allowing it to gain considerable speed and above 20,000 feet went supersonic.

Due to the lightness of the spacecraft, it took very little time to get the flying wing up to 100,000 feet where the spacecraft rocket engines lit off and separated from the flying wing and quickly went out into space.

They were flying off to a mining planet that was completely innocuous and deep inside Vekkar territory that seldom if ever had any Tramulite drones spying. There was nothing to see here but mining operations and most of it was underground therefore there was even less of it to see.

There was a spaceport on the mining planet to deliver and ship personnel and materials. Cargo Spaceships were the bulk of the air movements. Much of the mining materials were taken out in space via flying wing and spacecraft appearance like the size of the Intergalactic transports.

The purpose in picking this mining planet for training was the climate and landscape was very similar to where they were going to do the mission, at the Tramulite planet Anaserdova.

It took a couple days to reach the mining planet and soon the Intergalactic Transport was mated to the flying wing and landed at the spaceport. The men were led outside the Intergalactic Transport via the crew access into a small concourse that connected directly to the entrance of a VTOL. Nobody at the spaceport would see their arrival in case there were enemy spies around.

The VTOL took off and one hour later landed at the training camp. To Adrak's surprise Cajarington was already there and had been training for another mission before priorities shifted and he was reassigned to make up a team with Adrak for the Anaserdova mission. He was at the entrance waiting to be escorted in with the rest.

Colonel "Blackjack" Langardo was met by Spraticus who welcomed him and asked the rest of the group to come into the facility conference room where they could have a discussion.

When they were all inside the nice, air-conditioned conference room with drinks and snacks in front of their name placards, Spraticus, a high-ranking member of the Vekkar leader's inner circle began the conversation:

"I appreciate everyone arriving in the most rapid manner. It gives me good feelings the agencies involved appreciate what's at stake here. Since not everyone is privy, let me just say, failure to complete this mission could result in the loss of 100,000 Amphibian Forces which we can ill afford to experience such losses in this portion of the battle."

Spraticus paused for a moment and looked at the attendees and could see they were highly focused on every word he said. He then continued:

"The Amphibians were landed in a flanking movement that appears to have done what we wanted it to do which gives the tip of the sphere in our assault force some breathing room. Tramular's have discovered the Amphibians puts their defenses in untenable condition."

"I know we have a warehouse to knock out, can you give us a little more detail about what that's all about and how it fits into all of this?" Colonel "Blackjack" Langardo asked.

"As you can imagine this has become such a tactical necessity that Tramular leadership has decided to throw in the *Quasar-Sonic Stasijar Battlefield Penetrators* just now approved for use by their government to attack the Amphibians. The Tramular commanders are now reaching the point of desperation, transports and escorts are being sent to the planet Anaserdova to load up the first shipment and deliver them to the forces the Amphibians now face." Spraticus said.

"It seems to me that should not take a lot of time, maybe we are too late to launch the effort," Colonel "Blackjack" Langardo said."

"The Tramular's have painted themselves in a corner. We don't know exactly how much time we have but VIA's estimates is we have enough time to do several days of training then deploy," Spraticus said.

"What's delaying the Tramular's?"

"Even though Tramular's drove us away from *Heuronvale*, their force protection was poor and as a result we damaged a lot of heavy lift transports. Their heavy lift transports are stuck at Anaserdova with less than half their cargo unloaded and having serious issues unloading the rest before they can load up the weapons," Spraticus replied.

"What seems to be their problem unloading?" Colonel "Blackjack" Langardo asked The Amphibian Commander knows if he can delay the unloading long enough it will give us time to blow up that warehouse so his boys will not have to deal with those *Quasar- Sonic Stasijar Battlefield Penetrators.* Spraticus replied.

"How does the Amphibian Commander know about the *Quasar-Sonic Stasijar Battlefield Penetrators,* that' a heavily guarded secret?" Colonel "Blackjack" Langardo asked.

"You are right, I personally paid him a visit yesterday and explained it to him." Spraticus responded.

"That's a long distance, how did you get here so quickly," Colonel "Blackjack" Langardo asked.

"My boss knows this is a crucial battle we cannot afford to lose, so he gave me permission to use his emergency escape spaceship." Spraticus replied.

"Nothing like riding in style," Colonel "Blackjack" Langardo said.

"It will be difficult for me to adjust to slow transports," Spraticus replied with a wicked grin.

"Since we don't really know when those Tramulite Transports will get unloaded, and I'm not good at guessing, I want to do as much training as possible today to buy us time to get the job done and get the hell out of there before the escorts arrive with the transports," Colonel "Blackjack" Langardo said.

"Good idea. I'll suspense with the rest of the briefing since it can be gone over on the way to the target," Spraticus said.

"Since we'll be arriving at night, I would prefer to keep working into the night and get night operations training completed," Adrak said.

"I like your enthusiasm, 000050428A62315 (a.k.a. Adrak)," Spraticus said.

"Everyone in the room knows 000050428A62315 is Adrak along with Karoline Morganthau one of Tramulite's best spies, might as well just call him by his name," Colonel "Blackjack" Langardo said.

"That's not an envious position to be in, Adrak," Spraticus said.

"I'm going to request my identity be changed after this mission," Adrak said.

"Sounds like a reasonable request, I'll endorse it just as soon as you submit it to Transport Directorate, *Doctor Oxyuran Lepidotus Taipan.*

"I appreciate that sir," Adrak replied.

"Alright gentlemen, Toland has been here for a while ahead of you to work out the training curriculum. He'll now explain what we are going to do now," Spraticus said.

"As long as you guys are feeling motivated to work to get the mission down, I'm willing to stay with you as late as necessary," Toland said.

"We are." Adrak responded.

"Alright we are going up in a shuttle shortly to a mother ship. In that ship is a glider that is just like the one you used when you blew up the Tramulite research center," Toland said.

"Put up a picture of the warehouse," Toland said.

Artificial intelligence that was part of the conference room display technology suddenly put up the picture that was secretly taken by a spy they inserted as they were planning for the mission. From a distance a spy can photograph such a building with low risk, in a hidden position then be evacuated in the middle of the night in a shuttle.

"How did this picture get taken?" Adrak asked.

"VIA delivered one of their operatives via a shuttle at night who hid in a nearby wooded area and moved to a camouflaged area where observations could be made during the day. This is the building you are going to blow up," Toland said.

"It looks like it has some really good perimeter defenses including a couple concentric rings of fences," Adrak said.

"That's correct," Toland said. Then he added, you will come down in a disposable glider that will self-destruct after you leave via Portal to the mother ship."

"Any reason why we cannot come down via Portal," Adrak asked.

"We do not want you detected arriving. The Tramulite's might detect the Portal opening and you would be exposed. If they detect a Portal near this warehouse, especially now that it's been loaded up with *Quasar-Sonic Stasijar Battlefield Penetrators* they would not hesitate to send an entire Marine Division after you to capture you and find out why you are there."

"Just like the mission you did to destroy the research center; the glider will arrive via autopilot and the middle of a wooded area that has a small clearing. Show the clearing," Toland said."

"That does not look big enough for the glider to land in," Adrak said.

Toland explained:

"You are correct. The glider will deploy a parachute like the way an ejection seat works in a fighter-bomber, around 200 feet very close to the landing zone. We have a simulated landing zone set up where you will practice landing with four electronic towers that will feed the electronics in the glider to give you an artificial view on the heads-up display. When you come down you will have a view just like you see the trees on the holograph."

"Play one of the test landing videos," Toland said and artificial intelligence commenced.

The holographic imagery looked like a person would see in the cockpit coming down. The video had an elapsed time sequence starting from the time it left the mother ship with different view angles, coming down through planetary atmosphere, then right when it got near the landing zone at around 1000 feet, the video shift to real time as if the person was now in the glider coming down.

The video had a split screen. One side was an external view of the glider and the landscape, and the other was what the pilot would see in a heads-up display. It did not matter which seat the two spies sat in, they each had a heads-up display for situational awareness.

The screen with the external view of the glider showed at 200 feet the parachute deploying quickly catching the airflow and expanding just like one would see from a pilot ejecting from an aircraft about ready to crash.

The glider then had a soft landing.

"The glider will come down in autopilot. On your heads up display you will have a similar display, except the image on the left will have a ghost image overlaid which is the planned position. As long as the ghost image is on top of the real image, the glider is on course," Toland said.

After a moment to allow the current video to fully complete Toland said, "Now we are going to show a real heads-up display taken from an actual test flight here. Remember we have 4 towers that are set up for accurate measurement of the glider which gives the simulation electronics package onboard the glider to give you the imagery like you would see during the actual mission."

Now Adrak and Cajarington could see the ghosting on the image that was scaled for reasonable variance so as not cause gitter on the display.

At times the ghost image would shift slightly directly off the real image and as flight controls correct the ghost image would overlay perfectly on top of the real image. When they were overlaid, it gave the appearance of infrared or ultraviolet overlays done for night vision or during reduced visibility.

"Since this imagery was taken from a test flight, it it's assumed you will experience such imagery from the heads-up display," Toland said.

After some discussion, Toland informed Adrak and Cajarington: "Your helmets are on the table against the wall. During the mission you will wear a camouflaged set of pilot coveralls, but for now you are going to do a couple day test flights wearing the clothes you have on now."

"Alright," Adrak replied.

"Just like you had when you blew up the research building, you will find backpacks in the cargo bay of the glider. Those are identical to the personal drones you flew to the target during that mission.

"Each of you will also carry a satchel to place on the rooftop of the warehouse. The warehouse roof is nowhere nearly as strong as the research building you blew up, but you will have just as many explosives as you deliver.

"You are flying over dry land and not over a river. You will sit your satchels down on the top of the warehouse that has its lat-long programmed into your personal drone propulsion navigation system.

"Your helmet's microprocessor will arm the satchels automatically as you sit down and place them on the roof tops in the middle of the roof. You will not fly back to the drone.

"Why is that?" Cajarington asked.

"There will be a huge explosion when your satchels go off. Instead you will fly over to an escarpment and we have mapped out a flat spot that is twenty feet down on the escarpment that will protect you from high speed flying shrapnel and the shockwave," Toland said.

"You expect a large explosion?" Adrak asked.

"When all those *Quasar-Sonic Stasijar Battlefield Penetrators* cook off, we expect a huge explosion that would no doubt cut you down if you were standing up in the path of the shockwave caused by the detonation of an equivalent of several hundred thousand 1000-pound gravity bombs.

Upon landing on the side of the escarpment, your drone wings will recess back into the backpack and your artificial intelligence will tell you to get down low. Hug the ground for your own safety. We expect that even laying on the ground you will feel the shockwave."

"When will we be transported via portal via the mother ship?" Adrak asked.

"The mother ship will be monitoring your location, and they will have no problem seeing the fireball from space that will appear to be a small nuclear detonation. As soon as the dust settles and we feel its safe to extract you, the Portals will appear to bring you back to the mother ship.

"This all-sounds kind of wild," Cajarington said.

"One of the reasons why we picked this site to train is you will soon discover a skeleton rooftop put up and an actual escarpment you will fly to and get down and lay down for your protection."

"How will you simulate such a large explosion you anticipate we'll be subject too?" Cajarington asked.

"This will be live fire training. At the actual target site, the explosion will be a good distance away. But for a live fire to give you the sensation of a shockwave an explosion will go off 100 yards from you. As soon as the range safety officer confirms by his video monitor you two are laying on the ground on the side of the escarpment, the explosives will go off and you will get the sensation of a real shockwave and shrapnel flying past you which at the mission will be parts of the building blowing up."

"Understand," Cajarington said.

"Any questions?" Toland asked?

The two spies shook their heads.

Soon the men were escorted out of the conference room and outside the building where they discovered a space capable shuttle waiting for them as they carried their helmets. Everything else they needed was already packed in the glider which was now in the mothership in a geostationary orbit directly overhead in semi-low planet orbit.

Toland went up with them in the mothership. Spraticus and Colonel "Blackjack" Langardo remained in the conference room where they had a full holographic view of the test flight.

In the flight up and getting situated in the glider just before deployment, questions were answered.

This test fight was nothing more than a rehash of what they did before. They soon afterwards deployed from the mothership and did a practice run just like they would in the real mission. The glider parachuted and landed on the bullseye. The men got out opened the cargo bay of the glider extracted the two personal glider backpacks and a simulated satchel and hooked it onto their service belts that was part of the backpack fasteners.

The two spies deployed the drone wings and soon heard in the headsets; "Artificial intelligence will fly your personal drone. No movement on the straps is necessary."

This was a big surprise to the men.

Artificial Intelligence asked, "Are you ready to fly to the target."

"Yes." The two spies each answered, and they were soon airborne flying a mile in a circuitous route to the simulated warehouse roof where they deposited the satchels. They then heard artificial intelligence informed them: "The satchel has been armed. You are now flying to the escarpment."

The personal drone lifted them into the air and flew them approximately a mile to the escarpment and set down. Artificial Intelligence then said, "Lay down on the ground and when you are ready, I will detonate the explosives."

The two men laid down on the ground and each of them said, "Ready."

A moment later a big ass explosion happened that temporarily scared the living dogshit out of the two spies, but as they gathered their wits, they knew this was a live fire exercise and if the shockwaves they felt were like the real thing that would be sending shrapnel at them at supersonic speed, they were happy to be laying down. A moment later Artificial intelligence informed the two spies: in 5 seconds two portals will appear to extract you. It's now safe to stand up.

The two spies stood up, the portals appeared, and they stepped into them and soon found themselves back on the mother ship where Toland escorted them into the shuttle that soon took them back to the secret base.

While the men went through a critique, the staff retrieved the glider which was quite easy since it was on a concrete bull's eye that had a two-inch-thick martial arts rubber cover to soften the landing to help prevent any connections from coming loose.

The glider parachute rig was a module they could easily unbolt and replace with a module with a packed parachute. The glider's battery was also swapped out with a fully charged dual power supply dual battery module with more than sufficient power to handle several planetary arrivals.

A good-sized shuttle arrived and the staff using a mobile lifting device, and a lifting pad screwed into the center of gravity on the roof of the glider loaded it into the back of the shuttle with a large door.

The pilot and copilot would wear space suits because the shuttle would be depressurized, rear door opened and with a cable attached to a dragging eye pad on the rear of the glider would back up close to the mother ship glider bay that also had a large door.

Men inside the shuttle simply had to throw a rope like a Navy ship does when its mooring to attach to mooring lines to drag them on the ship.

Crew members aboard the mother ship took the rope that was attached to something that looked like a softball for throwing and pulled the rope attached to a small metal cable that would soon be connected to the tow line on a wench easily dragged the glider out of the shuttle and into the mother ship glider bay.

With the wench operating slowly to prevent damage the rear of the glider slid it on a Teflon sheet easily into the mother ship glider bay.

The rope used to send the tow cable over to the mother ship had already been pulled back into the shuttle and it was slowly moving away from the mothership with the rear door shutting. The mothership was now ready to support another test flight.

The critique didn't surface any issues, but they train like they fight and the more training you do the better proficiency you build. Concert pianists prove that philosophy every day.

As soon as the team was informed the glider was aboard the mother ship ready for another test flight, Adrak and Cajarington were escorted out of the building to the waiting shuttle carrying their helmets with them.

The two spies boarded the shuttle and were soon on their way back out into space. As before Toland was with them for last-minute adjustments or comments.

These iterations of glider flights eat up time going out into space flying back to the planet then going back out to do it again. The men didn't know it at the time and had no hunger pains, but they missed lunch and were now working during dinner time as the sun was getting low on the horizon.

They completed their next exercise and were taken back to the critique room where everyone was there reviewing the video with them and making comments if any were required.

At the end of discussion, noting the two spies were somewhat dirty from laying on loose soil, Spraticus made the statement:

"Adrak and Cajarington, you are going to be escorted to your quarters where you can take a shower, get cleaned up, get a change of clothing, and your meals will be provided to you."

"Alright," Cajarington replied, and the men all stood up.

"Follow me," Toland said and led them outside the conference room down a hallway and walked up to a door and entered a password and they entered.

As they walked down the hallway they came up to a room and Toland said, "Adrak this is your room. You can open the door since it's programmed for your facial recognition."

As soon as Adrak grabbed the door handle he felt the solenoid click and he opened it and went inside to a very nice room that happened to be senior officer quarters with all the amenities. Inside the room was a female there to assist him.

"Hello Adrak, my name is Melony, I'm your room assistant to take care of all your needs. In your bedroom through that door (she pointed), you will see a change of clothes laying on your bed. You can take a shower or a bath, it's up to you. But if you want to take a bath it is automated and, on the bathroom, tabletop is a container that says bath salts on it. Those bath salts have muscle relaxers and pleasurizers in them that will make you feel better if you want to take a bath."

"Alright," Adrak said.

"Adrak, I'm part of project KOBRA SPEKTR. I'm a professional who is called upon like you to make supreme sacrifices at times. My task is to make you happy. I'm well briefed on you and know your history and your missions. I also know all about your affection for Joanie. But since you will soon be going on a very dangerous mission and we never know what the outcome will be as the scars on your back prove, I'm more than happy to get in the bath with you and give you a message and if you desire copulation, I've already taken my pregnancy prevention medications and am willing to take you if you desire."

"That will not be necessary. I'll save it for Joanie who I already miss."

"Adrak, I knew you would say that. You are a prince and a gentleman, and I personally know Joanie and she knows what I do in my assignments to give spies their farewell sendoff because we know they are going on extremely dangerous assignments. I know I'm good looking and make a lot of men get *hardon's* and few can resist me. I've done a couple dozen honey pot schemes setting up enemy spies. You have confirmed to me personally what kind of a person you are. I know Joanie quite well and the fact you declined me because of your emotional bond to her pleases me.

"That's okay, I probably do not deserve Joanie, but I've taken a liking to her."

"I know you have and consider this a privileged conversation, and all the bugs are turned off in the room so you can speak freely."

"Thanks."

"Adrak, the psychiatrist treating Joanie because of her terrible trauma, she had terrible injuries, evaluated Joanie with severe PTSD. She was in a very bad state of mind. Her pain management was insufficient but that's the best the doctors could do with her injuries. Time must take its toll on the healing so that her pain will go away. But being crippled and in terrible pain and suffering and being a spy and a Tramulite prisoner, Joanie had a mental breakdown. With her PTSD the psychiatrist feared she would never snap out of it."

"Then suddenly you requested to see her. The psychiatrist noticed the remarkable change in Joanie, and she did an experiment that would be looked down upon by her colleagues. Because of her injuries and mental condition, the protocols state, she is not to have any visitors. The chief surgeon was the person who relayed your visit request to the psychiatrist who asked Joanie if she would like to see you."

"Joanie snapped out of her mental slump and completely changed and almost floored the psychiatrist. To be honest, Joanie was looking very haggardly, because she has been through far more than practically any woman who wasn't killed. The team prepared her so that you would see a good image of Joanie and I saw the images before and after and it was a remarkable change."

"You are a remarkable person Adrak. You are Joanie's prince charming, and you arrived just in time to save her. She will never forget you for the rest of her life. Her life now orbits around you."

"Thank you for telling me this. I am quite fond of Joanie, and I'm looking forward to completing this mission so I can get back to her."

"Adrak, she knows that. I contacted the psychiatrist an hour ago to get an update on Joanie's condition. According to the psychiatrist, she's going through a remarkable change now. Because she wants to enhance her healing and improve her pain management, she now is asking the therapists to take her to the gym that is set up for wounded patients where they can work out a little under medical supervision. I'm very proud of that woman because she is giving it all her best pushing herself unlike any other patient."

"That's good to hear she's doing it."

"She's doing it for one reason: you." Melony said with great articulation.

That statement hit Adrak in the gut and Melony could see the tears form in the corners of Adak's eyes knowing she hit a raw nerve. She then knew she had to back off immediately and said, "Adrak why don't you go ahead and take your bath and soak for a while. I'll be back in 30 minutes with your meal so that you don't have to rush and can soak a bit."

"Thank you I appreciate that." Adrak responded.

Melony then left the room walked to the cafeteria and gave the manager there the food order for Adrak which was an exclusive with a key code for senior officers, so he was going to get the absolute best.

Melony then went to her private office and had an interstellar communicator that operated off the neutrino broadcast system allowing real time communications to the home planet and VIA headquarters.

This interstellar communicator system was far better than the miliary had, but the spooks needed supreme communications for the extravagant missions they performed all the time.

Melany had Joanie's hospital room link up number and placed the call. Joanie had just bathed, had the bandages on her wounds changed, and a light meal. Joanie was sitting up in bed feeling good as the pain management protocol drugs were now starting to kick in.

The interstellar communicator system through artificial intelligence found Joanie's communicator and using surveillance video determined she was awake and her communicator close to her beside. The call came in and Joanie, curious, answered and discovered to her delight it was her friend Melony on the caller's I.D.

Hello Melonie, how are you?

"I'm doing great Joanie. The reason why I'm calling is I'm Adrak's room assistant to take care of all his needs."

"I hope he doesn't dip his pen in company ink."

"Not to worry Joanie, that guy is in love with you. You are the only woman he's interested in, plus I'm here to keep the bitches away from him. I'll protect him he's safe and will soon come back and see you."

"That's good to know."

"He personally informed me he just wants to get this mission done so he can get back right away and see you."

"You don't know how good that makes me feel."

"I must be honest Joanie I have a couple tears in my eyes thinking about all this. I don't know what you did to that man, but you have indelibly stained his psyche for you."

"Well, you know in our business if I told you what it was, I would have to kill you." The two women chuckled then got more serious.

"How's your exercises working out?"

"It's hard and I do have pain, but I know one thing, each day I push myself and even if it hurts at the time I'm doing it and want to quit, I find that later my pain management works a lot better. I can tell by the healing of my wounds and the scars I'm healing. A week ago, the bandages had to be changed a couple times a day because of the bleeding, and I had a couple blood transfusions. Now thanks to my exercises I only need the bandages changed once a day even though they do it multiple times."

"That's good to know. Is there anything you want me to tell Adrak?"

"Yes, tell him he gave me smiles today thinking about seeing him again soon."

"I will be most happy to inform him and in about 15 minutes I'm going to take his meal to him."

"Melany, I've known you a long time, may I ask you a question?"

"Sure?" Melany replied.

"Why did they send a high-level spy like you to be Adrak's room assistant?"

"I probably may get in trouble if they know I revealed this to you. I'm part of his personal security detachment to make sure he stays safe, and nobody can get near him with nefarious purposes."

"I kind of suspected that to be the case. I do appreciate they picked you of all people to do this."

"I was not aware of this mission because it's compartmentalized, but I will tell you that Interdimensional Transport Directorate, *Doctor Oxyuran Lepidotus Taipan,* personally requested me."

"Well, you do have a reputation."

"Is that because I cut off a few spies dicks?"

"No, I'd say it's how you shot and killed some female Tramular officers is why, it shows you have no remorse killing women."

"I look at it this way. They were Spy's not women. Sex has nothing to do with who a spy is. They are in a deadly business and sometimes as you well know, the perfect plan is foiled."

"I sure hope Adrak's plan isn't foiled, I'm not sure I would want to live without him."

"He'll do fine. He has some great people who you know on his team."

"Thanks that makes me feel better."

"Listen I can't call you too often or I'll get in trouble, but I promise you that as soon as I know he's heading back from the mission I will contact you.

"Thank you I appreciate that."

"Rest well Joanie and I think in about a month I might be able to come visit you."

"Melony, I will be looking forward to your visit and thank you very much for all you do."

"My pleasure. Rest well."

The phone line went dead, and Artificial Intelligence shut down Joanie's phone and she laid back and closed her eyes with a splendid smile. In a short time, she was sleeping.

Joanies, Delta and Theta brainwaves being monitored by sensors in her pillow fed the monitoring system that evaluated Joanie as in a mental condition of sleeping. Her Alpha, Beta, and Gama waves were at quiescence with low activity.

The psychiatrist and her medical doctor came into the room then to check up on their unique patient and could see the instrumentation was indicating Joanie was in a sleep pattern and all her vital signs such as blook pressure, respiration rate, etc. were in the green band. They knew Joanie was asleep with a big smile on her face.

Artificial intelligence that monitors patient activity gave a report to the psychiatrist that Joanie had received a phone call from an interstellar communicator source and the caller's I.D. was blocked from their viewing. Only the recipient of the phone call may know the caller's I.D. from an interstellar communicator source.

The psychiatrist who had a lot of interesting patients in the past knew this was a long- distance call and the smile probably had a lot to do with Adrak. The psychiatrist smiled and looked over the chart silently with the medical doctor then left and went back to the medical doctor's office where they could discuss the results of their patient visit.

"This patient is having a radical improvement. Your psychiatric evaluations are rather astonishing," the doctor stated.

"Tell me doctor about how her wounds are healing and how's the pain management working out?"

"To be honest, I'm quite surprised. Her physical healing graphs, pain management distributions, are almost changing as fast as your psychiatric evaluations. Also, the reports from the physical therapists are amazing."

"It's like the woman is driven," the psychiatrist said.

"I know there are some patient-psychiatrist privileges that I'm not entitled to know about because of patients' privacy requirements. But can you give me a hint of what is driving her?"

"Yes doctor, you are firsthand observing the power of love."

The psychiatrist stood up smiling and walked out of the doctor's office who was now in deep thought thinking about this remarkable patient.

Just like she promised, Melonie was back 30 minutes with Adrak's food that was also spiked with sleep enhancers.

"Adrak, as soon as you finish eating, the management would like you to take a nap and rest up. You will be awakened in the middle of the night to go do a night deployment test flight."

"Alright, I like that plan."

"One other thing Adrak, I have the means of communicating with Joanie and while you were taking your bath, she informed me she was feeling a lot better and was looking forward to seeing you as soon as you get back."

"That's good to hear."

"Enjoy your meal. After you finish eating a doctor will be here to give you a quick checkup."

"Thanks for the warning."

Melony went back to her office where she did a few items, then she went to her temporary quarters and took a nap knowing artificial intelligence would wake her up so she could help Adrak hustle out of bed, freshen up if necessary and escort him to the conference room where he would meet up with the key individuals.

In the middle of the night after Adrak freshened up and put on his change of clothes that would be the type he would wear during the mission including a Kevlar bullet proof vest built into the flight coveralls.

Even though it was not necessary they went over a few details including reminding them their helmets had infrared capabilities, and the starlight alone was all that was necessary to turn darkness into daylight and as the flew from the simulated building to the escarpment it was almost no different than what they did during the daytime. There would be one big change. They would not be igniting explosives that would wake up the base. Instead, artificial intelligence would say, "You can remain standing, there will be no explosions."

The shuttle took them up into space where the glider was prepared to go. The men got into the glider and were set to deploy. The mothership remotely opened the door to the glider bay. The mother ship was in geosynchronous orbit, and it then accelerated towards the planet using it's reversers (going backwards). With the glider untethered on sitting on the Teflon sheet when the mother ship sudden stopped and went in the opposite direction using its main thruster engines the glider was launched with centrifugal force doing approximately one thousand miles per hour vertically pointing the planet. With the planet's gravity and the velocity of the glider it took very little time to approach the atmosphere and head for the landing zone.

At some distance from the target, the glider under autopilot leveled off for horizontal flight towards the target. Before it leveled off, the glider slowed below supersonic speeds, and the straight horizontal flight bled the speed off as the glider got closer to touchdown.

On the heads up display the Flur-like device allowed seeing below in high resolution. The yellow surface tracking device on the heads-up display showing the target area in infrared and the ghost image soon gave a 5 second countdown to parachute deployment and that happened. The glider gently floated down the remainder of the distance and landed. Just like before the men working in the dark using their infrared prepared themselves, flew over to the simulated warehouse and deposited the simulated satchels, then flew to the escarpment where they were informed to remain standing because there would be no explosions at night waking up the base.

They went back to the conference room had a critique, then went back out in space and flew the glider back to the surface of the planet again.

After completing the simulated mission, they did another critique and were then taken back to their rooms to eat and rest.

The spy's world is all about drugs. Drugs to enable sleep, drugs to enable waking up, drugs for enhanced perception, drugs for invincibility, drugs for this and drugs for that. And sometimes they are fed drugs even when they do not know it. This is precisely what happened now. Adrak and Cajarington were drugged. This would not be the first time Spraticus and Colonel "Blackjack" Langardo did something like this. It happens quite often.

After their breakfast the two spies were directed to rest up to make them ready for the next series of test flights.

There would be no further test flights. In the private meeting between Spraticus and Colonel "Blackjack" Langardo (the Committee) they drilled Toland.

Committee: "If they deploy today, can they pull it off?"

Toland: They just worked a long shift and are about to have a rest period. I do not think they are physically ready to go now; after resting I give them an 80% probability of success."

Committee: "If we drug them and put them on the transport can they go now?"
Toland: "Sure but you will erode their trust in you."

Committee: "When they come back as victors, we'll shower them with praise and rewards, this insertion method will be quickly forgiven."

Toland: "Why the rush?"

Committee: "The Amphibian Commander doesn't think he can hold back the Tramular's unloading their transports much longer. That collapse in effort and support may happen very soon."

Toland: "May I make a suggestion?"

Committee: "Sure."

Toland: "The three of us will be on the transport with them. When they wake up us immediately have a meeting and explain the circumstances and simply state we drugged them so they would be rested well and not have time to think about the mission which could cause negative psychology."

Committee: "That's a reasonable suggestion."

Moments after they finished their meal that drugged them that would make them sleepy, they had Doctor's visits that wanted them to take a sleep enhancer. She already knew the precursor drugs they already ingested. The combination of what they ingested with their meal and what she gave them did the finishing touches. 15 minutes later, a medical team was in the room verifying the patients' conditions. A head ring was put on them that measured brain activity and it reported the obvious: [UNCONCIOUS].

The medical team slid the two spies onto carriers that had straps to secure their bodies and prevent them from being bounced around, possibly injured or woken up.

They were wheeled out to military ambulances and driven to the space port and put on a transport. The committee was with them.

The flying wing that took them up into space was a military enhanced version that would launch the spaceship at 150,000 feet saving phenomenal amount of fuel that would allow them to burn more fuel in transit to get them to Anaserdova much sooner than the Tramulite's could get there even if they finished unloading the transports in the war zone today.

The Mother ship carrying the glider, and a Portal system was already on its way to Anaserdova and would easily get there ahead of the rest.

The decision was made not to wake the two spies up for 10 hours. This would be the last sleep they would have before they would finish the mission.

Thanks to fuel savings and a straight shot flying dark avoiding reporting to planets they passed on the way, in 10 hours traveling at the faster velocity there were about to approach Anaserdova. The two spies were still strapped down on their medical carriers and were given a invigorative gas that would enhance their wakeup. With medical people present and the three members of the committee, Adrak was woken up first. He was still strapped down when he came to the medical team and the committee there.

"I just had the strangest dream. Where am I?" Adrak asked.

"Adrak, you have been asleep for 10 hours because we wanted you rested for your mission you were strapped down to protect you while we moved you." The doctor said.

"Where did you move me too?" Adrak asked.

"Adrak you are on a Transport and the men you work with are here with you." The doctor said then nodded at Spraticus who stepped forward.

"Adrak, you no longer need to be strapped down now that you are waking up, I'm going to release your straps so you can go use the toilet, if necessary," Spraticus said.

This was a transport of a type Adrak had flown on quite a few times. He knew where the toilet was and went there by himself.

After he urinated, Adrak looked in the mirror. It was evident that he had recently shaved and had a manicure. Out of curiosity he checked and discovered they also trimmed his toenails. *That was very nice of them*, Adrak thought.

Adrak went back to where he came from, and the group was in the process of waking up Cajarington. Cajarington wasn't quite as calm as Adrak was when he came too feeling he was strapped in and jerked around a little feeling restrained.

When Adrak said, "Relax Cajarington, you will be unstrapped so you can go use the restroom," That seemed to calm Cajarington down quite a bit.

As soon as all the restraints were disengaged Adrak held out his hand and said, "Let me help you up."

"Thanks," Cajarington replied. He then stood up and he too knew the direction of the toilets and went and did his number.

Flying towards Anaserdova, the mother ship arrived off the Transport's port side. Communication was via a tightly coupled laser so as to not give off any radio signals that could warn the enemy they were coming. Moments after communicating with the mother ship, Adrak, Cajarington, Spraticus, Toland, and Colonel "Blackjack" Langardo all went up the ladder via airlock into a shuttle that took them over to the mother ship. The Shuttle landed inside the mothership shuttle bay and would be going with them in the event a shuttle ride became necessary to rescue the spies.

As soon as they were aboard the mothership and one last quick laser communication happened, the Transport turned around and went back to where it came from.

Now on the mothership, familiar faces were there who they trained with in the past.

"You men will be flying down to the planet the glider in less than one hour." Spraticus said.

"I'm ready, I want to get it over with," Adrak said.

"I like that enthusiasm," Spraticus said.

"I have a cute girlfriend I want to get back to, so we need to finish," Adrak said.

"Isn't it kind of funny how love is an inducement to men?" Spraticus said.

"Considering how many wars have been fought over women, I would say so," Adrak a history buff responded.

30 minutes before launch, Cajarington and Adrak were in the glider bay, checking everything and double checking. The battery power in the glider was good for 12 hours.

They only needed less than one hour now. Systems were powered up. Health checks were ongoing and all automated preventive maintenance/fault location algorithms running were not indicating any faults.

When checking the helmet interface, a speaker in the overhead of each passenger said, "Put on your helmet. When ready to proceed, press [GO] on the control display health check screen.

After they had their helmets on and pressed [GO], health checks on the helmet were running in the background. All health checks remained positive, and launch came up quickly.

At five minutes before launch the two glider canopies came down and sealed the glider and a 15-pound air test were completed to demonstrate no air leaks. The 5 minutes went by quickly and suddenly the glider bay hatch opened while the mother ship was maneuvering towards the planet. When the mother ship reached the velocity desired it started its propulsion motors and the glider sliding on the Teflon was released and floating down towards the planet at around one thousand miles per hour picking up velocity as gravity pulled it towards the planet.

This ride down to the planet seemed exactly like the one they practiced and the images on the heads-up display seemed identical.

The glider came down and then shifted the pitch and leveled off and started reducing speed due to drag. Before long that yellow box went over the landing zone.

The big difference is this was the real deal and, in a few minutes, they would be killing living human beings who made the fatal blunder to be in warehouse at this moment. Sadly, a couple dozen of them were recording serial numbers for the bean counters. Every *Quasar-Sonic Stasijar Battlefield Penetrators* had to be accounted for by the box kickers (logistics technicians).

The glider came in with perfection on its navigation, and soon the parachute deployed, and the glider landed softly. The men jumped out and got their back packs out and strapped them on and latched the satchels on and were ready to go.

"In case we don't make it, I was proud to serve with you," Adrak said.

Cajarington grabbed Adrak's hand, and they moved in such a way as it looked like two arm wrestlers. This was the secret handshake for Portal Spies.

"Don't forget I got your six o'clock we'll make it," Cajarington said.

"Let's go." Adrak said.

They deployed their personal drones and were soon airborne flying in the middle of the night up to an altitude of six hundred feet.

It seemed like it didn't take long to get to the target. There were four perimeter guards, and lucky for Adrak and Cajarington. Three of them were sound asleep and knew they would wake up in the morning when the yard whistle went off indicating change of shift.

The box kickers were inside the warehouse recording serial numbers on those 45-centimeter inch long missiles all night long, being admonished that within twelve hours transports would be arriving to take the shipment and they needed to have a good accounting.

These men were slightly brain dead from recording serial numbers all night long and didn't realize the importance of the sounds they heard from the rooftop.

The eggs were deposited, and artificial intelligence reported the satchels were armed. In reality, both men could now feel good, they just saved 100,000 lives because without these *Quasar-Sonic Stasijar Battlefield Penetrators,* there would be no way for the Tramular's to do anything about the pincer attacks the Vekkar's could now continue until they crushed their enemy. With this one act, Adrak's legacy was painted in Vekkar history.

They now flew to the escarpment and just like they trained, artificial intelligence said, get down low. As soon as artificial intelligence saw the men were laying on the ground, the two satchels were detonated. The shaped charges sent a hot explosion that went down through the thin tin metal roof right into the middle of where the box kickers had pallets of rockets open writing down serial numbers. That explosion and shock wave was so hot within a fifty-foot radius it cooked off several hundred *QuasarSonic Stasijar Battlefield Penetrators* each with the explosive force of a 1000-pound gravity dropped bomb. Several hundred of these missiles cooking off at the same time created plasma that soon cooked off every missile in the building creating an explosion the size of a small nuke.

People on the mother ship saw the fiery explosion and were impressed with its illuminance. It created a miniature sun for that side of the planet that was dark in the middle of the night to daylight. The noise and vibration from the explosion set off earthquake monitors and the sound could be heard for several hundred miles.

Adrak and Cajarington bounced around on the ground hard and had injuries as if they had just fell ten feet. After the blast died down and it was quiet again and getting darker artificial intelligence said, "Stand up now your way home has appeared."

Cajarington was beaten up badly and Adrak who also was in severe pain managed to get him to his feet and shoved Cajarington into a portal and painfully walked into the other. They were now gone and appeared on the mothership that had already triggered the self- destruct on the glider that now blew up into a million pieces that didn't seem to bother anyone nearby since they were all dead.

The blast blew out every glass window within a 20-mile radius and fifty plus homes disintegrated. The adjacent factory that built the missiles also had severe collateral damage and would not be manufacturing anything anytime soon.

Because of their injuries they were sedated and cleaned up on the mother ship that had doctors who stated these men needed to be admitted to a hospital because they each had broken bones and one of them had some severe organ damage from being bounced really hard from the shockwave. But as it turns out, the spot on the escarpment was the very best place for them as a lot of the other area on the escarpment took a lot of plasma heat and had they been anywhere else they likely would have been cooked.

The critique for this mission would last several weeks. The reason why the explosion was a lot worse than they predicted is there were almost triple the number of missiles in the warehouse, so VIA information was not accurate enough.

Due to the secrecy of the mission and who was involved there was only one place where Adrak and Cajarington could be taken with sufficient security and seclusion. The same one Joanie was licking her wounds in.

The psychiatrist treating Joanie was now alarmed as soon as she found out who the two new patients were in private rooms with armed guards outside their doors.

To say Adrak was messed up really good was a mild way of putting it.

The psychiatrist decided to withhold the information from Joanie for a day or two as to not trigger more melancholy with her might have been a good plan. But like all good plans this one fell apart real fast.

Joanie was now to the point she could get around good with a cane and was just walking back from rehabilitation when she saw Spraticus, Colonel "Blackjack" Langardo, Toland and Transport Directorate, *Doctor Oxyuran Lepidotus Taipan,* leave one of the two rooms that had armed guards outside.

Joanie was a smart woman, an intel analyst and a deadly spy. She knew the odds of *Doctor Oxyuran Lepidotus Taipan,* walking with VIA, and Project KOBRA SPEKTR together meant the patient had to be someone she knew. And who was just sent on a mission? ADRAK!

With her cane and the psychiatrist coming up fast on her six o'clock Joanie virtually ran up to *Doctor Oxyuran Lepidotus Taipan,* who she knew wouldn't bullshit her and demanded, "Is Adrak in that room?"

She looked at their faces and the truth was written all over their faces, she panicked and made her way to the room and the security guard tried to stop her. She might be in pain but she still knew her martial arts and faster than anyone present could believe she knocked out the security guard and made her way in the room and there he was, her precious Adrak.

There was enough of Adrak showing to know damn well who he was. Adrak had medical attendants in the room who were on the other side of the bed and out of position to stop her. Adrak was coming out of a drug induced fog. He was on life support and in bad shape.

Joanie laid her head down on his chest and started crying. Poor Adrak had been through far too much for any person. The two medical staff people were approaching Joanie to pull her off Adrak when suddenly one of them had a hand on her and it was

Doctor Oxyuran Lepidotus Taipan, who said:

"Leave her alone, that's his lover."

The medical staff were now utterly shocked.

The psychiatrist came in and was also approaching Joanie and Colonel "Blackjack" Langardo grabbed her hand and put his finger up to his mouth and said "Shhhhhhh."

They didn't know if Adrak was going to make it. His prognosis was maybe 49%.

Then suddenly he started tapping Joanie on her back, and as much as it hurt, he said, "Thank you for welcoming me home. You saved me."

The psychiatrist who knew them both quite well, stood there shaking her head. She had never seen anything like this in her lifetime. She and the chief surgeon were going to have another great discussion.

Doctor Oxyuran Lepidotus Taipan knew that Adrak had earned this moment more than anyone said, "Would everyone please leave the room and give the couple a moment of privacy. He and "Blackjack" Langardo helped several of them out of the room.

Adrak knew at this very moment that he was now safe, and he would make it just fine. Patients' attitudes go a long way to enhancing their survival.

When they were suddenly alone in the room Adrak said, "I know you are kind of weak with your own injuries, but do you think you can help me sit up?"

"I'll help you honey," Joanie said.

They had to struggle but between the two of them they were able to get Adrak sitting up in bed. He had just been given some pain medications and lots of analgesics, and healing expediter drugs designed specifically for war wounded military people to make them ambulatory much quicker to get them out of the warzone fast.

"I feel so much better knowing you are here," Adrak said.

"Well, I feel a lot better knowing you are here and safe even if you are beat up a little."

Meanwhile the other men helped the security guard to his feet and sat him down in the chair put there so he didn't have to stand throughout his shift. Since he was in the hospital, Spraticus, who had a lot of control over VIA directed the medical staff to give him some first aid and verify he was okay. *Other than the embarrassment of getting knocked out by a crippled woman on a cane, he was doing okay.*

Adrak should have been going to sleep by now with all the sedatives and pain killers, but he was hungry and after they said all their lovely things to each other, Adrak mentioned "I'm getting really hungry."

"Why don't you press your buzzer and ask they give you something to eat."

"Good idea."

Adrak pressed the buzzer and the medical people being held outside the room suddenly ran in, fearing the worst that Adrak had a setback to find him sitting up in bed smiling and Joanie smiling as well.

The staff was shocked, and one could only ask, "What can we do to help you?"

"I'm kind of hungry, can I get some Kratchen soup?" Adrak asked.

A lot of Earth people would think Kratchen soup tastes like chicken soup or rattle snake meat soup.

The chief surgeon arrived after being informed of the circus that was going on to size it up himself and had read the prognosis of the patient giving him odds of less than 50% for surviving, just asking for some Kratchen soup, sitting up in his bed all smiles!

"That's a great idea," the surgeon said as he was taking it all in.

The staff immediately contacted the hospital chef who designed all the patient's meals and knew Kratchen soup had a lot of natural melatonin in it and responded, "That will help the patient rest better with his pain management regiment."

In due time Adrak was served his Kratchen soup and as he finished it the combination of his sedatives and the melatonin in his Kratchen soup that was delicious and filled him up was making him drowsy.

"Joanie, I'm getting sleepy now. I'll come see you when I wake up later."

"Alright dear, sleep well. I'll check in on you."

Joanie then bent over and hugged Adrak, feeling so wonderful with his touch. Adrak was soon laying down and falling to sleep with his brain monitors giving the printout [sleeping].

The psychiatrist helped Joanie back to her own hospital bed noticed her cheerfulness was quite robust.

"You know I may have a problem sleeping tonight." Joanie said. "Why is that? the Psychiatrist asked.

"I'm so excited Adrak is back and because of our injuries we'll be on convalescence leave for a while and can spend some time together."

"It's a shame the two of you have to get injured just to get time off together." The psychiatrist said and the two women laughed a little.

"I'll talk to the nurse when I leave here in a few moments and fix you up with something that will help you sleep comfortably."

"Thank you doctor."

"My pleasure."

The VIA men were now gone, but they would be back tomorrow visiting with Cajarington who was beat up by the shockwave just as bad as Adrak. The two men survived the explosion the best they could. They were sucking dirt as low as they got so they did all they could, but the force of the blast and all the tornadic air currents whipped their bodies around regardless. However, being low did keep them from being sliced up by shrapnel. Had either one of them been standing the shrapnel would likely have cut their heads off and they would have been blown a long way down the escarpment.

The next day after the explosion when the Tramular transports and their escorts showed up, members of that force had a sinking feeling that about all was lost now with that battle. There were no magic bullets left.

Thanks to Cajarington and Adrak, the battle soon reached the point where the Tramular's started evacuating their force off the planet to preserve the units for a fight at another time and place. What started out as what they thought was a quick and easy victory quickly turned into a slow agonizing defeat. In due time the remainer of the Tramular's abruptly evacuated on the same transports that were sent to pick up their silver bullets, the *Quasar-Sonic Stasijar Battlefield Penetrators*

One of the commanders in the battle assigned with the Amphibians was none other than Colonel Suzan Marklar. She had some VIA Intel people with her group and one of them was injured badly and sent to the same hospital and ward that Adrak was located. While visiting the VIA person she bumped into Toland and Lt. Colonel Tom Atractaspidi who came to visit Adrak.

They had a short conversation and asked who they were visiting, and they informed her it was one of her former students.

"How did he get injured?"

"He was sent to blow up a warehouse full of *Quasar-Sonic Stasijar Battlefield Penetrators* to prevent them from being used against the Amphibians in their recent battle."

"Oh my god, that's where I just came from. Was he successful?"

"Yep, that's why he's in the hospital, he blew up the whole warehouse which had a lot more missiles in it than INTEL knew about. So, it had a much stronger explosion than they anticipated. He and his partner Cajarington got tossed around badly with tornadic winds and the shockwave."

"Were you going in to see him?"

"Yes, would you like to come with us and say hello to him."

"Definitely, he probably did far more for us than he realizes. We owe him a lot."

"Alright, let's go see him."

"They went in the room and Adrak was sitting up in bed with Joanie sitting in the seat beside the bed in here own hospital gown."

"Guess who came to see you Adrak."

"Hello Colonel."

"Good to see you Adrak. I wanted to come and personally thank you for what you did. What you probably didn't know when you were doing your mission, I was with the Amphibians as part of a Joint operation, and your actions had a direct impact on the outcome of the mission. You don't know this, but you saved a lot of lives."

"I'm glad I was able to help out."

"Adrak I'm very proud that you are one of my former students." Colonel Suzan Marklar said.

"Thank you, Colonel."

Colonel Suzan Marklar looked at Joanie who was holding Adak's hand and thought that was unique two people in the hospital holding hands then she realized she knew this woman from some place. She looked down at Joanie and smiled and said, "I know you from some place."

"Yes, I was assigned to Project KOBRA SPEKTR," Joanie said.

"That's right, now I remember. Why are you in the hospital dear?"

"I was captured by the Tramulite's I was severely injured during the takedown. Bad luck. Adrak here saved my life."

"How did he do that if I may ask." Colonel Suzan Marklar asked.

"Adrak is a very brave man. He captured one of the top Tramulite spy's, a woman with the alias Karoline Morganthau. They did a spy swap to get her back. Me and my partner Corgrelius were swapped for her and another spy who is a Vekkar traitor and almost got Adrak killed several times," Joanie said.

"It's amazing how some of this all gets tied together. How about yourself are you making good recovery?" Colonel Suzan Marklar asked.

Yes, every day I'm anxious to do my rehabilitation and I'm getting my strength back and my pain management is getting better. I can now walk around okay with a cane." Joanie said.

"I need to go visit one of my men injured in the battle, so I will leave you two to have some privacy. Can you do me a favor dear?" Colonel Suzan Marklar asked.

"Sure."

"In a couple minutes tell these two guys to leave to give you some privacy with Adrak. You two sure earned it." Colonel Suzan Marklar said.

"Not a problem," Joanie said.

Colonel Suzan Marklar held out her hand to Joanie and smiled then she held her hand out to Adrak and grasped it and said, "I hope you recover fast, Adrak."

"Thank you, Colonel, and thank you for visiting me."

"My pleasure."

Chapter Nineteen

Recovery and Rehabilitation

Adrak's strength returned rapidly as the biological wound accelerators seemed to work well on him. He always went to Rehabilitation with Joanie and the two acted like a catalyst for each other which enhanced the wound recovery accelerators process.

Adrak had one substantial benefit from the last mission and the injuries he sustained. Adrak and Cajarington's lives were probably saved from the personal drone backpacks they were wearing when the explosion occurred at the Anaserdova warehouse that protected their backs while the helmets protected their head, though they were bounced around like a yoyo slamming against the rocky soil a time or two breaking a few bones and damaging some internal organs.

Each spy had to have internal surgery to make important medical procedures, or they would likely have died. When Adrak first arrived at the VIA secret hospital, and his prognosis was less than 50% the was probably a realistic number. Adrak might not have ever come back to consciousness had Joanie not triggered the emotional center of his brain that ultimately woke him up. The staff had nothing that would have awakened Adrak otherwise and with a decaying physical condition, he was destined to die.

The hospital was not in a rush to treat Adrak like before, and since they had to perform several surgeries and a skin graft, the Chief Surgeon so moved by everything he discovered about the two spies and the power of love, had a lot of influence over rehabilitative surgeries including dealing with scar tissue.

Colonel Suzan Marklar was now a very influential person and kept in touch with the chief surgeon at the VIA hospital as well as the psychiatrist. About the same time the chief surgeon was contemplating scar removal on Adrak, Colonel Suzan Marklar paid him a private visit.

"Thanks for seeing me, Doctor."

"It's my pleasure Colonel especially since you are a national hero and winning the battle with the Amphibians you commanded, it's an honor to meet you."

"Thank you doctor. I'm not exactly sure what the VIA or Project KOBRA SPEKTR intends to do with Joanie after all this, but she is very talented and has been a participant in some missions that had a huge impact on our present military status."

"My orders are to *stabilize and treat* the three patients Adrak, Joanie and Cajarington."

"Oh my God that is terrible. I've been around the block, and I know exactly what that means, they will carry their scars around for the rest of their lives."

"Yes, probably so."

"Doctor, I know you operate off your instructions, guidelines, and protocols, and do what management tells you to do. Unfortunately for the cases of Adrak and Joanie, *stabilize and treat* is a travesty when you stop to think about the contributions, they made such as allowing my force to survive the onslaught and achieve victory."

"Thank you for understanding." The chief surgeon replied.

"Doctor, I'm going to work on getting you more flexibility with these two patients Adrak and Joanie who are not going to be subject to any new missions for a while."

"What do you have in mind?"

"I'm going to visit Spraticus because he and I have some planning and implementation meetings for some new initiatives. I'm going to press him into a side bar so that I can get him to agree to give you new guidance and instead of *stabilize and treat*, I want the terminology added that says *restore*."

"Spraticus wields a lot of power if you can get him to send the hospital new official guidance for these two patients saying stabilize, treat, and restore, its true it will expend a lot of extra doctor's hours, but I've seen my cosmetic surgeons to some miracles. If we get the added tasking, I'll make it happen."

"I know Spraticus is going to want me to prepare for a new mission that will require a very capable female spy. For this mission we absolutely cannot have a woman with tattoos or several nasty looking scars. Expect to get re-directed real soon."

"I look forward to redirection and I do really want to *restore* since those two patients have paid a lot by their contribution to the war effort."

Colonel Suzan Marklar lived up to her promise and visited Spraticus and they talked about that future mission they both knew would happen.

Spraticus need a capable spy like Joanie, but he could not send a woman who had appearances of damaged goods because it would send up a red flag quickly this person might have been military or connected in some way to receive those scars.

The chief surgeon understood that Adrak previously had some compelling business to attend while being treated during the previous hospital stay. But now that Adrak was down and out and not clearable for any mission until the mandatory convalescent was completed, the chief surgeon instituted work on all the scar tissue on his back covering all those ugly bullet holes. Each scar tissue had a skin graft and reconstructive surgery. By the time Adrak left the VIA hospital, his back bullet hole scars were gone. With the skin grafts on his legs, Adrak wound up 95% cosmetically repaired from all his injuries sustained in missions.

Within three weeks Joanie and Adrak were moved out of the hospital and were now outpatients on convalescence leave. With their aggressive rehabilitation work, good pain management, and the biological wound healing accelerators, they were soon permitted to take a vacation which they did together as long as they only went some place near good medical facilities and get weekly remote checkups that were scheduled by Project KOBRA SPEKTR that took the lead on overseeing their recovery process.

Joanie and Adrak didn't have a lot of incentive to leave the Vekkar home world and searched for the ultimate nearby vacation locations. Down near the equator was a series of Islands that had a tourist area called Pàrgŏnzéfrās (pronounced: Par-goanezay-fress) that featured beautiful white sandy beaches, luxury hotels and a very good hospital.

The two spies were now fully mobile and could walk without a cane. They no longer had open sores, but they were still getting over painful episodes.

The Fĕicuì de Lùzhōu Resort they selected; had an air-conditioned exercise room they would make good use of. They also had numerous places to walk, that included guided walking tours.

The resulting cosmetic surgery was soon completed for Joanie and Adrak. They would appear to be a handsome couple walking around Pàrgŏnzéfrās.

Joanie and Adrak each had a lot of combat pay and INTEL HAZZARDOUS DUTY PAY which increased their salaries 35% while they were assigned to Project KOBRA SPEKTR and since they had no down time for a lengthy period, they each now had substantial credits to enjoy lavish vacations and joyous times together. Joanie and Adrak had free medical so they didn't have to pay for any of that and during their doctor's visits while enjoying time off there would not be any procedures needed.

Pàrgŏnzéfrās main hospital within walking distance of Fĕicuì de Lùzhōu Resort of where they were staying had dealt with a lot of VIA personnel in the past and it was not a big surprise for them when they had visitors informing them one of their doctors would be making appointments with them and oversee and report medical status to people who had concern in their cases.

The supervisory VIA doctors were of course quite satisfied their visits turned out to be restoration results monitoring to make sure the patients had no adverse side effects. Secret surveillance video was provided to the psychiatrist who monitored patients' mental well-being and was very happy how they progressed. But she knew the facts, these two individuals had some sort of magical healing powers towards each other.

One issue that seemed to never die down was Adrak's combined infrared/ ultraviolet blurry image taken while he was working out heavily. The researchers that were making noise about that and wanting access to Adrak to monitor him some more and perform some elaborate checks were pulled into a secret meeting and shown Adrak's severe wounds before *restoration* and advised the researchers it would be a while before he was physically capable to do any sort of strenuous exercise. Of course, all those wounds were healed about the time the researchers were gawking at the photos and decided it was prudent on their behalf to go away and not pester VIA for a while.

The two lovers had not experienced any happy times since Adrak had sworn he would not fall in love with Joanie. It was clear to both the situation had changed and even if they were adhering to that previous mindset, their injuries reminded them they were living on borrowed time, and it was time to throw caution to the wind and take gigantic risks in evolving interpersonal relationships.

Joanie had already made up her mind, if the VIA purposely kept them apart in the future like they did other spies that became romantically involved, she had another option, resign and become a domestic engineer.

Joanie knew it was only a matter of time before she would have to tell her handlers they risked her becoming a full-time domestic engineer if they got in the way of her relationship with Adrak. The other possibility they never contemplated, *what if they lost them at the same time and Adrak chose to pursue another line of work?*

Nevertheless, Spraticus was a smarter operator than many others, he would rather there be fraternization between the two spies than losing them. He also understood Adrak would soon be dipping his pen in company ink.

To get to Pàrgŏnzéfrās the couple had to fly halfway around the world on a stratospheric transport that flew on the fringes of the atmosphere allowing great speed without inflicting sonic booms on populations below them. It was almost as taxing as going to another planet via Intergalactic Transport.

When they checked in to the Fěicuì de Lùzhōu Resort they had a temporary identity. They had to protect themselves and act as if they were spies since they were still members of VIA and in the case of Adrak, Transport Directorate, *Doctor Oxyuran Lepidotus Taipan* remained his supervisor.

VIA had Alexis Tegaro and Sabastian Rollie programmed for them during this vacation. Those aliases were used at the tourist city of Kōrāll on planet Fŏrlāgér because they could not use their real names of Joanie and Adrak, because that would be the same as handing over to the enemy the NOK list for these two individuals if they met SMERSH agents accidentally here.

It was a far-gone conclusion SMERSH agents walked among the Vekkar people just like VIA personnel inserted blended in with the Tramulars's.

Occasionally SMERSH and VIA people ran into each other unexpectedly. In some cases, such as Karoline Morganthau, she had Adrak indelibly etched in her mind, so if any such accidental meeting happened, they would instantly know who the other person was. Surprisingly, such accidental meetings happened all too often. And when you have a mole in your group it happens even more often.

Adrak knew turning Karoline Morganthau loose would one day bite VIA in the arse. But at the same time, Adrak knew he would be crushed knowing Joanie was being routinely tortured by SMERSH and probably killed eventually. Turing one of the best SMERSH spies loose at least made him feel good knowing it saved Joanie's life.

Adrak wouldn't have minded inflicting great pain on the Mole 000090317A512941 (a.k.a. Zmeya Rembert).

But all that was behind them. Now they could unwind and live for the moment at least.

When they checked in their communicators loaded with Spĕctrāl de Dòngtài artificial intelligence, would help keep them safe as it was able to break into all the security and surveillance systems at the Fĕicuì de Lùzhōu Resort and practically everywhere they went.

If Spĕctrāl de Dòngtài artificial intelligence somehow identified a SMERSH agent, it would immediately put a tracker on the spy and VIA would immediately start tracking the spy through satellite links and other means.

If they accidentally came across Karoline Morganthau, VIA would be sending a task force to take the spy down rapidly. However, in the spy business there is no guarantee a top spy like Karoline Morganthau didn't have an elaborate bug out plan and the means to disappear, especially since there were traitors that existed on the planet, they had no idea who they were.

In the case of Mole 000090317A512941 (a.k.a. Zmeya Rembert), it took someone special like Adrak suffering great injuries to turn him, and they got lucky. Had SMERSH not overplayed their hand to give the appearance of apparent compromise, there never would have been a reason to go after Zmeya Rembert. But even with Zmeya Rembert taken out of the picture, they learned the hard way, SMERSH was still around as it was indeed a nine headed snake ready to strike from multiple directions.

The recent devastation of several Tramulite major initiatives by a single spy Adrak netted him on the top 10 kill list. Adrak would be a target until they killed him, and they would go out of their way to find him and set a trap. Loose lips sank ships and all they needed to do was find another traitor and the day of reconning was sooner than VIA was willing to entertain in their poor philosophy living on their laurels because of recent success stories.

Fĕicuì de Lùzhōu Resort immediately had Alexis Tegaro and Sabastian Rollie in their system including facial recognition since that's how all transactions were handled.

The two were escorted up to their room in the resort that was one of the better rooms with a fantastic view of the beach. Bellhops delivered their luggage, there was no physical exertion required on their part which was fine with the two.

Soon they were alone for the first time since they were at the tourist city of Kōrāll on planet Fŏrlāgér.

As much as they wanted to enjoy the celestial feasts, two things were happening, they were suffering from stratospheric transport lag (jet lag). They also were due to take their pain medications now or their pain management would fall apart.

"Listen Adrak, I'm very tired now. I want to take my medications and take a nap. Why don't you take your medication with me, then let's lay down and cuddle and rest." Joanie suggested.

"Sounds like a great idea," Adrak said.

The two took their medications, undressed and got into their large King Size bed and were soon falling asleep. The medications they took had several applications. First and foremost was pain management. The second was the healing accelerators for their internal injuries that were slowly getting better, and the third was a sleep inducer. In a matter of minutes their minds were somewhere else, but Joanie had a strange feeling. She felt very comfortable and safe.

When Joanie was cuddled by Adrak her Aura intersected his and that blurry image of Adrak when he was meditating dealing with exhaustion now intersected Joanie's Aura and strange effects occurred that were very pleasant.

It was now moments of peace and harmony and expansive happiness. Joanie, who would portray Alexis during this holiday, felt uplifted and extremely satisfied with the feelings she now felt.

Joanie knew what was in Adrak's heart, there was no mistaking it. She had warned him not to fall in love with her because she's a spy. It was her world, and she had no intentions of departing from it until recently.

Perhaps it was her terrible and painful injuries that made her feel like she almost wished she was dead to end the suffering.

But suddenly Adrak approached her in her greatest time of need and a mysterious development took place where Adrak snapped her out of it and made her want to go on living.

Adrak did it exactly at the same time he announced he was in love with Joanie.

Joanie then hospitalized in a lot of pain, also had the critical review created when her friend Melony called her to let her know she was with Adrak and assigned to look after him. She would contact Joanie when Adrak returned from the mission as planned. Unfortunately, the explosion wounded Adrak very severely and he didn't return and just like magic for some unknown reason,

Joanie found out Adrak was in the same hospital and in serious pain and about to die. That's when the fusion of their aura's occurred. Their power of love had tremendous effects and now at this very moment as they were resting peacefully, Joanie (a.k.a. Alexis) was receiving waves of love somehow through the ethereal and feeling better than she had in many years.

Due to the 12-hour time zone change, Joanie and Adrak slept through lunch. They did not become coherent until late in the afternoon, right about the time they felt hungry.

"I'm so hungry dear," Joanie said.

"This resort, like most of them probably has a bar/restaurant by their swimming pool. Let's go down there and get a bit to eat, then we can figure out what to do after that," Adrak said.

"I like that idea, it will not take me long to dress," Joanie said.

This was also going to be good for Adrak to check out the swimming pool since the doctors advised him not to swim in the ocean as he may get infections in wounds that could have minor exposures.

Five minutes later the handsome couple was out of their resort room and on the way to get something to eat.

While in the elevator they saw a map of the resort which gave them all the directions they needed. Adrak snapped a picture of the elevator MAP.

Just like Adrak assumed there was a restaurant by the nice pool, and they went inside. The Maître d' sat them down at a nice table with a good view of the pool and close enough to see the performers.

Most of the population on the Vekkar capital planet Vekkar Blesk appeared Caucasian and would easily pass for Europeans from Earth. Some of the Vekkar Territories at other star systems had people of complex racial makeup. The performers on the small stage were green skin women most likely from the planet Franzon where the Franzonian Philosophers lived in a cult like style that most outsiders avoided.

The only reason why the Franzonian Philosophers tolerated Vekkar's is because there were worse examples of humanity in the solar system that was utterly pungent to them. The Franzonian Philosophers tolerated Vekkar's mainly because of the *Modus Vivendi* built upon the philosophy of empire wide separation of church and state. The Vekkar government had stiff rules about not getting involved in any sort of religious matters.

The Franzonian Philosophers were very strict at what types of music they tolerated on Franzon. Even though inspiring young musicians and singers wanted to perform music on the prohibited list, at least their singing skills and instrumentation was second to none.

There were a few Fanzon's who traveled to other worlds for trade and commerce and thus were exposed to the great spectrum of musical styles. Some of them also had multiple discoveries of educational opportunities to improve their medical and technical skills that went along to building a better and more advanced world. Since Fanzon's were part of the empire and in good standing, providing military personnel for wars and precious resources such as metals and rare minerals, the children of these Franzon travelers had no issues getting accepted in institutions of higher learning and music schools. Since Franzon singers were significantly trained by incredible teachers, their vocal cords and dexterity were second to none.

Adrak and Joanie both had heard Franzon singers before, so this was not a huge revelation to them. This singing group was very good, and their musical output, based on general Vekkar entertainment standards, created splendid songs and music for the restaurant goers.

"What would you like to drink?" the waitress who came to their table right away asked.

"Do you have Trambrosier Elixirs?" Joanie asked.

That question immediately caused Adrak to think about the train ride with Martilene Chares. It would have created melancholy, but the Franzon singers were performing such a beautiful song, he temporarily sidestepped a dent to his heart.

The memories of Martilene triggered Adrak's thought, and he said, I would like a glass of Jiǎo Gǒu Yúyuè Qì (pronounced Jiow-Go You-Yea Chi) wine. This wine, known in many solar systems was a combined pleasurizers and some men thought it stimulated their libido. It was expensive and had quite an effect.

The waitress knew about the subtle effects of Jiǎo Gǒu Yúyuè Qì and wondered if the gentleman was ordering it because he had big plans for his girlfriend?

In a short time, the combination of the Franzon singers and the Jiǎo Gǒu Yúyuè Qì, created the psychological tapestry that quickly faded Martilene from Adrak's thoughts and put Joanie front and center that now created the ethereal content of his mind responding to the pleasurizers mixed into the wine.

Joanie wasn't fascinated by green skin women and sat down with her back to them giving Adrak the view of them. Joanie and Adrak were both hungry and not here for the entertainment, though it did add nicely to their atmosphere.

The waitress saw the couple scanning the menu when she delivered their drinks and thus asked, "Would you like a food order?"

Joanie said, "Yes. I would like the Dravergor seafood combination."

"That's a lot of food, mam, just so you know," the Waitress said.

"I'll share some of it with my sweetheart then."

"Sir what would you like?"

"Since I'm going to have some of her meal, I'll just order a side of *Hop and Swim* (frog legs and turtle).

"Good choice, our chef does a really good job on *Hop and Swim meats*."

Later when the entrées were served, Adrak noticed the meat was all boneless and someone took the time to strip the meat from the legs or carcass. The Fěicuì de Lùzhōu Resort Chef utilized the best of native Pàrgǒnzéfrās spices and herbs that created a flavorful and lovely aroma to the meal.

The waitress placed an extra dish on the table so that Joanie could share some of her Dravergor seafood combination with Adrak and like the waitress warned there was more food there than Joanie could handle.

Halfway through the meal they needed refills which the waitress gladly provided. Since this was a resort operating off facial recognition charging the meals to their room, part of the protocols including to ask the guest percentages for tips which Adrak had selected 18% since he was flush with credits₿. Upon ordering the meal the charge was made and the tip exposed. The waitress was naturally very accommodative because many of the resort guests were not so generous.

The second set of drinks created a pleasant atmosphere as Joanie and Adrak were now responding to the drugging that was part of their drink chemistry. The guests were responding exactly the way the inventors of the drinks inspired them to achieve commercial success.

It was a happy and joyous occasion, the calm before the storm. The two spies were not 100% healed but 90% was one hell of a lot better than what they were just three weeks ago. And even though internally they were still wounded, the cosmetic surgeons had done wonders and people that would observe them at the Fěicuì de Lùzhōu Resort had no idea how just three weeks ago their bodies looked ravaged.

Transport Directorate, *Doctor Oxyuran Lepidotus Taipan,* had visited Adrak just a couple days before and appeared at the rehabilitation swimming pool where Adrak was getting some good exercise.

As Adrak moved around drying off and putting on his swim/bath robe, *Doctor Oxyuran Lepidotus Taipan,* saw up close and personal the miraculous job these cosmetic surgeons had done removing all his scar tissue and restoring him. They sat down together at one of the tables provided for patients to congregate and talk during their exercise period when they took breaks.

"I'm glad they did a great job of restoring you Adrak," *Doctor Oxyuran Lepidotus Taipan* said.

"So am I, *Taipan*" Adrak responded using the personal name since they were alone.

"I want to tell you how you got such good medical procedures." *Taipan* said.

"Sure, I would like to know because one of the surgeons informed me it was extremely rare to get the full restoration like I did, because they assumed I would be killed probably in a couple years as a spy, so why bother?"

"That doctor had an astute observation," *Taipan* said.

"If that's the case, why did I get fully restored?" Adrak asked.

"You would have no way of knowing this, nor did I at the time. Colonel Suzan Marklar was part of a Joint Task Group and happened to be with the 100,000 Amphibians you saved when you blew up the warehouse on Anaserdova."

"If that's the case I'm glad I helped her in some way."

"She knows what you did because when she discovered you were at the hospital and met with the chief surgeon, she got involved."

"How so?"

"The chief surgeon informed her what your treatment would be. Since she must deal with war wounded and was there visiting a VIA rep that worked for her in a nearby room, she was almost floored when the chief surgeon said what he was ordered to do as part of your recovery which was stabilize and treat."

"That sounds like what I would expect," Adrak said.

"Colonel Suzan Marklar paid Spraticus a personal visit and demanded he direct the chief surgeon to add restoration to the tasking, otherwise you would be carrying those scars around with you the rest of your life."

"I hope to one day see Colonel Suzan Marklar again to personally thank her,"

Adrak said.

"I've already received requests from Project KOBRA SPEKTR to loan you to them for another future mission. I believe Colonel Suzan Marklar will oversee your training, so you will have the opportunity to thank her."

"How soon do you think this will happen?" Adrak asked.

"It can't happen until you are healed up because you are going to have to go through training like you did with Joanie in preparation for the Intergalactic Dreadnaught Carrier mission."

"That's some pretty rough training, I definitely need to heal up some for that level of exertion," Adrak said.

"You will be given the time. Project KOBRA SPEKTR is obviously interested in how effective those healing accelerators are working."

***

Adrak's mind shifted back to his current reality listening to the beautiful Franzon singers' music, keeping him in a joyous mood.

Joanie was feeling marvelous and since she had not had any Big-A in a while, her two Trambrosier Elixirs were putting her in the mood.

They were not in the mood to quickly finish their entrées, plus the tall dish was tall because it was three times as thick to accommodate the food warming surface warm throughout the meal. Digital temperature monitors kept the plate surface at a precise temperature expert had experimented with to derive the best temperature for the satisfaction of the patrons.

The dishes with built in food warmers turned on via wireless which gave status to the server the plate was almost empty thanks to digital scales to measure the weight of the contents. Also, a sensor in the plate electronics recorded lack of activity generated by customers finished eating brought the waitress to their table promptly to remove the dish and take additional orders such as deserts.

Long before they finished their entrée's the green skin performers finished the set and the four women walked through the customers greeting them and creating spontaneous conversations.

One of the green skin performers, Helénē came by Joanie and Adrak's table and introduced herself.

"Are you having a good time?"

"Yes, we are," Adrak said.

"What's your names if I might ask?" Helénē asked.

"I'm Sabastian and this is Alexis," Adrak said using their alias.

Adrak would not have noticed it, but a man at the bar smiled hearing his comments. Adrak explored the man and quickly ascertained it was none other than Lt. Colonel Tom Atractaspidi. And his disguise was not all that effective!

That discovery immediately put Adrak in a critical thought. Having a super spook like Lt. Colonel Tom Atractaspidi in this bar at this precise moment meant they were here. And why?It could be several reasons why, including assassination, one could never assume anything in the spy business. The other reason could be protection. He would soon come to find out he was indeed protected. Why is that?

During his stay at the Fěicuì de Lùzhōu Resort, Adrak would soon discover that if he was ever away from a base, he would have protection. He had not yet been informed he was now on the top10 list to kill any means possible. The Tramulars had tallied up the damage Adrak had done to them thanks to the mole and a second mole they would soon confirm. Few people, including the best scientists, had ever damaged them quite as badly as Adrak.

Numbers and statistics mean something. Not only do bean counters care about statistics so do planners and organizers of organizations like SMERSH. Simply by taking down Adrak they could save themselves irreparable damage. They knew the facts of life in the spy business 10% of the people do 90% of the work. Adrak was part of the 10% and he was now marked for life. SMERSH would do anything and everything to locate him and kill him and the 2nd mole was helping them in that regard.

Lucky for Adrak he had been on a Project KOBRA SPEKTR and would be going back to a Project KOBRA SPEKTR assignment which prevented the second mole from providing the information SMERSH was seeking so they could circle the wagons, trap Adrak and kill him.

Another dirty secret Adrak didn't know yet: he was the bait and part of an operation he didn't know had already started.

Adrak knew the woman was tired from singing and needed a drink and some rest and asked, "Would you like to join us?"

"Sure," Helénē stated slightly nervous because a lot of girlfriends got upset when a boyfriend asked her to sit down with them.

Helénē had no idea this couple were dangerous spies, and Joanie would simply kill her if she fooled around with Adrak. Adrak on the other hand had gone through some extraordinary times with Joanie and wasn't about to mess with another woman any time soon, which Joanie knew and thus would not be alarmed by Adrak's gentlemanliness in the offer.

"How's your vacation been so far?" Helénē asked.

"We just got here and are still working our way through travel fatigue."

"Did you have to travel a long distance?" Helénē asked.

"Yes, we came all the way from Crocus," Adrak said.

"I can understand why, that's a long trip," Helénē said.

"Are you from Pàrgŏnzéfrās," Adrak asked knowing these women were from Franzon.

"No, we are all from Franzon, but we were educated on other empire worlds and have performed on a lot of empire planets.

"I enjoyed your singing very much," Joanie said.

"Thank you very much, that means a lot to me," Helénē replied.

Joanie knew a lot about the entertainment business because sometimes she had to deploy as an entertainer in her missions. Joanie was a great singer and musician so when the VIA inserted her somewhere, that was her disguise, and it worked well.

One of the misconceptions a lot of people had about cabaret singers is they would never be smart enough to be a galactic class spy. Joanie decided one day she would sing for Adrak and surprise him. But she needed the right venue to do it in.

Adrak looked at Heléné mystical purple eyes. Her red hair and her perfectly rounded face created a tapestry of beauty. Up close Heléné looked far more beautiful than she did on the stage. Heléné's body was also unique. She was tall but she was thin. Her waist that was exposed with her costume was considerably narrower than her hips. She looked fragile yet wonderful. Heléné's voice was also very pleasant and Adrak could now understand why her singing was so wonderful.

Joanie knew the four Franzon singers were vulnerable and mistreated at times. Some of the producers were creeps and had no issues sticking their pen in company ink at the expense of these young girls' hearts. Joanie knew that for a fact and encountered it herself several times. Unfortunately for one producer who was the worst, Joanie took matters in her own hands because her controller was not intervening.

Joanie knew the VIA didn't mind this creep doing bad things as long as their spy was shielded from who she really was.

Just when the creep thought he was going to insert his Johnson inside Joanie for the grand gratification he soon found himself on his back with his penis in Joanie's hand and a knife in the other, informing him, "If you ever try that again I will cut your dick off. Do you understand? And if you try to fire me, I will slit your throat, so don't even think about doing it."

Joanie had some serious counseling afterwards because her abrupt activity almost screwed up the mission.

"So, you wanted me to take a bullet for the team (bullet a.k.a. load)?

"You are a spy, it's one of your weapons." Her VIA manager said.

"Since the mission was completed successfully without letting, the creep touch me, you have to admit there are other protocols we can use," Joanie said.

Joanie knew not to expect an answer and soon that appeared to be the case.

When Joanie looked at Heléné in her heart she knew the poor girl had to endure a lot of terrible situations to get into the position she was in with the three other singers. They were all victims of some creep like she herself had endured.

Joanie, being a body language expert could tell that after Adrak ordered Heléné a drink, she showed signs of gratitude as well as appreciation and satisfaction this lovely couple were treating her with such pleasantness.

There was almost a covalent bond between Heléné and Adrak. It was far more serious than Joanie realized. Heléné was no virgin and had been abused by her manager and her producer. Heléné was just recently emotionally and monetarily stabile enough to be in a position to no longer allow the creeps to take advantage of her and abuse her.

The situation had flipped her and three other fabulous Franzon singers were now in control of their own destiny and could walk out of the contract without any effort or repercussions and had hired a lawyer to represent them who then explained the four women had signed affidavits and if they did any more hanky panky, the lawyer would expose them and ruin their enterprise.

Helénē was given her life back to her and no longer had to suffer exploitations of the creeps as well as her three friends who now had a new lease on life, growing in popularity and flourishing as entertainers. Helénē had paid her dues.

Helénē had met a lot of people but strangely felt special with this nice couple who had no demands and were full of affection. She realized they were true decent fans and the satisfaction of being with them was mutual.

But Helénē had no idea the pain and suffering the two spies went through and their interactions with her in no way would expose such life altering events. She would thus adopt them as like a family if they kept coming to watch her performances.

Soon the break was over and the four lovely Franzon singers were back on the stage and Joanie and Adrak remained to watch half of the next set and then left waving at Helénē as they left. Even though they had a nap earlier, they took their medications which included pills for pain management and healing accelerators which had proven to be very successful in improving their overall conditions.

Even if they had big-A on their minds, the combination of medications, meals, and elixirs had them under hold each other entering a transdimensional transcendence.

There was no point in planning what to do for the evening because they remained in this transdimensional state until early in the morning when Adrak had to get up to urinate. In the process he woke up Joanie, which he tried to avoid, but as a spy she was acutely responsive to movement in her bed.

Adrak didn't know Joanie was awake and when he laid down again her eyes were still shut, but he suddenly discovered she was not sleeping when her sudden grip on his manliness gave him absolute confirmation of what her intensions were. As soon as she knew Adrak was rock hard she mounted him and inserted his manliness and proceeded to copulate creating great sensations and ultimate gratifications.

As Joanie was slowly and methodically moving up and down on Adrak mindful he was not fully healed, she substituted the bitch force with vaginal muscle control she knew would cause Adrak to quickly respond to her splendid vaginal control because of her unique training in seducing men for honey pot schemes spies must do.

Just like she predicted Adrak lost control and as prolactin was flooding the pleasure center of his brain, he uttered those three famous words that Joanie knew were true that caused a biofeedback with her multiplying the sensations she felt because the position she took and how she did it created the best clitoris contact possible.

The loving dovetailed nicely into some precious moments. They no longer needed sleep, and the interaction now was simply their emotions flooding with covalent bonding. But these two spies were now reaching the point where their injuries were no longer guiding their lives thanks to the healing accelerators.

After a while, Adrak asked, "I know it's still slightly dark outside, but would you like to go for a walk on the beach?"

"Actually, that's not a bad idea, it's still kind of nice and pleasant outside now. Later in the day it will get hot," Joanie said.

The two got up, put on shorts and t-shirts and beach shoes that appeared like sneakers and headed out to the beach area.

Security observed them leaving, otherwise it would have been difficult getting back in until later in the morning.

The two holding hands walked down the beach.

It was a moment of tranquility. Quiescence had been obtained.

There wasn't a lot of room to walk, in the area from the Fěicuì de Lùzhōu Resort.

Pàrgŏnzéfrās vacation beach and community existed in a natural deep-water harbor that protected shipping from rough weather when storms blew through. There was a Tsunami that hit a couple decades ago that created a lot of damage. The scars from that Tsunami were mainly healed.

Offset from the beach were tropical forests with tall trees. This area was no doubt altered by the resort owners, cleaning out a lot of brush making it appear very clean and delightful. Adrak could tell there was not a lot of native vegetation because of all the clearing. These were strange looking trees but closer to the beach were very tall palm trees mixed in with coconut palms. People who took vacations to the south Pacific would think they were there walking this way.

The gentle waves crashing on the shoreline gave a cacophony of pleasant noise. This kind of noise is often recorded and sold to people that needed a relaxer while they meditated.

This was very early in the morning exposing bright stars and planets. The two were not in a hurry and took their time simply enjoying the other's company. Words were not necessary. Their current gentle fabric of life and the temporal menagerie that lingered from their love making created a moment they would likely never forget.

Two spies, being in love, granted this rare moment of downtime, only because of their recent injuries without the knowledge those who wanted to press them back in service. As they walked past other areas, the brush was not removed, and flora abounded.

They were now walking past a nature reserve that allowed no entry or manipulation. The underbrush was so thick the locals would never traverse this area.

All along this walkway, the white sandy beaches existed off to the side in the most majestic manner. Adrak judged by visual interpolation from their vantage point to where the water slowly rolled up onto the beach, was probably 50 feet. It was still dark so they could not see the full spectrum of the beach. Three hours later they would see the aqua blue marine water that remained shallow for at least 100 yards. And in that space, there were outcroppings of coral reefs that sustained multitudes of beautiful colored fish.

They reached the end of the beach sidewalk and Adrak estimated to go beyond this point would require a lot of energy he didn't think the two of them had, so they turned around walking back to the Fěicuì de Lùzhōu Resort. Right when they came upon the resort, Adrak noticed a man observing them.

Is he friendly or is he a foe? Adrak wondered.

Adrak then suggested us continue up the beach in this direction to discover what's here.

"All right," Joanie stated.

The two spies were walking approximately 2.5 miles per hour, not in a big rush.

Adrak, constantly looking out towards the bay with an open view to space on the horizon, saw a cluster of stars he knew well. He had severe injuries twice from that location and one thing that helps you remember an image better than anything else is to obtain a severe injury from such places.

"Let's stop here a moment," Adrak said and was in the perfect position to rotate around to approach Joanie to give the appearance they were engaging in a romantic embrace.

This maneuver gave Adrak the opportunity to *"clear his baffles"* and do surveillance on someone possibly following them.

Adrak had to put on a show to make it look convincing he wasn't spying on a possible trailer. Even though Adrak had not planned to suffocate Joanie with romance this morning, he had to do it to mitigate any possible concern the trailer might have followed them until he figured out who, what, where, and why.

Joanie didn't know what was going on until Adrak whispered in her ear, "I think someone is trailing us. It might be friendly, but until we find out we need to be careful.

Act normal as if we never concluded he is following us."

Joanie got slightly emotional as she realized SMERSH might be in the process of ruining their vacation and down time, on their own planet. *When will the crap end?* Joanie thought.

"Kiss me and make it look convincing," Adrak instructed Joanie.

Joanie did as Adrak requested, then asked, "Was that convincing enough?"

"To the point you make me want to go back to the Fěicuì de Lùzhōu Resort and get back in bed."

"We can do that too."

"I have some Shǒuyǐn Bèidāo Stars (pronounced: Show-yen Bay-dow) in my small document holder in my shorts. Are you still proficient in using them?" Adrak asked.

"Yes. When I was in the hospital, I asked the staff to set me up a painter's easel with a dart board down in the rehab room. I started out throwing the Shǒuyǐn Bèidāo Stars (appear like Shuriken stars) a few feet away in low force and work my way up to full force with Bulls Eyes most of the time at twenty feet.

A shuriken (Japanese: 手裏剣 , lit. 'hand-hidden blade') is a Japanese concealed weapon used by samurai or ninja or in martial arts as a hidden dagger or *metsubushi* to distract or misdirect.

"Twenty feet is about the edge of an effective laser pistol range. It this person is a spy out to do us harm as he approaches immediately walk towards the water. We need to separate so he can't get a cheap shot at the two of us," Adrak said.

"Alright," Joanie responded.

"I always carry two packages of Shǒuyǐn Bèidāo Stars just in case. I'm slipping you one package in your hand now," Adrak said.

"Are your blades coated with *Seirinlectin*?" Joanie asked.

"Yes, how did you guess?" Adrak asked.

"May I ask you how you obtained the *Seirinlectin*?" Joanie asked.

"It's best I do not reveal my source in case sometime in the future you get neurotic investigations." Adrak said.

The *Seirinlectin* is a highly controlled compound made in a secret Vekkar lab exclusively for VIA. Only a few VIA agents who were considered master's at throwing Shǒuyǐn Bèidāo Stars were ever permitted to have stars coated with Seirinlectin. In many respects *Seirinlectin* acts like viper venom. It can kill the person hit with a *Seirinlectin* coated Shǒuyǐn Bèidāo Star, but it usually disabled them for several hours so they would not be a threat and could be apprehended.

Joanie would never rat out Adrak under any circumstances, but she now knew Interdimensional Transport Directorate, or Project KOBRA SPEKTR gave a small tube of *Seirinlectin* to Adrak to coat his stars. The stars were then coated with a thin cover of wax and unless it punctured the skin and got into the bloodstream it likely would not have an effect on someone throwing the stars.

The Shǒuyǐn Bèidāo Stars rotated in flight at an amazing speed. They were aerodynamically designed and the velocity of the throw that caused the initial spin by the thrower often increased the spin rate in flight as the aerodynamic properties worked like the sail on a sailing ship going sideways with the wind but obtaining a good headway.

Because of the spin, the Shǒuyǐn Bèidāo Stars were like mini-buzz saws that ripped into the flesh causing severe lacerations. During this ripping process the wax came off the blade exposing the *Seirinlectin* that had immediate chemical reactions with the person struck. In sixty seconds or less the person would be temporarily paralyzed as the chemical reactions with the *Seirinlectin* stopped all motor control functions in the brain sometimes interrupting the person's ability to breath and that killed them. However those deaths were rare, but they did happen. There would be no tears for an enemy spy killed by *Seirinlectin* coated Shǒuyǐn Bèidāo Stars.

Adrak and Joanie were very accurate with their Shǒuyǐn Bèidāo Stars which meant they conceivably could take down a half dozen spies quickly.

"Us walk a few feet towards the water to give this guy some room. If he follows us, he's fair game. If pulls out a blaster, nail him right away."

Since Joanie was closer to the man approaching she led them off the sidewalk and out onto the white sandy beach about fifteen feet to give them a margin of safety in case it was a spy and if he altered his direction towards them that was conclusive because VIA or Project KOBRA SPEKTR would not be approaching them for any reason this early in the morning and if they did for some official business, by now the person would have called out for Alexis Tegaro and Sabastian Rollie their alias.

The man came walking up the sidewalk but passed them and kept going. Either he was a person out for an early morning walk which is unlikely, or he may be a friendly doing surveillance on them. The man had another mile to go to get to the end of the sidewalk where he had to turn around if he were taking a walk or faking it.

The two stayed where they were on the beach with Adrak guiding Joanie telling her to act like a lover and as soon as the man was about a quarter mile away beyond hearing range with the surf noise, Adrak said, "Spĕctrāl send a special case SITREP, reporting this man walking past us including time of day and all the information. Any chance we can put a tracker on him?"

Spĕctrāl de Dòngtài-Sabastian immediately said, "Listening to your conversation with Alexis (he knew her code name), I had information already cued up. I had already initiated a tracker due to the odd hour of the morning. I have reports back from my agency controller, the person has a tracker on him and thanks to cued up imagery from Fĕicuì de Lùzhōu Resort that VIA has tapped into, his identity is now being checked. This entire stretch of beach has hidden surveillance video. He is never out of view from surveillance.

"Also, Sabastian (Adrak's alias) I've been directed to inform you not to move. Security personnel are coming your way in an electric cart to pick you up to take you back to the resort." Spĕctrāl de Dòngtài-Sabastian said.

True to Spĕctrāl's word, an electric cart with lights on came down the sidewalk and was soon upon them. The driver of the cart was none other than Lt. Colonel Tom Atractaspidi.

They hopped in the electric cart which turned around heading back to the resort.

"Is that guy one of our men?" Adrak asked.

"No, he does not work for VIA or Project KOBRA SPEKTR."

"He certainly does not work for Interdimensional Transport Directorate," Adrak added.

Adrak didn't quite know it yet, he was the perfect decoy. VIA had ever intentions of utilizing his fame to attract the enemy. One of the reasons why Lt. Colonel Tom Atractaspidi was here to deal with the second mole. If everything worked out as planned, they would catch the second mole with his hands in the cookie jar and that person would soon learn why Interdimensional Transport Directorate Executive Director, *Doctor Oxyuran Lepidotus Taipan,* had such an alias. That was not his real name. And his bite was far worse than a real *Taipan* that had poisons worse than vipers.

"Go back to your resort room and relax. Maybe I will run into you at the swimming pool later as I know you want to do some swimming to work out," Lt. Colonel Tom Atractaspidi said.

"Plus, I want to work on my suntan," Joanie said.

Chapter Twenty

Igor Duquesne

Adrak and Joanie were taken to a side entrance of the resort the VIA men had electronic keys to. Once inside the two were escorted to their resort room where Lt. Colonel Tom Atractaspidi asked, "May I come into your room for a minute to talk with you?"

"Sure," Adrak replied.

The three were inside the room and Lt. Colonel Tom Atractaspidi said: "We don't know who that person is yet, but we will soon find out. You saw who the men are with me, so you know who some of the team is that is here protecting you. This morning was a slight slipup because we didn't expect you to go out so early on a morning walk. But that will not happen again." Lt. Colonel Tom Atractaspidi said.

"Okay thanks," Adrak replied.

"From now on, if you leave your room, Spĕctrāl will notify us so we can have someone in position to assist you if necessary."

"How soon will we know about this guy we ran across this morning?" Adrak asked.

"As soon as we determine who he is, Spĕctrāl will be notified, and if the person is indeed a SMERSH agent, Spĕctrāl will brief you immediately." Lt. Colonel Tom Atractaspidi said.

"Thanks." Adrak said.

I know it might feel cumbersome wearing your conformal ear bud during your vacation when you should be having fun on your own home planet, but being able to hear Spĕctrāl communications might be in your best interests." Lt. Colonel Tom Atractaspidi said.

"Alright," Adrak replied.

"If we determine that man is SMERSH it means you might have to be relocated to another vacation site." Lt. Colonel Tom Atractaspidi said.

"I'm kind of taking a liking to this place," Joanie said.

"We'll keep you advised, enjoy your vacation and maybe I'll see you down at the pool later," Lt. Colonel Tom Atractaspidi said then left the room where two of his men were standing outside and walked away with him.

It was still somewhat dark, and sunrise was just starting.

"I think I want to take a shower now," Adrak said.

"Me too, and I think I want you to scrub my back," Joanie said.

Soon the honeymoon Hollywood shower commenced. Water was plentiful because Pàrgŏnzéfràs vacation beach and community had some of the most rain as anywhere on the planet. There was so much excess runoff that entrepreneurs set up a *Pàrgŏnzéfràs Water and Mineral Water Bottling Company* to export the pure drinking water.

Ships that brought in all the imported food stuffs and materials necessary to support the tourism industry, the same ships departed with exports such as bottled water, tropical wear, and processed Pàrgŏnzéfràs delicacies. Pàrgŏnzéfràs was slowly accumulating wealth and wealthy Vekkar's moved here building expensive second homes.

There remained a lot of untouched wildernesses around the island, but the wise elders had long ago established nature reserves to prevent it from turning into other tropical paradises that became a concrete jungle.

The negative ions from the shower, the manipulating of the scrubbing, and the overflowing affection created the atmosphere for a continuation of what they did earlier. No sooner were they dried off and comfortable, than they exercized the horizontal Tango on a theme from Paganini.

Joanie didn't want to lay drenched in sweat, so she got up and urged Adrak to take another shower with her. This time they cleaned themselves up and then looking at the time knew it was time to take their medications which included pain management and healing accelerators. They were soon lying in bed and Adrak said, "Spĕctrāl, wake me up at 9:00 A.M."

"Understand Sabastian, wake you up at 9:00 A.M." Spĕctrāl said to ensure Adrak knew his future activity.

The pain medications and the health accelerators were slowly helping the two spies become whole again. This morning, they walked three miles without thinking about it and felt good afterwards.

The sexual intercourse was also intense, but much of that was from a long period of abstinence. In essence they had a sexual appetite.

The resort rooms were designed to be quiet. With the shades drawn, a person would not know if it was day or night. Because of the way they walked and came back to bed after medications, Joanie and Adrak obtained a great Rem sleep. When Spĕctrāl woke them up at 9:00 A.M. they were fully rested.

"I'm sorry but I need to piss like a Tramular Racehorse (similar to Russian Race

Horse), Adrak apologized and made a bee line to the toilet. Once he relieved himself, Joanie was entitled to do her thing and not rush.

This served one very useful purpose. Adrak did not want to mess up Joanie's vacation. Because of what she went through in her very painful episode, she deserved days off with relaxation.

While Joanie was on the toilet doing her morning routine, Spĕctrāl delivered the bad news.

"Sabastian, the man you saw this morning is a SMERSH agent."

"That means they know we are here."

"Unfortunately."

"Any instructions as to what we are to do?" Adrak asked.

"As soon as Joanie finishes freshening up and doing her morning routine, I've been directed to inform Joanie the plan with you together."

"Alright."

Joanie took her time, put on some nice makeup to show Adrak some appreciation and finally came out of the bathroom.

"We are going to get a briefing from Spĕctrāl."

Adrak placed his communicator on a small table next to the bed and said, "Alright Spĕctrāl, Alexis is here for the briefing."

With the position of the communicator on the tabletop, Spĕctrāl with his vast artificial intelligence could see most of the room and record it if necessary. Spĕctrāl's AI quickly verified Joanie was sitting in a chair next to Adrak a few feet away.

"The man at the beach you saw this morning is a confirmed SMERSH agent named Igor Duquesne," Spĕctrāl reported.

"I wonder why he walked past us," Joanie asked.

"My speculation is he was coming in for a kill shot, and because we did the defensive move, he might have considered we were observing him as a potential hazard," Adrak said.

"Adrak you are very close to the truth. SMERSH agent Igor Duquesne has been detained by VIA and transported for interrogation," Spĕctrāl said.

"So, he was waiting for us to get a kill shot?" Adrak asked.

"Yes, that is correct," Spĕctrāl said.

"SMERSH agents never travel alone, that means more of them have to be here," Adrak said.

"Advanced Interrogation Techniques including neurological clarifiers are being used to obtain critical information from Igor Duquesne. We are slowly gathering information about his mission, but we have not yet identified who his accomplices are," Spĕctrāl said.

"What are we going to do?" Adrak asked.

"You are going to get dressed in swimwear and go down to the pool where you will accidentally meet Lt. Colonel Tom Atractaspidi and act like nothing happened. You are now part of an operation Code named "The Limping Lady." Spĕctrāl said.

"That's quite a name for an operation," Joanie remarked.

"Joanie, Mr. Spraticus gave the name to the operation since he's in charge of it. He named it after you," Spĕctrāl said.

Joanie was completely floored by Spĕctrāl's remark. To Joanie it meant her name was probably used along the line and she now had a real legacy as a spy with this new mission. Her question was:

"What does Lt. Colonel Tom Atractaspidi plan on doing with us two handicapped spies?" Joanie asked

"This afternoon you two will be taken to the medical center for a checkup after lunch. You will then go to a safe house after the medical treatment for a special briefing we cannot provide here." Spĕctrāl said.

"Alright," Adrak replied.

"I'm getting kind of hungry," Joanie said.

"You can order food at the swimming pool," Spĕctrāl said.

"Alright," Joanie replied.

"That is all for this special briefing, get ready to go to the pool," Spĕctrāl said.

In a brief amount of time the dynamic dual were heading down to the swimming pool. They found a couple of reclining chairs with leg rests next to a canopy table where they could sit up and eat a meal.

The pool was semi empty but there were a few barracudas already there to stake out their fresh meat for the day. A man with muscles like Adrak would quickly fall on their radar as these rich women knew they could drug him up and have hours of sex. They were not yet dazzled because Adrak had not taken off his bath robe and was with a sweetheart looking babe.

Adrak and Joanie had not shifted their chairs into recliners yet sat at the table looking like they wanted to order something. Moments later a waitress appeared and took care of all that. The two ordered snacks and elixirs. Like the old saying went.

When in Pàrgŏnzéfrās, do as Pàrgŏnzéfrāsians would do.

The morning snacks and elixirs hit the spot. Adrak's elixir was fortified with Vitamin B and so he was energized to some extent.

Shortly after Joanie and Adrak were finished eating, Lt. Colonel Tom Atractaspidi and a couple guys that looked familiar, sat down at a nearby table with reclining chairs.

Two of the men had what appeared to be beach bags people take with them to carry items such as suntan lotion, beach towels etc. No doubt their beach bags had a couple blasters in the beach bags including the extra's they could give to Adrak and Joanie who were expert shooters.

There were probably 30 people at the pool and half of them were there to eat breakfast, the other half to take a morning swim before it got too hot. Any of them could be SMERSH agents with an assignment to kill Adrak now a member of the top 10, kill any means possible.

Everyone at the pool was getting filmed and artificial intelligence was cataloging them and then comparing them to resort facial recognition records to obtain all the information on them. Anyone who came close to Adrak, now operating as a decoy without his knowledge, would get checked out completely.

As the day went by, the data poured in and Spĕctrāl de Dòngtài artificial intelligence was interacting with its AI controllers as well as AI on the network.

Spies get plastic surgery all the time. The Mole 000090317A512941 (a.k.a. Zmeya Rembert), discovered the hard way what happens to a former Interdimensional Transport Directorate Spy that was a traitor: "You now work for us, or we'll give you back to the Vekkar's."

Zmeya Rembert and Karoline Morganthau had 3D biological printing done to alter their facial recognition. Their palm prints and fingerprints also got changed to match people abducted from Vekkar planets who were away ostensibly on a vacation. Their identities were also stolen, and they were dispatched as soon as SMERSH determined they had all their personal information with nothing more to offer.

Zmeya Rembert and Karoline Morganthau were sitting on the other side of the pool completely innocuously. Zmeya Rembert was unhappy because there was no way he could visit his family who were probably highly monitored just in case he did something stupid and tried to contact them.

Karoline Morganthau viewed Zmeya Rembert as nothing more than a highly controlled prop to make it look real as a couple on a holiday. She had no respect for the traitor because he was interrogated as to why he betrayed Adrak. This was all part of the psychological study of Zmeya Rembert to best figure out how to control him and force him to continue being a traitor to the world where his family lived.

Like all spies, Zmeya Rembert had no tattoos or significant scars except for one minor one they thought would not be of significance in this mission. However, in the future, the scar tissue would be removed since it was an identifier. This is precisely what undermined their mission.

It would take up to a couple days to extract all the information concerning everyone now at the pool. Every major mark on their body was recorded and analyzed and compared to a relational database of known enemy spies and traitors.

Eventually VIA would find the small scar in the database and attribute it to none other than Zmeya Rembert. The traitor immediately had a tracker on him and anyone he encountered. This was one of the reasons for using Adrak as a decoy, even if he was killed in the process.

The woman with Zmeya Rembert was no doubt a SMERSH agent. With her disguise and her bathing suit on they could not fully vet who she really was. But VIA knew most precisely she was with Zmeya Rembert at the Fěicuì de Lùzhōu Resort because the MOLE still in the organization had betrayed Adrak.

There were two possible MOLES. Vekkar Interdimensional Portal Directorate, Executive Director, *Doctor Oxyuran Lepidotus Taipan* needed a decoy to decide which person it was. That Mole would then become a double spy without knowing it.

VIA immediately sent in plumbers who installed special fiberoptic tubing that end face was a camera lens. Bug sniffers would not be able to find it and they assumed SMERSH equipped these spies with sophisticated bug and hidden video sniffers to determine if they were under some type of surveillance.

Ingenious ways of installing the fiberoptic cables with the camera lens end face included in the shower head, the bidet toilet and electrical power jacks' maids plugged in vacuum cleaners.

When a power plug was pushed in the socket of the camera lens, a spring actuator shoved it back into position when the power plug was removed. Guests staying on either side of the two spies were shifted to other rooms for maintenance reasons.

A device that arrived in a large tube was unfolded and placed against the wall. Even though spies are taught to expect bugs, Karoline Morganthau and Zmeya Rembert arrived so quickly after the reservations were made informing the Fěicuì de Lùzhōu Resort the Hotel they were to stay at lost their reservations.

Karoline Morganthau and Zmeya Rembert didn't think things would evolve so quickly or that Igor Duquesne would be captured already. They were to meet up with Igor Duquesne before they did the hit on Adrak.

Karoline Morganthau and Zmeya Rembert made statements like unhappy wayward travelers about they had to pay a lot more for the Resort. But they didn't want their vacation ruined over a reservationist clicking on the wrong icon thus not saving the reservation in the system.

Unfortunately, this happened all too often at Pàrgŏnzéfrās vacation beach and community that had unscrupulous operators that did that trick to increase the price of their rooms based on scarcity.

Igor Duquesne was another John Wayne type and acted a lot like Tramulite SMERSH agent Sidis, who Adrak killed at planet *Drusyltania* during *Project Geyser.*

By a mere accident, Igor Duquesne had gone out to the beach for a smoke break and spotted Adrak walking with a woman. Due to the time of day, and total lack of people on the beach, Igor Duquesne had the element of surprise which meant he could kill Adrak with his blaster, then get an emergency extraction and be the hero.

Instead, Igor Duquesne was now in a safe house on the other side of the island undergoing enhanced interrogation techniques that would make the Gestapo or the KGB blush.

The installation of the plumbing was very easy because the two spies were down at the pool not realizing the peril they were in.

In the safe house interrogators surprised Igor Duquesne when they asked him:

"What is Zmeya Rembert doing here and *who is the woman*?

Igor Duquesne thought he could hold out for a couple days and by then Adrak would be dead, then he could admit everything and beg for leniency or hope a spy trade was initiated. He refused to cooperate and one of the chief interrogators informed him:

"If you do not cooperate with us, you will force us to amputate your penis and remove your testicles. The expert who will do that surgery will be arriving this afternoon. You will be restrained like you are now and he'll do the surgery with no antiseptics or anesthesia."

"You better hope to hell my government never finds out, we will kill him," Igor Duquesne said.

"You already tried, and you failed and now you are a prisoner, so think about what you will lose today if you do not reveal to us who the woman is that is with Zmeya Rembert.

"I do not know who she is," Igor Duquesne said.

"We know she's a spy, we could just haul her in now, but we want to know who else she is working with."

***

At the same time, Adrak decided he wanted to go for a swim.

"Do you want to go for a swim?" Adrak asked Joanie.

"No, I'm going to work on my tan," Joanie replied.

Adrak took off his bath towel and walked over and got in the water.

Karoline Morganthau and Zmeya Rembert watched Adrak get in the water and start swimming. They didn't know VIA had a *Big Ears* system pointing right at them.

"That's amazing his scars are all gone," Zmeya Rembert said.

"Someone must be planning on using him for a major mission," Karoline Morgan said in a very low voice.

They watched Adrak swim some laps which truly surprised them because just three weeks prior, the MOLE back at the Vekkar Interdimensional Spy Portal Directorate, reported Adrak was mostly seriously handicapped and would be out of action indefinitely or possibly permanently and medically retired.

In due time Adrak finished swimming and Joanie decided she had enough suntan and the departed to head back up to their room noting they had to get dressed, get a bite to eat then go somewhere with Lt. Colonel Tom Atractaspidi after their medical appointments.

Five minutes after Adrak and Joanie left the pool, Karoline Morganthau said to Zmeya Rembert:

"We need to go back to the room and make a report about Adrak's condition and Igor Duquesne missing. He missed his rendezvous with us."

Big Ears transcripts were now at Counterintelligence who now had a 95 percent figure of merit on who the MOLE was back at Vekkar Interdimensional Spy Portal Directorate.

Karoline Morganthau now gave away her means of communicating to SMERSH without discovery.

When the two spies arrived in their room, Karoline Morganthau typed up her report on her communicator and when she was all complete, she walked over to one of her high heel shoes and unscrewed on of the heels. She walked over to the window, plugged the shoe heel into her communicator that had a special connector on it that mated with the charge port of the communicator. Then she sent the message. It was a series of burst transmissions randomly spaced to give the appearance of static noise caused by lightning strikes from a nearby storm cloud. She then unplugged her shoe heel and screwed it back on the high heel shoe.

"It's kind of muggy, I'm going to take a sprite shower," Karoline said, then continued, "And don't try coming into the bathroom or I'll shoot your dick off."

While Karoline Morganthau was a prisoner prior to the spy exchange, she was drugged and unconscious and her body photographed with high resolution camera's. VIA had a lot of information such as exact dimensions on her nipples using an interferometer, as well as how she trimmed her pubis, the size of her clitoris, etc.

Before she took her shower, she sat down on the Bidet Toilet and did her business and didn't know she was being scanned. Her entire body was being photographed and she didn't know it.

All the imagery provided by the fiberoptic camera lenses was now analyzed by artificial intelligence and in a short period of time going down the probable lists, they got a match on Karoline Morganthau. Three indicators provided a confidence factor of 99%. Her nipples, her clitoris, and the way she trimmed her pubis.

Since the VIA now knew who this woman was, AI could then reconstruct her facial imagery and filter out the cosmetic surgery to produce a valid facial recognition.

The interrogators were soon informed and asked them not to inform Igor Duquesne who the woman was, because later when Adrak confronted him threatening to cut off his penis and his testicles, he could tell Igor he was lying if he did not identify her.

Karoline Morganthau sent in her report she questioned the validity of the MOLE's information including warning SMERSH he might be a double spy giving false information.

Since the video of Karoline Morganthau was time synchronized, the spooks could then check the time synchronized recorded RF spectrum and find signals that were transmitted precisely the same time as Karoline Morgenthau's transmissions.

Traffick analysis would soon reveal frequencies and the type of transmission. This would then allow signal analysts using wavelets, stochastic resonance, Fourier and Laplace techniques. There were some indicators that suggested SMERSH had started using cyclostationary processes. VIA researchers had developed new tools to deal with cyclostationary signals artificial intelligence would crack with machine learning and statistical analysis.

In communications, even burst transmissions end up with bauds. These are envelopes of information. Encoded in the baud envelopes is an encoding method. When VIA discovers spies transmitting signals, that raises the priority to spend a lot of effort into learning.

The communication technique Karoline Morgenthau used had never been detected before. How long has this technology been used?

VIA scientists analyzing the burst transmissions quickly developed a theory that Quaternions were used to convert the signals for transmission easily seen with sophisticated chirp filters.

Karoline Morgenthau's communicator had an artificial intelligence APP very similar to how Spĕctrāl de Dòngtài was employed. SMERSH AI as VIA referred to it. SMERSH AI would use crypto to encode the text and transfer the file to the sequencer. At this point in time the encoded file appears to be random numbers. The sequencer was essentially the firmware in the microprocessor that provided all the number crunching and communications. The overall signal could be described as random distribution of burst cyclostationary communication processes. They were short and sweet and extremely hard to detect and unless you had a spy like Karoline Morganthau transmitting it, even with a chirp detector, the best signal processing experts would conclude it to simply be random noise spikes caused by atmospheric conditions such as lightning strikes.

Through expanded monitoring elsewhere, it was now possible for VIA to find other SMERSH transmissions done elsewhere. In very complicated communication systems, it takes time to implement them and worse, yet it takes an even longer time to discover when the system was compromised.

Putting it all together, VIA knew a SMERSH agent would soon be contacting the MOLE for clarification about Adrak and most poignantly, about his multiple scars on his back that did not exist.

At this point in the operation, VIA could have sent in a team and arrested Karoline Morganthau but there was more to learn. Were there any other agents at the Fĕicuì de Lùzhōu Resort and who is the SMERSH agent the Interdimensional Portal Spy Mole communicated with and how?

Thanks to Karoline Morganthau, Vekkar Counterintelligence Agents were onto the Mole because he was requested to attend a physical meeting with the SMERSH agent who was going to throw the scar tissue issue into his face and accuse him of being a double spy, including possibly killing him if he didn't give the right answers. Vekkar Counterintelligence Agents realized the Mole might be killed so they had to be in a position to intervene and take the SMERSH agent down. A critical factor was identifying the SMERSH agent's watcher so he too could be arrested and prevented from sending a warning that would get back to Karoline Morganthau. It was going to be touch and go.

Yes, there were indeed more SMERSH agents present. Rule of thumb, if someone followed Adrak to the hospital, they were probably a watcher or a SMERSH agent.

Adrak and Joanie were soon ready to go to their doctor's appointments. They left their room, went out to the Fĕicuì de Lùzhōu Resort front entrance and got into a Limo. They were not dressed up, just wearing tourist clothing. They went directly to the hospital and went inside to the floor where primary care doctors' offices were and checked in with the receptionist.

The SMERSH agent had no idea how badly their mission had been compromised and since VIA was playing a very coy game and not exhibiting buck fever other than detaining Igor Duquesne, he was not surprised they went to the hospital based on the

Mole's report. He loosely followed the two to the waiting room where Adrak and Joanie now sat waiting to be called in for their examinations.

Joanie was called first and went through a door down a hallway and turned into another hallway where a nurse took her into an examining room, took her blood pressure, temperature, weight, height, and asked several medical questions such as if she was having any issues she wanted to discuss with the doctor.

Pàrgŏnzéfrās Vacation Beach and Community Hospital had visiting doctors all the time including specialists brought in for special patients that needed monitoring while on vacation for various illnesses. Today they had a couple visiting doctors.

Adrak was soon led to his examining room while the SMERSH agent sat in the busy waiting room that nobody (except VIA) was interested in. The fact he left the resort and bird dogged Adrak to the hospital gave away who he was. But to add icing on the cake, Karoline Morganthau texted him to come back to the resort they needed to talk. The SMERSH agent promptly went back to the Fĕicuì de Lùzhōu Resort.

The hidden cameras were able to correlate the timing between Karoline Morgenthau's texting and the SMERSH agent answering.

Adrak and Joanie got their independent examinations by VIA doctors who were pleased at how well they were improving and healing. They were also very pleased with Adrak's scar tissue and his reports of how well the swimming went today. The doctors had been directed to escort the two patients up to the rooftop after their examination because a Skycar would be waiting for Adrak and Joanie to take them somewhere. The doctors soon made their way out the front door of the hospital after they delivered the couple to the rooftop. The doctors took a private limo to the airport and flew back home and back to their VIA offices to brief the Gopher on the spies' physical conditions.

The Skycar took Adrak and Joanie to the safe house.

As soon as Adrak arrived, one of the interrogators gave him a rusty knife as a prop and informed Adrak: "The knife was sharpened nicely and gave him an apple to carve in front of Igor Duquesne.

Igor Duquesne was suffering from sleep deprivation, some minor physical abuse, and psychological side effects from interrogation drugs he was injected with. The last person he ever expected to meet here was Adrak.

"Igor, your doctor has arrived for your surgery," one of the interrogators said, then opened the door and Adrak and Joanie walked in.

Joanie was given heads up that Adrak would be spoon feeding Igor Duquesne some lies for psychological enhancement. VIA knew Karoline Morganthau and Igor Duquesne had been lovers in the past. The status of their relationship was unknown, but Adrak figured Karoline had her needs and used Igor as a sex provider. Igor was misled Karoline had any feelings for him. It was nothing more than sex for sex.

The rusty knife and the apple immediately got Igor Duquesne's attention

"Igor, I'm going to ask you one question one time, and if you do not answer correctly, I'm going to perform the surgery these fine gentlemen have promised you," Adrak said.

Igor started sweating profusely.

"Igor, is the woman with Zmeya Rembert, the illustrious spy Karoline Morganthau?"

"No."

"I'm sorry Igor that's a lie so you will get your surgery right after I tell you what I did to Karoline this morning."

Igor gave Adrak a strange look.

"Igor, I had sex with Karoline before I cut her throat with this knife." Adrak then nodded to Joanie who knew what she had to say.

"Igor, I helped tie up Karoline and I asked Adrak if he wanted to do something to the pretty girl before he killed her, and he said he wanted to leave a deposit."

"You are lying!" Igor screamed.

"Pull his pants down for me like you did for me with Karoline," Adrak said to Joanie.

"My pleasure," Joanie said then put on a pair of plastic gloves.

Igor's legs were restrained to the chair and could not move, and his arms were also restrained well.

To Igor's chagrin Joanie walked over and a lot faster than Igor could imagine, his trousers were yanked down exposing his Johnson. Joanie wrapped a small cable around Igor's Johnson and proceeded to tighten it like a tourniquet. Within a minute Igor's Johnson was swelling a lot larger than the typical "soft-off."

One of the interrogators handed Adrak a pair of gloves and Adrak handed him the knife and the apple to hold while he put on those gloves.

"No reason to get that blood all over my hands," Adrak said.

After Adrak had the gloves on the VIA agent handed him the Knife and the apple. "Igor, I'm a very good surgeon. I make very quick and nice cuts."

Just as if he had practiced it many times, Adrak sliced that apple up in just a couple seconds for further psychological enhancement of Igor.

"Igor, there is no reason why you need to have your dick cut off protecting Karoline, she's dead, I've already killed her."

Igor was now down to the breaking point and starting to mumble and whimper.

"Hold that Tourniquet nice and tight, I don't want his blood shooting all over me," Adrak said for effect.

Adrak then bent down and grabbed Igor's penis and moved the knife in position to cut it off.

"Please stop. I admit it is Karoline."

"Igor, you now need us to protect you because when I tell Karoline you identified her, she's going to want to kill you," Adrak said, then added, "Go ahead and release the Tourniquet, we are not going to cut off his dick quite yet. If he continues cooperating, he'll get to keep it and we'll trade him in a spy swap."

Moments later Adrak and Joanie were taken by Skycar back to Fěicuì de Lùzhōu Resort. Adrak and Joanie went back to their resort room and took their medications they knew would make them sleepy.

"Spěctrāl, wake me up at 3:00 P.M." Adrak said.

"Sabastian (a.k.a. Adrak), before you fall asleep, I have a mandatory briefing I must now give you," Spěctrāl said.

"Alright Spěctrāl. I'm just going to lay here if you don't mind, go ahead and show it," Adrak said.

Joanie was watching as well and could see all the imagery and the sound went into their conformal earphones which meant no enemy could hear the briefing.

"This is the updated image of Karoline Morganthau who is with Zmeya Rembert," Spěctrāl said. We have monitored their conversations in their resort room, and you now have the transcript you can read at your leisure after your nap," Spěctrāl said.

"Anything else?" Adrak asked.

Spěctrāl put up another image then briefed Adrak and Joanie about the person.

"Yes, this is a SMERSH agent who followed you to the doctor's office. Karoline Morganthau sent him a text message directing him to come back to the resort and make a report and receive further instructions," Spěctrāl said.

"Any other SMERSH agents here?" Adrak asked.

"We are monitoring Karoline Morganthau and if she comes in contact with anyone, we investigate that person assuming he/she's a SMERSH agent," Spěctrāl said.

Adrak then turned off his communicator and set it aside on the little table next to the bed. He then laid back to get a nap.

The SMERSH agent that followed Adrak and Joanie to the hospital gave a report to Karoline Morganthau in her resort room with Zmeya Rembert in attendance.

"They had a doctor's appointment?"

"Yes."

"Did they finish their doctor's appointment while you were there?"

"No, you recalled me, so I have no idea when they left."

"We have not been able to contact Igor Duquesne. Headquarters has informed us he might have been captured and to get the mission finished promptly because VIA may coerce him into disclosing us."

"It will have to be an opportunistic hit. We may not get the opportunity to take him out," the SMERSH agent said.

"At the risk of discovery, we'll have to do an aggressive trail to have an opportunistic hit," Karoline said.

"Alright," the SMERSH agent replied.

From now on wherever he goes, we follow and if it appears we get an opportunistic shot, we take it, then issue the bug out request."

"Understand," the SMERSH agent said.

***

Chapter Twenty-One

Night Life at the Zĭsè de Drakon

At 3:00 P.M. Spĕctrāl initiated the chimes and the awakening routine including statements Adrak received in his conformal ear bud:

"Adrak, it's time to wake up."

Adrak was slightly groggy but managed to swing around and sit up on the side of the bed and only got up then because he needed to use the toilet. After he did his deed, Joanie was right behind him and did her business.

While Adrak was back sitting on the side of the bed he asked, "Spĕctrāl, is there any good dinner night clubs away from the resort I can take Joanie?"

"Yes, Adrak, one club in particular you two would enjoy but you need to go in more formal clothes." Spĕctrāl said.

"What club is that?" Adrak asked.

"It's the Zĭsè de Drakon (pronounced: Zeise da Drakown [Purple Dragon])," Spĕctrāl replied.

"Does the Fĕicuì de Lùzhōu Resort have fashion designers that can rent us clothes for the night so we can go there?" Adrak asked.

"Yes, they do Adrak, would you like me to make a reservation?" Artificial intelligence Spĕctrāl asked via the ear bud.

"Yes, and please make reservations at the Zĭsè de Drakon for 9:00 P.M.," Adrak said.

Moments later Spĕctrāl reported: "Adrak your reservations are complete. The fashion designer said the earliest she could get here would be 6:30 P.M."

"That works just fine," Adrak said.

Joanie came out of the bathroom about that time and Adrak informed her of the plans, which she immediately responded in a positive manner.

"I think I can do some dancing especially if it's a slow dance," Joanie said.

"What do you want to do now, we have a few hours before the fashion designer arrives?" Adrak asked.

"I don't think I can last until 9:00 before I eat something," Joanie said.

"We could go down to the pool bar and restaurant and get a snack," Adrak said.

"Are you saying that so you can go down and see Heléné?" Joanie asked.

"I've never been with a green skin woman before. I doubt we have much in common," Adrak said.

"The purpose of a good spy is INTEL gathering. Perhaps you feel like you are in an investigative mode and your target is Heléné?" Joanie asked.

"My target is Karoline Morganthau. The big difference is she was sent here to kill me. When we leave here it's highly unlikely, I will ever see Heléné again the rest of my life, nor would I care. But since we are here in between our next great adventure, I might as well hear Heléné sing," Adrak said.

"You can look as long as you don't touch," Joanie said.

"My destiny is charted with you I seriously doubt Heléné can compete with you," Adrak said.

"As a lover or a spy?" Joanie asked.

"My valance is with you. Your sky belongs to me."

Joanie approached Adrak and got close and pulled him closer then took her right hand as she held his abdomen with her left hand and pulled his face closer to her and she gave Adrak a kiss that would gain her an A+ in her training in honeypot schemes.

Joanie had the expert ability to do such a seductive kiss, but now she also had the emotional vibrations that invigorated her in ways she rarely felt. If it were not for the fact she wanted to get something to eat and was mindful of their fashion designer appointment, she would have grabbed Adrak and thrown him on the bed and proved what a tough bitch like her could do to an unsuspecting male. And it didn't matter the condition of her healing injuries, she wouldn't care, she would go for keeps and Adrak would never forget. But there is a time and place for everything. Maybe after another week of healing she would be poised to show Adrak another side of her, he didn't quite know existed.

Moments later they were down at the pool bar and restaurant in a great seat to enjoy the four delightful young Franzon singers.

Heléné was happy the lovely couple showed up. She felt good around their sweet gentleness and loved watching couples that got along together so well.

Heléné suspected Alexis (a.k.a. Joanie) and Sabastian (a.k.a. Adrak) had quite a history together. She had no idea that such an experience and relationship could ever exist. She also had no idea the level of pain the two had suffered as the result of activities associated with espionage and sabotage. But about that time there were several people in the room that did.

Lt. Colonel Tom Atractaspidi and his two heavy guns were sitting at the bar with a nice mirror to view the entire restaurant. They had on their conformal earbuds just like Joanie and Adrak. Their communicators also had the Spĕctrāl de Dòngtài APP.

People often sat their communicators on the bar tabletop next to them to be more comfortable. Lt. Colonel Tom Atractaspidi was no exception. It gave him an added level of reconnaissance as his Spĕctrāl de Dòngtài APP utilized its multiple cameras with multiple angles for surveillance.

Lt. Colonel Tom Atractaspidi was always expecting data and information since he was the onsite coordinator of the VIA personnel sent on this mission code named *The Limping Lady.*

Accordingly, Lt. Colonel Tom Atractaspidi was soon informed that Karoline Morganthau and Zmeya Rembert were approaching the restaurant/bar. He was also informed another man already sitting in the bar/restaurant met with Karoline Morganthau earlier that day who had followed Adrak to the Hospital. The two shooters sitting on either side of Lt. Colonel Tom Atractaspidi mainly to provide some flanking protection from possible shooters received the same reports in their conformal ear buds.

Lt. Colonel Tom Atractaspidi had on advanced glasses that took imagery from his Spĕctrāl de Dòngtài in a mini heads-up display that only he could see because of his contact lenses. The mini heads-up display showed the enemy spies all with tracker symbols over their heads. Thanks to their access to the hotel security system VIA would never lose track of these spies until they left the area.

At this point, Joanie was dressed and looked like a plane Jane. She didn't care, later in the evening she knew she would look glamorous.

Fortified by Adrak's words up in their resort hotel room, Joanie was emotionally fortified and in a pleasant mood. She was all smiles and so was Adrak. While Helénē sang her heart out for the lovely couple that inherently motivated the band, the patrons were enjoying the great performance.

The elixirs and the snacks hit the spot. Quiescence was easily met. Now it was nothing more than enjoying their time before their makeovers. Spĕctrāl would give them a 30- minute warning followed by a fifteen-minute announcement, "You need to proceed to your resort/hotel room immediately."

Shortly after the waitress all smiles again because she loved the way the couple tipped, had their table cleaned off and was about to ask them if they wanted a refill when Helénē was taking a break with the band and came nearby and was offered to join them for a drink which she readily accepted.

"My throat gets so dry singing. That's why we really must take breaks," Helénē said.

"I can imagine," Joanie said having inside information having used being a cabaret singer in the past as part of her disguise.

The three had a lovely discussion while they were being monitored by multiple people from two major intelligence organizations.

***

Time was running out, the hit had to happen today. Karoline Morganthau knew it was not long before Igor Duquesne would crack. The SMERSH team had to do the dirty deed and get the hell out of here quickly.

Several miles down the beach were a couple boats that could be either pleasure boats or deep ocean fishing boats, staged for their bug out. They had to make a fast run over the horizon where a seaplane would come down and pick them up.

The seaplane was currently gassed up in a lagoon in a nearby island that would fly to the rendezvous point due west of the Fěicuì de Lùzhōu Resort over the horizon where the pickup could occur without being seen.

The seaplane with over 1500-mile range would fly to an island about 500 miles away the pickup location that was sparsely populated where a shuttle would fly down from space and pick them up while a diversion was being created on the other side of the planet.

At 6:00 P.M. Spěctrāl informed Adrak:

"Your fashion designer appointment is in 30-minutes."

Adrak had his communicator in his front left pocket where he preferred to carry it and did 3 taps on it in a way nobody could see happening. Spěctrāl took that as affirmation he received the information discretely.

The singers would be taking a break from the current set about the time of Adrak's appointment so for on the better part of valor, he said to Joanie:

"Let's go up to the room and get ready."

Joanie was pleasantly surprised Adrak would leave the bar earlier than he had to.

They stood up and walked out of the bar/restaurant. Fifteen seconds after they departed, the SMERSH agents stood up and went after them.

Lt. Colonel Tom Atractaspidi notified by his Spěctrāl APP the obvious, grabbed his communicator and pressed an icon nobody else could see because of the wavelength that was the [RED ALERT] button.

The VIA team swung into action as Artificial Intelligence notified three suspects were coming after Adrak and Joanie. Before they could get into a distance where they could apply a kill shot, a Bellhop who was a VIA agent with a luggage rack purposely rammed Karoline Morganthau which knocked her on her ass and allowed Adrak and Joanie to distance the three.

Zmeya Rembert was a YES man and not a self-starter. That's one of the reasons why he had a growing animosity towards Adrak who continuously made him look like an incompetent fool.

The third SMERSH agent was a chickenshit and wasn't going to go charging after two famous spies by himself. Zmeya Rembert didn't budge nor did the third SMERSH agent and Karoline looked at them in utter disgust.

In their ear buds Adrak and Joanie were warned Karoline Morganthau and two accomplices were coming at them quickly. Adrak handed Joanie a package of Shǒuyǐn Bèidāo Stars in case she needed to toss a few. It would please Joanie to no end to nail Karoline in the middle of the forehead with a Shǒuyǐn Bèidāo Star.

At the elevator was the Hotel Security Manager who had been notified not to let anyone in the elevator with Adrak and Joanie. The couple was soon at the door to their room. VIA men from rooms on each side of them were out in the hallway packing blasters if needed and one of them opened the door for Adrak and said, "You are safe, the three that were going to accost you are still down by the lobby."

The bellhop profusely apologized, and the manager was immediately on the scene and after notified by the Bellhop what happened, the manager immediately informed Karoline:

"We are so sorry this happened. I'm going to give you the resort room you are staying, the night for free, there would be no charge for her room for the day."

Karoline wasn't damaged in any way other than it screwed up her attack plan. She got herself together and told the two other guys, "Let's go for a walk at the beach."

Karoline had to have a big talk with these two incompetents.

Karoline was full of piss and vinegar and quite upset at the two SMERSH agent's conduct.

The beach was quickly abandoned for the evening and there were not many beach goers left so Karoline easily found a spot they could talk in privacy. At least that's what she thought. Big ears heard every word she said.

"You two idiots are almost worthless. You stood there like rookies and let them get away from us. Zmeya Rembert, I know why you were always jealous of Adrak, your buddy who also spies for us told us all about it. You are inherently a chickenshit afraid to take risks. That's why you were a failure at spying. The only spying you got right was being a traitor and we had to handle you like a baby or you would have got our spy captured."

Karoline knew if they blew this mission, she personally would be held responsible. SMERSH expected results from her even if she had to commit suicide to kill Adrak.

The next time we get in range to take down Adrak, I expect you to put forth and effort or I will shoot you in the back. Your performance has been completely unsatisfactory and you two are not worthy of working for SMERSH. You have one more chance to redeem yourselves.

Karoline didn't know it at the time, but she got to Zmeya Rembert in ways she didn't understand. The way she just talked to him changed him completely. He was no longer going to be a chickenshit. He was going to personally prove to Karoline he's just as good a spy as she is. He would show her his form of redemption when the time came.

They regrouped and Karoline took Zmeya Rembert back to their room where she would send a status report. The third man was sent as a lookout. His orders were to keep an eye on the entrance just in case the two went somewhere tonight, as it appeared Adrak and Joanie didn't know how close they came. But they did. They were well briefed by Artificial Intelligence Spĕctrāl.

Lt. Colonel Tom Atractaspidi sent Joanie and Adrak a message via Spĕctrāl:

"Get dressed up and act like nothing happened. You will still go to Zïsè de Drakon and there would be plenty of security," Lt. Colonel Tom Atractaspidi said.

"Alright," Adrak said sounding not too convincingly.

"This will draw them out and it will also help us determine how many players they have so we will know if we should go ahead and arrest them or kill them if they resist," Lt. Colonel Tom Atractaspidi said.

Adrak was now back in his spy mode. He wanted to go to Zïsè de Drakon, because he wanted Karoline Morganthau taken down and that peep squeak Zmeya Rembert.

The fashion designer and her crew showed up and they were fully vetted by VIA from the time the reservation was made.

Joanie received the full makeover, nails, hair style, makeup, and couture dress that revealed a little leg and cleavage and made her look utterly smoking hot.

Adrak was also made over including male makeup, hair style, manicure, and put in a black suit with a black tie. His body had no fat on it, and he was all muscle, so he fit the suit quite well.

The fashion designer and her crew promptly left, and the time was eight forty, plenty of time since the restaurant night club was nearby.

The two spies were escorted to the elevator, two VIA agents got into the elevator with them and were notified one of the SMERSH agents was at the front entrance. They informed Adrak of the plan on the way down. I will walk in front of you, and he will walk behind you like we are strangers, to the waiting Limo for you, a third person is now at the entrance asking the Bellhop some questions, they both work for us and will deal with the SMERSH agent if he poses any threats.

Adrak and Joanie got into the Limo and were on their way for a short drive. The SMERSH agent got into a waiting resort courtesy car and told the driver who happened to be a VIA agent to follow the limo, he wanted to go where they were heading. Once the Limo arrived at Zǐsè de Drakon, Adrak and Joanie got out and went inside the building and up the elevator to the top floor for the restaurant/night club.

There was a line waiting to get in, but Zǐsè de Drakon management had the couple escorted to the elevator as if they were VIP's. People in line wondered who the fashionable couple was, knowing they were likely celebrities they would find out.

The SMERSH agent got in line acting like a loner who would go to the bar, have some drinks and make himself available for the barracuda's and cougars that were likely to show up. He then called Karoline and said, "Hey if you guys are not busy, why don't you come on down to the Zǐsè de Drakon."

Karoline Morgenthau had a tracker APP on her communicator that could send via her artificial intelligence requests to the SMERSH agent's communicator, and that data showed up such as exact location where he was and what his situation was. The report back was the SMERSH agent trailed Adrak and Joanie to the Zǐsè de Drakon and they were going to for entertainment and dinner.

Karoline also got the details of the Zǐsè de Drakon. She quickly knew she had to dress up. Karoline had her own glamorous clothes with her. Karoline had no choice but to never travel without them just in case she needed them. Karoline's exotic clothes come from some of the wealthiest neutral worlds that have some of the best fashions in the galaxy.

"We need to get dressed up to go to that restaurant night club to get another shot at Adrak," Karoline Morganthau said.

"Understand," Zmeya Rembert said even though all he had on his mind was how he was going to do the redemption.

Zmeya Rembert had a few suits with him as well. Tonight, it would appear as men in black since that's what these two male spies were wearing.

***

The Maître d' put Adrak and Joanie at one of the best tables in the restaurant with a great view. Soon the waitress was there for their drink orders.

"I'll have a Blue Bǎixiāng Guǒzhī," Joanie said after she looked at the drink menu.

"Give me a Trambrosier Elixir," Adrak said.

Moments later after serving the drinks, the waitress took their food orders.

I'll have the Kǒngquè (pronounced Kong-Chea [Peacock])," Joanie requested. Adrak chose the Kǎohǔ (pronounce Kao-who [Barbecued Saber Tooth Tiger])

The food was great, and the music was lame. But that was okay, they had each other to enjoy.

By the time Joanie and Adrak finished their entrées, three people walked into the restaurant and were seated four tables over. Lt. Colonel Tom Atractaspidi, now sitting at the bar with special assistants on each side of him was alerted Karoline Morganthau, Zmeya Rembert, and another SMERSH agent had entered the restaurant and were sitting four tables from Adrak.

The team swung into action and was poised to intervene in the event Karoline triggered a gun battle in this room full of innocent bystanders. Adrak and Joanie were advised of the situation through their conformal ear buds.

With the music playing and the numerous conversations going on, Joanie could speak softly to Adrak without being overheard.

"This is getting a little old, that bitch showing up all the time," Joanie said.

"I know what you mean," Adrak said not happy SMERSH was screwing up his vacation where the two lovers were supposed to be enjoying each other and not on another mission.

About the time their table was cleaned off including changing the tablecloth and new place settings for entertainment and drinking elixirs as the venue was shifting from dinner hours to live music performances with a six-person band and singer.

People who came just for dinner were slowly exiting the Zĭsè de Drakon restaurant night club. The angry line down outside the building was starting to slowly move in and take their seats.

The music shifted from lackluster dinner music to dancing music and popular hits performances by the band. They only had one or two songs of their own, so they had to sing other artists' songs to fill in the sets.

The elixirs had a good effect on Joanie and Adrak which soothed their emotions despite feeling violated by Karoline and her gang.

Adrak wasn't too concerned about Karoline because he saw Lt. Colonel Tom Atractaspidi sitting at the bar with special assistants on each side of him. Likely they were not the only VIA agents there tonight packing blasters.

With drinks on the table with security tops placed over them while they got up to prevent someone from poisoning them, Joanie led Adrak out on the dance floor during the first slow dance of the night.

"Isn't that special," Karoline Morganthau said with disdain to the SMERSH agent sitting next to her. Zmeya Rembert was on the other side of the SMERSH agent giving an appearance of three friends out for the night enjoying the night life.

After the song, the two lovers sat down and continued enjoying their elixirs.

Joanie was no doubt the best looking and best dressed woman tonight at Zǐsè de Drakon with her designer dress and hair design. Adrak looked like the perfect escort for Joanie and the two were dressed just slightly above the level of the crowd. But sometimes celebrities or the super-rich came in and they were well dressed like these two tonight.

"You know I used to be a cabaret singer?" Joanie said.

"Really?" Adrak asked.

"Would you like me to sing you a song to show you how well I can sing and make Karoline a little jealous?" Joanie asked.

"I think you are already making Karoline jealous because you are certainly much better looking," Adrak said.

"You really know how to flower me with the right words at the right time," Joanie said.

"I hope by now you realize it comes from the heart," Adrak responded.

"I certainly do, and that's why it's so pleasant being around you," Joanie said.

The club's artificial intelligence noted Adrak and Joanies drinks were almost empty, so the waitress was notified to go to the table to get them refills. The waitress was more than delighted because when the couple ordered their meal and paid for it then which was the custom of Pàrgǒnzéfrās vacation beach and community, Adrak also paid the upper band of the tip selections. The couple not only looked the part, but they also acted it as well.

"Would you two like refills?" the waitress asked.

"Yes, we would like refills, but I have a question," Joanie said.

"Alright madam, what is your question?" the lovely waitress asked with a lovely smile because she loved the way the couple tipped her which also made her look good in the eyes of management.

"I'm a cabaret singer and I do sing very well professionally, and I want to sing a song for my boyfriend. Would it be possible for you to ask the band if I could have permission to sing one song? I promise they will not be disappointed." Joanie asked.

"Madam as soon as I get your drinks, I'll catch the band between songs and ask them," the waitress said.

"Thank you very much," Joanie responded.

This should be interesting, Adrak thought.

The waitress was back with their drinks and had notified the Maître d' what the beautiful woman had requested. The Maître d' had been briefed by VIA earlier about the situation in the Night Club with enemy agents present and assurances they planned to not cause a confrontation while present. The Maître d' looked at the beautiful woman who he knew now was a VIA agent and thought it would be most appropriate if she sang a song adding to the drama of the evening that electrified his thoughts.

The band has little short breaks between songs to discuss a couple technical matters typically and during one of those short breaks the Maître d' talked to the band's leader pointed out the woman and notified him: "The woman is a successful Cabaret singer and wants to dazzle her boyfriend with a song."

"As good as she looks, I'll take a chance on her," the band leader said.

"Thank you I will bring her right up," The Maître d' said.

The Maître d' knew Joanie's alias from the VIA briefing in the manager's office a couple hours prior and walked directly to the table.

"Excuse me Alexis, your waitress notified me that you wanted to sing a song. I personally asked the band. They are waiting for you to come to the stage now and sing your song. Will you please follow me," the Maître d' said.

Alexis (a.k.a. Joanie) followed the Maître d' to the stage where she stepped up on it and approached the band leader.

"What song do you want to sing?" the band leader asked.

"I want to sing '*You Came to Me When I Was In A Lot Of Pain.*' I can sing it a cappella if necessary."

We know that song, we can play it. Do you want the voice backup which we normally do since that's how the song is performed?

"Yes, I would like that."

"Our singer Jennie here will sing backup to you. I think it will add a lot of luster to the song with two female singers."

"I agree."

"What is your name dear?" "I'm Alexis."

"Alright, Alexis let me introduce you and then we'll start performing."

"Sure." Alexis replied

"Jennie, you stand beside Alexis and share the microphone." The band leader said.

"Not a problem," Jennie said who was interested in seeing how this was all going to play out.

The audience was lackluster because the performance all night long had been uninspiring, and the band needed an emotional tweaking to up their game. That was just about to happen.

"Ladies and Gentlemen, we have a pleasant surprise tonight. We have a cabaret singer Alexis who is going to join us for a song. I think you will like it," the band leader announced.

The music started playing and the band was proficient at performing '*You Came to Me When I Was In A Lot Of Pain.*'

Adrak was all ears and so was Karoline whose communicator artificial intelligence was recording the sound. Karoline placed her communicator on the table like many people do and the recording included live video.

Karoline had reports that Adrak and Joanie were lovers. But now Karoline was having doubts about their Inter Dimensional Portal Spy source who did not inform them about Adrak's scar tissue removal and here was his partner singing, she had never received any such reports.

It only took Karoline, who was a music connoisseur a moment to figure out Alexis the current alias for Joanie was an exceptional singer. The band, the waitress, the Maître d' and the crowd quickly came to the same conclusion. Bands hate to take risks like this but when a singer comes along and hits a base loaded home run so quickly, it makes up for all the losers they came across over time.

Alexis (a.k.a. Joanie) sent reverberations through the audience. They were immediately enthralled. When Joanie sang in the past as part of her cover, the crowds loved her so she knew she would get the proper response.

Joanie's only question now was, *how will my lover boy respond.*

The lyrics to '*You Came to Me When I Was In A Lot Of Pain,*' completely described their ordeal when Adrak first visited the broken woman in the hospital. Joanie knew she had come along quite a way since then. Adrak was first and foremost the catalyst for her fast healing and great efforts she put into her rehabilitation since he was with her every day encouraging her when she needed it the most and feeling intense pain at times even with pain management.

Now it all unfolded to Joanie as she saw the tears forming on the sides of Adrak's cheeks. He was only twenty feet away from the stage, so Joanie could easily detect the psychological transcendence Adrak now exhibited. This was raw emotion, the real deal. This was immediate feedback to Joanie who responded now almost like she did orgasmically when Adrak said to her he loved her right when she started her ejaculation and the intense vibrations and frequencies she felt then, she felt now.

It was almost like witchcraft as Joanie (a.k.a. Alexis) cast a spell on the audience as well as the band. Thus, the entire band upped their output a notch or two. The regular singer doing the backup to Joanie created a unique sound that any recording studio would love. The band's singer was energized standing next to Joanie and was motivated to do her best. She hoped one day to have this experience singing with a professional who was quite capable.

The lyrics of course were something that only Adrak understood fit over their experiences just like finding an important piece to a puzzle. It was a perfect match and foretold their future when they would overcome diversity and achieve the success they rightfully observed.

Lt. Colonel Tom Atractaspidi knew of Joanie's singing abilities because he had supported a couple missions where she performed the role of a cabaret singer enabling them to get close to a SMERSH official Cleitus Beroea the head of SMERSH 3rd Main Directorate. That operation resulted in the takedown of Cleitus Beroea's two top lieutenants. Joanie's singing brought back quite a few memories.

Karoline Morganthau and Zmeya Rembert were utterly stunned. Karoline suddenly felt some remorse she was going to kill Joanie tonight after this performance. At the same time Zmeya Rembert now had more ideas floating in his head about redemption.

Nobody wanted the song to end, but at four and a half minutes long, it was one of the lengthier song choices tonight since most of the rest were around three minutes.

The song ended and there was pure chaos in the standing ovation. This band had never experienced this response before. It was almost hypnotic and the only explanation to this kind of response is Joanie had to be a witch and applied her magic spell.

The singers bowed to the crazy cacophony of sounds and BRAVO's that were registering.

The Maître d' saw the manager come out and look at the situation full of smiles. If the manager could have this success every night, it would be like the lord parting the Red Sea so Moses and his clan could escape the Egyptians.

The two singers hugged each other as if they were lifelong sisters.

"You sang so great," the band's singer said.

"Your back up was utterly perfect. You resonated with my voice and added tremendously to the sound quality. As you can see this crowd is not use to this, but your singing helped make it possible by adding magic to the lyrics."

"To be honest, there was a portion in the song I had to struggle to not break down. And when I saw your boyfriend's tears, it hit me emotionally real hard." the band's singer said.

"You have no idea what it did to me," Joanie said.

"Say when we take a break may I join you and your boyfriend for a drink?"

"We would love you to join us."

"I want to bring the band leader with us. I could see how he was reacting. You moved him too."

"Sure, bring him, we have several spare seats."

The music played on and instantly the dance floor was packed. The manager saw that as well and could hear the delivery of the band seemed to have been picked up a notch or two.

One slight risky opportunity led to all this. *If this could just happen every day*!

Joanie walked over to their table and put her arms around Adrak who knew she was special. Besides being a very successful VIA operative, Joanie was quite a singer and if she ever wanted to retire and leave the agency, she could do well as an entertainer.

Karoline Morganthau was now contemplating getting it over with killing Adrak right here in the night club. She would send the SMERSH agent over to grab the elevator and hold it just before she stood up and killed Adrak then run to the elevator with Zmeya Rembert who could be her rear guard until they got into the elevator and escaped.

Based on their present location they were a lot closer to the two boats than they would be at the Fěicuì de Lùzhōu Resort.

Karoline Morganthau sent out an alert that went via randomly keyed cyclostationary signals. The two boats and the aircraft were now ready.

Just before Karoline was about to launch her assault, the band took a beak and the band leader as well as their normal singer approached Joanie and Adrak's table and were soon invited to sit down for a drink. Once Adrak paid for their food earlier, all later charges were put on his tab and charged automatically each time they served a new drink. When he was ready to leave, all he had to do is simply just walk out. He intended to do that as soon as the two band members left the table and went back to performing. He felt like he wanted to get away from Karoline and go somewhere that would restrict her movement and have the entire team ready to intervene, and that was back at the Fěicuì de Lùzhōu Resort.

"That was an excellent song you guys performed with Alexis," Adrak said.

"We perform that song a couple times each week. It's a well-established hit so we can't go wrong performing it since the audience knows the song. But we've never had two great singers performing it like tonight to show the song's true potential," the band leader said.

Adrak got a closeup of the band's singer and she definitely was cute up close. She looked good on the stage too, but up close exposed how lovely her skin is.

The typical discussion unfolded Adrak would have such as where are you from and what do you do in life. Adrak and Joanie had a cover story built around their alias Alexis Tegaro and Sabastian Rollie.

The conversation was delightful and Adrak could tell the band leader, and their singer truly appreciated Joanie because of how they turned the crowd on.

Chapter Twenty-Two

Showdown at the Fěicuì de Lùzhōu Resort

The band members soon migrated back to the stage leaving Adrak and Joanie alone and exposed and just as soon as Karoline was going to start issuing orders to the third SMERSH agent and Zmeya Rembert, their quarry was on the way to the elevator.

Per instructions from the manager the elevator operator was not allowed to let anyone else in the elevator while the couple were in it going down.

Karoline said, "Quick we need to catch up with them."

Adrak and Joanie stepped in the elevator and the operator pressed the close door button and five seconds later Karoline and her team were there wanting to stop the elevator and as soon as Karoline reached to press the open-door button, the operator who happened to be a tough VIA operative grabbed her hand and said:

"I'm sorry, nobody is going down in the elevator with the couple."

Lt. Colonel Tom Atractaspidi saw all this unfold and nodded at the manager that was a semaphore meaning, *follow me.*

Two seconds after the elevator operator grabbed Karolines hand, the manager asked, "Is there a problem?"

Karoline turned around and saw three bruisers behind the manager and realized the possibility they may be VIA agents thus had to quickly modify her modus operendus.

"No sir, I was just trying to press the down button until this man stopped me."

Now it was too late, the elevator was on its way down and since Lt. Colonel Tom Atractaspidi pressed the [ALERT] icon on his communicator, VIA operators were by the elevator door Adrak knew and they were led 30 feet to the waiting Limo and driven back to the Resort.

Lt. Colonel Tom Atractaspidi could have taken the three down, but he wanted to make sure there wasn't a fourth SMERSH agent involved.

Because of the failed attack earlier in the day, SMERSH directed one of their agents at the boats to come ashore and go to Fěicuì de Lùzhōu Resort to provide another set of eyes and ears to replace the missing agent Igor Duquesne.

Karoline Morganthau was advised while at the restaurant eating, the 4th agent was at the resort as a lookout to report if Adrak and Joanie arrived or left. By the time the SMERSH agents made their way down the elevator, Karoline led them to their vehicle to go back to Fěicuì de Lùzhōu Resort and received the message from the 4th agent Adrak and Joanie arrived and went to the pool bar and restaurant where they were enjoying Helénē's singing.

Helénē got to see Joanie in all her glory, the beautiful princess and it clearly became obvious why Adrak had the *strong affection* for Joanie as she was a movie star quality beauty tonight.

Adrak and Joanie, all dressed up and looking so magnificent, motivated Helénē to perform better for her friends. The other Franzon singers were also motivated by Helénē's uptick in her performance and followed suit creating a nicer environment.

SMERSH had used their cyclostationary transmitters far too often during this mission. VIA signals intelligence people had wavelet processors and chirp filters fully monitoring this area. Thanks to traffic analysis and triangulation techniques, the fourth spy that was bird dogging Adrak was identified and had a tracker on him. Now was the time to close the net.

Lt. Colonel Tom Atractaspidi and his two bruisers were at the Fěicuì de Lùzhōu Resort pool bar and restaurant just a few minutes after Adrak and Joanie arrived. There were no tables available since the place was now packed. But they had intended on sitting at the bar regardless of if any tables were available.

On the way driving to the Fěicuì de Lùzhōu Resort, Lt. Colonel Tom Atractaspidi explained to his men, "We have the 4th person identified who's their lookout. We are going to do the takedown tonight."

Lt. Colonel Tom Atractaspidi had to get Adrak and Joanie out of the bar and use them as a decoy to get them to lead Karoline Morganthau and her accomplices out of the bar. The best place to do this was out on the empty beach. Nobody was there now.

Adrak was warned via his conformal ear bud the SMERSH agents were behind him in the bar. Moments later Adrak and Joanie received a notification via their conformal ear buds, "Commencing SRV RF [Special Reaction Venture & Resolute Finish]."

SRV RF really meant: *all hands-on deck, repel borders*!

During an SRV RF event the handles and controllers would give special instructions to VIA operatives.

Adrak, invite Joanie to go for a walk on the beach. If at any time you feel unsafe, jump in the water and swim away from the beach. We have a support boat coming in now.

The BEPB (black electric powered boat) was built stealthily with radar absorbent paint and panels and had a low profile.

On a dark night BEPB was almost impossible to spot. 80% of the hull was under water in sealed compartments until they blew ballas (water in tanks). Then 50% of the hull would be above the waterline so they could pick up agents in the water doing a swim out during a mission.

Lt. Colonel Tom Atractaspidi had every intention of forcing the SMERSH agents to surrender because they were far more valuable alive than dead.

"Would you like to go for a walk with me on the beach?" Adrak asked after Helénē left their table from this break and started singing again.

Joanie already knew those were his instructions and to expect the question.

"Yes, I would love to go for a walk on the beach," Joanie replied.

Because nobody, since Igor Duquesne had any interface with VIA Karoline knew of, she didn't know the net was closing in on her and she was now leading her team into a trap because she was paranoid Igor would break and rat them out.

Karoline had no idea there were drones and probes flying around looking for anything that transmitted the randomly distributed cyclostationary signals. Artificial Intelligence doing machine learning and statistical analysis, combined with traffic analysis was able to pinpoint a flying boat aircraft in a lagoon at a nearby Island. That meant there was probably a SMERSH agent onboard. Indeed, there was. A SMERSH agent who worked directly for Cleitus Beroea, the head of SMERSH 3rd Main Directorate was on that airplane and was the overall controller for the operation.

That's how bad Cletus Beroea wanted to kill Adrak who had caused him severe embarrassment and put him in a bad light with his boss when SMERSH got a report from the MOLE, Adrak blew up their new Intergalactic Dreadnaught Carrier, blew up their warehouse full of essential *Quasar-Sonic Stasijar Battlefield Penetrators,* and killed his protégée Sidis.

Cletus Beroea wanted blood revenge and wasn't going to allow Karoline to screw it up when she had buck fever and just knew she could take out Adrak with no serious repercussions.

Cletus Beroea's top agent in charge of the operation was somewhat in a hurry, mindful the VIA would likely break Igor Duquesne any minute.

Just like Karoline thought, Cletus Beroea's top agent in charge of the operation sent a randomly distributed cyclostationary immediate (RDCI) action burst message to the two boats that would transport the spies from the beach to rendezvous. The two boats were to report coordinates off the beach when they arrived.

As soon as the two boats did their report as they were directed, real time wavelet and chirp filters detected and classified the transmission as a SMERSH RDCI transmission and pinpointed the location of the transmissions on the escape boats.

The VIA's BEPB was directed to relocate near the beach area where the takedown was about to begin preventing the two boats from assisting the SMERSH agents going after Adrak.

Karoline and her group were about 50 yards behind Adrak and Joanie who were advised how close they were. The BEPB could see everyone on the beach and because the new moon had very little florescence it was a dark night with just starlight, but substantially enough for infrared imaging via the BEPB's telescope that could extend upwards to 10 feet in the air via a telescoping mechanism. At this time the SMERSH lookout at the rear entrance of the hotel acting as a rear guard was hit with a dart gun and fell over unconscious.

Karoline was suffering a little with Buck Fever to get the takedown and leave. Each of the two support boats had a single white light and she could visually see they were coming towards her as she approached Adrak and Jonie who were directed to walk towards the water right in front of the BEPB.

It was totally empty on the beach and Karoline suddenly got the notion to abduct Adrak because she knew Cleitus Beroea the head of SMERSH's 3rd Main Directorate would love to personally take Adrak to the hog farm and feed him to starving Zvetchen hogs that had razar sharp teeth and would tear into Adrak bound and still alive but cut in a few places to make sure the Zvetchen hogs would smell the blood and if they hadn't been fed in a couple days, there would be an orgy like flesh tearing due to their terrible hunger.

Adrak handed Joanie a package of Shǒuyǐn Bèidāo Stars as Karoline and her crew were twenty-five feet away approaching. Karoline got such Buck Fever when she flipped the safety on the laser pistol, she selected stun instead of kill.

Karoline's denigration of Zmeya Rembert was now about to boil over and he was going to show Karoline what true redemption was. He had nothing to lose. He lost his family and spying for SMERSH no longer appealed to him.

***

Chapter Twenty-Three

True Redemption

It all happened so quickly that Adrak did not respond throwing the Shǒuyǐn Bèidāo Stars until Karoline was in range to attack. Karoline shot Joanie not realizing her laser weapon was in stun mode until she made the shot and just as soon as she had moved the safety from stun to kill Zmeya Rembert had his laser pistol pointing towards Karoline and said, "Karoline, drop the weapon or I'll show you a little redemption."

Snipers were about ready to blow Karoline's head off, but Lt. Colonel Tom Atractaspidi directed them to hold their fire, he wanted to see what this was all about, with Zmeya Rembert pointing his gun at Karoline.

The other SMERSH agent, a chickenshit saw enough and started running down the beach and towards the white lights on the two boats sent in to pick up the SMERSH agents.

The small boats were coming in fast to assist Karoline and saw something on the beach had gone awry. Within a minute they had the third SMERSH agent aboard and continued approaching the group on the beach when suddenly, the BEPB blew its ballast and popped up and shined powerful searchlights on the two boats causing the one that picked up the SMERSH agent to accelerate and maneuver away from shore and speed up to fast speed probably making 30 knots.

"I said drop your weapon," Zmeya Rembert said.

Karoline didn't know what to think. She suddenly thought maybe Zmeya Rembert had been a double spy all along and she was now in a trap with no way out. Karoline sure as hell was not going to be captured again. The VIA was not nice to her the last time she was a prisoner.

Now knowing her laser weapon was set to kill she turned towards Zmeya Rembert with every intention of shooting and killing him, but he did not waiver. All he had to do is pull the trigger. Just as Karoline Morganthau was about to pull her trigger Zmeya Rembert pulled his trigger and said, "This is my redemption."

The two spies then shot and killed each other.

Adrak immediately went to Joanies aid, and she had been stunned a lot worse in the past and because Karoline had buck fever shooting too far away thinking her laser weapon was on kill, Joanie came to in Adrak's arms who was weeping thinking she was dead.

When Joanie looked up at Adrak who had the resort lights shining on his face, his crocodile tears were easily observable.

Before Adrak could move or register the awareness, Joanie placed her hand on the side of his head and rubbed away some of those crocodile tears and said, "Adrak I'm a spy and I shouldn't have done it because it's bad for business, but I fell in love with you."

As the electric carts came upon Adrak and Joanie saw the two spies kissing and smiled and just shook his head. *Romance right in the middle of a firefight!*

The BEPB had missile launchers and carried eight missiles that were three feet long and six inches in diameter and could easily blow up and sink much larger boats and ships

Lt. Colonel Tom Atractaspidi directed the BEPB not to sink the boat that was running to the Rendezvous. They had their own float planes and Sky-cruisers that were repurposed from law enforcement to VIA and Coast Guard operations. The Vekkar Coast Guard Sky- cruisers carried the same missiles as the BEPB that had dual roles A/S and A/A.

The second SMERSH small boat had some shoulder fired missiles designed to take out aircraft like the Sky-cruisers or other boats and ships, but a couple attempts to shoot at the BEPB flew by harmlessly as the seeker and proximity device was not able to activate on the stealth vessel.

The BEPB was ordered to sink the second boat that had several SMERSH agents on board and the two missiles fired back at the SMERSH small boat had no problems in destroying the boat and killing everyone onboard.

All the lights suddenly went on in the hotel. People were awakened by the sound of the explosion. They were looking out trying to see what was happening.

The second small boat blew up into thousands of pieces and immediately sank in about fifty feet of water. Photonics on the BEPB saw nothing was left nor any survivors and shut off its searchlight and was then directed to trail the small boat that got away just in case they needed to sink it.

The BEPB transitioned to its hydrofoils and was soon flying at 90 miles per hour towards its target easily tracked by infrared especially since the fools were not bright enough to turn off their one masthead light. As soon as the BEPB closed to within a couple thousand yards of the SMERSH small boat it dropped down slowing and retracted its hydrofoil. The bugout boat was over the horizon from the beach now and the SMERSH boat slowed down.

The BEPB flooded its ballast tanks dropping down into the water and observed the small boat at a safe distance.

Just as VIA expected the float plane came in and landed and pulled up next to the small boat to extract the SMERSH agent chickenshit and find out what happened on the beach and why he ran away from the fight.

About that time a half dozen Sky-cruisers arrived and the BEPB was ordered to turn its search lights onto the float plane. Additionally, VIA agents came in on float planes and pulled up to the SMERSH group who were told to stand by the side of the boat with their hands up and not to move. The float plane was informed that if it started its engine, it would be blown up by a missile.

The boat and the SMERSH float plane were boarded, and all the occupants were removed and cuffed and had leg restraints put on and flown back to . Pàrgǒnzéfràs vacation beach and community and quickly put on aircraft and flown to a VIA facility where they would have the pleasure of receiving aggressive interrogation techniques.

VIA thought they had gotten all they could out of Igor Duquesne, and he was separated and ultimately traded in a spy swap.

The SMERSH agent that turned out to be a chickenshit was broken without much effort. He was very instrumental in identifying the mission commander who happened to work directly for Cleitus Beroea, the head of SMERSH 3rd Main Directorate.

Making Adrak a decoy turned out to be very provincial because Cleitus Beroea's agent identified the MOLE. They now had complete evidence of who it was.

***

From the time Adrak and Joanie left to go for a walk on the beach until they returned to the pool bar and restaurant, was only 45 minutes.

Joanie informed Lt. Colonel Tom Atractaspidi, "We want to have a couple of drinks to unwind and rejoice survival."

"SMERSH got snakebit pretty bad tonight, we took down their entire apparatus associated with this mission, I'd say it's safe to say, you can enjoy yourselves now."

"I want to spend some time running on the beach and swimming to build up my strength," Adrak said.

"I have some good news for you Adrak, you will have a personal workout instructor arrive tomorrow to assist you."

"Oh yea. Who's that?"

"I don't want you to say anything to him about it because I don't want it to go to his head, but Toland volunteered to come here and work out with you."

"I can appreciate that."

"Would you mind me joining you and Joanie for a drink?"

"Actually, what you just put us through, I insist you buy the drinks for the rest of the night."

"You got a deal."

Besides all the excitement and people wondering what was going on that now had no trace of anything happening, when the bar started to slow down this time of night it got busier. It was a full house.

The dynamic duo plus one was being served their drinks right about the exact time of the next break for the performers. Heléné made her rounds and found Adrak and Joanie sitting with another man, and she was invited to join them.

Lt. Colonel Tom Atractaspidi had the pleasure of experiencing time spent with a Franzon woman in the past when was there for a while on official business. He knew the great pleasures they could give a man, and he immediately took a fancy to Heléné who was what some would think low hanging fruit ready to be harvested.

It was a joyous night of celebration and relief. Other than Joanie getting stunned that she quickly got over, VIA had no casualties or people wounded in the take down.

Chapter Twenty-Four

The Vacation Ends Another Mission

Zmeya Rembert's actions were recorded and observed by VIA officials. In interviews with Adrak they learned *Zmeya Rembert carried out his redemption.*

Zmeya Rembert no doubt saved Joanie's life because Karoline had switched her laser weapon from stun to kill and the results are easily observed in the dark. Karoline fried Zmeya Rembert's heart, and he fried her heart at the exact same moment instantly killing each other and with the third chickenshit running away, the two spies Adrak and Joanie were saved.

Zmeya Rembert's body was returned to his family for a decent burial. Nobody knew he had been a defector and betrayed his country. As far as anyone knew he was on an assignment. VIA is great at fabricating a story for their own propaganda purposes and the new story that was put out the second mole spoon-fed to SMERSH was Zmeya Rembert had been a double spy all along.

The second MOLE was given his life back by agreeing to be a double spy. And he did a fantastic job at it. But eventually SMERSH caught on to the Mole and had him assassinated. VIA didn't have to take any action as the enemy did their dirty work for them.

The next two weeks at Fĕicuì de Lùzhōu Resort were fantastic for Adrak and Joanie.

Toland showed up and worked with both spies running up and down the beach, swimming, and time in the resort's gym for clients. Low intensity martial arts were practiced including forms and minor sparing.

Every week Joanie and Adrak had more medical examinations showing vast improvements thanks to the health accelerators and other medications.

Joanie felt like she wanted to do some more singing and convinced Adrak to take her back to Zǐsè de Drakon restaurant night club where Alexis Tegaro and Sabastian Rollie became quite popular with the band, the manager, and the staff. It seemed Joanie's magic transfixed the nightclub into a highly successful venture.

In some of the visits to Zǐsè de Drakon restaurant night club Alexis Tegaro and Sabastian Rollie brought along Helénē and Lt. Colonel Tom Atractaspidi during Helénē's day off. Helénē was mesmerized observing Joanie sing.

During the last night of their vacation Joanie, Helénē, and the band's singer sang a song together with the three other Franzon singers. Since all the Franzon singers were enjoying a night off, they were just having fun and with as much perfume as these women brought in with them. The Franzon singers were easily approachable for dance requests. The Zĭsè de Drakon restaurant night club had one of its finest nights ever.

Just when the manager thought it couldn't get any better, with all these women up on the stage together singing a couple of the Franzon songs, the club was truly rocking that night.

Now it was time for Adrak and Joanie to go back to work.

Adrak had not been back to the office for quite some time. Employees there didn't think he still worked there and may not be alive.

After a couple days of dealing with administrative functions, Interdimensional Spy Portal Directorate Executive Director, *Doctor Oxyuran Lepidotus Taipan* walked into Adrak's office and said, "I'm taking you somewhere now. This will involve your future assignment."

"Alright *Taipan,*" Adrak said since they were alone.

The two men made their way to the rooftop Skycar parking area and were soon underway via Skycar administration navigation (SAN).

Adrak was not surprised when he discovered they were heading towards Project KOBRA SPEKTR facilities.

The Skycar landed on the hilltop landing pad shortly after the camouflage shifted out of the way. As soon as they were out of the Skycar heading down the elevator. SAN took the Skycar to an area where visitors had parking under camouflage.

Taipan led Adrak into the familiar conference room which had several familiar faces including Colonel Suzan Marklar, the Gopher, and Spraticus. Also notable in the room was Joanie who was all smiles because she knew what Adrak had not been informed of would soon be revealed.

They were soon all seated waiting to hear what the Gopher had to say.

"Welcome everyone. I'm here for two reasons. First and foremost, I'm here to give Adrak and Joanie awards for several missions our supreme commander has decided their missions have been some of the most heroic acts in recent history.

"Secondly Adrak, since you did such a good job in the past you were given a new assignment; we will soon reveal it to you. It will be another dangerous mission and you may get killed, but in our business the thrill of victory and the agony of defeat is what drives a super spy like you.

"Based on your health status the doctors have said, and Mr. Toland coaches' comments, we think it's only fitting to now give you the opportunity to again taste the thrill of victory."

"Adrak, you know from your debriefings that Cleitus Beroea, the head of SMERSH

3rd Main Directorate has been your nemesis. Your assignment will involve sabotaging an important SMERSH 3rd Main Directorate facility where General Coenus has set up his command center for their upcoming attempt on Plexisplatoria.

"Adrak, your new assignment is perhaps the most important for the VIA this year. We know we need the very best team to pull it off and that's why Colonel Suzan Marklar, who will oversee this operation personally asked for you."

Adrak looked over at Colonel Suzan Marklar who was now smiling.

This was going to be a big operation so there would be more briefings in the future.

The meeting soon ended and before Adrak left traveling with *Taipan* to go back to his office, he said:

"Give me a couple moments to talk to a couple people."

Adrak then walked up to Colonel Suzan Marklar and announced:

"Colonel, I want to thank you for looking out for me and demand my restoration.

You have no idea how good it makes me feel with all that scar tissue removed."

"Adrak, you earned it more than anyone, plus you will be given some tasks in the future that will allow you to earn it again." Colonel Suzan Marklar said.

The two shook hands, then Adrak walked over to Joanie and the two evolved quickly into a temporal oasis where time has no boundaries and love persists.

"I am just about caught up with all my administrative BS so we can meet and be together," Adrak said.

"I'm sorry honey to be the one to have to inform you, Toland doesn't think he'll have enough time to train us unless we move back in the trailer again and do our workouts like we used to."

"When is this supposed to take place?"

"See how your buddy *Taipan* is smiling? I think he forgot to tell you something."

The days passed and Toland lived up to his reputation getting the two trained. He then felt obligated to inform Colonel Suzan Marklar, "Remember when we discovered Adrak's infrared and ultra-violet imagery blurred?"

"Yes, what about it?" Colonel Suzan Marklar asked.

"Joanie's imagery is now blurred the same way." Toland said.

"Don't you dare call in those aura researchers!" Colonel Suzan Marklar said and the two broke into a soft laugh.

Paul D. Escudero July 6 2024 San Diego, California.

Author Note

This Novel is a work of fiction. It takes place on Alien Planets and is not associated with any person from planet Earth. The technology is different and appears far more advanced in the future than what exists today on planet Earth.

If Skycars and Artificial Intelligence develop on this planet the way I think those products will, that aspect of the Novel will become true for us as well.

There are sophisticated drones, submarines, gliders, and of course the Inter Dimensional Portals that provide the fabric of the story.

For now, Portals are far-fetched, right?

Conspiracy theory is theory until proven to be fact.

A lot of people that bombast conspiracy theorists are now eating their words on a few items, so be careful to not discount something you are not aware of or have any means to vet the story.

One of the Conspiracy theories that influenced me using portals in my Novel is the internet story that President Obama went to Mars in 1981 and again in 1983 as a CIA intern via a portal of sort in a transporter that Aliens ostensibly gave the CIA to allow transporting people to Mars and the Moon. According to the various sources people who go to Mars or the Moon in these means of transport get there in mere minutes about the same time it takes light to travel there.

Whether the story is true or not, I thought Portals would be something fun to write about.

There are numerous sources about the story Obama went to Mars twice. This book has nothing to do with that, just reporting what inspired my story. Conspiracy theory: Obama went to Mars as teen (nbcnews.com)

I have no way of knowing if this is true or not, only Obama and a few handfuls of people know for sure. Will Obama one day come clean and admit it if it is true? The White House already denied it, but what else did they deny they lied about? Just listen to the Presidential Campaign going on and you will hear all kinds of accusations.

I have also published novels on Transporters and Time Machines.

Amazon.com: Clandestine Transporters: Unconventional Delivery: 9781963718096: Escudero, Paul D: Books

Time Travel Spy: A Time for Memories and the Unthinkable - Walmart.com

The Life of a Time Travel Spy by Paul D. Escudero | Book Video Trailer (youtube.com)

As I mentioned, there is technology and there is artificial intelligence in this book.

Artificial Intelligence in this Novel manifests certain communications and activities that otherwise could not happen. In some of my other books I have write-ups on what countries in the world are investing in artificial intelligence.

Sometimes you get machine learning people upset if you cross over and describe artificial intelligence doing something they think is machine learning.

My thoughts are machine learning creates artificial intelligence just like human learning creates intelligence.

I read a lot about China all the time. It's an interesting place. I enjoy watching major construction projects that turn nothing into something.

China has 3 priorities. They make no bones about it. China considers all three dual use and anyone who might think otherwise is rather foolish.

China's priorities are Space, Robotics, and Artificial Intelligence.

One might ask, why is robotics such a high priority in China?

China like Japan has an aging population problem. Young adults more and more do not want children as they feel the world is no longer suitable to raise children. There are so many obstacles for Parenting, they feel they are doing the world a favor by reducing population and drain on the environment.

A lot of Chinese now live in cities and are no longer part of a vast agrarian society of the past where a family had to raise 4 or 5 children to do the farming and chores. As a result, China fears 10 years from now there will not be enough younger people to take care of the elderly in an aging population.

China's goal is to replace the younger caretakers with robotics and help the elderly through artificial intelligence. China figures they have 10 years to accomplish the development they need to eliminate the need for a young person to take care of an elderly person because a robot will be there to do what is necessary.

Artificial intelligence is a priority because that's how they will regulate society. As they figure out better ways of doing things, it will be implemented with artificial intelligence including their criminal justice systems and their courts. The reason why I'm mentioning China's development is so that when you read my Novel and think it's all farfetched, you might discover the Chinese are already doing it, such as an INTEL APP on their cell phone.

Space is an obvious necessity because since it's a dual use technology, peaceful civilian space exploration and development will dovetail nicely into newer weapon systems loaded up with AI to make the weapons smarter and robotic functions such as in drones and unmanned military craft.

China has many super intelligent people. China has over 2,000 Einsteins capable of creating new algorithms and different approaches to mathematics and signal processing.

Since espionage and sabotage can have an element of signal processing involved, I have some of that in this book. If you google some of the terminology, I used in describing secret communications the aliens are using, you will discover Russian and Chinese principal investigators involved in the research.

Moore's law says every 2 years computational ability will double.

New technology can also double every two years and eventually these 2,000 Chinese Einsteins will communicate directly with AI personalities that will take their comments and develop them. Hence the 2000 Chinese Einsteins will just be the guide and AI will do the actual development.

You might think this is something Einstein would never do unless you read his biography.

Einstein had 3 mathematicians do all his calculations.

All Einstein did was give guidance to the mathematicians in what he wanted calculated as he knew they would know how to number crunch it, using log tables, trig tables, integral tables, slide rules, and the other mathematicians' tools at the time. Two of Einstein's mathematicians won Nobel Prizes.

The same thing will be what happens with artificial intelligence.

Even though the spy in the Novel Adrak has Portals he can travel to, he cannot be inserted via a portal because that would quite probably get him detected. A spy needs the element of surprise.

On the other hand, when Spies are escaping and bugging out, the enemy already knows they are there and leaving the fastest way possible is highly desirable. So, you see there is a time and place for everything. Penetration must be carried out via classical means whether via gliders, aircraft, parachute, or Wing Suits.

In the chapters where the spies are inserted via wing suits, dropped out of shuttle craft at 60,000 feet with helmet and life support, it mimics some of the insertion techniques special operations developed in the Vietnam war by the Green Beret and others.

Do you think this would be a good way to insert a spy who will perform sabotage on critical infrastructure?

In this novel the spies do something like this and at the end have a parachute, but they use a Wing Suit to travel horizontally to the target area then deploy the parachute to land. Here a video showing American Green Beret soldiers jumping in Latvia. How far do you think that is to Moscow?

https://www.youtube.com/watch?v=39nykGC5AhQ

Do you think spies and the military would be interested in Wing Suits? GoPro: Wingsuit Flight Through 2 Meter Cave - Uli Emanuele (youtube.com)

This would be one hell of a movie.

In the Novel the spies use laser weapons and other devices which I get into. Will there be laser pistols in the future? I suspect with the new SUPER CAPACITORs laser pistols are a foregone conclusion.

Laser pistols might only have 3 shots, but with a laser pistol you only will need one shot to kill someone when you burn a hole through the heart. Will the accuracy of the shooter matter? No because artificial intelligence will aim the beam with great accuracy right at the heart and in one second the victim's heart will stop forever as it's instantly fried.

This book has romance and other aspects of the human condition. In one case two spies must fake love because they are staying in an organized crime hotel that they know likely has surveillance cameras and microphones.

Would a government train two spies to have sex so they would do it in the field to give the appearance they were a couple?

What if creating that image is necessary to take down a significant major enemy weapon system. What do you think female spies would do for victory?

Just like in this Novel, female spies in WW1 and WW2 experienced the thrill of victory and the agony of defeat.

Some of the stories of French resistance women associated with MI6 and the OSS during WW2 experienced firsthand how a spy encounters the agony of defeat.

Not all female spies suffered, Einstein was seduced by a Russian Spy, Margarita Konenkova (1895-1980) never experienced the agony of defeat.

Einstein's love, Stalin's agent: How a Russian woman won over the world's greatest mind - Russia Beyond (rbth.com)

GLOSSARY

Note: Names are listed in the Dramatis Persona.

SMERSH had already started their operation, Clover (Sidis involved).

Geskar found a file that pertained to the research center on the planet

Drusyltania

VIA wanted destroyed.

Emerald Jasmine Resort ready to commence the extracurricular activities at the

Rumors and Romance Night Club on the top floor of the Resort

Tramulite Planetary Security Cruisers, are significantly enhanced Skycars, launched a couple plasma vortex weapons. These hypersonic weapons took only a moment to cover the distance and hit the Skycar.

Tour de Cymbidium [like a Tour de France sexual tryst that included Cunnilingus].

Lotos de Solodka (pronounced Lotus de Sa-lād-ka [Lotus and Licorice]). Karly's drink at Rumors

Shǒuyǐn Bèidāo Stars 手隱備刀 Hand Hidden Blades

Artificial intelligence Spĕctrāl

Wingsuit Gliding Trambrosier Elixirs

Quasar-Sonic Stasijar Battlefield Penetrators Cobana Kāfēi, a nice drink laced with caffein. Rose Trambrosier Elixir

Zygov fighter bombers

Intergalactic Dreadnaught Carrier

Spratz prototype fighter bombers

Intergalactic Transport destined for planet *Heuronvale*

Labrodralger, resembled the typical small lovely fluffy dog.

Kokoshes (like popcorn)

È-long (pronounced uh long) elixir

"Gānbēi (pronounced: Gun Bay, means: Cheers)"

Jiǎo Gǒu Yúyuè Qì (pronounced Jiow-Go You-Yea Chi) wine.

Kratchen Eggs comes with a white tart *marmeladny sous* on top

Khrustal'ny Zverinets Wine (pronounced Crew-sh-tal-knee Zver-E-Nets).

Baked Phasianidae (pronounced Fay-she-awn-e-day) [pheasant].

Pastukhi Pie (pronounced Puss-tue-he Pie)."

Blue Bǎixiāng Guǒzhī (pronounced Blue Bye-schung Gwo-jhee) [Blue Passion Fruit] Canyon known as Láng Xiágǔ (pronounced: Lang Sha-goo).

Local Medved's (appear like Brown Bears).

Sanicar Qudrellas (Turtle Meat).

Wúliáng Huāmì (pronounced: Wu-long Hwa-me [Unscrupulous nectar])

Emerald Jasmine Resort where Karli Pauli sang at *Rumors and Romance* night club.

Tramulite planetary security cruisers, which were significantly enhanced Skycar launched a couple plasma vortex weapons. These hypersonic weapons took only a moment to cover the distance and hit the Skycar.

Doctor Oxyuran Lepidotus Taipan has assigned the mole to travel to planet *Craterus* where a set piece takedown is being staged.

Hello Adrak, my name is Melony, I'm your room assistant

Vekkar capital planet Vekkar Blesk

You are now part of an operation Code named "The Limping Lady." Spĕctrāl said.

DRAMATIS PERSONA

Polina Raduga Waterfall

The tourist train stopped at Potryasayushche Krasivo (pronounced Putra-seeya-su-cha Cra- seva) artist community

VIA Vekkar Intelligence Agency

Melony VIA spy who assisted Adrak during training and friend of Joanie

Alexis Tegaro alias for Joanie during mission with spy partner Adrak

Sabastian Rollie alias for Adrak during mission with Joanie

Igor Duquesne SMERSH agent.

Helénē, is a Franzon singer at Fěicuì de Lùzhōu Resort pool bar and restaurante.

Pàrgǒnzéfrās vacation beach and community

Fěicuì de Lùzhōu Resort located on the Island of Pàrgǒnzéfrās

Anaserdova location of warehouse during sabotage mission

Spraticus high ranking VIA official

Colonel "Blackjack" Langardo special operations trainer and task force commander

Omnicrom Reticulum Planetary system

Cornelius Bragrand, one of the three Inter Dimensional Portal Directorate Amigo's and a Mole who betrays Adrak.

Mole 000090317A512941 (a.k.a. Zmeya Rembert) who betrayed Adrak and part of the three Amigos with Cornelius Bragrand.

Gopher high ranking government official who works directly for the Supreme Commander. Spraticus works for Gopher.

Arapakar Town near Tramulite Air Base

Rokko's *Terrain Sportster* rentals where Adrak obtains rental for mission.

Cobana Kāfēi, a nice drink laced with caffein.

Rose female XXXX

General Maunoury, Major Divico Training for the Tramular Inter Dimensional Portal Research Campus saboutage mission, *Project Geyser.*

Blue Băixiāng Guŏzhī (pronounced Bye-shung Gwo-chee) elixir.

Planet *Heuronvale* where PROJECT KOBRA SPEKTR facility exists.

Spĕctrāl de Dòngtài: the artificial intelligence APP on each of Alexis Tegaro (a.k.a. Joanie) and Sabastian Rollie (a.k.a. Boone a.k.a. Adrak) communicators.

Nètsòn de Plàtinā Resort one of Adrak's temporary residences during missions.

Kōrāll tourist city of planet Fŏrlāgér

Colonel Suzan Marklar head of training for Project KOBRA SPEKTR

Vekkar Meditatsiya Institute

Doctor Svirepy Drakon, who is the lead researcher in Portal Technology

Zhēnabscoto (fragrant orchid) masseuse who treated Adrak

Project KOBRA SPEKTR secret VIA project Adrak loaned to.

VIA agents Astor and Sorge in charge of Adrak's training during portions of Project KOBRA SPEKTR training.

Lt. Colonel Tom Atractaspidi, military training expert worked for Colonel Suzan Marklar, and was task force commander during mission.

Karoline Morganthau *a.k.a. Agnes Renceladus* SMERSH agent sent to kill Adrak.

Corgrelius and Joanie VIA agents who transported Adrak to training. Joanie becomes Adrak's partner during missions Boone Whitaker alias for Adrak during mission

Planet *Heuronvale* location of Adrak's training.

Jămbŏdià Càrŭzŏ mountain resort town visited during train ride.

Tramulite City of Klamagore visited during train ride.

Tramulite City of Praxiskrowtious where Adrak fights Sidis and meets Martilene and Blue Băixiāng Guŏzhī (pronounced Blue Bye-schung Gwo-jhee) Blue Passion Fruit elixir.

Planet Drusyltania *Project Geyser*

Major Divico at training center

Vekkar Interdimensional Spy Portal Directorate Executive Director of Vekkar, *Doctor Oxyuran Lepidotus Taipan*

Geskar's home on Davenkret Street Martilene Chares

Geskar's wife Mildrayd was taken from him at an early age in a terrible accident.

The interdimensional spy Adrak, whose identity was so secret, was known only by VIA identifier. 000050428A62315.

000040972A48795 (a.k.a. Cajarington) Vekkar agent's official identifier. Cajarington Inter Dimensional Portal Spy who is with Adrak during several missions.

Note: Cajarington is named after Carrington, friend of mine who works for City of San Diego. Note the Carrington event in 1859. Carrington Event - Wikipedia Sidis One of Tramulite's best Spy who Adrak fights in an epic battle.

Commander Ptolemy Soter Tramulite Planetary Defense Force Commander

Mildrayd, Geskar's wife who died form an accident

Geskar, identity Adrak stole to allow him to operate as a spy in the Tramular City of

Praxiskrowtious

Martilene Chares Adrak's lover in the Tramular City of Praxiskrowtious. Adrak used her as a prop. Unfortunately, by the end of the mission Adrak became emotionally involved knowing he would have to leave her behind.

Sidis works directly for Cleitus Beroea the head of SMERSH 3rd Main Directorate Emergency room at the Space Force Hospital in Leaperring Valentina.

Karli Pauli Cabaret singer at the Maracava Castilshasta Night Club in the Tramulite City of Praxiskrowtious location of Adrak's mission. Adrak has an affair with Karli Pauli and ends up with some emotional tremmors.

Planet Craterus where set piece spy takedown of SMERSH agent was being staged.